SEEKER

KIM CHANCE

Mendota Heights, Minnesota

First Edition
Second Printing, 2019

Book design by Jake Slavik
Cover design by Jake Slavik
Cover images by Phovoir/Shutterstock, Kamenetskiy Konstantin/ Shutterstock, andreiuc88/Shutterstock, faestock/Shutterstock

Flux, an imprint of North Star Editions, Inc.

Library of Congress Cataloging-in-Publication Data
Names: Chance, Kim, author.
Title: Seeker / Kim Chance.
Description: First edition. | Mendota Heights, MN : Flux, an imprint of North Star Editions, Inc., [2019] | Sequel to: Keeper. | Summary: "Teenagers Lainey, Ty, and Maggie struggle against the Master, an evil force who could destroy the world"— Provided by publisher.
Identifiers: LCCN 2019015455 (print) | LCCN 2019018167 (ebook) | ISBN 9781635830392 (ebook) | ISBN 9781635830385 (pbk.)
Subjects: | CYAC: Witches—Fiction. | Wizards—Fiction. | Magic—Fiction.
Classification: LCC PZ7.1.C478 (ebook) | LCC PZ7.1.C478 Se 2019 (print) | DDC [Fic] —dc23
LC record available at https://lccn.loc.gov/20190154554

Flux
North Star Editions, Inc.
2297 Waters Drive
Mendota Heights, MN 55120
www.fluxnow.com

For my mama,

who always took me to the library, bought me a million Sweet Valley Twins and Goosebumps books, and gave me the exact pep talk I needed to write this one.

Thanks for always believing in me, Mom! I love you!

CHAPTER ONE

TY

Emerald embers dotted the sky.

The metallic taste of rust coated my tongue, and I coughed, my lungs shuddering against the thick coils of acrid smoke that clogged the air and burned my throat.

The ground around me was littered with debris—scraps of singed fabric, glass fragments, splinters of scorched wood— and all sound was muted by a shrill ringing in my ears.

I closed my eyes, trying to get my bearings. Nothing made sense. My brain was foggy, out of focus.

Flashes of green light illuminated the darkness behind my eyelids. The unusual color pulled at me, reminding me of something. Something important. Hands full of crackling green lightning. An emerald amulet. A pair of irises of the exact same hue belonging to—

My eyes shot open.

"Lainey!" I lurched forward, stumbling. My stomach

pitched and rolled in waves, much like the ground underneath my feet. The sky tilted toward me, and I staggered backward until my back hit the trunk of a tall cypress tree. I clung to the rough bark, waiting for the dizziness to pass.

As the world finally began to right itself, the ringing in my ears diminished, only to be replaced with a dissonant symphony of screams.

I stood at the edge of the tree line surrounding the smoldering wreckage of a large plantation. The house's blackened skeleton burned wildly and unruly, with tall bottle-green flames licking at its wounds.

The lawn was littered with bodies.

My eyes zeroed in on the figure nearest to me. A woman knelt in the grass, sobbing, her elegant ivory gown stained with the blood gushing from a wound on her forehead. Crimson rivulets dripped down her chin and mixed with her tears as she wailed. A man, unmoving and pale, lay cradled in her lap, a jagged shard of wood embedded in his chest.

Similar scenes were everywhere I looked. People stumbling around, disoriented and afraid. Others trying to help the injured. Hacking coughs from the thick grit in the air. Blood seeping into the ground. Many lying alone and still in the grass. It was exactly like a scene from one of those end-of-the-world disaster movies. But this wasn't a movie. It wasn't the end of the world that had caused so much destruction.

It was a witch.

Lainey Styles, the last remaining DuCarmont Keeper, had obliterated the house with her magic. I had a hazy recollection of running toward her after she collapsed, trying to reach her, but people had raced in all directions, pushing and shoving toward the exits. The ballroom was incinerated in a matter of minutes—that unnatural, magical fire burning fast and hot. When the heat from the flames and the electric energy from Lainey's magic had reached a boiling point, there'd only been time to suck in a breath before the whole structure blew apart—and the rest of us still inside along with it.

Beads of sweat rolled down my neck, and I hissed, swatting at an ember that landed on my cheek. The sizzle of skin broke through the shock from the devastation, and I rushed forward, scanning the lawn. "Lainey!" I yelled again, searching the faces around me.

Then I felt it—the connection between us. A strand of feeling, a sense of knowing, a bond forged by magic—*my* magic. It was faint and growing weak, but it was enough to know that I wasn't going to find her here on the lawn. I let out a deep breath, thanking the stars that my Praetorian senses were still working, that I could still feel her. It meant she was alive.

But what about—I glanced around sharply, then stopped myself. If Lainey was gone, so were Maggie and Serena. I wasn't sure how, but they must have all gotten out of the mansion in time and escaped in the aftermath of the explosion. Lainey never would have left without the people she cared about.

Which is why you're still here, I thought, trying to ignore the sharp twist of my stomach. A Praetorian who is separated from his Calling is like a lighthouse with no lamp or lens—utterly without purpose.

But it's more than that, the voice in my head whispered. *She's more than that.* I let out a slow breath. True or not, it didn't change anything. No matter what I was feeling, I deserved it for what I'd done to her.

I forced away the image of Lainey in her long green dress, the feel of her soft lips against mine. *In the end, the sacrifice will be worth it*, I reasoned. *It won't be for nothing.*

I turned back to face the wasteland of the plantation. So many bodies on the ground, so much destruction. Was it possible that *he* had been swept up in it? Hope burned through me like a fever, fast and hot, as I scanned the crowd for the face that dominated my nightmares.

A discordant, yet familiar boom of thunder echoed across the sky. Potent and guttural, it filled the open space, erasing all other sound—and eviscerated my wishful thinking.

"Dammit," I muttered. *He's alive.*

The night sky grew darker, snuffing out the light from the stars and the moon. The cries from those on the lawn morphed into something new—terror. Those who could ran for the trees and out toward the road. I watched as two young Sprites clung to each other, crying. Their pale green skin looked more sallow than usual in the dimming light of the flames.

"You better hurry," I whispered in their direction. "Before he sees you."

As if they heard my warning, they dashed behind a looming live oak and disappeared in a flutter of Spanish moss.

Shadows—heavy and draining—surrounded the rest of us, slinking through the trees and blotting out even the emerald glow from the fire. I groaned as they wrapped around me, beckoning.

I stepped forward right as another wave of dizziness washed over me. I must have hit the ground harder than I thought when Lainey's magic blasted apart the plantation. I put my hands on my knees and took a couple of deep breaths to steady myself.

Out of the corner of my eye, the last of the dying green flames tiptoed through the rubble, scattering ashes to the wind. I imagined what Lainey's face would look like if she were here surveying the wreckage, the bodies in the grass.

The responding wrench of my heart made me squirm, reminding me of another look: the flash of hatred that burned in her emerald eyes as she spat in my face.

"My name is Tyler Marek. I am one of yours, my lord."

My betrayal. My lies. My horrible truth reflected in Lainey's eyes. It didn't matter why I'd done it or what I'd lost that led me to this place.

The gnawing in my chest deepened as my father's voice—preserved so perfectly in my mind—whispered in my ear, a conversation from long ago. *"Pain is earned, son,"* he said, *"but you get to choose whether it limits you or reminds you of how hard you've fought. Win or lose, loss or gain, how we acknowledge our pain defines us. It is the tether that links us to who we really are, who we are meant to be."*

I used to think he was referring to physical pain only, but as a crushing weight—the truth of who Ty Marek really was—pressed against my heart, I finally understood.

If pain is a tether, then I am unbreakable chain—each link forged through blood and iniquity.

"So, what now?" I muttered, kicking a piece of debris—a crumpled strip of blackened fabric—with my shoe. *What now?*

My link to Lainey was a tiny fraying thread, but it pulled me toward her, and it was enough that my feet itched to start moving. Yet something else tugged at me, pulling me in the opposite direction. Just like the mark across my chest, it was a permanent reminder that I wasn't one of the good guys—and I still had a job to do. The choice was decided a long time ago, my mind already made up.

"But what of your heart?"

"You don't understand," I hissed, shaking my head. "It's complicated."

"What's so complicated about it?" My father's voice was clear, almost as if he were standing next to me. *"You're a Praetorian."*

It was a simple statement. Three words—yet they cleaved through me. "I don't know what I am anymore."

Another peal of thunder resounded, and I moved, not away but toward it. The scrap of fabric by my feet fluttered in the movement, unfurling to full length and stopping me in my tracks. An "H" was stamped into the fabric. It wasn't just a random piece of material. It was a calling card.

I picked it up, a half smile curling on my lips. So, our plan had worked; Lainey had found them after all. *Oh, he's going to love this.*

Others were heading in the same direction I was. Each of us bearing the same mark, answering the same summons. The dark shadows snaked around us, pulling us farther along. One slithered across my neck, and I cringed—the icy sensation grated against my nerves like fork tines on ceramic. I clenched my jaw, ignoring the ache of my grinding teeth, and walked stiffly through the trees.

On the opposite side of the wreckage, a man wearing a crisp black suit waited, his hands clasped in front of him. Four men in long black robes—his personal attendants, the Alium—stood behind him, their faces solemn. He watched as we, members of his Guard, approached. His slate-colored eyes gave nothing away. The curling onyx shadows rippled around him, the tangible fingers of his magic.

The Master.

The hair on the back of my neck rose, and every muscle in my body tensed. My fingernails dug deep crescents into my palms as I fought to keep from launching myself over the small expanse of open space between us.

But as always, I held back. Played my part. It was the only thing I had left.

There was a loaded pause as the thirty or so of us who'd answered his summons waited for orders.

The Master opened his arms as if to embrace us all, but his face was far from welcoming. "Where is she?" The words weren't loud, but all of us standing there felt them deep in our bones.

No one responded.

The Master let out a soft, sinister chuckle. "Let me try that again." He gestured to the smoldering wreckage. "Has anyone seen the little witch who burned down my house?"

Still no response.

The Master sighed. "So disappointing," he drawled. "That means we have a problem. That girl, the one no one can seem to find, was wearing the DuCarmont Grimoire." His face quickly lost all traces of amusement and morphed into a feral snarl. "I need that book and that girl back. You lot let her ruin my lovely party—not to mention escape." He swept an arm out, indicating us. "So, the question is, what am I going to do with you now?" The malign shadows around him billowed outward, undulating wildly around his shoulders.

One of the Alium stepped forward and spoke quietly. The Master's harsh angular features relaxed, and he grinned, baring a row of sparkling white teeth. "Ah yes, bring him forth."

The Alium inclined his head and beckoned to someone from behind. A man limped forward. The stark white of his shirt glowed against the backdrop of darkness. His face was swollen, bruised, and oozing blood, but I recognized the long, stringy hair that hung over his shoulders. The Scavenger from the fair, the one who tracked us at the Gathering and ruined everything. Heat flooded through me, and I growled, my fists aching to be put to use.

The Master circled the Scavenger.

"My . . . my lord," the man managed, his voice hoarse through cracked lips.

"Well?" The Master's voice was eerily calm. "Did you find it?"

"No, my lord." The Scavenger was visibly shaking now. "I . . . I tried but—"

"Ah, ah, ah," the Master tsked, moving his finger with every enunciated syllable. "Let's not make excuses, shall we? It does little for my mood." His face grew darker with every word as he turned to address us.

"It seems we have another problem. This dog guaranteed that if I spared his life, he would locate the DuCarmont girl. He is the one to have tracked her first, after all," the Master sneered. "But now it appears he has failed. *Again.*"

"My lord." The Scavenger pushed forward. "Please, you have to understand. There are traces of her," he said, wringing his hands, "but they don't extend very far past the house. It's like she . . . it's like she went in but didn't come out."

I stared at the Scavenger's gaunt face. In the Master's presence, he was far from the fierce and dangerous Shifter we'd first encountered at the fairgrounds; he was a simpering pawn now. I almost felt sorry for him. *Almost.*

The Master's eyes narrowed to slits. "Impossible."

"There's no trail to follow, my lord," the Scavenger continued, his voice cracking. "There are faint traces, but they're old. I can't pick up anything fresh . . . She's just gone." As if to illustrate his point, he reached down and scooped up a handful of dirt and sniffed it. Shifters didn't have as keen a sense of smell as Lycans, but they still made decent trackers, and he was right. I didn't know where Lainey was, but she wasn't near here. I tried not to smirk.

"Well, she couldn't have just disappeared into thin air, now could she?" the Master growled. A muscle twitched near his jaw, and the shadows contracted around him, a pulsing silhouette.

"I can't explain it, my lord." The Scavenger wiped his hands, scattering the dirt back to the ground. "But she's not here."

"So, what you're saying is that you have, in fact, *failed* me."

The Scavenger paled, his eyes going wide. "My lord . . . I . . ."
He didn't get to finish his sentence.

In a flurry of shadow and darkness, the Master threw out his arm. Like sharpened arrows, the shadows shot toward the Scavenger. He screamed and tried to run, but the ribbons of darkness wrapped around him, disappearing inside his nose, his ears, and his open mouth.

The Scavenger stood there, stunned. Then the screaming began in earnest. His whole body convulsed, and his cries were ear-shattering. He clawed at his head and neck, leaving angry red trails down his already bruised and swollen skin. Frothy black foam bubbled from his lips, and his screams cut off suddenly, giving way to a sickening gurgle. The shadows expelled themselves the same way they entered and flew back toward the Master, who caressed them with a finger.

The Scavenger lay dead in the grass, thick black liquid oozing from his pores.

The Master touched the cuff of his jacket where a small patch of the black liquid spotted the fabric. "That's too bad," he said, attempting to wipe away the stain. "I really liked this suit."

Eyes flashing, he glared into the crowd. "I need that witch," he said as casually as if he had just placed an order for coffee.

"Find her, and you will be rewarded handsomely. Fail me, and . . ." He looked back over at the Scavenger, his face lifting in a terrifying, brilliant grin.

Heat rushed through my veins. I'd seen that grin before. The night my father was murdered.

With roaring in my ears, I stepped forward. "My lord," I called out.

"Marek," the Master said, chewing on my name.

"I believe I might know why the trail has gone cold." I let the fabric dangle from my fingertips, the stamp facing outward. "If the witch is gone, it's because she had help."

"The Hetaeria." The Master's words were barely louder than a whisper, but the venom behind them was the worst kind of poison. Reaching out, he took the scrap of material from my outstretched hand. He stared at it, his frame trembling with rage.

My fingertips began to tingle, then my whole hand. It was like I'd shoved my fist into a basin of ice-cold water. I shook it, my eyes widening as the sharp stab of a thousand icy needles moved up my arm to my elbow, my shoulder, to my chest and torso. I gasped as the pain turned sharper, moving inward and twisting my insides.

The Master watched me squirm under his magic, his lips curling. Teeth bared, he crumpled the fabric in his hand. It felt like my bones were being crushed along with it. I sank to my knees, locking my jaw to keep from screaming.

"The Hetaeria," he growled. The shadow tentacles writhed around him, striking through the air like vipers.

A high-pitched ringing filled my ears as I fought against the pain. It exploded inside me like shards of glass puncturing me from the inside out.

Around me, the other members of the Guard dropped to the ground, writhing and squirming like I was. Some began to scream. The shadows closed in.

My heart pounded against my chest, and each pump of blood caused the ice in my veins to grow colder. My teeth began to chatter, and I shivered, layers upon layers of goosebumps covering my skin. The pain deepened, and I cried out. A chorus of yells rose up around me, my own voice mixing in the agony.

You've failed! the voice in my head shrieked. Anger stabbed at me, adding to the torment, as I waited to welcome death. Seconds later, the misery evaporated, and warmth flooded back through my body.

I yelped and rolled over to my back, sucking down large mouthfuls of air.

Crickets chirped loudly, and overhead, thin streams of moonlight trickled through the darkness, making a patchwork quilt of the grass. The shadows were nowhere to be seen.

"My lord," a quiet voice whispered.

I was the only one close enough to hear; I turned my head.

The Master was on his knees, his chest heaving. All the vitality had been leeched from his tawny skin. His eyes were glazed and heavy. He coughed—a raspy, wet sound.

One of the Alium knelt at the Master's side, a curved dagger in his hand. As the Master wheezed, the man sliced the dagger across his palm. Blood spilled from the uneven line. Tightening his fist, he held it in front of the Master and squeezed until a small puddle of blood seeped into the ground. Then he pulled a black handkerchief from his pocket, wiped the dagger clean, and bound his injured hand.

The Master lifted his arm, beads of sweat forming on his forehead from the effort, and held his shaking palm over the bloody ground. He whispered an incantation, and black steam rose from the soil, absorbing into his outstretched palm. The moment it hit his skin, he let out a deep sigh. The shaking stopped, and his cheeks flooded with color.

He stood up and dusted the dirt from his suit, then nodded at the Alium—though the look of disgust on his face was clear.

A cold shiver ran down my spine. Blood Reaping was an ancient and cursed form of magic. In order for it to even work, the blood had to be given willingly. Human sacrifice.

The Master rolled his shoulders and took a deep breath. He eyed me and the rest of the Guard lying in the grass.

"Find her," he commanded, the sound echoing through the trees.

Then he stalked away, the Alium close behind.

I struggled to my feet. The residual effects of the Master's magic left my limbs stiff and aching.

The rest of the Guard picked themselves up off the ground. Tidbits of their conversations floated toward me as I moved through them and back toward the main road.

"I've heard rumors of a Hetaerian basecamp up in the Catskills," a tall Strigoi said eagerly, pulling up a map on his phone.

Next, a pair of Nixies were whispering feverishly to one another, their voices carrying. "If we find the witch first, imagine the favor the Master will grant us," one of them said, her friend nodding in agreement.

"What do you think he'll do to her when he finds her?"

"Kill her . . . though he'll likely make her pay for outsmarting him tonight."

"Better her than us." They cackled loudly, the sound shrill.

By the time I was alone, engulfed by a grove of tall trees, everything inside me was screaming.

Find her! my brain howled. *Find her before they do!* My

heart was in my throat, and instinctively, I felt for the thread between us. That small, faint pull was all I had left, but it was something. I changed directions before I even registered it, my feet following the instinct, pulling me toward her.

"No," I said, forcing myself to a stop. The other thread, the one forged from blood, still tugged at me.

A battle raged inside me, building in my chest until it throbbed. I clasped my hands behind my head and exhaled sharply, waited for the warring sides of me to decide.

"Pain is a tether," I whispered, aching for my father's wisdom one last time. "Pain is a tether."

I closed my eyes. Lainey's face floated before me in the darkness. Her long dark hair framed her face, her emerald eyes staring at me. The hurt and anger shined brightly in them, but there was something else too. Then my father's face replaced Lainey's. His broad grin, the soft laugh lines that creased his skin, warm brown eyes.

How could I choose?

What if you don't have to choose? The words came from somewhere deep inside me, my own voice whispering my answer.

I knew what I had to do.

I started walking.

CHAPTER TWO

LAINEY

Murderer.

The word, cold and unyielding, slithered down my back. It draped around me and stole the warmth from my skin, despite the rays of afternoon sun pooling around me. I shivered.

The ever-present ache in my chest, sharp and marrow-deep, throbbed in time with the rapid beat of my heart. I placed a hand there, applying just enough pressure to keep the pain from stealing my breath.

But it was still there, lingering in my thoughts—that horrible truth, the one that still woke me, screaming, at night.

Murderer.

"Multiple casualties," they had told me only a few days after we arrived in Hudsonville, Michigan—where the farm that served as the Hetaerian basecamp was located. The power that had consumed me, those electric green flames that burned as brightly as my grief and rage, had done more than incinerate the mansion where the Master's Gathering was held. So much more.

Magic always leaves a mark.

I shook my head, forcing myself to think of something else. The direction of the sunbeams—perfectly positioned overhead—or the growling of my stomach. The stone-faced witch whose glare I could feel penetrating the blindfold that covered my eyes. *Anything* else.

"You just have to focus, Lainey," I grumbled under my breath, mimicking Zia's high-pitched tone. "Center your energy."

I huffed, arching my aching back. Hollywood made it look so easy: swish and flick. Bibbidi bobbidi boo. The weird nose-twitch thing.

But magic didn't actually work that way.

Concentrate, Styles.

I reached up to adjust the blindfold, ignoring the way it dug into my skull. A dull pounding had taken up residence in my temple, but I ignored that too. Limiting my senses was supposed to help me tap into my magic, the energy within me. Mostly, it made me feel ridiculous.

Just focus. You can do this.

I shivered again, this time from the crisp wind whipping long strands of my brown hair into my face. Even with my thick wool sweater, jeans, and leather boots, I got chilled easily. Winters in Michigan were known for being dreadfully cold, and there were already a few snow flurries floating through the air.

I ignored the layer of goosebumps covering my skin and went back to imagining a blank slate. A chalkboard wiped clean. A fresh sheet of paper without a single mark or blemish. Focus and control.

The grass—deadened and brittle—pricked my skin as I dug my fingertips deeper into the dry soil, energy crackling through me.

I inhaled deeply, letting the air rush back out through my mouth. Then I whispered the necessary words aloud, the incantation Zia had given me. *"Floredia Flosium."*

The magic inside me began to sing. A warm current of energy sprinted through my veins, a song that filled every inch of me. Like a crescendo, the melody grew louder with every rapid beat of my heart. It swirled through me before finally bursting from my fingertips and into the dirt.

The rush of magic always surprised me. Two weeks had passed since the Gathering, and it didn't matter that I'd been training every day since we'd arrived; every time I used my magic, it was like the very first time: the rush of excitement, the wild, electric pull of my power, the fear that gnawed at the deepest parts of me.

I never got used to it.

I sagged as the last bit of magic faded, leaving my limbs weak and noodle-like.

Did it work?

A flat, pinched voice broke the silence. "You've got to be kidding me."

I ripped off the blindfold.

The bush I had parked myself in front of that morning was a gigantic ball of blossoms, overflowing like a bridal bouquet gone wrong. I'd been focusing on a single branch and a single bloom, but instead, the entire bush had been affected—erupting into thousands of brilliant white azaleas. The ground was littered with them. There were even azaleas covering me. On my lap, in my hair—everywhere.

A laugh bubbled up in my chest only to slam against the lump that was lodged in my throat. The sight of the deadened ground, covered in bright out-of-season flowers, was proof that my magic was active. The overabundance, however, was yet another reminder of just how little control I actually had over using it.

I turned to Zia, my self-appointed taskmaster, and grimaced. Her arms were crossed over her chest, her mouth set in a hard line. Waves of her vibrantly dyed red hair pooled around her shoulders and formed a curtain on either side of her tan face. Her dark eyes, ringed with thick black eyeliner, bore into mine.

Next to her, my best friend, Maggie, sat on the low stone wall that fenced in the long lawn, her coils of thick, curly black hair dancing in the breeze. Her light-brown cheeks lifted in an encouraging smile, but her eyes shifted over to the stoic witch glaring at me, and the smile faded.

"I don't know what happened," I said, focusing on Zia,

whose mouth was still set in a hard line. "I thought I had it that time."

She let out a huff. "You lost your focus." Her tone was both firm and condescending, as if she were talking to a small child. "You have to concentrate."

"I know," I said through gritted teeth. "I'm trying."

Zia's eyes swept over the lawn, at the sea of flowers, and then back to my face. "Not hard enough." She punctuated each word, three separate jabs that hit me square in the chest.

It had taken a week to travel from Georgia to Michigan after the Gathering—mainly because Zia had insisted we circle around and back again to throw off anyone who might be on our trail—and since the moment we'd stepped foot on the farm, all I'd done was focus my energy on my magic, on learning how to use it. Not trying hard enough wasn't the issue.

"I've been out here for hours," I said, hopping to my feet. "I'm giving it everything I've got. What more do you want from me?"

Zia's face didn't change; she merely lifted a thick eyebrow. "I want you to *focus*."

"Gee, why didn't I try that?" I said, heat flaring through me. "Ever think that maybe it's your stellar teaching skills that are the problem?"

"Ever think that if you stopped whining for five seconds that you might be able to perform the simplest of spells?" Zia fired back, completely unfazed. "You're making this harder than it is. You have to focus on the outcome, what you want to accomplish, and then channel your magic into that outcome." She pointed at the azalea bush and held up a hand. "*Floredia Flosium.*"

There was a quick flash of scarlet light, and then a single white azalea bloomed from the exact spot I'd been aiming for with my own spell.

"See the end result in your mind and will it into being with your energy," Zia said. "It's that simple. Got it?"

I bit down on my lip to keep another retort from coming out, though my mind supplied definitions on instinct, an echo of my old life.

Abrasive (adjective). Tending to annoy or cause ill will; overly aggressive. Vexing (verb). To irritate; to annoy; to provoke. Tyrant (noun). Person exercising power or control in an unreasonable way.

"Got it," I grumbled.

"Then try it again," Zia barked. "It's not a difficult spell. Focus and control."

"Zia."

I jumped at the sound of a deep voice behind me. Julian, a Skipper and Zia's second-in-command, walked toward us. Serena, the only family I had left, trailed a few paces behind him, her face blank, a thin sheet of paper in her hand.

The vise that had been permanently clamped around my heart since the Gathering tightened. I still wasn't used to seeing Serena like this. Her long black hair hung in a limp braid over one shoulder, and her russet skin was lusterless.

The blue lace agate medallion she always wore still hung from her throat, but her simple collared shirt and jeans were a far cry from the long, flowing skirts and loose tops she'd favored before—

The vise around my heart squeezed again, this time stealing my breath and leaving me aching.

Gareth.

I tried not to think of my uncle, the man who raised me, tried not to feel his blood on my skin, but when I wasn't burying myself in magic, it was hard not to. He was everywhere I looked—the golden sunrise, the stack of worn books in my room, the soft faded-blue color of my jeans. Everywhere.

I knew Serena felt it too. We didn't talk about it—we didn't talk about much of anything anymore—but I could see it in her eyes, her mannerisms, and even in her appearance. To her, Gareth was color—vibrant and bright. Her true love. Without him, the world was leeched of hue, nothing left but gray scale.

And her own color was fading, right before my eyes, but there was nothing I could do or say to stop it.

"Serena," I said, giving her a hopeful smile. "I was hoping you'd come today. I've—"

"I'm here with news," Serena broke in, turning to Zia as if she hadn't heard me. I swallowed, choking on the pain of her dismissal. I'd been asking her for days to come to one of my training sessions; I thought she might be able to help, but no. *She's gone, too,* I thought bitterly, chewing the inside of my cheek.

Serena handed Zia the piece of paper, a small hand-drawn map. "We've seen Scavengers in the area," she said, her tone dull and flat. "The other Seers and I are watching for more movement, but mainly it's here"—she indicated the map—"and here. Best we can tell, anyway."

"We'll need to revisit the boundary and concealment wards," Julian added. "Make sure nothing slips through the cracks."

Zia nodded. "Do it." She turned to Serena. "Keep watching and report any further movement to me immediately."

"Of course," Serena said as her eyes found my face. She lifted a hand in my direction, as if to reach for me, but then dropped it limply to her side. "I'll leave you to your training."

"Thanks," I muttered, watching as she moved like a wraith back toward the farmhouse. I turned to Zia. "How can I help?"

"Focus on your training," she replied, not even looking up. "When you've mastered control of your magic, we'll talk."

"That's not good enough," I argued. "I can't just sit here hoping it's going to click while every day the Master is one step closer to bringing war to our doorstep. I need—"

"What you *need* is control," Zia cut me off. "Don't you get it? You're a powerhouse, and we have every intention of unleashing all of that power on the Master and his forces—but *not* until you've learned to manage it, to use it properly."

Her tone wasn't unkind, but it was firm, unyielding. It was the same thing she'd been telling me since we'd arrived on the farm.

"We both know I'm not making any progress," I said. "I'm trying but . . . You need to send me out with the scouts. Let me—"

"No."

"Just give me a shot. I know I can do more if I'm out there actively helping our cause, instead of being stuck here all the time."

"Not a chance."

"Please, I know I can help, just let me—"

"I said *no*," Zia snapped. "The last thing we need right now is for you to leave the farm, magic unchecked, and lose control again. We can't afford any more losses as a result, and we certainly don't need the Master knowing exactly where you are. You want to help? Then stay here, behind the wards, and learn control."

Murderer.

I stepped back, recoiling from that ghostly whisper in my ear. "I want to help," I murmured.

"And you will. But for now, focus on your training." With a wave of Zia's hand, all the azaleas disappeared. Then, with a nod at Julian, the two of them swept past me without another word.

"How does she do that?" I grumbled, turning toward Maggie, who was now at my side.

"Years of practice, I guess," she said, watching as Zia and Julian disappeared inside the house.

"Well some of us didn't get that luxury."

Sparks of green lightning crackled through my fingertips.

I felt the urge to press against that spot on my chest, against the stinging raw edges of that wound, but I kept my hand at my side.

"You okay?" Maggie asked, reading the grimace I was trying hard not to show.

No. Not at all. "Yeah," I said, not meeting her gaze. "I'm fine."

"You might be a witch, Styles, but you're a terrible liar."

I let out a slow breath. "Things just haven't been the same since . . . " My throat ached thinking about it. "Since we got here."

Since Gareth. Since I'd been told the truth about what I'd done.

"They expect me to just shrug it off," I whispered. "To just pretend it didn't happen. But how can I be the all-powerful witch they expect me to be when, every time I close my eyes, Gareth's blood, those people's blood . . . it's all I can see."

The look in Maggie's eyes caused warm tears to well up in mine. I blinked them away.

"It's not your fault, you know," she finally said, her words soft.

"Don't—" I shook my head. I didn't want to hear the lie anymore.

"No, listen to me, Styles," Maggie pressed. "You have to let it go. You couldn't save Gareth. His death is not on you." She grabbed my hand and squeezed it. "And what happened with the others? It was an accident. You have to forgive yourself for it."

It sounded so simple, just let it go. Forgive. But I couldn't.

"Magic always leaves a mark," I murmured with a little sigh. Given my now-green eyes and the emerald tattoo on my wrist, I'd always assumed that all magical marks were physical ones.

I knew better now.

The cost of my actions would mark me for the rest of my life.

"I just wish Zia would let me do something," I huffed, needing to change the subject. "The Master could be knocking on the front door right now, and I'm still sitting here trying to figure out Magic 101."

"Nah," Maggie shook her head. "The wards around this place are no joke. Julian was telling me about them. You'd have to be freaking Dumbledore to get through all the barriers."

"Still, I'm not getting any better, Mags. If anything, I'm getting worse. There has to be something else I can do to help."

"Maybe if you told Zia about the Grimoire, she'd—"

"Maggie!" I cut her off, looking around frantically for anyone who might have overheard. There were several people running sparring drills near the barn, and a handful of others were doing target practice, but no one was within earshot. "You swore you wouldn't say anything."

Aside from Maggie, I hadn't told anyone about what

Josephine had said to me the last time I saw her—that the DuCarmont Grimoire was no longer a physical book, that *I* was the Grimoire.

"I haven't," Maggie said quickly. "But maybe you should?"

"I can't. They already have big plans for my power: Lainey Styles, the last DuCarmont witch. What do you think they'd do if they found out that I have generations of magic locked inside of me?" I shook my head. "I can't ever tell them the truth."

"But what if it helps—"

"Don't you understand? If I can't control my magic, then it could happen again. And what if it's Serena this time . . . or you?" My voice cracked on the word. "I can't . . . I won't—" The lump in my throat grew; I swallowed hard. "What if I can't ever control it? What if I never—"

"I'm going to stop you right there." Maggie bumped her shoulder with mine. "I know it doesn't seem like it right now, but you *will* learn to control your magic. It might take time, but you will. Want to know how I know?"

"How?"

"Because you, Lainey Styles, are a DuCarmont witch, Keeper of the Grimoire, and total badass. It's in your blood. Josephine and your mother believed in you, and I believe in you too. As corny as it sounds, it's true. You just have to believe in yourself."

Her words were as warm as the sun. Maggie had powers of her own: the ability to turn the tide of a conversation, to find hope when it felt like none existed. She made things easy. "I'm surprised you didn't manage to squeeze a comic book reference in there."

"Oh, it's coming," Maggie said, raising her hand. "Give me a sec."

She cleared her throat and then looked at me with mock seriousness. "Rogue couldn't always control her powers either. In fact, a lot of your comic book heroes struggled with it, but I like Rogue, so she's the comparison you get. And to give you some hope, she eventually figured it out. True, she nearly sucked some people dry, and she did some pretty terrible things when she was a baddie. Nearly killed Ms. Marvel when she took her powers, and she *did* put Belladonna in a coma . . ." She trailed off, realizing she'd gone off on one of her tangents, and grinned. "You will figure this out. In the meantime, you could always take up gardening." She eyed the azalea bush in front of me to make her point.

"Oh, shut up," I said, cracking a small smile. "What about you? Managed to Shift yet?"

Maggie's face dropped slightly, though her eyes still sparkled. "No, not yet. But I was *this* close to growing fur this morning." She held up her hand, inspecting it closely. I winced a little thinking of the scar, raised and bumpy, on her skin—the Shifter bite that had started it all. Maggie said it was her ticket to the comic-book life she'd always dreamed of, but to me it was just another dagger of guilt that stabbed me whenever I looked at it.

Maggie studied my face for several long moments. "Listen,

Styles, you're not gonna like this, but as your best friend, I have to say it." She took a breath. "I understand why you don't want to tell Zia about the Grimoire. But is it possible that there's another reason, something else holding you back?"

"Like what?"

Maggie shrugged. "I don't know, trust issues? I mean, after everything that's happened, especially with—"

"Please don't say his name." A crack of green lightning lit up the sky.

My body trembled, and every cell underneath my skin flooded with warm energy. That place inside of me—where I kept *him* buried—rattled.

Maggie opened her mouth, but then shut it. I knew she wanted to say more—she never shied away from calling me out on crap or telling me things I didn't want to hear—but for once, she kept quiet. "Okay."

"It's just—" I held up a hand.

"You don't have to explain anything to me. I get it."

Maggie always seemed able to read my mind. "Thanks."

"Well, I think I'm going to head inside, grab a cup of hot chocolate, and then maybe work on my fur a little more. Want to come with?"

"No, you go ahead." I pointed at the azalea bush. "I might give this one more try."

Maggie waved as she headed toward the house that offered little refuge. Members of the Hetaeria were always coming and going. There was rarely a moment of quiet or solitude, and there were eyes everywhere. Every time I turned my head or turned a corner, someone was staring at me or watching me like I was a ticking time bomb likely to detonate at any moment.

I waved back, trying to smile. The throbbing in my head had intensified, and another crack of lightning split the sky.

Just breathe, Lainey. Just breathe.

But the air was thick. It clung to my nose and stuck in my throat.

I headed in the opposite direction, jumping over the low fence around the pasture, and kept walking until I was surrounded by open space. I sank to my knees, grateful for the solitude, the fresh air.

I ran a thumb over the small emerald tattoo on my wrist. *Be brave, Lainey. As you always are.* Josephine's last words to me flooded my thoughts.

"I'm trying, Jo. I really am," I whispered. "You should come see for yourself." A spark of hope ignited in my heart as I scanned the trees around me, but she wasn't there.

The ache in my chest billowed out like a sail, spreading through me and filling me until there was little room for anything else.

For the briefest second, since my walls were already dangerously low, I thought of him—of Ty. There were moments when he felt so close, I would turn around and expect to see him standing behind me. Sometimes, I even heard his voice, saying my name in that way of his, his warm eyes and smile appearing in my memory more times than I'd ever admit out loud.

But it wasn't real.

Just like everything that had been between us.

How appropriate that the Master's mark was inked exactly where his heart should have been.

"I hate you, Tyler Marek," I muttered, pushing the image of that stupid crooked smile of his out of my head.

A few feet away, a row of brittle bushes sat tucked against the tree line. "One more try," I said, closing my eyes. *Focus and control.* "*Floredia Flosium.*"

The pungent smell of scorched wood stung my nose. My eyes flew open. Engulfed in green flames, the bush turned to ash in a matter of seconds. I held up my hands, both surprised and unsurprised to see smoke rising from my fingertips.

The entire bush, charred and ruined.

Something else dead because of me.

It didn't matter that I hadn't meant to, that I wasn't trying to erupt with fatal power. I couldn't control it. I didn't even know I was doing it.

Maggie's words floated in my thoughts. *It was an accident. You have to forgive yourself for it.*

Standing up, I wiped the dirt from my legs and sucked down a shaky breath. "I am not a murderer," I said, testing the words out loud. They tasted all wrong.

I turned away from the blackened corpse of the bush and started walking back toward the main house. "I am not a murderer," I tried again.

But no matter how many times I said it out loud or how much I wanted to believe it, those words were a lie.

Murderer.

CHAPTER THREE

LAINEY

With so many people on the farm, it wasn't easy finding a place to lie low—and that's exactly what I needed. So, I headed for the barn. Its red brick walls and crisp white trim were a bright spot against the dull backdrop of the gray sky, and the mixture of hay and manure wafting through the air was oddly comforting. I'd taken horseback riding lessons when I was a kid and had always found the barn and the horses to be incredibly therapeutic. So, naturally, the barn was a place of refuge—the only spot on the farm where I could breathe easily. The horses and goats weren't exactly masters of conversation, and that suited me just fine.

I slid the barn door open and walked toward the back stall, digging into the small bag I'd brought with me.

Birdie, the chocolate-brown quarter horse I'd befriended, whinnied when she saw me coming. "Hey, you," I said, smiling. "Look what I have for you."

I held out my hand, making sure my fingers were flat and straight. A baby carrot sat in my palm.

I extended my hand until it met her wide, flaring nostrils. She snorted and sucked the carrot from my palm. It crunched loudly as she chewed.

I glanced over to the large round clock on the wall. I was *supposed* to be finishing up a training session with Zia, but I'd skipped it. Yesterday's incident with the gardenias and the scorched bush had rattled me.

"I just need a break," I said to Birdie, as if she cared why I was hiding out in the barn. *And if I'm not using magic, then no one else gets hurt. Maybe I can just hide in the barn forever.* It wasn't a good plan, but at least it was a plan. "I think I'll just stay here with you. What do you think about that, girl?"

Birdie snorted again and nudged my shoulder, snuffling for more carrots. I chuckled, handing her another one.

"Someone has a new friend."

She found me, I thought, jumping at the sound. Tensing, I waited for the reprimand that was sure to follow, but the voice that spoke wasn't dripping in sarcasm or disapproval. It was kind.

I turned around. A tall woman with a long salt-and-pepper braid stood with a grooming kit. Her golden-brown skin was slightly creased from age, and she was wearing jeans, a flannel shirt, and a friendly smile.

"It's probably just all the carrots and apples I bring her," I said, smiling back.

"Oh no, dear. It's more than that." The woman came forward and ran her hand along the ridge of Birdie's back. "Horses are very perceptive animals. There's nothing you can hide from them—they can see right into the soul." Opening the door to the stall, she led Birdie out to be groomed. I followed as she pulled a curry comb from the bucket and began running it across Birdie's back in a circular motion.

I looked up at Birdie. Her large brown eyes were fixed on my face. *What do you see, girl?* I leaned closer, the weight of my burdens bearing heavily upon me.

Murderer.

The whispered echo in my thoughts made me flinch. I stepped back, frowning.

"You really believe that?" I looked at the woman.

"It isn't difficult to see what a person is trying to hide if you look hard enough. The problem is, humans rarely take the time. Animals, however, live very differently than we do. I've never met a horse who wasn't an excellent judge of character."

As if to make the point, Birdie leaned forward, nuzzling me affectionately.

"See?" the woman said. "She agrees."

I grinned and held out my hand. "I don't think we've met. I'm Lainey."

"Ah yes," the woman said, recognition in her eyes as she shook my hand. "The DuCarmont witch who thwarted the

Hetaeria's plan at the Gathering and managed to escape the Master at the same time?" she chuckled. "You might say your reputation precedes you."

I wasn't sure how to respond to that, though my face automatically twisted into a grimace.

The woman continued, her smile still kind. "Everyone here calls me Teddy."

"I haven't seen you at the big house before. Did you just arrive?" More and more members of the Hetaeria arrived on the farm every day. It was difficult to keep them all straight.

"Oh no, I've been here for over a decade now," Teddy said. "I own this place."

"Oh," I said, surprised. "I'm sorry, I had no idea."

Teddy waved her hand. "I like to keep to myself mostly."

"You're not part of the Hetaeria?"

Teddy paused, lines creasing her forehead. She opened her mouth and shut it again as if she were choosing her words carefully. "Well . . . I suppose the easiest answer is yes, I am, but like most things in life, it's a little complicated." She gave Birdie a pat on the rump and turned toward a shelf behind us that held more grooming supplies. The curry comb she'd been using continued to move across Birdie's back as if an invisible hand were holding it.

I started slightly, though it shouldn't have surprised me to see magic used so casually. Everyone on the farm was a Supernatural.

"You're a witch too."

"I am."

I watched the brush move by itself. "You make it look so easy."

"Isn't it?" Teddy cocked her head.

"Not for me," I sighed. "I can't seem to get the hang of it. Every time I try to use my magic, it goes horribly wrong. I overshoot it or something. Zia keeps telling me it's a matter of focus, that I'm not concentrating hard enough, but I'm trying."

Teddy regarded me thoughtfully. "Might I give you a little bit of advice?"

"Please. I'm willing to try anything at this point."

"Magic isn't a one-size-fits-all type of thing. For some, it comes from here"—Teddy touched her forehead—"and for others, it comes from here." She placed her hand over her own heart. "Perhaps you belong to the latter camp. It's important to remember that either way, our magic is a part of us. It lives and breathes as we do. It feels everything we feel."

I shook my head. "If my magic is a part of me, shouldn't I be able to control it?"

"You're looking at it all wrong, dear. Magic isn't about control. It's about letting go. If you want your magic to respond to you, you have to respond to it."

I was quiet for a moment. "I don't know how to do that."

Teddy's clear, dark eyes focused on mine. Her eyebrows furrowed as she looked at me, *really* looked at me, and I shifted from one foot to the other, squirming under her gaze.

"Perhaps your magic isn't the problem. The burdens we carry can very easily wreak havoc on our psyche, on our ability to feel the magic within us." She paused, swallowing. "So ask yourself, Lainey . . . how is your heart?"

The words crumpled a wall in my chest.

Ty.

Gareth.

The people at the Gathering.

Murderer.

I pressed a hand to the aching spot, the pressure of my fingers like a bandage, barely keeping the wound from bleeding out.

My lower lip quivered. "I . . . I . . ."

"Just open yourself up," Teddy said, reaching over to squeeze my other hand, understanding alight in her eyes. "And don't be afraid to let go."

The barn door slammed open, making me jump. Birdie skittered a little and stamped her feet. Teddy stepped back, and I quickly wiped the tears that had welled up in my eyes.

"Back here," she called out.

Zia stalked toward us, the usual scowl on her face. She stopped midstride when she saw me standing next to Teddy. A muscle twitched in her jaw as she glared at me for a split second before focusing on Teddy. "There's a council meeting in a few minutes."

"Yes, I heard," Teddy replied. Her back was ramrod straight, and her warm smile was gone.

"And are you planning to attend?" Zia ground out the words.

"No, I think I'll stay here." The conversation was benign

enough, but an unnamed energy crackled between the two women, sending a chill crawling down my spine.

"Look . . . we need you there," Zia tried again. "There's a lot of planning to be done, and we could really use your *expertise*. If you could just—"

"I believe I made myself perfectly clear on the matter," Teddy replied, her voice quiet but steely.

A flush of color rose up Zia's neck and into her cheeks. "Fine," she spat.

Teddy frowned, but quickly schooled her features into a more neutral expression. "Well, I think I'll let you finish up here." She handed me the brush in her hand. "It was a pleasure meeting you, Lainey."

"It was nice meeting you too."

She gave me one last small smile and disappeared around the corner.

With a sigh, I tossed the brush back into the bucket on the ground and led Birdie quickly back into her stall. When I stepped out, Zia was still standing there glowering at me. "Well?" she demanded.

"Well what?" I asked, though I knew what she was asking.

"We had a training session, and you weren't there. Why?"

"I lost track of the time," I said, avoiding her stare. I had zero poker face, and my lie sounded feeble even to me.

Zia's hands lifted, then curled into fists that she shoved down at her side. "That's bullshit, and you know it."

"What if it is?" I asked. An ember of warmth coiled in my gut, ignited by my own bold response.

"Do you think this is some kind of game?" Zia growled.

"No," I muttered.

"Then you better have a damn good reason for skipping that session."

I straightened, trying to find the right words, the words that would make her understand. "The training sessions aren't working, and it's . . . it's complicated. I'm just trying to figure stuff out. I didn't ask for any of this, and—"

"And you think we did?" Zia rolled her eyes. "Guess what, little witch? None of us asked for this." Pain flashed across her eyes, but it was quickly replaced with her usual icy-cold glare. "We're on the brink of war, don't you get that? We all have a job to do—every single one of us. My job is to make sure we're ready, and your job is to stop whining and learn some focus and control so we can actually use you. You want to help us win this war? Train. Do the work. Fight the Master. That's it."

I sucked my bottom lip between my teeth and bit down. "I'm not whining. I just . . . don't want to hurt anyone else. Can't you understand that?"

"Is this about what happened at the Gathering?"

"Of course it is," I said.

"Do you think you're the only one with blood on your hands?" Zia laughed, the sound rancorous. "What do you think happens in a war? People die."

"I know that, but—"

"But what?" Zia's face was flushed, the shrill tone of her voice rising.

"I know I'm not explaining this well, but you have to understand. Using my magic is . . . different for me than it is for everyone else."

"Oh really? Is it because you're a DuCarmont witch? Or because you think you're better than everyone else? What is it?"

The heat boiling beneath my skin erupted. "It's because I'm the Grimoire!" I yelled. My secret echoed across the barn, out there like a breath I couldn't suck back in.

"Just because you—" Zia stopped, my words registering. "What?"

"I'm the last remaining DuCarmont witch and Keeper of the Grimoire . . . but the thing is, *I'm* the Grimoire," I repeated, slower this time. "Before my mother died, she did a spell. A spell that's never been done before."

The image of my mother—the one Josephine had showed me in the Veil—was burned into my mind. The book that burst into glowing green flames. My mother's whispered words. Me, as a child, asleep in my bed.

"She transfigured it, transferring everything to me. All the spells, all the history, everything—it's all inside me. The DuCarmont Grimoire no longer exists . . . at least not in book form. I'm the Grimoire now."

Zia stared at me, her eyebrows lifted.

"Don't you see? That's why I skipped training. I'm already powerful thanks to my lineage. Add in the power of the Grimoire, and I'm . . . *dangerous.* You saw what happened at the Gathering. I killed all those people, and I can't let something like that happen again. What if it's Serena next time or Maggie—" My voice broke on the word. "I won't let that happen."

"Does the Master know?" Zia's voice was quiet, serious.

"No," I said. "He only knows that I'm the last remaining Keeper. I was wearing what he thought to be the Grimoire when we escaped the night of the Gathering. There's a spell he wants that's inside the Grimoire, a spell that will allow him to siphon away magic from other Supernaturals."

"Serena told us about the spell and how you snuck into the Gathering to steal back the DuCarmont Grimoire," Zia said, looking confused. "But she didn't tell us—"

"She didn't know," I cut in. "I found out after the fact. I didn't tell anyone except for Maggie, and I made her promise to keep it a secret."

"Why would you keep something like this a secret?" Zia yanked a hand through her hair. This changes *everything.*"

I let out a breath. "I'm sorry, but after I found out what happened . . . it seemed safer not to. I can't seem to use magic the way you or anyone else can. I guess it's because of my mom's spell."

"It's a possibility, but I believe there may be more to it than that." Zia's face softened, something I hadn't thought possible of her severe features. "You've been carrying a lot around with you, haven't you?" Her words were uncharacteristically gentle, and they made it hard to swallow.

"You could say that," I said, "but I want to help. I want

to fight the Master, but I'm scared if I keep trying . . . Can you help me?"

"No," Zia whispered, shaking her head. "No, I can't."

My heart sank. Was I a complete lost cause then?

Zia shook her head again. "Some matters are more complex than my particular skill set. I don't think I can help you." She paused. "But I know who can."

"Who?"

She sighed. "My mother."

CHAPTER FOUR

MAGGIE

"Okay, guys. We need to have a talk." The whole gang was there: Spiderman, T'Challa and Shuri, Wolverine, Storm, Ms. Marvel, and Captain America—all my favorites, lined up in a row.

I plopped down in front of them, and they stared back at me from the colorful, glossy covers of the comic books I'd propped up against the lower rung of the long wooden fence bordering the farm. Julian had gotten them for me—my own collection still safe at home in Georgia—and I was grateful for the company.

"I need some advice," I said, scanning the lineup. "I'm having a bit of trouble with the whole Shifter thing. By now, I thought I'd be Shifting like a pro. Squirrel to cat to owl to dog to bear. Bam, bam, *bam*!" I clapped my hands together for emphasis. "But . . . so far, nothing. Any advice?"

Wolverine glanced back indifferently. T'Challa, Shuri, and Ms. Marvel had the decency to eye me sympathetically but didn't really have much to say otherwise. Spiderman was . . . well, it was hard to tell behind the mask. Captain America stood in his power pose, his wide smile seeming to mock me.

"What are you smiling about?" I grumbled, more annoyed than I wanted to admit by that smug grin. "I'm gonna get the hang of this, you know, and when they write comics about *me*, they're gonna be way more popular than your patriotic ass, so watch it."

I cleared my throat and closed my eyes. Serena used to harp on Lainey all the time about the power of visualization. Maybe it was worth a try. "Okay, Maggie, you got this. You are a squirrel. Imagine your long, bushy tail. Oh, look! An acorn! You want the acorn. *Be* the squirrel."

I waited, expecting to feel a rush of energy or a prickling sensation, but as far as I could tell, nothing was happening.

"You have short arms and a little button nose. You *are* a squirrel. Be the squirrel."

I opened my eyes and held out my arms in front of me. My skin was the same, not even the slightest hint of a reddish-brown coat. I reached up and touched my face. My nose was the exact shape I was born with. I didn't need to look over my shoulder to know that the bushy tail I'd been imagining wasn't there. I groaned and turned back to my comics. It wasn't just the Captain smirking this time. They all seemed to be having a grand ole time at my expense—even

Spiderman, whose body language was clearly indicative of laughter.

"You know what? Not all of us get off easy with spandex and web slingers, dude. I'd like to see you grow fur." I let out a huff and leaned forward. "Can you guys keep a secret?" I swallowed. "I think something might be wrong."

Inching the sleeve of my long sleeve T-shirt up, hissing through my teeth as I did so, I stared down at my scar—the one from the Scavenger bite. For the last few days, it had been incredibly sore. Now, the skin around the edges was raised and hot to the touch. I poked it with my finger, wincing as a stab of pain shot down the rest of my arm.

"Nope," I said, "this is definitely not good."

I eyed my comics. "I know what you're thinking. I should tell someone, right?" I shook my head. *At least tell Lainey.* I waved the thought away. "She's got enough to deal with right now. We all do. War and . . . stuff. Nah, it's probably nothing. No big deal." Yet, as the words came out of my mouth, they did little to remedy the uneasiness coursing through me. Something was wrong. I could feel it in my gut. My instincts were usually pretty accurate; this time, though, I hoped they were wrong.

I plastered a smile on my face. "I just have to keep practicing and focusing on my Shifting. I'll get it! Practice makes perfect, right guys?"

Someone chuckled behind me. "Are you talking to your comic books?"

I yanked the sleeve of my shirt down and turned around.

Julian stood behind me with two dripping water bottles in his hand.

"Yep," I said, shrugging. "But they're not exactly being supportive, so I'm kinda thinking of giving them the silent treatment from now on."

Julian laughed, a loud, cheerful sound, and my cheeks automatically quirked up. It was hard not to feel cheerful around Julian. He was older than me by several years, and he was like a giant teddy bear—one that could promptly kick your ass—but a teddy bear all the same.

"How's it going with the Shifting? Any luck yet?"

"Have I told you lately how much I hate that question?" I groaned, my smile fading. "Everyone keeps asking me that. Like it's easy or something. Can *you* turn into an animal at will?"

Julian whistled through his teeth. "I don't think anyone wants to see me attempt that. Skipping, however, now that's my specialty." With a wicked grin, he snapped his fingers and disappeared, only to reappear two feet away from where he was originally standing.

"Show-off," I grumbled. "Until you grow a tail, you're dead to me."

Julian laughed, opening one of his water bottles. "The key is not overthinking it." He took a long pull, nearly draining it. "Just relax. And stay hydrated." He threw me the other water bottle, and I grabbed it out of the air before it smacked me in the face.

"Why didn't I think of that?" I rolled my eyes. "I guess I

just thought it would be instantaneous, you know?" I pointed to the comics. "They make it look so easy . . . but it's a whole lot harder than I thought it would be. Peter Parker was climbing on buildings on day one. We've been here awhile now, but I haven't completed a Shift yet." I straightened. "I'm determined, though. If Bruce Banner can figure out a way to control his anger, then I can at least learn to Shift into a freaking lizard or something."

"I wasn't great at Skipping at first," Julian said, crumpling the now-empty water bottle. "I kept smacking into stuff. Walls, doors, parked cars, you name it. Eventually, I got the hang of it, though, and you will too."

"I know." I picked a blade of grass and began to tear it into tiny pieces. "I just kinda wish there was another Shifter I could train with . . . or at least ask a few questions." I looked up. "Got any random Jedi masters or mutant professors around this place?"

Julian chuckled. "Fresh out of those, I'm afraid. Why don't you just talk to Oliver?"

"Who's Oliver?"

"He's our top scout . . . *and* he's a Shifter."

"Wait," I said. "I'm confused. When we first got here, Zia said there weren't any other Shifters around."

"That's because there weren't. We use most of the Shifters in the Hetaeria as scouts, and they're gone a lot. Being able to Shift into different animals makes it pretty convenient for them to slip into places unknown. The majority of our intel comes from their scouting missions."

"Oh," I said. "And this Oliver might be able to help me?"

"Most definitely. Oliver is the best of the best. He just got back two days ago. Want me to introduce you?"

I jumped to my feet. "Is Iron Man's name Tony Stark?"

Julian laughed. "Follow me."

We headed over to the area behind the barn. There were a few smaller buildings spread out, but mostly it was open space, set up as different training arenas. We walked past several Fae practicing archery and a group of Nymphs conducting hand-to-hand drills, before stopping at a patch of yard that was covered in equipment. There was a long row of wooden poles placed incredibly close to one another, and next to it were several hurdles of various heights. Beyond that was a tall, skinny catwalk and a brush jump. A large triangle-shaped structure and what looked like a canvas tunnel finished off the area.

I'd seen similar equipment before, but its presence here on the farm was confusing.

"Is that a . . ." I leaned forward over the fence railing to get a closer look. "An agility course?" I used to go to the rodeo with my parents every year. The dog shows were always our favorite event.

Julian smirked at me. "Just watch."

My eyes widened as a large German shepherd shot out from behind one of the buildings and launched up and over the triangular structure. It leapt over the hurdles with ease and through the canvas tunnel. With both grace and speed, it raced across the catwalk, over the brush jump, and began to weave in and out of the line of poles. It moved so quickly and so precisely that it didn't even look like it was moving, save for the dust flying up around its feet.

"Whoa," I said. As the dog finished the course, I raised my hands to applaud, but with a soft pop, the dog Shifted. A bushy black fox perched on its haunches where the dog had been. It sniffed the air for a microsecond before it was off, running through the course at the same breakneck speed. The movements were different this time—a fox moves much differently than a large dog—more bounding but still exact and full of speed.

At the end of the course, there was another *pop*. This time, an orange tabby flew through the obstacles. There were two more Shifts after that: a small field mouse and a brown tree squirrel.

Once the squirrel had cleared the line of poles, it leapt toward the fence where we were standing. With a final *pop*, the squirrel disappeared, and a muscular figure stood in its place.

Oliver.

He was tall with broad shoulders and younger than I expected. When Julian mentioned him, I assumed he was a middle-aged dude. This guy didn't look much older than me. He had dark hair and eyes, and his skin was a rich umber color. He wasn't wearing a shirt—only a pair of faded gym shorts— and his entire torso was glistening with sweat.

"Whoa," I said again, and Julian snickered.

Oliver stalked toward the fence where a white towel was hanging from one of the posts.

"Oliver!" Julian boomed. "Welcome back, man! How was it out there?"

Oliver mopped his face and neck with the towel. "Julian." His voice wasn't as deep as I'd expected, but it had a gravelly rasp to it. "It was . . . the usual." His eyes flicked to me for the slightest of seconds before he focused back on Julian. "What can I do for you? Does Zia need something?"

"No, you're good, man. Got someone I want you to meet." Julian shoved me forward. "This is Maggie. She's a Shifter too."

Oliver's eyes narrowed on me. "Oh?"

"I got bit," I blurted out, my brain too busy stumbling over itself to come up with something more normal to say. Heat flooded my cheeks. I let out a laugh, trying to seem carefree, but it came out sounding a lot like Goofy's famous *hyuck.*

Annnnddd . . . I officially want to go and die now.

After a few awkward seconds, Julian shook his head. "So, uh . . . Maggie here's been having a little trouble with Shifting. Since you're back now, I thought maybe you could give her some pointers."

"Yes, teach me your ways, Obi Wan," I joked before I could stop myself. *Dear God, woman. SHUT UP.* I made a mental note to slap myself later.

Oliver didn't even crack a smile. He ran a hand over his face, rubbing his eyes. "No." He shook his head. "I'm getting ready to head back out. I don't have the time."

Julian frowned. "Come on, man. Zia told me just this

morning that she was going to give you a break, let you stick around for a while. Just give Maggie a few pointers." He clapped his hands on my shoulders, shaking me slightly. "Trust me, she's a fast learner."

I nodded, though it was hard to tell if the fluttering in my stomach was from the anticipation of him saying no . . . or yes.

Oliver groaned. "Fine. But just a couple of lessons."

"Dude, that'd be awesome!" Julian held up his hand for a high five. Oliver paused for only a second before he returned it.

"I really appreciate it," I said, "I promise I'll—"

"0600." Oliver's voice cut through mine.

"Huh?"

"Six in the morning," he replied in a tone that I was quite sure was the audible version of an eye roll. "If we're going to train, we need to do it early."

"Oh. Got it. Should I meet you here?"

"South pasture. By the tree line." He didn't wait for a response. With a nod at Julian, Oliver tossed the towel back over the fence and turned toward the agility course. He started to run, and in seconds, his two legs became four. He was back in his first form, the German shepherd, and he began running through the course again, even faster than he had before.

I looked at Julian. He was trying not to laugh.

"Well, that went well," he managed, his whole body shaking as he tried to keep the laughter in.

I ignored him and headed back the way we came, my cheeks still burning. "I can't decide if I should thank you or punch you!" I called over my shoulder.

He jogged up, chuckling. "Trust me, Oliver really is the best. If anyone can help you with Shifting, it's him."

"Fine . . . but is he always so serious? The guy makes Magneto look like a cuddly kitten."

"Well, let's just hope your Shifting abilities are better than your jokes," Julian teased, turning his head as one of the Nymphs called his name. Waggling his eyebrows, he winked once at me and then jogged over. "Ladies!" he called out in a booming voice.

I rolled my eyes, imagining a preening peacock as I watched him puff out his chest. I wasn't quite ready to go back to the main house, so I wandered over to where the Fae archers were practicing. I didn't want to disrupt their concentration, so I was quiet, settling down on a shady patch of grass a few feet behind them.

The one on the right, tall with long red hair, pulled his bow back with what looked like very little effort, releasing the arrow. With a loud smack, it landed directly in the center of the bull's-eye. "Not bad," the other one, with long black hair pulled up in a bun, said, surveying the target. "Try a lighter hand."

The two Fae shot a few more arrows between them while images of the shirtless wonder ran through my thoughts. My face warmed, and I fanned my cheeks. *Get it together, girl.* I moved my hand a little faster.

My entire body was hot—too hot. I squeaked a little as black spots appeared before my eyes, completely obstructing my view. I swallowed hard, swaying a little as a rush of dizziness washed over me. My arm throbbed, and I put my hand over my scar. I could feel the raised skin through the fabric of my skirt.

I waited for the dizziness to pass. When my vision cleared, the two Fae were turned in my direction. "You okay?" the one with the bun asked.

I ignored the stabbing pain in my arm. "You bet." The two Fae shared a look, shrugged, and resumed nocking more arrows. As their focus returned to the targets, I stood up, careful not to move too quickly.

When I was sure the dizziness wasn't going to return, I let out a huge breath and carefully tugged my sleeve up. The bite mark on my arm looked angrier than it had before.

My heart gave a small stutter, and I yanked my sleeve back down.

Something is definitely wrong.

I headed for the main house. Lainey would be finished with her training session soon. *I'll tell her as soon as I see her.*

I passed the fence where I'd stopped earlier and scooped up my comics from the grass where I'd left them. The bright colors and smiling heroes on the covers always made things seem better, but in this case, even they couldn't lighten the rock in the pit of my stomach.

"I don't suppose any of you might be willing to tell her?" I asked, staring down at their faces.

SEEKER

There were no volunteers.

I sighed. "Didn't think so."

CHAPTER FIVE

LAINEY

The cottage was small, but homey. The front windows were large and oval-shaped, and perched beneath them were brightly colored window boxes full of herbs. There was smoke rising from the brick chimney, and a tiny, dormant vegetable patch sat adjacent to the building. It was a cozy-looking place, but I had my doubts about the woman we'd find inside. If she was as delightful as Zia, I was in for a real treat.

The formidable look on Zia's face was anything but warm, and as we walked up the worn path and knocked on the door, I thought of Hansel and Gretel. They'd almost ended up in an oven—what in the world was about to happen to me?

When the door opened, however, the woman I'd been expecting—beastly, with the same severe expression as Zia—wasn't standing there. Instead, Teddy, the kind witch I'd met in the barn, stood wiping her hands on a blue dish towel, a half apron wrapped around her waist.

She looked back and forth between Zia and me. If she was surprised to see us standing on her doorstep, I couldn't tell.

"Mother," Zia said, her tone flat, as if it pained her to say the word. With them standing so close to each other, it was easy to see the resemblance: same bone structure, same complexion, same thick, furrowed brows, and a fierceness that could only be inherited. I was surprised I didn't see it before.

"Zia," Teddy replied. Her tone was equally flat, but then she turned to me and smiled. "Hello, Lainey. I wasn't expecting to see you again quite so soon."

I smiled back. "Neither was I."

"Mother, we need to talk."

Teddy looked us both over again and pushed the door open wider, gesturing for us to come inside. "I was thinking about doing some baking," she said, following behind us. The counter in the small kitchen was covered in what looked to be supplies for making a pie: flour, evaporated milk, eggs, and various spices.

"That will have to wait," Zia barked.

The smile faded from Teddy's face. "If this is about the council meeting, I've already told you—"

Zia held up a hand. "It's not. It's about her." She pointed to me.

Teddy's eyes darted over to mine. I resisted the urge to give a little wave.

"I need you to train her."

Teddy cocked her head. "You? Or the Hetaeria?"

Her question caught me off guard, but Zia only blinked, her stoic expression unchanging. "Both," she answered, her upper lip twitching in annoyance.

"We've had this discussion many times before. I do believe you know where I stand." Without waiting for any kind of response from Zia, Teddy walked over to her kitchenette and began pouring flour into a measuring cup.

"For once, can you stop looking at everything through your own selfish lens?" Zia's face had finally cracked. Her eyes were wide and flashing. "This is about more than just you, Mother."

Teddy whirled around to face her daughter. I could have sworn the temperature in the room dropped dramatically. I shivered, watching as mother and daughter had an entire conversation with their eyes only. I was eyeing the door and wondering if I should give them some space when Zia snapped her fingers at me.

"Tell her what you told me," she said sharply.

Annoyance surged through me, but I kept the sarcastic retorts rolling through my mind to myself. Instead, I told Teddy about the spell my mother had cast and how the DuCarmont Grimoire was no longer a book, but a living, breathing person.

When I finished, Teddy's face was softer, her eyes full of concern. "Such a thing has never been done before," she whispered.

"It was the only way to protect us both," I said, the thought of my mother tugging at my heart.

"This sort of magic is unprecedented," Zia looked at her mother. "*And* she's a DuCarmont. She needs someone who can train her to use her own magic, but also someone who can help her access the Grimoire and use it."

"A task that you yourself are fully qualified to do," Teddy argued.

"No," Zia shook her head, her eyes landing on me. "There's more to it than just an uncharted level of magic." She shifted from one foot to the other. "She's blocked."

"You don't have to talk about me like I'm not here," I snapped.

Zia ignored me. "You know I'm not the best at that sort of thing. She needs someone who understands. She needs *you*, Mother."

Teddy was quiet, staring at me as if she were trying to decipher a complicated puzzle. "I'm sorry," she finally said, her voice soft. "I can't help you."

Zia growled. "Can't or won't?"

Teddy frowned, her eyes full of sadness. "Does it make a difference?"

"You can't just blow this off, Mother!" Zia stomped across the floor. "This war is happening whether you want it to or not."

I winced at Teddy's words. If she wouldn't help me, who would? Zia continued arguing with her mother, but I was lost in my own thoughts. The tiny seeds of fear and doubt were growing roots, creeping through me.

"You asked me earlier," I said, focusing on Teddy, "about

my heart." I let the words carry over the yelling until both women had fallen silent. "To answer your question . . . it's broken. My heart. My magic. *Me*."

My words hung suspended in the air.

"Please, Teddy." My voice cracked on her name.

Teddy closed her eyes for a moment, then opened them again. "Okay," she breathed.

Zia's eyebrows rose. "You'll do it? You'll train her?"

"I can't promise anything." Teddy looked to me. "But I'll try."

Zia's eyebrows lowered, and she looked less likely to jump out of her skin than she had a few moments ago. "I'll leave you to it then." She stalked out the door, not sparing either of us another glance.

The moment the door slammed behind her, it was like fresh air had been blown back into the room. Everything was lighter and brighter.

Teddy smiled kindly at me. "She's a bit of a thundercloud. Too much like her father, I'm afraid." She motioned for me to sit on the cushy blue sofa across the room.

"I think a snow-cone maker in Alaska is warmer than she is," I said, the words slipping out.

I winced, realizing I had just insulted her daughter, but Teddy laughed.

"You're probably right," she agreed. "Though to be fair, she wasn't always like that."

It felt odd to be prying into Zia's personal life, but I was curious. "What happened to her?"

SEEKER

"Life." Teddy's answer was simple, but there was a deep sadness in her eyes. "But let's not talk about her any longer," she said with a flick of her hand. "We have quite a bit of work ahead of us, and we'll need to get started right away."

She untied her apron, dropping it on the countertop, and walked over to a wooden bookshelf. She pulled a thick brown leather book from the shelf and placed it on the coffee table in front of me. She pointed at it. "Open the book to page 112."

I moved toward the book, my hand outstretched.

"With magic," Teddy corrected, her voice kind. "I need to see what we're working with."

"Oh, right. Sorry." I swallowed and tried to clear my mind. Closing my eyes, I focused all my attention and energy on that book. *You can do this, Lainey. Just focus on lifting the cover and turning the pages.*

My body began to warm and buzz with energy. *Turn to page 112.*

Tiny jolts of electricity pricked my skin, and when I heard the familiar sound of pages turning, satisfaction pulsed through me—I was sure it was working. But when I opened my eyes, the pages of the book were flying back and forth as if they were caught in opposing wind streams.

I huffed, throwing my hands up in the air. "See? It's like I told you in the barn: My magic never responds the way it's supposed to."

Teddy studied me, her face revealing nothing. "It's like that for all of us in the beginning. Those early manifestations are either accidents or emotional outbursts." She gave me a knowing look.

My earlier attempt with the azaleas flashed in my mind. "You don't say," I muttered.

Teddy continued. "Without understanding how your magic works, you've been blindly channeling all your emotions into your magic—neither of which can be easily controlled. But think of it like this: You don't have any control over your lungs, yet they expand and contract on their own, exactly as they're supposed to. Magic is like that—you can't try to control it or dictate how it works. That's your problem." She pointed to the book, whose pages were still flipping wildly back and forth.

With a quick flick of her wrist, the pages stilled and the cover of the book snapped shut. "You're trying to force it—focusing so much on the outcome that you're creating a pocket of power with a mind of its own. The things that you're feeling, or trying *not* to feel, are fueling it."

She took a step forward, her eyes darting from me to the book. In a quick flip of pages, the book lay perfectly open to page 112, with hardly any effort at all. "Having magic isn't something that you can just focus really hard on and expect to see results." She looked at me pointedly.

"Instead, magic is like having a sixth sense, a feeling, an urge, an awareness beyond what other, non-magical people have. Just like with the other five senses, it's something that feels natural. If you were to lose one of your senses, your brain would shift its energy and processing power to the remaining senses, thus giving you a keener awareness of them. It would take some time to get used to, however. Magic is like that, but the opposite."

She smiled at me. "Instead of losing a sense, you've essentially gained one. You need to retrain your whole body to tap into this new sense. It's a matter of energy and processing, not control. It's a natural process that your body is already hardwired for. But you must also learn to separate your magic from the caverns in your soul, the aches you carry."

"Try again," she said, pointing to the book. "Only this time, remember that you don't have to force the magic. You just have to trust it will do what you need it to. You have to let go of whatever fear or pain is blocking you. Let your body do what it already instinctually knows to do."

"I'll try." I closed my eyes again and took several deep breaths, letting them out slowly.

Okay, Lainey. You have to—. I stopped myself. *No. Clear your mind. Don't force the magic, feel it.*

I waited, focusing on my breathing and keeping my mind clear.

And then I felt it.

The warm current that always shot to the surface whenever I attempted to use magic was there. I could feel it trapped beneath a barrier—one of my own creation.

I could see now what Teddy meant. Without realizing it, I'd placed walls around it. My fear, my doubt, my grief—the mortar and bricks. Every now and then, I was able to punch through the walls, but instantly the hole would repair itself, containing the magic once more. Like a tiny finger, it prodded gently at the barrier, simply waiting to be acknowledged.

With several deep breaths, I imagined the walls crumbling piece by piece until the barrier was nothing but ash, but the bricks barely budged.

Murderer, the voice in my head whispered. *MURDERER!* it screamed, throwing images of Gareth at me, the knife in my hands, the blood pooling around me. The mansion I'd reduced to rubble.

No, I whispered back. *That's not who I want to be.*

A crack ripped through the wall, the fissure not large, but wide enough that a bolt of electric-green lightning shot from its seams. I gasped as a warm rush of energy pulsed through me, threads of current stretching and weaving into my core: in my chest, my fingertips, down to the balls of my feet. Everywhere.

The threads burst into a thousand tiny sparks, emerald flames that grew with every heartbeat, riding the current beneath my skin.

Something else cracked inside my chest, and I let out a wail, gripping the sides of my head.

"No, no, no," I murmured, trying to quell those green flames—to keep them from growing, from spreading . . .

At the Gathering, the sconces had reacted first, shattering into a thousand pieces. The chandelier was next, a shower of crystal fragments and flame that ignited the walls, the tapestries, the tablecloths. The mansion had become an emerald inferno.

And it was all my fault.

I shoved my magic away with all my might, severing the connection with such force, it sucked the air out of my lungs. I choked, my eyes flying open.

Teddy sat next to me on the sofa, but her gentle smile was gone. Around us, a tornado of books whirled around the room, spinning and smacking against one another.

"I'm so sorry!" I yelled over the noise, raising my hands. Sparks of bright green light were shooting intermittently from my fingertips. "I don't know how to stop it."

Teddy studied me, seemingly unsurprised and not the least bit bothered that the entire contents of her bookshelves were swirling above us. "You're scared," she said, her voice carrying above the noise. "But you don't have to be. Your magic is part of you—it won't hurt you."

The words slammed into the gaping hole in my chest. "It's not me I'm worried about," I said, buckling under the ache. "I couldn't save Gareth, and my magic is the reason he and so many others are dead."

The books picked up speed, whipping and swirling around so quickly, a low train sound echoed off the walls. A particularly thick leather-bound book got off track and careened into the floor lamp, knocking both to the floor, loose pages flying everywhere. I winced. "I can't . . . I won't . . . I . . ."

"Lainey." Teddy leaned over and gripped my shoulder. "It wasn't your fault."

"It was."

"No," she said firmly. "It wasn't. You no more could've

saved Gareth than I could've saved—" She cut off, swallowing. "We've all lost people. What happened with your magic was an accident. You can't keep blaming yourself for it."

The books slowed. "I don't know how. Every second of every day, it's all I can think about."

"It may take time," Teddy replied, "but you have to forgive yourself. Let go of all that pain and fear."

A tear rolled down my cheek, and the books slammed to a stop, frozen midair. "I can't."

"You don't have to be afraid of your magic," Teddy continued, her voice soft. "Just let it *in*."

I thought of my magic, of that wall, still standing around it. Standing, but not impenetrable. The crack, that rip in the rock, was proof.

I let out a breath, and the books fell, landing in a heap around us.

"I'll try."

Teddy gave me a half smile. "Good. It's a start." She began stacking the fallen books on the coffee table.

"I'm really sorry about . . . um, the mess," I said, reaching for the books nearest me.

"Not the first time this has happened," Teddy chuckled. "Zia's my daughter, remember. Quite the temper on that one. Now, if you'll excuse me, I have a pie to bake." She stood up and bustled over to the kitchen area, already reaching for the bag of flour on the counter.

"Oh." My eyebrows scrunched together. "Are we done?"

"Yes," Teddy answered. "For the day. But I expect to see you back here tomorrow. Same time?"

The wound in my chest ached, and I felt deflated and weary. Could I really return and face it all again tomorrow? Did I have a choice?

"I'll be here."

❧ • ❧

I left Teddy to baking and headed back up to the main house. The emotional journey had taken its toll; my eyelids drooped, and I couldn't stop yawning. I needed a cup of coffee or a nap. I'd settle for either.

When I walked up, Maggie was sitting on the front porch, a borrowed laptop atop her legs.

"Hey," I said, sitting on the porch swing across from her. "I didn't see you at breakfast this morning."

Maggie looked up from the screen. "I got up early and went for a run. I was hoping it might help me clear my head, maybe help with the Shifting."

"And did it?"

"Nope. Nothing." Maggie sighed. "It's going to happen soon, though. I can feel it."

I squirmed in my seat, though it was comforting to know I wasn't the only one struggling with my magic. "How do you know?"

"Animal instincts, of course!" Maggie grinned at me, and I had to laugh. "What have you been up to?" she asked.

"Magic training with Zia's mother."

Maggie's mouth dropped open. "What?"

I laughed before launching into a recap of the morning and my training session with Teddy.

"What are you doing?" I tapped the laptop, ready for a subject change. "Catching up on YouTube videos?"

Maggie rolled her eyes. "To do that, we'd actually have to have decent Wi-Fi around here." She shook her head. "No, I was just writing a quick response to the email my parents sent me."

The corners of her smile drooped a little. The mention of her parents always had that effect.

"How are they?"

"They're good from what I can tell. It seems Dad is still driving Mom nuts with all of his impressions, but at least nothing's changed."

"Mags, I'm really sorry that—"

She held up her hand, stopping me. "Don't start that again, Styles. You need to quit blaming yourself for everything."

She'd said the same thing over and over in other conversations, but that didn't stop the guilt from churning through me. "But if it weren't for me, you'd—"

"I wouldn't be a Shifter, and I wouldn't be with my best friend who, by the way, would be totally lost without me."

I cracked a tiny smile. "Can't argue with that." I let out a sigh of my own. "But you miss them."

"Of course I do," Maggie said, "but it's safer for them

if I stay away. Besides, Serena said the spell could always be reversed later. I'm just glad Zia was willing to do the spell, even over the phone. I'd rather them think I was studying abroad than in any kind of danger. Or know the truth. At least not yet."

"Yeah, it's probably best."

Maggie turned her attention back to the screen. She was silent for several minutes, the keyboard clicking as her fingers flew across the keys. The droop in her features was still there, and when she closed her laptop, her face was solemn.

"I'm sure even if they knew the truth, it wouldn't change how they feel about you," I said, taking a guess at her worry.

"It isn't that." She bit down on her lower lip, rolling it between her teeth.

"Then what is it?"

"I need to tell you something."

There was something in her voice that made the hair on the back of my neck stand up. "What?"

She paused, chewing on her bottom lip, as if she were thinking hard about something. Then, as if a flip had been switched, she broke out into a wide smile. "I think we should get out of here for a while."

"Wait . . . what?" I let out a breathy laugh.

"Think about it, Styles. We've been cooped up on this farm for ages now. I'd kill for some new comic books and a decent cup of coffee, and you can't tell me you wouldn't like to escape Zia for a few hours."

She had a point. The idea of being out from under Zia's glaring eyes was more than appealing.

"They'll never let us leave."

"I wasn't suggesting we ask permission," Maggie said with a wink.

Sneak out? It was a terrible idea, reckless even. But a few hours where I didn't have to be Lainey Styles DuCarmont, murderer and broken witch?

I grinned. "Let's do it."

CHAPTER SIX

TY

Despite the gray sky and the cold breeze, Washington Street was buzzing with people. I scanned each face as I walked, more out of habit than anything else. I knew Lainey wasn't there—my Praetorian senses told me as much—but that didn't stop me from carefully scrutinizing the brunettes who had the misfortune of walking beside me on the sidewalk. One such girl gave me a wide berth as she passed by, no doubt due to the scowl on my face.

Grinding my teeth, I shifted my backpack from one shoulder to the other and headed for the striped white and green awning at the corner. A mom-and-pop coffee shop sat cheerfully between a children's clothing store and a hair salon. Inside, the rich aroma of coffee hit me like a jolt to the system. I immediately perked up, despite the exhaustion that clung to every inch of me like a second skin.

The line was long, which I always took as a good sign. I didn't mind waiting. I had all the time in the world, it seemed.

"You new in town?"

A young girl with shoulder-length brown hair and wide hazel eyes stood behind me in line, her perfectly white teeth glistening behind a strawberry-colored smile. She had ivory skin and a light smattering of freckles on the bridge of her nose. The purple sweater she wore matched the bow at the top of her head. She looked to be about twelve or so.

"Something like that," I grumbled.

"I thought so, small town and all. You on some kind of backpacking trip?"

I snorted. *If only that were true.* I'd been traveling for three weeks now, tracking Lainey. The Praetorian bond was intact, but weak, and using it as a compass wasn't an exact science. I'd hit more dead ends than anything, and while I was sure she was close, I couldn't pinpoint her exact location. She was hidden behind magic—that much was obvious—but Praetorian bond or no, I'd yet to discover a way to get around it. I had my hands in the hay, but finding the needle was taking a lot longer than I thought.

The frustration coiling low in my gut had been my constant travel companion for days. I was beyond the ability of making small talk.

"It's too bad you didn't come through during the summer," the girl continued, not bothered by my lack of response. "That's tourist season. Lots of people, lots of crowds. Plenty of unsuspecting visitors."

It was an odd thing to say. The girl's face seemed to flash as she said it, and the gleam in her eye sent an alarm bell off in my head. My fingers moved quickly, reaching for the knife in the inside of my pocket, but the girl just smiled sweetly and skipped around me—jumping my place in line.

After the barista handed her a cup of hot chocolate, she gave me an angelic smile and whisked toward the door.

I shook my head. Clearly, the days of travel and very little sleep were getting to me. I stepped up to the register and tried not to grimace at the girl working the cash register. "Large espresso, please," I said, digging into my back pocket for my wallet. It wasn't there. I checked the other pocket. Nothing. I glanced around to see if it had fallen out on the floor, but it wasn't there either. It was gone.

Swearing, I fished a few spare dollars out of the bottom of my backpack and handed them over. As I wrapped my fingers around the warm Styrofoam cup, a phantom giggle crested over my shoulder. I whirled around, but the elderly gentleman standing patiently behind me just gave me a vacant smile and moved to place his order.

The wind bit at my cheeks as I stepped back outside. On the sidewalk, a block ahead, I saw the girl in the purple sweater. She stared at me, a wide grin lifting her cheeks. Then she held up two fingers, and dangling between them was a familiar brown square. My wallet.

What the— "Hey!" I yelled.

With a laugh, she jolted down a side street, disappearing faster than I would've thought possible, given her short legs.

Then it hit me. The flash of her face and the mischievous look in her eyes. It only took me a second to put two and two together.

I jogged after her, piping-hot espresso spilling over my fingertips as I ran. "Shit!" I hissed.

When I turned the corner, the shady side street was empty. The girl in the purple sweater wasn't visible, but I knew she was still there.

"I know you're here," I called out. "You might as well come out." A musical laugh came from the shadows. "You know, for being masters of disguise, I'm pretty disappointed in your Glamour. You could have at least made yourself a little taller. Old enough to walk into a bar at least." This time, it was a hiss that came from the shadows. I continued my goading. "But I guess it's true what they say of Tricksters: lots of magic, but not a whole lot of brains."

With a wild yell, the girl leapt out of the shadows and snarled at me. Her wide purple eyes were catlike and shining. They'd been a perfectly normal hazel back in the coffee shop. Now that I knew what she was, it was easy to see behind the Glamour she wore to blend in with the humans. Her cheekbones were sharper and more angular. Her teeth, though still pearly white, were pointed like canines.

"What do you know about my kind, human?" Her voice was low and gravely, but still tinkled.

"Enough to know that you're either alone and lack training, or you're too foolish to care you've attempted to trick a Supernatural instead of a human."

The girl cocked her head.

I pointed at myself. "Praetorian."

She held up her hand. My wallet was sitting casually in her palm. "More like succeeded."

"Only because you caught me decaffeinated," I said, smirking.

I held out my hand for the wallet, which she placed in my palm with a grumble.

"So, which is it?" I asked.

She cocked her head again, not understanding my question.

"Are you alone or foolish?"

The girl stared at me for a few long seconds before she shrugged. "Alone. Half my family was killed by the Guard. The other half follows *him* now."

I didn't have to ask who she was referring to. "And what about you? Whose side are you on?"

She stared at me again, and this time, behind the Glamour, the conflict that warred on her face was familiar. I saw the same fire and flood every time I looked at my own reflection.

"You know," she said, her voice soft but strong, "I haven't decided yet."

I wasn't sure how to respond. My path had been decided for so long, it was the only course I was sure of.

"I can take care of myself, though," the Trickster said quickly, her Glamour flashing as she hissed.

"I believe that," I said, and then, "What's your name?"

"Cora," she said with a grin that sent a chill down my spine.

"Well, Cora. I think—"

There was a loud crash at the end of the street as several aluminum trash cans fell over. A low growl echoed off the brick walls, and Cora's face instantly fell.

"What is it?" I asked, keeping my voice low.

"Troll," she squeaked back. Then, without another word, she dashed toward the main street and disappeared around the corner.

I couldn't blame her. Trolls were nasty creatures. Strong, powerful, and terrible tempers—provoking one was basically a death wish.

I moved quietly, backing up the way I came, careful not to make any sudden movements. I couldn't see the Troll, but they were masters of camouflage, and I didn't want to get close enough to get a better look.

When I was safely back on Main Street and I was sure it wasn't following me, I let out a breath. Trolls were aggressive, but rarely attacked without reason.

I downed the rest of my coffee and headed down the sidewalk. The pathway leading to the water was up ahead. I walked with my head down, pulling the collar of my leather jacket up around my neck. The few people I passed were moving in the opposite direction, and before long, I found myself alone on the shore of Lake Michigan.

Despite the biting wind coming off the water, the sand was warm from the afternoon sun. I'd grown up near the

Gulf, so I was used to the white sand salt beaches of the Florida panhandle. I'd been a little surprised when I'd arrived in town and saw that the shore here was, in fact, very beach-like.

Even now, as I watched the ebb and flow of the waves, there was a part of me that was still surprised, though my brain was whirling much too quickly for me to dwell on it for long. The gray clouds were starting to spit out snow flurries, and patches of ice chunks dotted the water near the pier. The brilliant red lighthouse and the fog-signal building were a stark contrast to the otherwise dull backdrop of the overcast sky.

The lullaby of the waves was familiar enough, and listening to their hypnotic rhythm reminded me of another beach, in another place and another time. I closed my eyes, and for a moment, I let my guard down. I let myself get lost in time . . .

ڡ · ؟

The boy's fingers were as stiff as the long wooden staff he gripped in his hands, his knuckles aching. The muscles in his arms quivered from the hours of practice, and his shoulders were tight and knotted. Sand clung to his sweaty skin, an abrasive rash that chaffed when he moved, and the skin underneath the grit was red from both the sun and the friction.

He ground his teeth and tried not to let his misery show on his face.

"Remember, son. Pain is a tether." The older man seemed to be reading his thoughts. "It can be a limit or a reminder. The choice is yours."

The boy sighed. His father's sun-browned skin glistened with sweat, but his eyes held no trace of the exhaustion or agony that riddled the boy's bones. The identical staff in his hands was worn from years of practice and use, a natural extension of the man's movements.

The boy's own stick still felt clunky in his hands.

With a groan, the boy dropped his stick and plopped down on the warm sand. The sea lapped at his toes, the white foam soothing his hot skin.

"I can't do it," he murmured, swallowing the lump that had formed in his throat.

"Yes, you can," the older man said gently. "It just takes practice."

The boy sniffed. "I'll never be as good as you are."

The man wrapped an arm around the boy's gritty shoulder. "When I was your age, I thought the same thing, but I kept practicing, and eventually, I got the hang of it. You will too."

The boy flexed and unflexed his sore fingers. "If you say so." He glared at the offending stick laying in the sand. "How much longer are we going to do this?"

His father chuckled, the lines crinkling around his warm brown eyes. "Just awhile longer." He squeezed the boy's shoulder. "What do you say we give it another shot?"

"Okay. But just one more," the boy said, grabbing his staff and hopping to his feet.

His father did the same, and they moved away from the surf and back onto a flat expanse of the beach. Standing apart, they faced each other, their staves held at the ready.

The father inclined his head ever so softly, the words between them unspoken. They bowed to one another, and as a large wave crashed to the shore, they moved, swinging their staves in a careful, practiced rhythm—their movements as fluid and as strong as the sea.

Like cobras, they struck, the staves bashing each other with a loud smack.

The boy let his voice out, releasing a yell as his staff struck the man's.

"Good!" the father encouraged. "Stay light on your feet. Make sure you have complete control over your stance."

The boy moved again, his feet advancing in the careful, practiced steps, and his limbs already anticipating their next move. "Excellent, son!" his father shouted over the cracking of wooden stick on wooden stick.

The man's words filled the boy with confidence, and he grinned. He whirled around, feeling success within his grasp. He was rewarded with a sharp thwack on the shoulder.

"Stay focused. Never assume victory until you're holding it in your hand," the older man said, his staff gripped at the ready.

The boy's smile disappeared. He readjusted his stance, holding his staff loosely.

When the older man struck, he was prepared.

His body moved exactly where it needed to without much thought. Muscle memory and focus aided him, and for the first time, his staff spun through the air with ease—natural and graceful.

When the man swung again, the boy blocked the blow and twisted, throwing his opponent off balance. Seizing an opportunity, he dove forward to strike.

They stood facing each other in the sand, chests heaving, and the boy's staff was inches away from the man's throat.

"See?" the man said, breaking into a wide grin. "I told you. All it takes is practice."

Whooping, the boy dropped his staff and threw his fists in the air.

His father watched the boy until he had finished celebrating. "Just remember, son. Being a Praetorian isn't about winning every fight. It's about doing what is right. You must remember the difference."

"Aren't they the same?" the boy asked.

"It might seem that way, but no. Doing what is right does not guarantee that you will end on the side of victory. You must do all you can to protect your Calling, defend those who cannot defend themselves, and fight battles that threaten what we as the Praetorians stand for. Do you remember the oath?"

The little boy nodded, crossing his arm and placing his fist over his heart.

"To live by light and each day's breath. To serve, to give, and others protect. To fight, to love, and do what's right. This spoken seal, my word, my life," he recited.

"Good. Promise me you'll never forget."

"I promise."

"I'm proud of you, Ty." The lines around his father's face were crinkled as he smiled broadly.

"Thanks, Dad."

That moment, preserved perfectly in my mind, seemed so long ago. Another lifetime, even. I didn't recognize that boy anymore. He certainly wasn't me.

"I'm proud of you, Ty."

My father's voice was crystal clear in my mind. Lately, I'd been hearing his more than my own.

By the time the memory faded completely, my chest was tight and heaving. The bone-deep ache resonating throughout my entire body was a looming and steadfast shadow, just as it had been for years. They say time heals all wounds, but not for me. The fire inside of me only grew hotter, and my heart . . . only colder.

"That's not entirely true," my father's voice whispered.

Lainey's face flashed in my thoughts. Her long brown hair and emerald eyes.

"You care for her."

I shook my head, ignoring the ache I'd felt since the

Gathering. "She is my Calling. Nothing more. It's the bond. I don't care for her like that, I—" I stopped myself. The lie tasted sour on my tongue, even though there was no one to hear it.

Briefly, I thought back to the dance we'd shared, where for a single moment in time, I had forgotten my pain. How, for the briefest second, something other than hate and bloodthirst had filled me, a ray of light that had cracked open the darkness, a warmth flowing through my cold and unfeeling system. A breath of fresh air.

I swallowed, imagining my father's eyes—open to the sky, lifeless and unseeing. I squeezed my fists together, remembering how that steady rhythm, the familiar beat of his heart, slowed and finally stopped beating beneath my palm.

I'm sorry, Lainey.

The Master killed my father, and I was going to kill the Master. Whatever else was inside me was nothing but chaff and fodder that would come to no end.

You have a choice. This time it was my own voice in my thoughts, my advice to Lainey coming back to haunt me.

Free will and choice.

But I didn't have a choice. My soul was stained black. There was no coming back from it.

Taking a deep breath, I stood up and wiped the sand from the back of my pants. I stepped toward the boardwalk when an agonizing sensation ripped through me, doubling me over and robbing me of breath. A high-pitched ringing echoed in my ears, and it was like my whole head was being split open.

Distorted images flashed before my eyes. A patch of blackened ground. Fingers wrapped in smoke. A windstorm of . . . books? And a single word shouted repeatedly and wrapped in such raw emotion, it brought me to my knees.

"Murderer."

"Lainey," I gasped. My Praetorian senses were going haywire, and the connection between us sparked like a jolt of electricity through me.

I collapsed in the sand, and everything stopped. There was nothing but the gray clouds overhead and the rhythmic sound of the waves crashing against the shoreline.

I lay there for several minutes, my chest heaving as my body recovered. When I could breathe easily again, I sat up slowly. A heart-wrenching feeling ached deep in my chest, but it wasn't mine. It was hers.

Something had changed. Our connection had been weak since the Gathering. I knew Lainey was cloaked in magic, but I'd also assumed she'd built her own wall against me. Given how we parted, it hadn't surprised me when she'd easily managed to block me out—but now, the walls were gone. She was devastated and heartbroken . . . and I felt it all.

I swallowed, surprised by the lump that had formed in my throat, and forced everything I was feeling down into the smallest parts of me.

Think. I commanded myself. *Focus.*

I closed my eyes, concentrating on the thread linking the two of us. I could feel her even more now—she was no longer in a single location. She was moving. And she was getting close.

You have a choice.

This was it. I wasn't sure what had happened, but she was no longer cloaked in magic. If I moved quickly enough, I could get to her. I could find her.

Or you could leave her in peace. Let her go so that you don't hurt her. I wasn't sure if I was hearing my own voice or my father's.

No, I had to find her. Lainey was the key to everything I wanted.

Despite the ache that throbbed through my chest, I quickened my pace and headed back to town.

I needed to manipulate the situation. Lainey would never come to me willingly. Unless there was a reason—a big reason.

I thought about our open connection. Perhaps it could be exploited. She wasn't blocking me now—she was sending me everything she was feeling. I could do the same. Even if it weren't real.

A plan began to form.

I walked up and down the sidewalk, scanning the faces of those I passed. This time, I wasn't looking for Lainey; I was looking for a little brunette with a purple bow.

I found her on the corner of Washington and 1st Street where she was tricking a pair of boys out of their skateboards.

"Hey, kid!" I called out. The boys took the opportunity to grab their boards and run in the opposite direction.

She turned around and immediately rolled her eyes. "Go away, Praetorian. You suck the fun out of everything."

"That may be true, but listen, I need your help."

She put her hands on her hips and glared at me, her purple eyes flashing through Glamour. "And why would I help you?"

I reached into my backpack and pulled out an iPod. "How about a trade?"

Her eyes immediately lit up, and she reached for the music player, her fingers twitching.

"Not yet," I said, pulling it out of reach. "You have to help me first."

"Fine," she grumbled. "What exactly do you want me to do?"

I swallowed. It was now or never. *Lainey, I'm sorry. Father, please forgive me.*

"I need you to help me trap a witch."

CHAPTER SEVEN

LAINEY

"It should be just up ahead somewhere," I said, surveying the road. The sky was painted with streaks of orange, and it would be getting dark soon. I picked up the pace. There was no sidewalk, and dead leaves crunched loudly under our boots.

Maggie pranced beside me, her curls bouncing like tiny springs all over her head. "This is so exciting!" She threw her arms out and inhaled deeply. "Smell that?"

"What? The trouble we're gonna be in when Zia finds out we're gone?"

"No," Maggie swatted at me. "*Freedom.* It's just you and me and wherever this road takes us." She grinned.

"Assuming this road actually leads to the bus stop," I said with a snort.

Cars zipped past, but no one stopped. *Good*, I thought.

It had been easier than I'd expected to leave the farm—we'd literally just started walking toward the main road—but I guess the wards were designed to keep unwanted guests out—not to keep us in.

Sneaking out had appealed to me initially, but now that we were traipsing along an unmarked road, I had a bad feeling.

You should probably turn around, the wiser, much quieter side of me whispered. *You never know what might be lurking out here.* The words were meant to frighten me into action, into running back to the farm, safe behind the wards.

But I didn't turn around. *You need this*, I reminded myself. A reprieve, however short-lived it might be, would be good for me. A chance to clear my head, to think about everything Teddy had said.

I felt for the dagger Gareth had given me, just to make sure. It was strapped to my belt, just like it had been since the day he'd given it to me, the cool metal a comforting weight against my hip. I smiled at Maggie, resolved.

Up ahead, there was a busy intersection. A wide green bench perched on the corner with a harbor transit schedule posted behind it.

"Aha!" Maggie exclaimed. "You were right, Styles!"

"Yeah, I—" I stopped.

Maggie stopped, too, scanning my face. "What is it?"

"I don't know, I just got a really weird feeling." It was like someone had called my name, a little twinge or tug that I couldn't place.

"Think we should go back?" Maggie's smile was gone.

"No, I'm probably just being paranoid. We've made it this far. We might as well see this plan through—at least get a decent latte, right?"

We plopped down on the bench, scanning the list of stops—though being new to the area, neither of us had any clues of where they were.

"Whatcha thinking?" Maggie asked, scanning the list.

My eyes fell on one stop in particular. *Washington Street, Downtown Grand Haven.*

"Washington Street," I murmured. The name was familiar in a way, though I was one hundred percent positive I'd never been there before. Something about it pulled at me like a memory. "Let's go to Grand Haven." The words were automatic.

Maggie didn't argue, and when the bus pulled up, we paid the exact fare to take us to Washington Street.

It wasn't a long ride, and the other passengers were quiet, minding their own business. Even Maggie's usually chatty demeanor was subdued by the gentle rocking of the bus on the winding road.

I stared out the window, watching the rural landscape become more suburban the closer we got to town. I'd never given Michigan much thought before, but there was no denying it was a beautiful state.

The houses were small, but charming. Craftsmen and bungalows, all with their own style and timeless personalities. One house, in particular, caught my eye. It had a wide wraparound porch and was painted a light blue color, one shade lighter than robin's egg blue.

Like his eyes.

I sat straight up, shaking my head. Where had that come from? I didn't think about Ty—not if I could help it.

But you could, you know.

I shook my head again. "No," I whispered, trying to get the image of his crystal blue irises out of my mind. But it was too late. Maybe it was the fact that I was already at my emotional limit after my session with Teddy, or maybe there was a tiny, selfish piece of me that wanted to get lost in those eyes again. Either way, the flood gates opened, and every suppressed memory and emotion flooded my senses.

"You feel that?" Ty had asked at the Gathering, placing my own hand over my heart. *"It's the one thing he can't take away from you. Do you understand?"*

"You're wrong," I whispered to the memory. The Master had known exactly how to hurt me. Gareth's blood was a stain on my hands that I could never remove, a wound that would never fully heal.

And Ty . . . he had broken what was left of my heart.

The landscape outside blurred together as more and more memories resurfaced. For the first time since the Gathering, I let myself feel them . . . It was only a tiny bit of the punishment I deserved.

But then a new feeling welled up inside me that didn't make sense—a feeling that wasn't my own. My entire body broke out into a cold sweat, and my heart jolted as adrenaline coursed through my veins. Sheer terror and pain, sharp enough to make my eyes water, sliced through me. I doubled over, wrapping my arms around my torso. Air whistled through my clenched teeth.

"Styles?" Maggie's worried voice was in my ear and her hand on my back. "What's wrong?"

Within seconds, the sensation disappeared, leaving me hunched and gasping. I sat up slowly, my chest heaving. "I don't know."

We were nearing the Grand Haven city limits now, and as the bus began to slow, another wave of pain crashed over me. *Washington Street.* I had to get there.

"Someone's in trouble," I choked out. The pull to help end the agony was so strong, I could hardly stay seated. When the bus finally rolled up to our stop, I leapt from my seat and was at the door before the wheels had even stopped turning.

"Wait!" Maggie called after me, jumping off the bus behind me. "Lainey! How do you know?"

I scanned the sidewalks, my head whipping back and forth as my heart slammed against my chest. "I can't explain it. I just have a feeling. We have to find them."

Maggie wrinkled her nose. "Are you sure that's such a good idea? We don't know—"

"I'm not going to let someone else die just because I didn't try to help." I ground my teeth as another wave of pain propelled me forward. Maggie's lips were pressed into a line, but she followed me down the sidewalk.

The sky was dark enough that the streetlamps were already starting to flicker on. Washington Street looked like something off a postcard, with the picturesque local shops lining the sidewalk, but I didn't pause long enough to appreciate it.

The ache radiating through me wasn't mine, but it was real enough that I winced at each new pulse.

"Are you all right, dear?"

A kindly older gentleman sitting on a bench with a little fluffy white dog stared at us, his wrinkled face lined with concern. I realized my face was twisted into a worried grimace. "I'm fine, thank you." I forced a softened smile and hurried past, trying to walk as normally as possible. *But someone isn't.*

Another stab of pain jolted me, and I gasped, hot tears springing to my eyes. It felt like someone had taken a baseball bat to my ribcage.

I pressed my hand against the spot, and even though I knew I wasn't really hurt, I lifted my shirt and poked at the skin there, expecting it to be tender.

"Lainey?" Maggie's voice was high.

"It's not me," I tried to explain. "But we're getting close."

At the end of the street, a crosswalk led to the concrete boardwalk that lined the channel. It was mostly empty, but there were a handful of people walking near the water, bundled up against the chill. None of their faces held any sign of worry or trouble.

Where are you? I scanned the area.

My entire body throbbed; I kept moving, dashing down

the boardwalk and following the channel that led to the wide mouth of the lake. The lights from a red lighthouse at the end of the pier sparkled against the backdrop of the darkening sky.

The foot traffic lessened the closer I got to the water.

Several yards ahead, there was a tall ship mast erected in the middle of a concrete amphitheater. Several large antique steel buoys were centered around it, casting shadows in the grass. Something else was there, too, but it was so oddly shaped, I couldn't quite make it out. Then it moved.

I gasped, realizing that it was alive, whatever it was. Maggie stilled beside me. "What is that?" she asked.

"Only one way to find out." I ran closer, using the grass beside the walkway to muffle the sounds of my approach.

The hulking shape moved again, and this time, I got a better look at it. It was nearly seven or eight feet tall, with sallow, yellow-brownish skin, broad shoulders, and a neck like a tree stump. Its head was covered with patchy wisps of scraggly brown hair, and two black eyes sat perched on the bridge of a badly misshapen nose.

A squeak tore from my throat as I staggered backward, nearly tripping over my own two feet and running into Maggie. *What is that thing?!*

"It looks like the freaking Hulk!" Maggie whispered. Though I wasn't as well-versed as Maggie, I immediately made the connection to the burly green monster in her comics.

As we watched, a boy our age darted out of the darkness. He wore jeans and a hoodie, and his white-blond hair was slick with sweat and glowed in the dim light. One hand clutched his side—ribs that were likely broken, if my own were any indication.

The Hulk opened its mouth and roared, lunging forward with its massive arms swinging. The boy ducked and rolled to the side, narrowly missing another blow. He was back on his feet in seconds, though the effort cost him—his face was twisted in a grimace that my own mirrored. The Hulk moved again, springing forward with speed and accuracy that I wouldn't have thought possible for a creature of its size. It landed inches from where the boy was hunched over, panting.

With another roar, the Hulk's massive fist connected with the boy's face. The boy went flying, and I screamed as my head erupted in pain—as if it were being split open. I sank to my knees, ears ringing, and the boy's body landed in a heap several feet away. He made no move to get up.

"Holy crapkittens!" Maggie shrieked beside me.

I took a step forward, but she grabbed my arm. "What are you doing?"

"I have to go help!"

"You can't! That thing will kill you!"

"If I don't, that thing will kill *him*!"

The Hulk crept toward the boy, its shoulders shaking as if it were chuckling to itself. It rubbed its large, meaty hands together.

"I have to help him, Maggie! I can't just stand here and watch."

Alarm bells rang in my head, warning me to run, but the thrum of energy crackling through me kept my feet rooted to the ground. Maggie looked like she wanted to argue, but instead she said, "*We* have to help him."

"Right." I gave her a half smile and then let out a breath. "I'll distract the Hulk. You go see how bad that guy is hurt, get him out of the way if you can."

"Okay," Maggie said. "Then what?"

"Then we try not to get killed." My magic was waiting, warm underneath my skin, but I pushed it away. Instead, I pulled up the hem of my sweater and ripped my dagger from its sheath and ran forward. "Hey!" I shouted, leaping onto the concrete.

The Hulk turned to me, its wide black eyes narrowing on my face. It cocked its head, surprised to see me standing there.

Behind it, the boy was still and pale, sprawled on the concrete. A scary-looking puddle of blood was growing underneath him.

Then Hulk made a high-pitched sound—a laugh maybe?—and changed directions. Behind him, Maggie darted toward the boy on the ground.

The Hulk took one step and then two . . . then it was running, covering the distance between us in seconds. I tried to jump to the side, but I wasn't fast enough. One of its legs hip-checked me, sending me flying. I landed in a heap on the concrete, pain shooting through my body as my joints absorbed the impact. The dagger had been knocked from my hand. I scanned the ground quickly, but couldn't see where it landed.

The Hulk turned to charge me again. This time, it seemed

to move in slow motion as my brain whirled, trying to come up with some kind of plan. I had no weapon and no real combat training.

What were you thinking, Lainey? a tiny voice screamed at me.

I did the only thing I could think to do: I dashed back along the boardwalk and darted up the grassy hill, looking for anything I could use as a weapon. There were a few sticks laying around, but nothing that would inflict much damage.

I shrieked as a loud crack overhead filled my ears, and the tree next to me was yanked out by the roots. The Hulk growled, tossing the tree aside as if it weighed nothing.

I ran forward, avoiding the second tree he threw at me. I sprinted back down the hill toward the water and the concrete amphitheater. *The dagger! Find the dagger!*

The Hulk was right behind me as I scrambled across the flat surface, frantically searching the ground for my fallen weapon.

I cried out as something hard clipped my right shoulder and sent me flying. I landed in a heap on the concrete, and a huge chunk of brick clattered next to me. The Hulk had ripped it right off the retaining wall that surrounded the amphitheater. Hot tears sprang up in my eyes. I couldn't move my right arm, and when I tried, fire seared down my arm and up through my neck. I bit down hard on my lip to keep from sobbing.

The Hulk edged forward, smug victory already etched across its ugly face.

Then, out of nowhere, a shadow moved. It leapt at the Hulk and clamored up its back. I swiped at my eyes, trying to see what it was.

It was the blond boy, clinging to the Hulk's back like a monkey.

"Styles!" Maggie ran to my side. "Are you hurt?"

"It's my arm," I said as she carefully helped me stand. We watched as the Hulk roared, clawing at the boy and spinning around to try to throw him off. Something glinted in the light. It was my dagger.

Using one hand to hold on to the writhing creature, he used the other to raise the dagger and plunge it between the Hulk's shoulder blades. The creature roared, angry and in pain, and spun wildly. Its movements were enough to dislodge the boy and the dagger, and both fell to the concrete right beneath the creature.

With a growl, the Hulk seized him, its large hand wrapped around the boy's throat.

The boy clawed at the Hulk's fingers, and his legs swung as he tried to kick his way free. He opened his mouth, and a raspy gasp flooded out as the Hulk grinned and squeezed.

"Put him down!" I screeched at the same time Maggie shouted, "No!"

My right arm was throbbing, and a whimper rose in my throat at the movement, but I swallowed it down. *Do something, Lainey!*

I held up my left hand. Sparks of green lightning were already there, dancing between my fingertips. My body shook with warm energy. The Hulk barely looked at me, not the least bit intimidated.

Maggie stared at my hand, my magic reflecting back at me in the dark pool of her eyes. "Are you sure?" she asked.

I wasn't sure if I'd be able to control it, and using magic outside the wards was risky. Anyone could track it. But when the boy's arms and legs went slack, it made the decision easy.

I nodded at Maggie. "Just stand back, okay?"

I limped forward, and Maggie darted for the boardwalk, a safe distance away. I sucked down a breath of air and thought about what Teddy had said: *Magic isn't about control. It's about letting go.*

Closing my eyes, I reached for my magic. It responded immediately, the familiar rush of heat igniting my skin. I opened my eyes and, with a roar of my own, released a brilliant stream of green fire from my open palm. It shot forward and collided directly with the Hulk, blasting it backward.

The impact knocked the Hulk's hands loose. The boy lay on the ground, hacking and wheezing, but breathing.

"Grab the dagger!" I shouted to Maggie. I ran up to the boy, all too aware that though the Hulk was unmoving, its chest was still rising and falling. It wasn't dead. Just stunned.

"Come on," I said. I reached out my good hand to the boy, ignoring the throb in my other arm. "We have to go now!"

A look, both familiar and foreign, flashed across his features. When he placed his hand in mine, something inside me broke apart, and a huge current of energy jolted through me. I hissed, but the boy didn't let go. He let me pull him to his feet.

"Thank you," he rasped, dropping my hand and pressing against his ribcage again. There were marks around his neck that were already beginning to purple, and a deep gash in his forehead was pouring blood.

"We've got to get you to a doctor," I said, scanning the rest of him. "Do you think you can walk?"

"I think so. I twisted my ankle pretty badly, but I can walk on it." He took a tentative step forward, wincing as he put weight on his injured foot.

"Here," I said, maneuvering around him so that I could pull his arm up and over my shoulders. Hissing, I clamped my jaw against the pain of his weight on my injured shoulder. Maggie ran over, my dagger in hand, and grabbed the boy's other arm. We stabilized him between us as we hurried as best we could toward town.

"Do you think it will come after us?" she asked, sparing a look over her shoulder for the Hulk.

"Trust me," the boy said. "We don't want to be anywhere in the vicinity when it wakes up."

We picked up the pace, hobbling along like a creature in the night.

As we neared the main intersection, a black sedan screeched to a halt in front of us. I shrieked, but instantly calmed when the driver's side window rolled down and Julian's familiar face appeared. Pain and exhaustion were starting to wear on me. Julian got out of the car, his usual jovial face carved in a grim seriousness I'd never seen before. "Get in," he growled. "We've got to get back."

Next to me, the blond boy sagged. His face was deathly pale, and I could tell from the unfocused glaze in his eyes that he was only seconds away from passing out.

"Help us!" I said, struggling under the boy's weight. Maggie, too, was fighting to stay upright. "Hurry!"

Julian didn't move, his eyes narrowing. "Who is he?" he asked.

"I don't know," I snapped. "He was in trouble, so we helped him."

"Come on, Julian," Maggie pleaded. "This guy is seriously heavy."

Julian stared at us, his eyes darting back and forth between the bloodied boy and me. "Leave him. We've got to get back to camp. *Now.*"

"What?" I shrieked at the same time Maggie said, "Julian!"

"I'm not just gonna leave him here!" I shouted as loudly as I could manage. "Can't we at least take him to the hospital?"

"No," Julian said. "I'm on Zia's orders to get you back to camp immediately." He looked around. The wind had picked up, and thick, fluffy snow flurries were beginning to drift down. There weren't many people crowding the sidewalk, but I did notice the elderly man with the dog from earlier staring at us from the corner. A cell phone perched in his hand.

"Now," Julian said. He opened the back driver's side door. "Get in."

"Can we take him with us?" I said, tightening my grip on the boy, whose eyes were rolling backward. Next to me, Maggie squeaked as the boy passed out. His legs went limp, and his weight rested entirely on our shoulders. I yelped as the pain in my injured arm intensified.

"Please," I said. "We can't just leave him here."

Julian's face hadn't changed.

"You might as well agree, dude," Maggie said through gritted teeth. "She doesn't give up once she sets her mind to something. I'm sure someone can wipe his memory or something once we're back on the farm, right?"

A police car was rolling down the street and stopped where the elderly man stood, still staring with wide eyes.

Julian threw a nervous glance at the police car. "Fine. Just get in."

Maggie and I half pulled, half dragged the boy between us to the open car door. I got in first, and with Julian's help, we managed to get the boy in the car, lying across the backseat with his head in my lap.

Maggie ran around to the passenger side, slamming the door and throwing her seatbelt on. "Is he breathing, Styles?"

I placed my palm against the boy's chest. It was moving slowly up and down. "Yeah, I think he's just unconscious. He's lost a lot of blood."

Maggie handed me a bandana she pulled from a backpack on the floor. "Here, use this."

I pressed the bandana against the wound on the boy's head, trying to staunch the blood.

Julian was driving as fast as the side streets would allow. When flashing blue and red lights lit up the darkness behind us, he swore under his breath but didn't stop.

"Do we stop?" I asked, uneasiness washing over me.

Julian shook his head. There was a look on his face that I didn't understand. There was something he wasn't saying.

"What is it?" I asked.

"We've got to get back to the farm right away."

The police car behind us sounded its alarm, a quick little blast to get our attention.

Julian responded by jamming down the gear shift and making a sharp, seemingly impossible turn down a side street. He raced down the main highway, the one that would take us out of Grand Haven. The cop car followed, its lights still flashing.

"How much farther?" Maggie asked, seeming to understand something I didn't.

"Just a few miles," Julian responded.

I wasn't sure what they were talking about. The farm was still a good twenty-minute drive from where we were.

Julian stepped on the gas; the car lurched forward.

We drove for a few minutes more, Julian dodging traffic and the wail of the siren behind us. Then, all of a sudden, the cop car slowed. The cop turned off his lights and turned on a turn signal instead, maneuvering into the gas station on the corner.

"Why's he giving up?" I asked, confused.

"The wards," Maggie said. "He can't get through them."

Any human who comes near them suddenly remembers they have somewhere else to be and turns around."

"Oh," I said, my voice low.

Julian grunted in response, his eyes focused on the road. Maggie gave me a strained smile, but didn't say any more.

The only sounds that filled the car were the hum of the tires on the highway and the boy's soft breathing. The bandana I was holding to his wound was soaked through, and his skin was a green, ashy color.

Don't worry, I thought. *I've got you.*

My chest warmed as a sudden thought occurred to me. *I used magic to fight the Hulk.* For the first time since I'd arrived on the farm, I'd used my magic and it had responded exactly as it was supposed to—just like Teddy said it would.

I might have killed people at the Gathering with my magic, but today I had used it to save this boy. It couldn't make up for what I'd done, but it was a start.

When we rolled up to the farm, it was a flurry of activity. People were running in all directions, and Zia was standing in the thick of it all, barking orders. When she saw us pull up, she marched toward the car. My smile vanished.

"Brace yourself, kids," Julian said. "She had Serena and the other Seers on you." He got out of the car and opened my door.

"What the hell is wrong with you?" Zia fumed, gesticulating wildly with her hands. "Do you have any idea the jeopardy you've put this place in?"

"I'm sorry, but—"

"You're sorry? You used magic, Lainey!" she exploded. "You might as well have sent a gift-wrapped GPS to the Master."

"You're a DuCarmont," Julian said calmly beside me. "Your magic is incredibly potent, which makes it stand out—easy to track."

"Especially fused with the power of the Grimoire," Zia growled.

"I know," I argued, "but he was going to die." I indicated the blond boy. "I couldn't just stand there and watch. I didn't have a choice."

"There is always a choice," Zia said, quieter this time, though her tone was still laced with fury. "Send a team back to town," she ordered several of the Hetaeria standing behind us. "Check for witnesses and anyone who might be tailing us or tracking the magic. Maybe it's not too late to clean up this mess."

I was vaguely aware of Julian yelling for a healer as I sat still in the backseat, heat burning in my cheeks.

"Now, we prepare for the worst," Zia said. "Pack up the farm, get ready to move." Zia stepped aside as a dark-haired witch who specialized in healing ran up to the car. With Julian's help, the witch managed to pull the blond boy from the backseat and onto the ground. I followed, wincing at the pain in my injured arm.

Lynlee, the healer, questioned me about the boy's injuries and my own, and I answered as best I could. It was only after I'd finished that I realized Julian and Zia were having a heated argument behind me.

"What were you thinking bringing him here?"

Julian shrugged but looked over at me. "We were drawing attention from the humans. She wasn't going to leave without the boy."

"And you thought bringing some random Supernatural into camp was wise?"

"I was just—"

"Wait," I cut in. "Did you just say Supernatural?" I looked down at the boy and then back up at Zia. "He's human."

"Are you willing to bet your life on that?" Zia asked coolly. "Or everyone else's here?"

"I-I . . ." I stammered. "I mean, I just thought . . ."

"Clearly, thinking was the last thing you were actually doing today." Zia stomped over and kicked the boy's shoulder with her boot. "This boy is no more human than I am."

"And," the healer piped up, "he's cloaked in Trickster magic."

"What does that mean?" I sat back on my heels.

"It means," Zia said, waving her hand over the boy's face, "that not everything is as it appears." She waved her hand again, and this time, the boy's facial features began to distort. In and out like a mirage, they faded and twisted until finally, the magic disintegrated and the Glamour fell away.

Heat flooded my senses, and all I could see was red.

"No," I whispered as fingers of green lightning cracked across the sky. *No.*

Behind me, Maggie gasped.

The unconscious boy lying on the ground was no longer the blond boy I'd saved from the Hulk.

It was Ty.

CHAPTER EIGHT

LAINEY

A bark of laughter tore from my lips, but it was a bitter sound—the kind that leaves a stale, metallic taste in your mouth.

I ran the hand of my uninjured arm across my face, squeezing my eyes shut and opening them again. But it was still there—that face that crept into my dreams, the one I swore to forget.

Ty.

My chest cavity hummed with warmth, but a chilling cold permeated through the rest of me, numbing me down to the bone. I hissed and clawed at my chest, but then my hand moved. Those traitorous fingers of mine reached to brush the wisps of dark hair from his forehead. Like a magnet pulled to its opposite, the urge to touch him was strong.

Frowning, I slapped my own hand down with the other,

relishing the ache of my injured arm. The pain was an excellent reminder of just how much I hated the boy lying in the grass—magnetic connection or not.

Maggie knelt down next to me, her face searching mine. "Styles, I—"

I shook my head fiercely, cutting her off. I wasn't ready to talk, wasn't sure what to say. His face looked exactly the same. Strong jaw, straight nose, and full lips that knew the shape of a crooked smile all too well. I didn't have to see his eyes to know their exact shade of piercing blue. There was even a bruise forming on his cheek, already beginning to purple.

Just like the night we first met.

I tore my eyes away, looking up at Zia instead. She was staring, her gaze flickering back and forth between me, Ty, and Maggie. Her eyebrows lifted, and she stood with her hands on her hips.

"What is it?" she demanded, her voice gruff.

"His name is Ty Marek," I said, my voice strong and clear despite the shaking in my limbs. "He's a Praetorian . . . and he works for the Master."

Julian and Zia began to speak at the same time, their voices blending on top of one another, making it difficult to hear either clearly. Lynlee, the dark-haired healer, cut off her healing incantation with a gasp and held her arms up and away from his body as if touching him would burn her.

I couldn't blame her. Touching him burned me, too, just in a different way. I didn't want to think about it.

"This is the boy who betrayed you at the Gathering?"

Zia asked, finally holding up a hand to silence Julian so she could be heard. Her face was beginning to flush, and she was tapping the side of her leg—a nervous or angry tic, I wasn't sure which.

I settled for the facts—the simple ones. "Yes. He has the mark," I responded with a shrug. I reached out to show them the exact spot, and again, the magnetic pull to touch him caused a small gasp to erupt from my lips. Once more, I yanked my hand back, swearing not to get that close again.

"On his chest," Maggie said, clearly reading my mind. "Just there." She pointed, her finger making the briefest contact with his body. The touch had no effect on her, but I shuddered just the same.

Zia elbowed Julian, who stalked over and pulled down the collar of Ty's shirt. The onyx triangles, forming an unmistakable "M," were as plain as day. Inked across his heart, they were a stark contrast to his pale skin.

The sight of them made bile rise in my throat. I swallowed hard and turned my head, looking away.

Zia stared at the mark, her eyes narrowed in an expression that I couldn't read, but the flush that colored her cheeks had spread down her neck and chest in angry, splotchy patches.

"We thought he was on our side," Maggie said, her voice soft, "but . . ." Her eyes darted over to me.

I cleared my throat. "But we were wrong." The words were sawdust on my tongue.

"Well, what's he doing here? How did he find you?" Zia's

words were clipped. "Did you tell him about us? Have you been communicating with him?"

"What? No!" I scoffed. "I haven't spoken to him since that night." I bit down on my lip to keep from trembling and let out a huff. If my suspicions were correct, I knew exactly how he'd found me.

The remnants of a forgotten conversation floated back to me, ringing clear as a bell in my mind. *"We're drawn to the people we're meant to safeguard, and they to us. It's the Calling. I wish I could explain it more than that, but it's just a feeling we get. The instinct to travel in a particular direction, to be in a certain place at a certain time, to speak to someone we've never met."*

Zia waved her hand. "Praetorians are decent trackers, yes, but he would've had to have some intel as to your whereabouts. He couldn't just track you out of thin air, even if he is a Praetorian."

I swallowed as Ty's voice filled my head again. *"I knew it was you from the moment I saw you. And in the gym, when I touched you . . . I've never felt so drawn to anyone in my life."*

"He is, but . . . he's also *my* Praetorian."

Julian's and Zia's heads snapped toward one another, but it was the healer witch who said what they were thinking out loud.

"You're his Calling," she said, her voice soft, her eyes a mixture of distrust and pity.

"Is that true?" Julian barked.

I nodded, and both he and Zia swore.

"And you didn't think to mention that to us?" Zia was officially the color of a summer tomato.

"You were there! You saw what happened," I said defensively. "I can't even say his name without—" I broke off, breathing deeply. "I just wanted to forget about him, okay? I didn't even think to tell you; I didn't realize it mattered."

Zia groaned. "Well, it does. Praetorians and their Callings share a bond, a magical connection. Not only could he have easily tracked you through it, but there's no telling what sort of information you've given him."

"I told you: I haven't spoken to him since the night of the Gathering."

"A Praetorian bond hardly needs words," the healer said, her eyes narrowed. "You might have shared more than you realize."

The implication of her words yanked any remaining warmth from my body.

Zia glared at me. "Like I said, this would've been extremely helpful to know prior to bringing you here."

"Well, excuse me," I said dryly. "I was a little too busy thinking about how I had to kill my own uncle to give you a thorough list of all the people who might have a supernatural connection to me."

"To be fair, I knew about him too," Maggie said, nudging my shoulder slightly in a silent show of solidarity. "I don't think either of us really thought there was a chance he'd find us, especially with the wards. Besides, Lainey and Ty"—his name rolled so easily off her tongue—"didn't part on the best of terms. We don't talk about him."

"She's right. Calling or no Calling, he's nothing to me."

My words were clear and loud. Maggie's eyes darted over to mine, but I refused to look at her. A single word floated through my thoughts like a balloon on a breeze—*liar*.

I shook my head to clear it.

"Nothing, huh?" Zia was examining my face for fallacy.

"Nothing at all."

She gave a curt nod. "All right, then. Guess you won't mind if we get rid of him. Julian, Skip this traitor to the nearest cliff and drop him over the side."

I could no longer breathe.

Zia's eyes bore into mine, an unspoken challenge. "Unless you have a problem with that?"

"No, be my guest," I managed to choke out, ignoring the screaming protest inside me.

"Lainey!" Maggie hissed beside me.

Julian rubbed his hands together and stepped forward.

"Wait!" Maggie sprang ahead, stepping between Ty and Julian with her hands outstretched. "We can't just kill him."

"Any ally to the Master is an enemy to the Hetaeria," Julian said. "It's that simple."

Maggie rolled her eyes. "Okay, Frank Castle, slow your roll. No need to go all Punisher on us. Don't you think we better ask a few questions first? Styles?" She looked over at me, her eyes full of expectation, but I was numb. There weren't words.

"Just hear me out." Maggie turned back to Julian and Zia. "This is exactly like when Dumbledore used the veritaserum on Barty Crouch Jr." They stared back blankly. "Oh, come on! You know? *Harry Potter and the Goblet of Fire*? I mean, you're *witches*." When they continued to stare at her blankly, Maggie waved a hand and continued. "I'm going to just blow past your horrible lack of essential knowledge and get to the important stuff. Before we . . . drop him off a cliff or whatever, we need to find out what information he has. He works for the Master. Wouldn't someone in his position have information that might be useful to the Hetaeria?"

Zia cocked her head. "It's possible. Though I'm not in the habit of having conversations with traitors." She looked over at Julian, who grunted his approval. "We'll ask a few questions first. *Then* he goes cliff-diving."

Maggie nudged me with her elbow, but when I didn't say anything, she gave me a strange look and let out a sigh. "Fine," she finally said.

Julian had walked over to the car and popped the trunk. He returned a few seconds later with a thick rope. "I'll tie him up and get him moved somewhere more secure. He good to go?" He looked to the healer.

"He'll live. A few broken ribs and maybe a concussion, but nothing serious that would prevent him from answering questions."

"I want a guard on him at all times," Zia said. "In the meantime, we need an emergency council meeting. Even the slightest chance that someone could track her magic"—her eyes cut over to me for the slightest second—"is cause enough for the plan to change. We need to get everyone on board."

"Roger that, boss," Julian said.

Zia stomped away, and he began knotting the rope around Ty's limp wrists. I stood rooted to the ground, breath hitched in my throat.

"You're not serious, are you?" Maggie hissed, knocking into me. "You can't let them kill him."

"Can't I?"

Maggie stared at me hard. "Lainey, you need to talk to him."

"Why? He betrayed me, Mags. What more do I need to know?"

Lynlee finished dressing Ty's wounds and turned to me. "Here," she said, reaching for my injured arm. "Let's take a look at that. It's at least partially dislocated."

I was grateful for the distraction. The throbbing in my shoulder was nothing compared to the blooming ache spreading through me, but I still cried out when she popped my shoulder back into its rightful spot. The pain dulled instantly and even more so when she rubbed a thick, creamy balm over the skin. "Let that soak in," she instructed me. "You'll be sore for a day or two, but you should be just fine after that."

"Thanks," I mumbled, watching as Julian directed two Supernaturals—one tall Fae with a severe expression and a young warlock—to carry Ty to the tack room in the back of the barn. I tried not to look, but I scanned him from head to toe as they carried him away, taking in every detail. His tall, lean frame. The fighter muscles in his arms and shoulders. The scrapes and bruises that covered his knuckles.

Wait . . . It was the sight of his hands that made me think of it. The way he had wrapped those hands in the gym to protect them from injury. Ty was a skilled fighter—skilled enough to avoid serious injury or, at the very least, outmaneuver the Hulk long enough to get away. My stomach dropped.

"Hey, Julian," I called out, jogging to catch up with him. "Can I ask you a question?"

"Make it quick."

"What was it?" I asked, assuming that the Hulk had also made an appearance in Serena's vision. "The creature?"

"It was a Troll."

Troll? In spite of everything I'd seen since discovering my Supernatural lineage, this surprised me. Everything I knew about Trolls was limited to the little singing cartoons with neon hair. "It's funny," Julian continued. "You don't usually find Trolls in largely populated cities. That one must have been scavenging for food."

"Are they super aggressive?"

"Not usually." Julian shrugged. "Trolls are strong and skilled fighters, but they're simple creatures, mainly sticking to themselves. They rarely congregate with their own kind, much less with other Supernaturals. They don't attack without cause. You'd have to be an idiot to pick a fight with a Troll."

The wheels in my head were turning. It didn't make sense.

"But why . . ." I stopped, Julian's words sinking in. *You'd have to be an idiot to pick a fight with a Troll.* "Or," I grumbled, walking away, "trying to set someone up."

"Lainey," Maggie said, coming up beside me. "I really think we should talk about—"

"It was a trick," I cut in. I didn't need her to confirm what I was thinking; the weight of the truth already bore down heavily on me.

"What?"

"The Troll. He must have provoked it on purpose."

Maggie looked confused, so I told her about the Hulk and what Julian had told me. "Think about it, Maggie. Ty is a Praetorian. He's a skilled fighter. Not only would he have known better than to anger a Troll, but he also would have been able to at least hold his own or get away. But when we showed up, the Troll was practically tossing him around like a rag doll. He had to have been *letting* the Troll hurt him."

"Why would he do that?"

I sucked in a shaky breath. "Because he knew I would save him . . . He played me, Mags." I swallowed. "Again."

Maggie looked down at the ground and then back up at me, trying to sort through it all herself. "Maybe there's some kind of explanation. I mean, how many people would just let a Troll kick their ass like that? Don't you think there's a reason for it?"

"No, I know the reason. He's a lying snake. That's it. He's just trying to finish what he started."

"You don't really believe that, do you?"

I stared at Maggie. "Why are you defending him? He betrayed us. From the day I met him, every word out of his mouth was a lie. He's part of the Guard. He's working for the man who killed my mother. Hell, he killed my whole family. He probably told the Master our plan, told him we were coming. Everything fell apart at the Gathering, and it's all his fault!" Hot tears sprang up in my eyes, but I refused to let them fall. I would *not* cry any more tears for that traitor.

"I'm not defending him, Lainey. I just . . . I don't know . . . something tells me there's more to the story."

"Look, Mags. Life's not a comic book. There isn't always a funny one-liner and plot twist at the end. We can't all walk through life with Marvel-colored glasses."

Maggie's eyebrows shot up, and I knew my words had hit their mark. I should've felt bad, but in that moment, I didn't.

"I know that," Maggie said, not responding to my dig. "And I know what Ty did. But I also saw the look on his face when the two of you were dancing. The way he was looking at you . . . And I saw his face when the Scavenger grabbed me, the moment it all fell apart. Lainey, he cares about you. I know it."

"He was just acting!"

"I don't think so. You can't fake a look like that."

"You don't know what you're talking about," I said.

"Maybe not," Maggie lifted her shoulder, then dropped it. "But don't you think you should at least talk to him? Life may not be like a comic book, but if I've learned anything from reading villain origin stories, it's that what you think you know is usually wrong. Take Venom, for example. He blamed Peter Parker for everything that had gone wrong in his life, but he eventually realized he had it all wrong. He even became the New Venom and ended up working for the government—as one of the good guys!"

I stared at her.

With a sigh, Maggie shoved her hands into her pockets. "Just talk to him, okay?" She gave me a meaningful look before walking away.

Talk to him? Is she nuts? Every cell in my body was electrified. I was shaking, and overhead, deep rumbles of thunder echoed across the night sky.

My magic writhed underneath my skin, and I thought about what Teddy had said about channeling my emotions into my magic. Swallowing a breath of air, I let it out slowly, reaching inside to soothe the electric current running through me. *Just calm down. Deep breaths.* My magic calmed instantly, as did the thunder.

Teddy was right. Respond to magic, and it will respond to you. A small smile lifted my cheeks. And then a sharp "Lainey!" came from behind me.

CHAPTER NINE

LAINEY

Serena marched toward me, both fury and relief shining in her eyes. She reached out a hand as if to touch me, but then it fell limply down by her side. She shifted from one foot to the other, chewing on her bottom lip. Her expression was hard. "What were you thinking, running off like that, huh?"

I ran a hand over my face and sighed. "Can we please not do this right now?"

"I just can't believe you would be so reckless, so irresponsible," Serena continued, throwing her arms up as she began to pace. "If I hadn't Seen you, hadn't known to send help, who knows what might have happened! And a Troll!? Do you have any idea how dangerous they are? You could've been killed!"

"Well, I wasn't." Watching Serena fume and rage like an exasperated parent sent flames of resentment and anger flickering through me.

"You *know* better than that. After everything we've been through, I thought you would've learned by now that—"

"Stop acting like you care!" I screamed, unable to control the words that poured out. Not that I wanted to.

Serena went silent, her face pale. "How can you say that?"

"It's true," I said, the words puncturing the stitching of my beaten and worn-down heart. "Ever since we got here, you act like I don't even exist."

She didn't even bother to deny it, and I had to bite down on my lower lip to stop it from trembling.

"I'm doing the best I can." Serena's voice was flat, that single sentence her only explanation—and a weak one at best. Her face was blank, her expression completely unreadable. If she saw how difficult it was for me to hold it together, she didn't react at all. Instead, she fidgeted with the hem of her plaid button-down shirt. The sight alone made me ache, made me wish for the days of her peasant tops and chiffon skirts.

For a split second, I forgot my anger. Instead, I stared at the woman in front of me with tears in my eyes. *Who are you?* Gareth's death had been hard on us both, and I knew that even if we survived the war, his absence would cling to us—but I'd always thought we'd have each other.

But this person in front of me wasn't the woman who always made snickerdoodles because she knew they were my favorite, the woman who made me wings three Halloweens in a row because I was obsessed with Tinker Bell, the woman who had held me close and helped me change when Gareth's blood had stained my clothes and covered my skin.

"It's like you died right along with him," I whispered, a tear rolling down my cheek.

Serena sucked in a breath and let it out slowly. She looked down at her clasped hands and then back up at me, her own unshed tears sparkling in the moonlight. "I did," she murmured.

We stared at each other for a long while, neither of us speaking.

"Don't go running off like that again," she said, finally breaking the silence. "Now, come on. Zia called an emergency council meeting, and she wants you there."

She didn't wait for me to respond before walking back to the big house, nor did she turn her head to make sure I was following.

With my fists clenched tightly at my sides, I stomped after her.

ॐ•ॐ

Zia stood at the head of the long, polished oak table, and seated around it were the council members. I didn't know all of their names, but I'd seen them around the farm enough to know what their role was.

"Thank you all for coming so quickly," Zia began. "There is much to discuss, and considering what happened tonight, time is of the essence."

My face flushed as I listened. No one was looking at me, yet I could feel the stare of every single person in the room.

"Lainey, I need you to tell the council what you told me earlier today. About the Grimoire."

The faces in the room turned to look at me; their eyes—full of anger, surprise, annoyance, and worry—sought the story in mine. I stood up and cleared my throat. "There is a spell inside the DuCarmont Grimoire that would allow a magic-wielder to strip away the magic of others. This is what the Master wants. If he can get it, he can use it to rid himself of the dark magic he's dependent on and siphon magic from other Supernaturals instead."

I swallowed. "Well, as far as the Master knows, I stole the Grimoire from him at the Gathering. But that's not exactly true . . . There is no Grimoire. At least, not a physical one."

I barely paused, but every single member at the table began speaking—even Serena, who was looking at me with wide eyes, questions on her lips.

"My mother cast a spell," I continued, speaking loudly over the other voices. They immediately quieted down. "She transferred the Grimoire—all of its contents—to me. The book no longer exists, at least not in book form. It's in me." I tapped the side of my head. "It's in here."

This time, silence filled the room. I waited, unsure of what to say next.

"But what does it mean?" Serena finally asked.

"It means that we have one hell of a weapon to use against the Master," Zia said from her position at the head of the table. Every head snapped back in her direction, and my blood ran cold. *Weapon?*

"Lainey is a DuCarmont. The blood running through her veins already makes her powerful. Add in her family's Grimoire, and she's unlike anything our kind has ever seen. If anyone can rival the Master and the dark magic, it's her."

Another murmur of conversation filled the room, only this time it was laced with tones of excitement and wonder, instead of confusion and distrust. Anger coiled low in my gut.

"This is awesome," Blake, one of the Skippers, said, clapping his hands together. "The Master won't know what's hit him!"

"I agree," Zia said with a grin. "He'll never expect it. We'll start planning right away," Once Lainey is ready, we'll—"

"No," I said loudly, glaring at Zia. "You've been planning to use me as a weapon since I got here. Grimoire or not, I'm not just some tool you can wield however you see fit."

"I know you're worried about hurting someone, but you're training now to make sure that doesn't happen."

"But it could," I argued.

"Regardless, this information does give us the upper hand in a way," Zia said, bringing everyone's attention back to her. "According to our scouts, the Master's forces are growing. They outnumber us three to one. We need allies." She leaned forward, placing her hands on the table. "We need to reunite the factions."

"It can't be done," a tall Sage with a severe expression argued. "The factions haven't united since the original Hetaeria decades ago. Most are so distrustful of anyone outside their own faction, even borrowing supplies would take a small miracle."

"They won't be easily persuaded," Serena agreed. "I've Seen it. Everyone is too afraid of the Master's retaliation."

"Of course they're afraid. But we have to make them see that the possible outcome is greater than the risk," Zia countered. "If we come together, we can defeat the Master. We don't have to live in fear anymore." Zia's eyes were bright. "We just have to show them that we can win."

Serena's brows furrowed. "How do we do that?"

"We don't." Zia pointed at me. "She does."

"What? You want *me* to convince the factions?"

"If the factions know we have a weapon to use against the Master, that we stand a chance against him, they'll join us. I know they will."

"I'm *not* a weapon," I growled.

"If it helps us win over allies, then I say you are," Zia said with a shrug. "You're powerful, Lainey. Embrace it."

"Wait, no—"

"I propose we invite faction representatives to a Summit meeting here," Zia said, cutting me off. "We tell them we have a weapon that can defeat the Master. Once they agree to ally themselves with us, we'll have the numbers we need."

Voices filled the room as the council members expressed their agreement.

"Julian," Zia said, "I don't think we can wait. Can you and Blake—"

"We're on it," Julian said, nodding to Blake. Within seconds, they disappeared, Skipping out of the room.

The remaining council members talked excitedly, their conversations blending into a hum that made it impossible to distinguish individual words, but their faces were easy enough to decipher. I marched over to Zia.

"What the hell?" I demanded.

"Look," she said, rolling her eyes, "you're the most powerful witch we have on our side. Call it what you want, but you're our best shot at defeating him. You know that."

"My magic can't be trusted." *But what about earlier with the Troll?* the voice in my head whispered. I shoved the thought away.

"Maybe for now, but it won't be like that for long."

"You can't know that for sure."

Zia shrugged. "For the sake of the alliance, I'm willing to risk it."

As Zia and the others continued to make plans, I sank down into a chair, glaring at anyone who looked in my direction.

With a sharp crack, Julian and Blake reappeared, windblown and grim-faced.

"They're ready to listen to what we have to say," Julian began without preamble. "But they want a demonstration."

"They want to make sure our 'weapon' is as powerful as you say it is," Blake added.

Every eye in the room landed on me.

Murderer.

"No," I leapt to my feet and shook my head. "I won't do it."

I ran from the room and outside, my heart hammering. I shoved all notions of magic and of me being a weapon aside. I needed a distraction.

The farm was bustling with people and activity. As I watched them work like ants, my plan to think of something other than how everything had gone to hell evaporated. There was a reason why everyone was moving quickly. I'd used magic tonight, and in doing so, I'd put everyone at risk. Guilt rose up in my throat, and I swallowed.

I thought of Maggie and the way I'd spoken to her.

The dull, lifeless look in Serena's eyes.

The way my heart had leapt at the sight of Ty lying there in the grass.

A streak of green lightning cracked across the sky, and I stalked toward the barn with one purpose in mind. There was so much uncertainty. I needed some solid ground to stand on.

Standing out front were the Fae and warlock guards.

"I need to see him," I said.

"He's under lock and key until he can be questioned by the council. Zia's orders."

I rolled my eyes. "You know I can blow that door right off its hinges, right?" I held out a hand. Green electricity crackled between my fingertips.

The guards looked at my hand and then back up at my face.

"He's still unconscious," the warlock said, stepping aside. "The minute he wakes up, Zia will want to know."

"Fine." *But I have a few questions of my own for him first.*

The Fae twisted the knob and pulled the door open for me. I walked inside, jumping a little when the door slammed shut behind me.

The room was dark and cool, but a lamp sat on a box in the corner, casting the room in a cozy orange glow.

Ty lay on his back on a cot in the corner. His hair had grown longer since the Gathering, and the strands were hanging over his forehead and into his eyes.

I hated myself for it, but I reached out and brushed the hair out of his eyes. Fury raced through me, but there was something else too.

Watching his chest rise and fall, I slid my back against the wall until I was seated across the small room from his inert body.

There was nothing else to do but wait, so I pulled my knees up to my chest and wrapped my arms around them.

In the still of the room, I counted his breaths and mine as I waited for the boy who betrayed me . . . and broke my heart to wake up.

CHAPTER TEN

TY

*T*here was no moon overhead. The bright silver orb had vanished, the cloak of darkness thick and unwieldy. Shadows hung from the trees like vines, and the boy could barely see his own hand in front of his face. It was as if all the light in the world had been snuffed out.

His father stood next to him, a heavy hand on the boy's shoulders. His forehead creased. "Ty," he said, his voice thick with emotion the boy didn't understand. "You need to go inside. You need to hide."

"No," Ty protested, marching over to where his staff leaned against the side of the cabin. "You won't have to face him alone. I'm ready. You said so yourself."

"You are ready, but not for this." His father knelt down and looked him in the eye. "I need you to trust me. Please, go *find a place to hide. You have to promise me that you won't come out, no matter what you see or hear."*

"But—"

"Promise me."

Ty swallowed. "I promise."

A groan slipped through my lips before I could even open my eyes. Every inch of me ached, and a pounding in my head made me wish I were still unconscious. My stomach rolled with a wave of nausea, and it felt as though I'd been hit repeatedly with a sledgehammer.

No, I corrected myself. *Not a sledgehammer. A Troll.*

I cracked open one eyelid, then the other. It was dark, but there was a small lantern casting a golden glow in the corner of the room—just enough light for me to see that I was in a small tack room with a dirt floor. There was a haybale in one corner, with a few crates stacked opposite. I was lying on the floor in the other corner, a thin straw mat beneath me.

Leaning against the closed door, with her knees pulled up to her chest and her eyes pinned on me, sat Lainey.

The Praetorian side of me was content. My Calling was safe. Another side, the side of me that I trusted the least, ached to see those eyes look at me the way they used to, before the Gathering. And then there was one last side—a side that was satisfied that my plan had worked. It made my stomach turn.

I didn't need a mirror to know my ruse was up, that the Trickster magic was gone—the look on her face said it all.

I swallowed. "Hey."

She glared and didn't respond. She didn't need to. Given our close proximity, the connection between us was strong. I sensed the words she was screaming in her mind.

I winced, hating the way those unspoken words stung. I expected her anger, deserved it even, but seeing the fire that burned in her eyes and knowing I was the one who put it there made it difficult to look at her for long.

A thick rope was wound securely around my wrists. I wasn't surprised, though it did make it more difficult to ease myself into a sitting position. Lainey made no move or offer to help as I struggled against the restraints and the shooting pain in my abdomen.

"You had a couple of broken ribs and a gash on your forehead. Maybe a concussion, but nothing major." Lainey's voice was low and dull. "One of the witches here healed you, but you'll likely be sore for a few days."

I nodded. "Thank you."

"Don't thank me. I wasn't the one who healed you."

"No, but you still saved my life tonight."

Lainey scoffed, rolled her eyes. "Don't do that."

"What?"

"Don't pretend this was just some coincidental act of heroism." Her cheeks were flushed, and her fingertips emitted tiny green sparks. "You tricked me. I don't know how you did it or why, but you knew I would come, that I would save you." She shook her head. "If I had known. . . I would've let that Troll crush you."

Her words were stabbing knives, even though I could feel the lie in them. "You're lying."

The same two words I'd spoken to her what felt like a lifetime ago. Her eyes flashed, and I knew she remembered that moment too.

"You still think you know me, Ty, but you don't know anything about me." She tore her gaze from mine, focusing hard on the dirt underneath her shoes. "I hate you," she finally whispered.

Another stab of the knife, though these words were laced with such truth, they cut deep—a far worse pain than any injury I'd received from the Troll. I winced.

I had accomplished my goal. I'd manipulated the Praetorian bond to get what I wanted—access to the Hetaeria. *"But was it worth it?"* my father's voice whispered in my ear. I started to shake my head, an argument already forming, but I couldn't deny the ache resonating in my chest, the emptiness of my hands that craved to touch her, hold her. *Stop it*, I ordered. *What's done is done.* But the warring sides of my heart and the voices in my head couldn't agree.

"I know," I finally offered, hating the way those words sounded, hating the way they made me feel, as if the Troll had landed a punch square into my chest where my heart rested.

Lainey looked up at me. The fire in her eyes was still there, but it wasn't as bright. Something else was there, too, a weariness that traced her features—something she didn't want anyone else to see.

"Why?" she said. She brushed an errant strand of hair back behind her ear. Her hand was trembling.

My own hand lifted in response, reaching for her, but my restraints inhibited the movement. When I realized what I was doing, I was grateful for the rope. I bit down hard on my own tongue. *Don't lose yourself now*, I chided. A warm rust taste spread throughout my mouth from the broken skin. It was an excellent reminder. *Pain is a tether.*

"Why?" she said it louder this time.

There were so many questions packed into that single word. So many things I had to account for, atone for. I opened my mouth and closed it again. My brain whirled, but the words were jumbled, and none of them seemed right.

"Just speak from the heart," my father's voice whispered. *"Tell her the truth."*

The truth. Did I even know what that was anymore?

Was I ready to tell it?

I shifted on the cot, trying to find a position that would alleviate some of the pressure on my sore ribcage. Lainey was waiting, staring at me with wide green eyes.

"It's a long story," I said.

"I've got time."

"Okay." Ready or not, this was it. "It would be easier if I showed you."

"Showed me?"

"Through the bond," I explained.

Lainey huffed, her eyes narrowing. "Fine. Show me."

ৎৎ◆ৎৎ

Logs dug uncomfortably into his back, the rough bark scratching against the sliver of exposed skin where his shirt had ridden up. The large wooden hamper on the side of the house was mainly used to store firewood in the winter, but there had been just enough space for him to squeeze inside. Lifting the lid a tiny crack, Ty peered into the dark.

A man cloaked in shadow faced his father, flanked by a dozen others wearing identical sneers. A shudder ran down Ty's back. It was the Master, the man his father so often warned him about.

"Marek," the Master boomed, his hand open as if in friendship. "I think you've been avoiding me."

"Not at all," Simon Marek replied, his shoulders rigid. "Just been doing a little traveling."

The Master cocked his head. "Ah, well, then perhaps we'll just get down to it. Have you given any consideration to my offer? I could use a Praetorian like you among my ranks, training my men."

"I appreciate the offer, but . . ."

"Oh dear," the Master said, cutting him off. "That sounds very much like the beginning of a rejection, and I just don't like those." He surveyed the area. "Where's that boy of yours?

I can see you need a little convincing." He bared his teeth then, a hideous grin of glistening canines.

"Stay away from my son!" Simon roared, losing his calm composure. He lunged at the Master but was quickly restrained.

Ty whimpered, but stayed hidden like he promised.

"Now, now. That's hardly hospitable," the Master crowed. "Here's the thing, Marek. It's not a choice. You either join us, or you die." He placed a hand on Simon's forehead.

There was a scuffle of feet as Simon tried to pull away from the hands that held him. Then a horrible wailing shattered the quiet of the night. His screams of agony echoed through the trees. Ty covered his ears to block out the blood-curdling sound, but he still felt it. It reverberated through him, etching itself on the lining of his heart.

Hours seemed to pass before the screams subsided.

Lifting the hamper lid once more, Ty looked for his father.

Simon hung limply from the arms of two of the Master's men.

The Master knelt down, his shadows hovering around him. "I'll ask you one more time, Marek. Join us?"

With what little strength he had left, Simon Marek lifted his head and spat. "Go to hell."

A harpoon of shadow shot forward. Simon cried out, impaled on the tendril of writhing darkness sticking from his chest.

Ty gasped, sinking back down as hot tears dripped down his cheeks. "You promised," he whispered over and over, guilt *and grief flooding through him. "You promised." He wanted so badly to fly from his hiding spot, to fight the men in the yard. But he had made a promise.*

And he kept it.

I let the connection between us fade, my throat thick. "I was twelve when the Master murdered my father."

Lainey's face was flushed, tears sparkling in her eyes.

"I swore to him that I wouldn't move . . . and I didn't. Not until they were long gone and my father's heart was barely beating. I was beside him when it finally stopped." I sucked in a shuddering breath.

"I buried him myself. Took me two whole days, but I couldn't just leave him there like that. And from then on, I felt nothing but an unyielding desire for revenge. I must have thought of a thousand different ways I would do it, all the pain I wanted to inflict on the Master—to make him feel even an ounce of what I was feeling. But I knew I wasn't strong enough."

"You were just a child," Lainey said.

I shook my head. "I stopped being a child the second the Master took my father from me. I threw myself into my training. I was completely consumed with being faster, braver, stronger than the rest. When I was fourteen, I presented myself to the head of the Master's Guard, a Lycan named

Crow, and begged a spot among the ranks. I proclaimed my own father a fool for refusing to join up and declared myself a vessel to take up the call that he had denied. It broke me into a thousand pieces to say those words, but I had to convince them. Crow laughed until I punched him square in the jaw so hard it knocked him over."

The memory brought a small smile to my face. "They let me join, but they gave me the worst assignments and frequently used me as a punching bag. I could hold my own—my father had taught me well—but one against ten is tough odds for a fourteen-year-old kid."

Lainey's eyes were wide. "I don't understand. Why would you join his Guard? After what he did? Why would you want to be a part of something like that?"

I inhaled and let it out. "I didn't want to be a part of it, but I had no other choice. To avenge my father, I had to get close to the Master. Close enough to kill him. I couldn't do that on my own. I kept training, doing whatever they tasked me with until I was good enough, if not better, than the best in their ranks. I earned their respect. I was nearly seventeen by then."

I stopped talking. The rest of the story was a bit more complicated. I'd be lying if I said I wasn't worried about how she'd receive it.

"She deserves to know the truth," my father urged me on.

But at what cost? I asked, rubbing my chest where a deep ache had settled in.

"Pain is a tether, son," my father replied. *"And some things are worth everything."*

"Pain is a tether," I repeated, low and under my breath. Lainey was still watching closely, waiting for me to continue. "How much do you know about Praetorians?" I asked.

"Not much. Just what you've told me."

"Well, I promise they're not all bastards like me." I gave her a half smile, then cleared my throat. "There's an oath that we live by. It's taught to us as early as possible. My father taught it to me.

To live by light and each day's breath.

To serve, to give, and others protect.

To fight, to love, and do what's right.

This spoken seal, my word, my life."

The words flowed from my memory. My heartbeat seemed to echo the rhythm of the oath, and something deep inside me warmed at the words. It'd been years since I said them out loud.

"We're meant to be Guardians. To safeguard others. To live in the light and do the right thing. When I joined the Master's Guard, I betrayed that oath, but you have to understand, there was no other way. I couldn't let my father's death go unavenged. I couldn't let his life mean nothing. I thought I'd be able to withstand it, to do what I had to do without succumbing to the darkness that permeates those who serve the Master. I thought naively that I'd still be able to be the man my father raised me to be . . . but something happened along the way . . ."

I swallowed, the words thick in my throat. "I got lost, Lainey. So lost in darkness, I couldn't see the light anymore. It was like I couldn't tell what was right and what was . . . not. The Master had us do terrible things in his name. At first, I convinced myself that it was for the greater good. I could do anything—even kill a man—if it brought me closer to my goal. But soon, it got easier, and I didn't have to convince myself any longer . . ."

I tore my eyes away from Lainey's face. I didn't want to see the judgment I knew would be there. Instead, I stared down at the rope that bound my hands. There were red rings of irritation forming on my wrists from the rough material chaffing against my skin.

"It was all supposed to be an act—just a role I was playing, but after so long, I realized I wasn't just playing a bad guy, I was one." I shrugged. "I liked how that power made me feel. The bloodlust was easier than the grief that suffocated me. It was easier than thinking about how lost I felt without my father, easier to just accept that this was who I was now, instead of dwelling on how much I'd disappoint my father if he were still alive. But then something else happened that changed everything." I stopped, dragging my eyes back up to hers. "You."

"Me?" she blurted out.

"I was just passing through town, only planning to stay a few days. Then you marched up to me at that comic book shop and wrapped your arm around mine." I smiled, a full one this time. It was the first time I'd smiled in weeks. "I knew the minute you touched me. The minute I looked into your eyes, I knew everything was going to change. It was only later that I realized what that feeling was. You're my Calling, Lainey, and I've never felt something so strong in my life." I stopped, the words hanging between us.

"It was like a defibrillator to a dying man," I continued. "You shocked my system and brought me back from the dead. Helping you find out the truth of who you are and, later, to find the Hetaeria gave me a new purpose. And when you looked at me, you didn't see what I see when I look in the mirror. I wanted to hang on to that for as long as possible."

"Why didn't you tell me any of this before?" she asked. "I would've understood."

"Would you? I've done unspeakable things—the things of nightmares. Every night, I see the faces of my victims. I can never wash their blood from my hands."

Lainey grimaced. "Believe it or not, I understand more than you think I might . . . Still, you lied to me."

"I know, and I'm sorry. I didn't mean for it to happen like that, but it was the only way I could think of to help Maggie. I was going to tell you eventually, but the timing never seemed right. I wasn't sure how to explain it. And . . ."

"And what?"

"There was a side of me that wasn't ready to let it go." I paused. "I care about you, Lainey." I placed my bound hands across my chest, a gesture I knew she would recognize. "My hands, my blade, my life. I meant every word."

"Stop it," she said, shaking her head. "Just stop. Every word out of your mouth is a lie."

"Not everything," I said. "I'm not a good guy, and I'm not sure I'll ever be. But you awoke a side of me I thought was long gone. My Praetorian upbringing, the man my father wanted me to be. You reminded me, and I'll never stop being grateful to you for that."

Lainey jumped to her feet, her cheeks flushed. "Stop lying!" she yelled, gripping the end of her long ponytail in frustration. "If you really cared about me, you wouldn't have lied to me. After everything you saw with Serena and Gareth"—her voice cracked on the word—"you knew how much I needed the truth. But you continued to lie to me, and you're lying now."

The anger I saw on her face and the pain I felt through our connection gutted me. I wanted so badly to wrap my arms around her, to show her how sorry I was, but I stayed seated. I had to stay the course. "Everything I've said tonight has been the truth."

"Really?" Lainey threw back her head and laughed. "Then what about the Troll? And that stupid disguise? It may not have been an outright lie, but it was still a deception. You tricked me tonight."

I shook my head. "You're right, I did. I laid a trap that I knew you would fall into."

"But why? You act like you care about me, but then you resort to trickery and deception."

"After what happened at the Gathering, I knew you'd

143

never let me get close enough to you to explain." To be completely truthful, I added, "And I knew that you were my best bet at getting to the Hetaeria." I said it matter-of-factly, but inside, guilt surged to life, attacking my defenses.

"What's the Hetaeria have to do with anything?"

"I *do* care about you, Lainey. That's not a lie. But as much as I care about you, there are . . . other things that matter more. You woke me up, that's true, but as much as I want to be the man my father raised me to be, I can't just change from the man I've become. I can't let my father die in vain. I can't ever move forward until the Master is dead. I thought joining the Guard was my way in, but I was wrong. I'm too weak, too likely to give in to the darkness. And I realized that the Hetaeria had a better chance. The only chance. And they have you."

Lainey flinched. "I'm *not* a weapon." Her voice was sharp, bitter.

I stared at her hard. "You're my best bet at getting what I want. No matter what else I feel, avenging my father is the only thing that matters." *Liar*, my heart seemed to whisper, thrashing in my chest. But I couldn't lose focus—I couldn't admit how close I was to crumbling. My plan, my goals, everything that led up to this moment was laid out on the table.

"I knew it," Lainey said, her lower lip trembling. "You're not here to make amends with me at all. This whole conversation is just another manipulation. You're here to use me, to use the Hetaeria to get what you want."

I shrugged. "Wouldn't anyone in my shoes do the same?"

The callous words were another manipulation. I hated myself for it.

"No," she spat. "When you care about someone, you don't use them as a pawn in some twisted game, a game where no one wins."

She began to pace. "I want to know how you did it. How did you find me? How did you know that I'd come rescue you?"

"That part was fairly easy. I used the Praetorian bond to track you."

"Like some weird Supernatural GPS?"

"No, it doesn't work like that, unfortunately. It's not nearly that specific. It's a feeling, almost like an instinct, of knowing where to go. It's like the south pole of a magnet. We're drawn to our magnetic north. I was able to get a sense of where you were, but not your exact location. I could sense magic, too, and I knew there were magical wards being used. That's why I had to lay the trap, to draw you out so that I could find you."

"And how exactly did you do that, draw me out?"

I grimaced, not wanting her to know this particular piece of information. "I manipulated the bond."

"You what?"

"I was able to send my thoughts and feelings to you through our connection. Not direct thoughts, mind you, but enough to give you a sense of danger and get you moving in my direction."

"And the pain?" Lainey rubbed absentmindedly at her ribcage.

"That was definitely real," I said with a small laugh. "Once the Troll was on the scene, he did the rest. I didn't have to fake that."

Lainey was quiet for several minutes, trying to process everything.

"Say something." The words slipped out, my aching heart pounding. I'd thought that finding Lainey and tricking her to take me to the Hetaeria would be the hard part of all of this, but staring at her now, I realized I was wrong. *This* was the hard part.

"I don't know what to say," Lainey said, sliding back to the ground. "I can't decide if I'm angry at you or I just feel sorry for you."

The words hurt, knives again, stabbing at the most vulnerable parts of me.

"I know none of this changes anything. I know you hate me, but please try to understand."

"I don't know if I can."

Her words were raw and honest, but they hurt just the same.

"For what it's worth, I really am sorry." It was the truth, but the other truth, the one that had fueled me so long, burned brighter than anything else. I sighed. "I'm not sorry for what I did. Selfish bastard, remember?" I gave her a half smile, which she did not return. "But I am sorry for hurting you. If I could change that, I would do it in a heartbeat."

Lainey swallowed. "I wish I could believe that."

"I hope someday you will. And I hope on that same day, you'll be able to forgive me for what I've done to you."

Lainey let out a deep breath, her eyes flashing. "Ty, I—"

The door to the tack room flew open. A red-haired witch stalked toward me, her eyes narrowed on me with disgust and distrust.

Lainey jumped to her feet. "Zia, I was just about—"

I recognized her name. Zia was the head of the Hetaeria— the woman we'd been trying to find the night of the Gathering.

"I told Julian no one was to come in here until he was questioned," she growled, glaring at Lainey.

Lainey put her hands on her hips. "I had a few questions of my own that needed answering."

The two stared at each other, locked in a silent showdown. Zia gave in first. "Did you get what you needed?"

Lainey looked over at me and shook her head. "No, but it's a start." She turned back to Zia. "He's all yours."

She walked out the door without looking back.

It hurt more than I wanted to admit. *Maybe it's for the best.*

Zia motioned, and two guards approached. The tall one pulled me up roughly, not caring at all when I hissed from the pain in my ribs.

"Now you answer *my* questions," Zia said.

The men dragged me outside, slamming the door to the tack room behind them.

CHAPTER ELEVEN

TY

They didn't take me far. When we stopped, we were standing behind a tall, worn building. The expression "if looks could kill" came to mind as other Hetaeria members gathered around, their faces hard.

Hisses of "traitor" and "Oathbreaker" floated through the air, the words ringing in my ears. *Oathbreaker.* It was the worst of insults. One reserved only for my kind, for Praetorians who do not fulfill their duties and break their oath. It was true. I was an Oathbreaker, but it was a word that I'd only ever allowed to seep into my nightmares. It hit me square in the jaw, a right hook that threw me off balance. But I kept walking, trying not to squirm under the weight of the word.

Off to the right of the crowd, Lainey stood with arms folded across her chest, her face unreadable. Maggie was standing next to her, and I was relieved to see her alive. Her face was solemn, and she was giving me a well-earned side-eye of disapproval, but hers was one of the few faces in the crowd not carved in hatred.

The guard holding my arm yanked on the restraints. I stumbled, almost losing my footing while the crowd jeered and the guard smirked. "Bring him forward," Zia called out. The guards pushed me ahead the last few steps and shoved me to my knees in front of her.

Zia walked around me, studying me. "What's your name?" The edge in her voice was sharp.

"Tyler Marek," I answered. "Ty."

Zia glared, her lips pursing. "How long have you been working for the Master?"

"Since I was fourteen."

"And why are you here?"

"Because of her." I glanced in Lainey's direction. The crowd's disapproving voices grew louder. Splotches of pink colored Lainey's cheeks, and overhead, a low peal of thunder rumbled. I didn't have to see the green lightning in her hand to know where it came from.

"What do you want with her?"

A pang of uncertainty mixed with anger pulsed through me, and my eyes darted over to Lainey. If she was aware she was sending me her feelings through the Praetorian bond, I couldn't tell. "The Master has promised to handsomely reward whoever returns both the DuCarmont witch and the Grimoire to him." I said it matter-of-factly, as if it were the most obvious thing in the world. It wasn't a lie per se, but it was a redirection. Zia's face didn't change, but Lainey's eyebrows furrowed, and there was another rumble of thunder. Maggie elbowed her.

Zia leaned forward, her eyes narrowing. "And so you thought you'd cash in?"

"If not me, then someone else," I said with a shrug. "I figured it might as well be me."

"You know we're going to kill you, right?"

I shrugged again. "We all die someday."

Zia's face was turning red, the muscles in her jaw twitching. "Are you alone, or did you come with others?"

"It's just me."

"How do we know you're not lying?"

"You don't."

Her lip curled up, and I knew my short, nondescript answers were getting under Zia's skin. It probably wasn't the smartest move on my part, especially given the request I was going to make of her, but she made it entirely too easy.

"Do you know what the Master is planning?"

Every eye in the crowd was trained on my face.

"All I know," I replied, "is that finding the DuCarmont Grimoire and the witch who goes with it is his number-one priority."

"Well, if that's all you know, then you are of no value to us," Zia sneered. "But I think you're lying."

"He is," Lainey stepped forward. "I can feel it." She knelt in front of me, the voices of the crowd rising again. "Tell them," she said out loud. "Whatever it is, tell us what you know." The next words—the ones that came through our bond—were meant for me only. *You owe me.*

I owed her far more than that, but this was something I had planned to do anyway. I tore my eyes from hers and addressed Zia. "I do have information you may find valuable. A secret the Master would very much like to remain a secret."

Her eyes were narrowed. "Okay then, Oathbreaker," Zia said, placing a hand on her hip. "Spill it."

"I'm not stupid," I said, cocking my head. "And neither are you. You want the secret; I want something too. There's a mutually beneficial agreement to be made here."

"You're not exactly in a position to be bargaining."

I gave Zia a half smile. "Aren't I?"

She glared at me, then stomped over to a cluster of Supernaturals who I assumed were members of the council. I couldn't hear their hushed conversation, but their unhappy expressions made it clear I had them exactly where I wanted them. Lainey still knelt in front of me, but the connection between us was blocked. I couldn't read her, couldn't tell from the look on her face what she was feeling. Despite whatever smug satisfaction I had in knowing my plan was working, the distance between us killed me. The ache in my chest I felt whenever I looked at her throbbed sharply.

"We don't bargain with traitors," Zia declared, stalking back over to me. Her sleek hair was ruffled from where she'd run her fingers hastily through it. "But tell us what you know, and we'll spare your life."

"Not good enough. If I'm going to give you the key to winning the war, to defeating the Master, you have to give me what I want."

"You don't care if you live or die?" Zia spat. "Does your life mean so little to you that it's hardly a bargaining chip?"

"My life was taken years ago. Now I want something better."

"Well, don't keep us in suspense."

I pulled against my restraints, leaning forward. "Do you give me your word that you'll do as I ask?"

Zia responded, moving in closer herself, "How do we know the information you give us will be credible and worth your price?"

I picked up my hand and placed it across my chest. "I swear on the Praetorian oath that what I have to tell you will change everything."

"On the oath?" she scoffed. "That's hardly worth the dirt under your feet, Oathbreaker. You've already broken every single word."

She was right, and I hated her for it. "Fine." I let out a breath. "I swear to you on my father's name that the information I share with you will not only turn the tide of war, but it will also be the key to the Master's undoing."

As the words poured from my mouth, the ache in my chest ignited. A swear against my father—who had I become? I tasted bile.

"On your father's name?" Zia asked. "Is that supposed to convince us?"

I flinched, her words digging into me like salt in a wound. She continued. "I hardly think—"

"Wait," Lainey stepped forward. "It's good enough." Her eyes were locked on me. I had no idea what my face looked like, but it didn't matter. She knew what my vow had cost me—she could feel it.

Zia studied both of us for a long time before she spoke again. "What is it that you want?"

"I want to join you. Let me be a part of the Hetaeria, and I'll tell you what I know."

Zia burst into laughter, as did many of the others who were standing around. Lainey and Maggie didn't laugh but looked at me with wide eyes.

"You must think of us as incredibly stupid."

I raised an eyebrow. "You don't have much of a choice if you want this information."

Zia considered this. "Why now? You're a member of the Master's Guard. Suddenly, you want to change sides? You can't expect us to believe that."

"It's simple, really. I want to be on the winning side of the war. It's self-preservation, nothing more."

"And what makes you think we'll win?"

"You have her." I looked at Lainey. "My reasons are simple. The Master murdered my father. I joined the Guard thinking it would get me close enough to the Master to avenge him, but that wasn't the case."

I was glossing over most of the details I'd shared with Lainey, but the overall story was the same. "I honestly don't care what side of the war I'm on as long as it ends with the Master dead and my father's memory honored."

Zia narrowed her eyes. "You've been loyal to the Master all these years. How can you—"

"I'm loyal to no one but myself," I broke in. I was tempted to look at Lainey, the oath I'd swore to her in the back of my mind, but I didn't move, didn't break the eye contact with Zia. She didn't need to know all of my lies . . . or my truths.

Zia moved to again consult with the other council members.

"There's one more thing," I called out to her retreating back. "When it comes down to it, in the end, I get to do it. I get to deliver the killing blow."

The words hung in the air, thick and potent.

She didn't respond, just continued speaking in low tones with the others. When she stomped back over to me, her face was tight.

"We agree," Zia said, "but there are conditions. You must take the Depreherium before we move any further. Once we know that you're speaking the truth, that your intentions are honorable, we'll agree to your terms."

The Depreherium was a magical ritual performed between two Supernaturals. It allowed one to probe through the other's consciousness, seeking out any lies or deception. It wasn't overly dangerous, but it wasn't pleasant. I'd never done it myself, but I'd seen it performed on others many times. It required a neutral third party—usually a very powerful witch or warlock—to perform the ritual.

"Agreed," I said.

Zia motioned to a woman with long braids and dark skin from the back of the crowd. "Hattie, if you please."

The witch stepped forward. She eyed me carefully and then lifted her hands, placing her long, slender fingers on either side of my head. She waited, and when Zia motioned for her to continue, she began to whisper an incantation under her breath.

A piercing sensation ripped through my skull. I squeezed my eyes shut against it, hissing as the witch searched my mind. Like a mouse darting through a maze, she moved her fingers across my scalp, probing and reaching, magically exposing my intentions.

The throbbing in my head from the Troll was bad, but this was worse. I winced, trying to focus on my breathing, but black spots dotted my vision, and I felt light-headed. A blistering light shot in my eye sockets, and I had to grit my teeth to keep from crying out. I was vaguely aware of a loud hiss and then a voice speaking from beside me.

". . . a concussion," Lainey was saying. "I don't think this is a good idea."

"Worried, are you?" Zia asked. "Seems quite contradictory coming from the girl who said this boy meant nothing to her."

Lainey didn't respond.

Then the witch's magic brushed against the connection, the bond linking Lainey and me. Her voice blended with mine as we both cried out.

No! I wanted to break free, to find a way to stop the pain I was feeling from reaching Lainey, but the witch's hold was strong. Lainey cried out again, the sound slicing through me.

Then it was gone. The pain vanished, and everything came shooting back into view. I was hunched over, panting. My eyes landed on Lainey, who was leaning heavily on Maggie, her chest heaving. She looked alarmed, but unharmed.

Hattie looked to Zia, flipping her long braids over her shoulder. "I detected no deception in his claims. He is telling us the truth."

The crowd murmured, and Zia knelt beside me. "Good, now tell us what you know."

It took a few minutes for the breath to return to my lungs, but once it did, I struggled back upright, swaying slightly. "The Master is using dark magic. It's what makes him so powerful."

"We already know that!" Zia hissed. "If you think we'll spare your life for that—"

I held up a hand to silence her so I could continue. "What you don't know is that the Master is also Blood Reaping."

The crowd fell silent. I kept going.

"I saw it with my own eyes. Dark magic weakens the Master over time. He can only sustain that level of power for so long. It drains him—of both magic and physical strength. He's Blood Reaping to counteract the effects of the dark magic—taking the strength of others to replenish his own."

Zia's eyes were wide. "I've heard whispers of Blood

Reaping, but never known anyone to actually do it. It requires willing human sacrifice. Only those who wish to gamble their own souls would ever take such a risk. To Reap the life force from others is blasphemy." She shivered. "Who would agree to do that for him?"

"It was the Alium I saw, but really, any of his followers would do it. They worship him. But if we can somehow prevent the Master from Reaping—"

"Then we can use that to our advantage," Zia continued.

"We wait until the dark magic has drained him," I said. "We wait until he is at his weakest, and then we attack him with everything we have."

"Yes, we can draw him out and force him to use his powers. Once he's weakened and unable to recharge"—she turned to Lainey—"we'll unleash our greatest weapon against him." Lainey's cheeks colored.

Zia's eyes darted back to me. "You earned your life today, Oathbreaker. Don't make me regret not killing you." She stalked off, and the crowd dispersed behind her.

Julian, the tall Scavenger, stepped in front of me and bent to remove the rope from my wrists. "You can sleep in the barn," he grumbled, fixing a large brown eye on me. "Betray us, and I skin you like a fish, got it?"

"Got it." It seemed a moot point to mention that the witch would have seen any plans of betrayal in my mind.

He shuffled away. Only Maggie and Lainey were left.

I reached for her, but the look in Lainey's eyes made me pause. I lowered my arm back down to my side. Tapping into our connection, I tried to send reassurance her way, hoping she would understand. Everything I'd told her inside and every word I'd spoken here was the truth. I'd done a lot of lying and omitting facts in the past, but deep down I wanted her to look at me like she used to. I wanted her to trust me.

But she didn't. Without a word, Lainey swept past me in the darkness, not even bothering to spare a glance in my direction.

Maggie waited until she was out of earshot before she walked over, her hands on her hips. "You're back," she said.

"I'm back."

"You really screwed things up, you know."

"I know," I said. "But for what it's worth, I never meant to hurt her."

Maggie eyed me carefully. "I don't know why, but I believe you. You may be working for the Master, and I'm getting a major Gambit vibe from you with the whole not knowing what side you're really on, *but* you protected me at the Gathering. When the Scavenger grabbed me, you fought like hell to get me back, to save me. There's more to you than meets the eye, I know it."

She glanced to Lainey's retreating shadow. "I don't know if she'll ever forgive you."

"I probably don't deserve it."

"Jean Grey always forgives Wolverine. She can't help it," Maggie said, giving me a small half smile. "Just give her some time."

She nudged me with her shoulder, then swayed backward, off balance.

"Whoa." I grabbed her arm to steady her. "You okay?" I hadn't noticed it earlier, but up close, her eyes were red, and a sheen of sweat dotted her brow.

"Yeah," she said, waving me off. "I'm fine."

"Are you sure? If you're sick, I'm sure there's—"

Maggie straightened and shook her head. "It's nothing."

I wasn't convinced. "Maggie, I really think—"

"That you have enough to be worrying about right now," Maggie finished. "Yeah, you do." She gave my shoulder a little pat and smiled. "Don't worry about me, Pretty Face. I'll manage."

She walked off, following the same path Lainey had taken, leaving me alone.

The barn loomed in the distance, and I headed that way. For the first time in weeks, I felt like I was exactly where I was supposed to be.

My body still ached from the excursion with the Troll, and the Depreherium hadn't helped much either. By the time I made it inside and collapsed onto a big pile of hay, every nerve ending in my body was screaming.

Lainey's face hovered in my thoughts, and my heart gave a pitiful pang. I shook my head to clear it.

It was worth it, I reminded myself, opening my mind to the ache. It was worth it.

Pain is a tether.

Pain is a tether.

CHAPTER TWELVE

MAGGIE

It wasn't long after I'd talked to Ty when it happened again. I'd been walking around aimlessly, just trying to clear my head when the dizziness hit me out of nowhere. I swayed, stumbling to keep my footing, but managed to stay upright. Breathing in the cool air, I closed my eyes and waited for the world to stop spinning. The vertigo only lasted a few seconds, but it was longer than the last bout I'd had. They were becoming more frequent and lasting longer.

I pushed the sleeve of my shirt up and ran my finger over my scar. The raised skin was even puffier now, inflamed and angry-looking. It was incredibly sensitive, though I didn't need to touch it to feel the heat coming off it. Faint dark lines were starting to branch off from the site, running up and down my arm in different directions.

Looks like I was right, I thought. *Something is definitely wrong.*

I let out a sigh and kept walking. I'd been meaning to tell Lainey or Serena, but with everything that was going on, it just didn't seem the right time. *Maybe tomorrow.*

Despite the fact that it was getting late, the farm was busier than I'd ever seen it. Most of the outer buildings were lit up with people bustling around. My eyes flitted to the main training area. Oliver was stacking boxes next to a pickup truck parked beside one of the smaller buildings. He had a T-shirt on this time, but even in the darkness, I could see his lean muscles moving underneath the thin fabric.

Holy crapkittens. I swallowed, heading in his direction. "Hi!" I called out.

Oliver looked up, his eyes narrowing on me in the darkness. "Hey."

"Need any help?"

He regarded me for a second, scowling, then pointed at the boxes. "I'm almost done, but you can help me finish loading up if you want. The boxes aren't that heavy."

With a spring in my step, I walked over and grabbed one of the boxes, expecting it to lift easily. When it didn't, my knees buckling under its weight, I shoved my heels into the ground and steadied my legs. *Not that heavy?* "Geez," I said, struggling to make it over to the truck. "You got dead bodies in here or something?"

Oliver rolled his eyes and took the box out of my hands.

"Supplies. Mostly medical, but a few other things we might need if we have to relocate. Zia wants us ready to go."

"Is it really that serious? Do you really think we'll have to leave the farm?"

"It's a real possibility, thanks to your dumb little friend." His scowl deepened.

Heat flooded my cheeks. "Whoa." I held up my hands. "That's my best friend you're talking about. Don't call her dumb."

"I call it like I see it," Oliver shrugged. "Her actions tonight were reckless and foolish. She may have cost the entire Hetaeria just because she couldn't keep her magical shit together."

"I know it's not a great excuse, but—"

"There are no excuses for what she did," Oliver cut me off. "The Master doesn't know where we are, but that could all change tonight if someone tracks your friend's little show."

The heat in my face grew hotter. "We don't know for sure that anyone is tracking her magic. And if they did, the Seers will be able to See any threat long before it gets here, right?"

Oliver muttered under his breath as he continued to load the boxes.

"Right?" I said, a little louder.

"It's possible the Seers might See something before it happens," Oliver growled, "but the Master is powerful and smart. He knows how to trick a Seer's Sight. We won't necessarily know a threat is coming until it's here."

"Look, she did what she had to do. I don't think either of

us realized we'd have to save someone from a freaking Troll. If I'd known that, I never would've suggested we sneak off the farm. I just thought—"

"Wait," Oliver said, putting the box he was holding back on the ground. "*You* suggested it?"

"I thought we could both use a break."

"And you just left? Without telling anyone?" Oliver stared at me like I had three heads. "Are you kidding me?" he yelled, throwing his hands up in the air. "Do you have any idea how stupid that was?"

I stepped back, a little surprised at the fury flashing in his eyes. "Excuse me?"

"When you arrived on the farm, Zia told all of us what happened at the Gathering. She was very specific in saying how imperative it was that the witch stay within the wards."

"Her name is Lainey," I said, putting my hands on my hips.

"Whatever," Oliver spat. "Zia wasn't trying to micromanage. She was trying to keep your dumb little friend alive."

The expression on Oliver's face—ugh! That stupid scowl—made me see red. "She's stronger than you think. And she's definitely not dumb."

"That may be true, but your friend might just cost us this war. Is it really worth the price?"

The rock in my stomach tripled in size, but I shook my head. "If Lainey's magic gives away our position, then . . . well, then that sucks. But we're not going to lose the war."

"You don't know anything."

This time, it was me who rolled my eyes. "Are you always this much of an asshat, or I am just special?"

Oliver jerked back and grunted—it was almost a laugh. "Listen, I have a lot of work to do here, so if you're done yelling at me . . ."

"I'm sorry. I'm not trying to be difficult. She's my friend, and I look out for her. I didn't mean to cause problems, and neither did she. We're both new at this, you know? We're trying."

Oliver grunted again but didn't say anything.

"Don't be mad," I said, walking a little closer. "We have to work together, right? You said you'd start training me. I just want—"

A wave of vertigo slammed into me. This time, it was so strong I couldn't keep my bearing. I swayed and tumbled to the ground. The heat in my face spread to my neck and chest. I was suffocating.

My ears were ringing, but over that I could just make out the sound of my name. Oliver was gripping the tops of my arms. I opened my mouth, but no sound came out.

It took a long time for the spinning to stop. When it did, I leaned over and vomited all over the grass.

"Here." Oliver had one hand on my shoulder and in the other was a tin cup full of water. I took it gratefully and swished the water around before spitting it out. Another sip to soothe my raw throat.

"Can you stand?"

"I think so," I said, my voice cracking.

Oliver stood and then reached down to help me up. The minute I hit a vertical position, I swayed again. Oliver caught me around the waist and helped me walk to the back of his truck. Sitting on the tailgate, I took another sip of water.

"Thank you," I said.

He was looking at me with concern in his eyes. It was a stark contrast to the anger and annoyance that had been there just moments earlier. "I'm fine," I waved a hand. "Just a dizzy spell."

"You look like shit," Oliver intoned.

Annnnd . . . he's back. I snorted. "Man, you sure know how to charm the ladies." I swallowed another mouthful of water.

Oliver put a palm against my forehead. "You're burning up."

"So . . . you're saying I'm hot?"

Oliver just stared. I let out a sigh, pulling away. "I'm just flustered. Trust me, I'm fine."

As I moved to hop off the tailgate, Oliver grabbed my arm to help me down. I yelped when his fingers dug into my scar, sending sharp pains shooting up my arm.

Oliver's eyes were wide as I cradled my arm against my chest, tears burning in my eyes. "I'm fine," I repeated, trying to muster a smile.

Oliver wasn't convinced. He eyed my arm. "Show me."

I shook my head.

"Just let me see." He held out a hand. "If you're injured, I can help."

"A Shifter and a doctor?" I attempted to joke.

"When you run with animals, you learn a thing or two about first aid." His hand was still outstretched.

The pain in my arm radiated down to the bone and made me dizzy. The feeling in my gut was clear. I held out my arm to Oliver.

He wrapped his fingers gently around my wrist with one hand and then carefully pushed the sleeve of my shirt up with the other.

He whistled through his teeth when he saw the scar. It was worse than it had been only a few minutes ago. The wound was red, incredibly swollen, and throbbing with heat. The dark lines branching off of it were even more pigmented, and they stretched up almost to my elbow.

Oliver's eyes flicked back up to mine before he leaned to inspect my arm more closely.

"What's the verdict, Doc?" My voice was shaky, and my nervous stomach was threatening to pitch its contents again.

Oliver let go of my arm and stepped back. "How long has it been like that?"

I shrugged. "A few days?"

"A few days!" Oliver wiped a hand across his face. "Why didn't you tell anyone?"

"I was going to. I planned to tell Lainey this afternoon, but she's dealing with a lot, and I didn't want to get everyone in a tizzy over a little irritation."

"A little irritation?" Oliver reached for my arm again,

raising it to eye level. "This isn't a *little* irritation. It's bite poisoning."

"What?"

"It happens," he continued. "Most who are bitten transition just fine. Others are completely immune. But for some, Shifter bites are dangerous."

I heard the words, but I was struggling to make sense of them.

"It's like a toxin running through your bloodstream. We need to get you to a healer right away."

"But I don't understand. How could it be bite poisoning? After I was bitten, I got sick, but then I got better. Zia said it was from the transition."

"There are rare cases of delayed reactions," Oliver said. "There probably wasn't enough toxin in your blood to cause a full reaction—your body was doing its job to fight it off. But now, over time, you're losing that ability."

He looked up at me. "It's getting worse every day, isn't it?"

"Yes." I didn't want to admit it, but it was the truth. "Okay, so I need some kind of Shifter antivenom, right? I get that, I get better, and then I'll finally be able to Shift right?" There had to be an easy solution to this problem.

"Maggie." It was the first time Oliver had ever said my name. "If your body is rejecting the bite, then that means—"

Please don't say it. Everything inside of me was tense, waiting for the words I knew were about to come out of his mouth.

"You're not a Shifter, Maggie. You never were."

No. I wouldn't accept what I was hearing. "You've got it wrong. I was bitten by a Shifter. I got sick right afterward. Zia said I was transitioning. I'm sure this is something else, something . . ." I trailed off, all the wind having left my sails. The rock in my stomach had now morphed into an anvil that sat on top of my head. Every inch of me was heavy.

The feeling in my gut was as strong as ever.

The truth was etched on the hard lines of Oliver's face. "I wish it were, but I've seen this before. And it's only going to get worse, until . . ."

"Until what?" The anvil pressed harder, and I was sure the heels of my feet were sinking into the ground beneath them.

"I'm not an expert; we need a healer . . . but in most of the cases I've seen, the person bitten isn't able to overcome the toxin. It's irreversible. Lethal."

"I'm going to die from this?" It was getting harder to breathe. "Please tell me this is some kind of sick joke."

The look on Oliver's face was resolute. The blood drained from my face, and I swallowed. *It wasn't true . . . was it?*

"We should tell the others, tell Zia," Oliver said, clearly uncomfortable having to be the one to explain my fate to me.

His voice became muffled as I tuned him out.

Not a Shifter.

Poison.

Lethal.

The more I tried to decipher those words, the dizzier I felt. The world began to spin again, and the ringing returned, completely drowning out the sound of Oliver's voice.

I stumbled forward, my hands outstretched. Every inch of my skin was on fire, and my lungs were so tight it was difficult to draw breath.

Oliver's hands were on me, and I forced my eyes open as wide as they would go. The fuzzy, distorted image of his face appeared in front of mine. He was shouting, but I couldn't hear a word he was saying.

With one arm around my shoulders, Oliver reached down and knocked my legs out from underneath me, catching me behind the knees.

I think we were moving, but it was hard to tell with the world already rotating around me like a kaleidoscope. I gasped and arched my back as waves of pain enveloped me, sending hot and cold chills across my skin.

The last thing I felt was Oliver's hands cradling me to his body. There was a rumbling in his chest, a murmur of words that I couldn't hear or make out.

Then I sank deep into a sea of darkness.

CHAPTER THIRTEEN

LAINEY

I burst into the room, the door slamming the wall behind me. The sound echoed down the hall of the otherwise quiet house, but I didn't care. "Maggie!"

She was lying in bed, a worn patchwork quilt covering her. The rich brown of her skin had lost its usual radiance, and her eyes were bloodshot. Her pale lips quirked up in a weak smile when she saw me. "Hey, Styles."

I rushed over and eased myself gently down beside her on the bed. Lynlee, the healer, had broken the news only seconds ago, and panic burned through me, resonating in the exact spot where my heart was pumping erratically. "Oh my god, Maggie. Why didn't you tell me?"

She lifted a shoulder and then let it drop. "I didn't think it was that serious, and you've had a lot on your plate. I didn't want to add any more."

The words lanced through me. "You're my family,

Maggie." My voice cracked as a lump began to form in my throat. "Nothing is more important than you, got it?"

"Yeah, I got it." She gave me a soft smile I couldn't return. "Can I see?"

Maggie pulled her arm out from beneath the quilt. Bile rose in my throat at the sight of the scar, now open and oozing with pus. The black lines of toxin that branched off from the wound looked like veins, a starburst of creeping fingers inching their way up and down her skin.

"The toxin is moving through her system incredibly fast." Lynlee's words echoed in my ears. *"At this rate, we may only have a few days before . . ."* I tore my eyes away from Maggie's arm. "I'm the world's worst friend," I said, burying my face in my hands. "If I had known, maybe I could've done something, maybe we'd—"

"We'd be in the same position we're in now," Maggie said, cutting me off. "There's no cure for bite poisoning. My body is either going to fight it off, or it won't."

The bitter taste of more bile filled my mouth. "It will."

"Well," Maggie said with a half smile, "that's the plan." She let out a sigh and pulled the covers a little higher. "You want to know the worst part about it? I mean, aside from the possible impending death thing?"

I snorted. "What?"

Her eyes filled with tears. "I'm not a Shifter."

The look on her face almost made me lose grip on the very thin thread that was holding me together. "Oh, Maggie, what matters is—"

"No, you don't get it, Styles." She sniffled. "This was my chance. My one shot to be more than just plain ole Maggie."

"You're not just plain ole Maggie. You're the strongest person I know. And you're my best friend. I wouldn't be here if it weren't for you." I reached over to squeeze her hand. "Batman and Robin, remember?"

"Batman and Robin," she agreed. "I just thought . . . I don't know. I guess I was just really looking forward to being a Shifter, to being part of something bigger than myself."

"You already are. Shifter or not, you're part of this, Maggie."

"If you say so . . . I guess I just have to figure out how not to die." She let out a breathy laugh, but there was a noticeable quiver in her voice.

The words twisted my insides. "We'll figure it out together. There *has* to be some kind of cure out there, and we'll find it, I know it. You're gonna be okay."

"I hope so, Styles," Maggie said. "If Deadpool can kick cancer's ass, I can beat some stupid toxin, right?"

"Right," I grinned, though my insides were still bent and burning.

She narrowed her eyes. "What about you? Are you okay?"

It was a hard question to answer. Aside from my best friend facing a life-threatening poison and the impending war, there was something else dominating my thoughts. *Someone.*

Ty.

From the moment the Trickster magic had lifted and I'd seen him lying there in the grass, he was all I could think about. Our conversation from the tack room played on a constant loop. *"I do care about you, Lainey. That's not a lie. But as much as I care about you, there are other things that matter more."* The words weren't any easier to hear the hundredth time in my head than they'd been when he spoke them the first time.

I hate you, Tyler Marek, I thought. But I didn't have to dig very deep to feel the lie in those words. It had been easier before I knew his story, heard the raw honesty of it all. Ty wasn't a good guy . . . but it wasn't as simple as saying he was a bad one either.

My head wanted to write him off completely—his story, as tragic as it was, changed nothing.

But my heart—my foolish, traitorous heart—couldn't stop thinking about a twelve-year-old Ty watching his father die in front of his very eyes. I knew all too well that was a pain that never faded. I never stopped seeing Gareth's blood on my hands.

I ached for that boy as much as I ached for myself. And when he looked at me, those piercing blue eyes staring into mine, that stupid heart of mine beat faster. Every single time.

"My hands, my blade, my life. I meant every word." His voice echoed in my head, and I absolutely hated the way my body responded to it.

"Honestly?" I let out a deep sigh and shook my head. "I have no idea. There's a Summit meeting the day after tomorrow. Zia told the faction leaders that she had a weapon to take out the Master."

"A weapon?"

I swallowed. "She meant me. They want a demonstration, some kind of show of my power, but I can't do it, Maggie. I made progress with Teddy, but I'm not ready for something like that. I could kill someone by accident . . . again."

"You're Lainey Styles," Maggie said. "You can face anything."

"I'm not ready."

An alarm clock chimed on the bedside table, signaling the hour. It was nearly midnight. I yawned, suddenly very tired.

"You look wiped out," Maggie said, readjusting the pillow behind her head.

"Long day," I said.

"Why don't you go get some sleep?"

"Sleep is the last thing I'm worried about. You're my number-one priority."

"I'm not going anywhere, Styles." Maggie shoved my shoulder. "Go get some sleep."

I stood up, grumbling. "Fine, but tomorrow, we start looking for a cure."

"Deal. And, Styles?"

"Yeah?"

"You're *not* a bad friend. You're the best friend I've ever had. You're my family too."

"I know," I said. "Night, Maggie." I gave her a soft smile and then eased into the hallway, shutting the door behind me.

Bumbling toward my room, I barely reached my bed before I collapsed in a heap, not even bothering to change my clothes.

Squeezing my eyes shut, I started counting from one, my brain aching to focus on something other than the events of the day. I made it to 729 before I finally drifted off to sleep.

∾•∾

It was still dark when I headed outside, the sun lazily hanging on to its slumber. I wish I could've done the same, but after a fitful night of sleep, I'd finally given up and headed down to the kitchen to make a pot of coffee.

A steaming camper mug in my hand, I walked out on the front porch, shivering at the crispness in the air. Julian had told me it wouldn't be long now till the first snowfall, and though I wasn't a fan of being cold, I was oddly excited by the idea. I'd never really seen snow before, but I imagined the world looked far less complicated and a whole lot more beautiful when covered in a layer of pristine, fluffy snow.

I sipped my coffee and tried to let the quiet of the morning clear my head. It wasn't working. The sun was just beginning to peek over the horizon, and hazy fingers of warm orange light streaked across the sky. Soon, the farm would be awake, bustling with activity. I hoped—no, *needed*—to have my head together before then.

On top of finding some way to help Maggie, I still needed

to practice my magic. I swallowed the rest of my coffee and headed for Teddy's cabin.

She opened the door seconds after I knocked, fully dressed and bright-eyed. She didn't seem surprised to see me at such an early hour.

"Ready for more training?" I asked, moving into her living room.

Teddy nodded. "I am."

"Good, then let's get started."

❧ • ❧

By lunchtime, my brain felt like a bowl of oatmeal. We'd spent all morning working on basic magic skills and fine-tuning my ability to feel and work with my magic instead of trying to control it or force it into action. The more I practiced, the easier it was to call the magic forth, to use it to do the things I needed it to do. Teddy had been right all along: Once I gave myself over to it, my magic just *was*.

"Unlocking the Grimoire might take some trial and error," Teddy said. "Given that the spell your mother performed has never been done before, I don't know what parameters she placed on it."

I wish there was a way to ask her. There was a pang in my chest as I thought of my mom, a woman I never got a chance to know. Thanks to the Master.

"As you did with your own magic, I believe you'll need

to connect with the Grimoire. It's already a part of you. You just need to reach for it. Close your eyes," Teddy instructed.

I was already sitting on the couch, but I moved to the floor, crossing my legs and straightening my spine. I closed my eyes, relaxed my shoulders, and placed my hands, open, on top of my knees.

"Take a few deep breaths. Focus on your breathing and the sound of my voice. Tune out any other distractions."

I followed Teddy's instructions, paying particular attention to the flow of my own breath, in and out. Settling into the darkness of my mind, I smiled. My magic was waiting for me there, swirling, a bright vivid green that embraced me like a long-lost friend.

"Now," Teddy said, her voice soft and low, "I want you to look deep inside your mind, inside your heart. Reach out and feel for the magic. It should feel different from your own magic."

I inhaled a few more deep breaths. Then I leaned into my magic, letting the now-familiar and friendly current warm me from the inside out. I imagined reaching out a hand and swirling it in the energy there. The sensation was like sticking my hand out a car window and moving it up and down in the rhythm of the airstream. Flow and resistance. Peace.

I let myself float in the stream of emerald green warmth, following its path to the deepest places of myself.

Then I felt a beacon of warmth, both bright and familiar. It hummed like my own magic, but it was stronger, more vibrant. I reached further, dug deeper.

Deep within my core, safely nestled there, waiting for me to find it, was the Grimoire. The overwhelming feeling of love that radiated from that place made my chest ache, and a lump formed in my throat. As I reached for it, closer and closer, the most beautiful sound filled my ears. *"Lainey."* My name, whispered in a hundred different voices, beckoning me forward. *My family.*

It shined so brightly it was hard to focus on, but I reached for it anyway. My fingertips grazed the surface, just the tiniest nudge, and I ignited.

I gasped as power surged through me. If my own magic was a thousand tiny sparks that warmed me like a blanket, then this magic was fireworks, a million starbursts of the brightest colors bursting apart, filling every inch of me.

Fire seared through me, but it didn't hurt. I was burning, but these flames were my history, my ancestors, my lineage coming to life within me. I gasped again, needing more oxygen as the flames licked through me.

The voices began to speak louder, the sounds mixing together in a symphony of melodic whispers that infiltrated my thoughts. Each voice a different note in the same song. I couldn't make out individual words, couldn't differentiate the voices, and yet I knew every one of them—a seamless melody engraved upon my heart.

It was getting more difficult to breathe, but I didn't care. I was exactly where I wanted to be: with my family. Magic always leaves a mark, and for the first time in as long as I could remember, I felt entirely whole—a mark I would gladly bear.

Then, slowly, ebbing and flowing like the tide, the melody began to decrescendo, until the sound was nothing but a whisper in my ear. The flames receded, too, and after a few moments, both were gone, and I was left once again in silence. There was still a warmth flooding my senses that burned a little hotter than my own magic. The two blended together to forge a powerful alloy of energy. It filled me, consumed me, completed me.

I opened my eyes.

Teddy's eyes were round and wide. She didn't speak, just waited.

"I found it," I whispered and then burst into tears.

Teddy grabbed a box of tissues off the coffee table and handed me one. "Here, dear." Her motherly tone made me weep harder, and I squeezed my eyes shut, aching for Josephine. For my mother. I was whole again, but that didn't stop me wishing my family existed outside of my own mind.

Once my tears had stopped, I wiped my face with a tissue and sniffled.

"Here," Teddy said, handing me something else. It was a small oval pocket compact. I opened it. My face was red and splotchy, but it was my eyes that drew my attention.

My emerald irises—DuCarmont green—were glowing with flickering green flames.

I let out a bubble of laughter, remembering how freaked out I'd been when my eyes changed colors the first time. Now, seeing the flames only made me feel lighter, closer to my family. I stared at those flames until they extinguished and my usual green eyes stared back at me. "Magic always leaves a mark." I snapped the compact shut.

"So it would seem," Teddy said.

"What now?" I asked. "I can feel the magic, and I was able to reach it, but I don't understand how I'm supposed to use it. You were right—it does feel different from my own magic. I'm guessing that using it will be different too?"

"Well, I'm grasping at straws here," Teddy admitted. "But I assume the process is similar to flipping through a book."

"I don't understand."

"Before your mother turned you into a living and breathing Grimoire, it existed in book form," Teddy said, rising from her spot on the sofa. She walked over to the bookshelf against the wall and pulled down a thick, ancient-looking leather-bound book. A small square of white paper fluttered to the ground. She scooped it up, shoving it randomly inside the book while she flipped through the pages. "A coven's Grimoire houses their ancestry and their magic. Whenever a witch or warlock needs to access that magic, it is simply a matter of turning to the correct page."

"Okay . . ." I said, though I still wasn't quite sure what she was saying.

"While some magic is innate, most requires an incantation or a spell. This is what would have been housed inside the Grimoire—what is now housed inside of you."

"It can't be as simple as just knowing the incantation," I argued. "I *don't* know any." I quickly racked my brain, but there was nothing there that I could recollect.

"But maybe you do." She opened the book in her lap and scanned the pages until she found the passage she was looking for. "This is my family Grimoire, and this"—she pointed to the page—"is a list of rudimentary incantations for beginner witches, which appears in all Grimoires. What's the incantation for wind?"

"*Ventius Ictuum.*" The words came out automatically. My eyebrows shot up. "Whoa. I have no idea how I knew that."

Teddy tapped the side of her head. "It's already up here. These basic spells would've been included in your family Grimoire. Let's try another one." She scanned the page. "Rain?"

"*Uteas Pluviamato.*" Again, the words came without any prompting. "Oh my gosh," I said, gripping the top of my head. "This is incredible. How did you know it would work like that?"

Teddy smiled. "I didn't know for sure, but as a mother, if it were me, I'd have made it as easy for my child as possible. Your mother must have been in a terrible position, but it seems that she thought much like I would, crafting the transition spell to make it simple for you."

She closed the book and stood up. "Now it's a matter of putting the incantation to use. You need to learn how to connect the words to the magic. It's not just knowing the words; it's knowing how to use them."

I jumped to my feet, eager to practice. "Well, let's get started." I rubbed my hands on my pants and made to head outside.

"Wait, Lainey," Teddy called after me. "A word of caution is needed here. There's a lot we don't know. What your mother did is entirely unprecedented. I do know this, however: This sort of information, magic, was never meant to be funneled into one single person. That's why it was always housed in a book. I'm not sure what the repercussions of using the Grimoire in this way will be. Magic always—"

"Leaves a mark," I finished. "Yeah, I know." I took a breath. "We won't know anything until we try, right?" I didn't wait for Teddy as I plunged through the open door and outside.

The sky overhead was a gorgeous blue, with patches of white puffy clouds.

"When using an incantation"—Teddy stepped up beside me—"the key is opening yourself to your magic and letting the words guide you. Understand?

"I think so."

"It should be fairly easy," Teddy said, "but you're pulling from magic that wasn't intended for one person to possess. I'm afraid I'm not sure if the mechanics are the same."

I pushed my sleeves up. "Then it's time to put it to a test."

Teddy looked like she wanted to argue. Instead, she backed up a safe distance. "Take it slow," she said. "If you feel anything strange, stop."

I looked down at my hands. The tiny green lightning I'd grown accustomed to crackled between my fingertips. I felt the hum of my magic under my skin, the tiny sparks igniting as one, nestling up against me. But there was something else too. Now that I'd found it, the power of the Grimoire hummed within me, calling to me.

I pushed my hands out. In a loud voice, I called out, *"Ventius Ictuum."* Sparks ignited beneath my skin, and my magic crackled to life. The alloy of both me and my ancestors heated up. A gentle breeze began to blow.

"Good!" Teddy called from behind me. But I wasn't satisfied.

"Ventius Ictuum," I said, louder this time. I closed my eyes, pulling more of the mixed energy from within me. A burst of wind blew across my face, harder than the last.

"Ventius Ictuum!" I shouted, pulling the warm current as hard as I could, bending it and twisting it to my will. Pain lanced through my limbs as the magic spilled from me. The wind rose with a gust so hard it nearly toppled me. I stumbled backward, flames igniting inside me—this time, they burned painfully. I cried out, but the sound was lost in the howling wind. Alarm bells howled in my head, but I couldn't turn it off, couldn't make it stop.

Then a loud voice commanded, *"Ventius Ictuum Probhiberiata*!" The wind instantly began to slow.

Teddy stood beside me, and for the first time since I'd met her, a chill ran down my spine. Energy pulsated from her body, and her eyes were dark with power, with magic. Now I understood why Zia had insisted Teddy train me.

When the wind died completely, she looked down at me, her face softening. "Are you all right?"

"Yeah." I stood up, dusting off my pants. "I don't know what happened. It was like I stopped using the magic and it started using me."

Teddy didn't look surprised. "We'll work on it, go slowly. There's a balance—we simply have to find it."

I didn't get the chance to respond. Zia and Serena were rushing toward us.

"Sorry!" I called out. "That was me." I assumed the worried expressions on their faces were due to the accidental wind gusts. "Everything's fine."

"It's not that," Serena said, her words coming out in short spurts of air.

Zia's face was grim. "We need you to come quickly. It's Maggie."

CHAPTER FOURTEEN

LAINEY

"How long has she been like this?" I pressed the cool, wet washrag against Maggie's forehead. She was burning up, but shivering as though chilled. "When I checked on her last night, she seemed okay."

Lynlee checked Maggie's pulse and looked at me. "Her fever has been steadily rising since this morning, and her condition is worsening. Her body is struggling to fight the toxin."

I looked down at Maggie's arm and nearly gagged. The edges of the wound were slightly macerated, and the bite itself had opened, oozing a pungent, yellowish substance. Ink-black lines branched all the way to her elbow and disappeared beneath her sleeve. The toxin was spreading fast. "We have to help her."

She shook her head. "I'm afraid there's not a whole lot we can do. With no cure, it's only a matter of time before her systems start shutting down." She let out a deep sigh. "The best we can do is keep the fever down and control any pain she might be feeling. We can make her comfortable. Maybe we should consider calling her parents?"

"No," I said, tossing the washcloth back into the water basin on the bedside table. "You're telling me that with all the Supernaturals in this place, there's not some magical remedy we can conjure up?"

"No," Zia replied from her position in the doorway. "There are some things not even magic can fix." Her tone wasn't unkind, but the candor in it made tears well up in my eyes. Serena was sitting on Maggie's other side, her eyes red-rimmed.

"We can't sit here and do nothing," I said. Maggie was asleep, but the fever made her fitful, and her eyes moved erratically beneath her eyelids. "I won't lose her too." I looked down at my hands, where the stain of Gareth's blood was always visible to my eyes. "I can't."

Zia and Lynlee said nothing, but shared a silent look.

My throat was aching as I choked back tears. "I need some air," I managed to get out. "Will she . . . Can I . . ."

"You've got time," Lynlee assured me. "She tough, and she's hanging in there."

I squeezed Maggie's hand before fleeing into the hallway. The air wasn't much better out there, so I flew down the stairs and into the office. Gasping, I scanned the bookshelves, desperate for anything that might help. But even as I did so,

I knew there was no book in the entire room that could give me the answer I was looking for.

With my back against the shelf, I slid to the floor, chest heaving.

"There's no time for that now," a cool voice said from the doorway. Zia stood there with her arms folded in front of her. "I know what you're feeling, but we need to stay focused. The Summit meeting is tomorrow, and we need to discuss—"

"Stay focused?" Heat flooded my cheeks and my neck at her words. "My best friend is dying!"

"I know it seems cold, but—"

"I already told you: I won't do it. I won't be your weapon." I leapt to my feet. "And I refuse to just turn off my emotions. I'm not a robot like you are, Zia."

Fire flashed in Zia's eyes. "You think you're the only one with things at stake here? The only one with people you can't stand to lose?" Her voice rose. "Every single person here has lost someone; many have lost their entire families. I lost . . ." She stopped. "No one is asking you to forget or pretend. Stop being so selfish."

"*I'm* being selfish?" I yelled. "All you care about is your stupid meeting."

"That meeting," Zia fired back, "could mean allies for us. Without them, we're all as good as dead. Like it or not, you *have* to do this."

Murderer.

"No," I said, thinking of Gareth, of what happened at the

Gathering. Even if I wanted to help, I couldn't trust myself not to lose control again. "I can't."

Zia's eyes narrowed. "You're scared, I get that, but you have to think about something more than yourself. You have to be willing to give it all for the greater good. If you're not, then this war is already lost. The Master has already won."

Her words cleaved into me, splitting my already battered heart. *Was* I being selfish?

From the moment I'd arrived on the farm, I'd been consumed by my own pain, my own struggles. The backdrop of war was nothing but an afterthought. I hadn't even noticed when Maggie got sick. How had I not noticed?

When Gareth died in my arms, something broke inside me. That pain infected all parts of me, spreading like a virus until I had burned with it—quite literally. The explosion of power, my loss of control—all because I couldn't see past my own pain.

Selfish. Selfish. Selfish.

Shame colored my skin.

"You're right," I said, my throat thick with unshed tears. "I am selfish." My voice cracked on the last word, my lower lip trembling.

Zia's face was still severe, but her eyes softened a tiny fraction. "You're also braver than you realize, and the Hetaeria needs that courage. We need you to do what no one else can." She moved toward the large table where only yesterday, the council had met to call the Summit. "It's a lot to ask, I know, but every one of us must be willing to risk it all if we're going to have a chance. And when we win this war, when we are finally free to live our lives without fear, every sacrifice we have made will be worth it." The look in her eyes was resolute. "I swear it."

It all came down to this. The wounds inside me ached, raw and still gaping. I was far from healed. I couldn't will away my grief. I couldn't snap my fingers and make all the guilt and fear that plagued me go away.

But I could stop focusing on myself.

It was time to fight back.

Swallowing the lump in my throat, I joined her at the table. "Okay. What do we need to do now?"

If Zia was excited by my change of heart, it didn't show. "We need to discuss what you'll do at the Summit to convince the faction leaders." She walked over to the door and motioned someone inside. Teddy crossed the threshold, wringing her hands. "My mother filled me in on your training from today. You're able to tap into the DuCarmont Grimoire's magic?"

"Yes, but it's not the easiest thing in the world, and"—I looked over at Teddy, who nodded as if she were reading my mind—"there are risks."

"There are always risks," Zia replied, waving a hand. "My question is, can you do it? Can you show them your power in some way?"

"Yes. I can do the wind incantation, or I—"

"No, we'll need something bigger, something more *impressive* than a windstorm." Zia began to pace. "We need to show them that you are what we say you are: a weapon to use on the Master. They have to believe that with you on our side, we can win the war."

"How is that even going to work?" I asked. "With the Grimoire, I'm powerful, yes, but . . . how do I weaponize that? What exactly am I—" It hit me. Like pulling the curtain away from the Wizard, the answer was as obvious to me as it had been to Dorothy. "Oh my god," I whispered. "That's it."

"What?" Zia demanded.

"The spell the Master wants allows him to steal magic from other people, right? What if we used it on him? What if instead of stripping away magic to make him powerful, we strip away *all* his magic, making him—"

"Human." Zia's eyes were wide. "Oh my god," she echoed, both hands on her head. "I . . . we . . ." She whipped her head around to face her mother. "Reverse the spell? Would that even work?"

Teddy's face had paled. "Yes," she said, her voice barely louder than a whisper. "In theory."

"It won't be easy," Zia said, talking more to herself than anyone else as she began to pace. "But if we can find a way to use the spell on him—"

"Then we can defeat him," I said.

A laugh bubbled from Zia's throat, and the first genuine smile I'd ever seen from her played on her lips. "Yes! This is what we'll tell the faction leaders. There's no way they'll turn us down now. You'll have to show them. Only a demonstration will convince them."

"I can do that . . . I think." I swallowed. "But how?"

Zia was still pacing, murmuring under her breath. It was Teddy who spoke, her voice soft. "You'll need a volunteer."

The words were heavy, weighted. Zia stopped pacing.

"Who would do that?" I asked. "Who would be willing to let me siphon magic from them? For show? Would they get it back?"

"I don't think it works like that," Teddy said. "Once the magic is siphoned, it cannot be restored."

"It wouldn't have to be a lot," Zia said, her tone uncertain. "Just enough to prove that the spell works. We'll find someone."

Teddy looked at me, and I looked at Zia. No one said anything.

The doors to the library opened, and Lynlee walked in, her face serious.

"Is it Maggie?" I demanded. "Is she—"

Lynlee held up her hand. "She's okay, still sleeping. I gave her a cooling draught to help with the fever, but it's getting difficult to control. If we can't get the fever down . . ." She shook her head, her eyes narrowing in on my face. "She doesn't have long."

My heart stuttered. *No.*

Then, for the second time that day, the answer was clear.

"Oh god," I breathed, pressing a hand against my hammering heart. I turned to Zia. "I know how to save Maggie."

〜•〜

"Here," Teddy said, handing me a shoebox. "Let's try this." She smiled at me, a reassuring gesture, but it didn't reach her eyes.

I took the shoebox, carefully lifting its lid. Inside was a small field mouse. I scrunched my nose.

"Better a mouse than a person the first time, don't you think?" Teddy said, reading the confusion on my face.

"Yeah, I guess so . . . but what exactly am I supposed to be siphoning? It's just a mouse."

"True," Teddy said, leaning forward to wave her hand over the shoebox. The mouse's fur began to shimmer, turning from brown to vibrant pink. "But now it's a pink mouse, and if I'm understanding how this spell works, you should be able to siphon the magic of the Glamour, thus turning the mouse back to his original color."

I peered into the box. The little mouse was scurrying back and forth. "Will it hurt him?"

"I don't know."

"Will it hurt me?"

Teddy shook her head. "I don't know that either. A spell like this . . . there's just no way to know." She took the box from my hands, setting it carefully on the table in front of me. "Lainey, if you don't want to do this—"

"No," I argued. "I have to at least try. If it works on the mouse, then that means I can siphon away the magic of the bite and the poison that's making Maggie so sick. Saving her is the only thing that matters."

Teddy frowned. "Okay, then. Let's give it a try. I want you to take several deep breaths. Close your eyes and focus on nothing but your own breathing. When you're ready, reach for the magic within you. If anything doesn't feel right, stop and let me know."

I did as she instructed, opening myself to the now-familiar current of my magic within me. I smiled at its warmth.

"Now, find the spell the Master wants, the one that will allow you to siphon away magic from another." There was a shake in her voice, a tone that I couldn't decipher. I searched inside, embracing my magic and allowing it to flow through me. *Show me*, I urged it. *Show me where it is.*

There, in the tiniest corner, in the darkest of places, it sat. I probed at it, hissing through my teeth at the immediate icy burn that shot through me.

"What is it?" Teddy whispered. "Is everything alright?"

I nodded.

"Good. Do you know the incantation?"

The words appeared in my mind as easily as they had when Teddy asked for the incantation for wind—but something was *wrong* about them. They were laced with something cold, something dark. As they echoed in my thoughts, chills crawled up and down my spine. A cruel voice began to whisper. I couldn't make out the words, but there was something in them that made my insides twist and the hair on my arms stand on end.

I prodded the magic again, gasping as another stab of pain, both ice and flame, shot through me. Something sinister resonated deep down into my bones. Left dormant, it was harmless, but to awaken it . . .

Dark magic, I realized. The spell was imbued with it, black and menacing. I recoiled, every instinct in my body urging me to pull away.

No. I fought against the panic rising in my chest. *Stop being so selfish. You have to do this for Maggie.* The voice screaming in my head was both mine and Zia's, the sting of her words—and the truth—still sharp.

More voices filled my head.

"Don't do it, girl."

"Stop, Lainey. You mustn't do this."

"This isn't a good idea."

"Dark magic is not to be toyed with."

They blended together, a chorus of pleas to walk away, to let sleeping monsters lie, but I ignored the calls of my ancestors.

I opened my eyes. "I think I'm ready," I said to Teddy.

She nodded, though her eyes were wary. "Place your palm over the mouse. With a spell like this, directional assistance is necessary, I think." She indicated the mouse. "Whenever you're ready."

I reached out, holding my hand over the shoebox. The

magic was there, waiting. "*Et Caperia Fineum*," I whispered, pulling ever so lightly at the malevolent energy. Just a touch, a pinch, a whisper.

Ice shards exploded beneath my skin, and I gasped as the cold turned to a scorching heat that licked through my veins.

A wisp of pink vapor floated toward my hand and absorbed into my skin, sending even more sharp stabs up my arm.

When sensation subsided, my entire body was trembling. I cracked open my eyes. "Did it work?"

Teddy, seeing that I was relatively unscathed, was already dipping her hand into the box. When she pulled it out, the small brown mouse sat in her palm, its little nose twitching as it sniffed the air. "It worked," she said, breathless.

Tears of relief welled up in my eyes, and I sagged back against the couch cushions. "It worked," I repeated, ignoring the uneasy churn of my gut, the magnetic pull of that cruel energy. Like a wraith in the darkness, it waited, awake and ready for me to call upon it again.

You should tell Teddy, the ever-present voice of reason demanded, and it was right. I *should* tell Teddy that the spell was made from dark magic, but if I did, would she allow me to use it again?

Stop being so selfish. The words rang in my ears, loud and clear.

I shook my head, my mind made up. If this spell was the only way to save Maggie, then so be it.

No one had to know.

CHAPTER FIFTEEN

LAINEY

To say I was nervous was the understatement of all time. My stomach was in knots, and what little bit I'd eaten had already made its way forcibly back into the world. I wasn't stupid enough to try again, even though Zia kept shoving packets of crackers at me every time I walked by. The entire farm was on edge, awaiting the faction leaders' arrival.

Zia said their agreement to come at all was a good sign—that the faction leaders were eager for a way to protect their people. In less than an hour, the Summit meeting would begin, and I would have to use an incredibly dangerous spell on my best friend—a spell made from dark magic. I shoved the thought away. *If it saves her, it will be worth it*, I reminded myself.

Maggie's condition continued to decline. She was stable enough for now, but she was rarely conscious for more than a few minutes.

I trust you, Styles, she had whispered when I told her the plan, but her words did little for my confidence.

"Excuse me." I looked up from my spot on the porch, and a tall guy with dark skin and broad shoulders stood in front of me, frowning. "I was wondering about Maggie. How's she doing?"

"Oliver, right?" I eyed the Shifter. I'd seen him around, heard Maggie talk about him, but I'd never met him. He nodded.

"She's the same. Stable for now, but not doing so great."

Oliver rubbed the back of his neck with one hand. "Okay, I wanted to . . . I just thought I'd . . ." He broke off. "Thanks." He started to turn around.

"You can go see her if you want," I offered. "Lynlee says it's good for people to talk to her, and we've got a little time before the Summit starts."

He hesitated, scowling. "Why would I do that?"

"I don't know," I shrugged. "Just thought you might want to."

He stared at me and then, without a word, turned and stomped back toward the outer buildings.

I couldn't help it—I let out a laugh. *What in the world? I can't wait to ask Maggie about that one.* The thought sobered me, and I stood up.

Serena stood at the door. "How are you?" she asked.

She looked thinner than usual, and there were dark circles under her eyes, but the slacks were gone. I almost cried at the sight of her long, flowing skirt.

"I don't know," I answered honestly.

Serena gave me a half smile. "I know what you mean."

"Look, Serena—" I began at the same time she said, "About the other night—"

We each broke off awkwardly. I opened my mouth to try again, but Serena held up a hand. "No, please. Let me go first." She came a little closer, clasping her hands together.

"I've been thinking a lot about what you said, about how it's like you lost both of us, Gareth and me." Her voice wobbled when she mentioned him, as it always did, but she kept going. "I owe you an apology, Lainey. I've been lost without him . . . and I've been taking out my grief on you. I'm so sorry."

I shook my head. "You don't have to apologize. I understand. I just missed you, that's all."

Serena's eyes pooled with tears. "I've missed you too. I'm sorry I was so hard on you the other night." She reached for my hand and gave it a squeeze. "When I found out you'd left the farm, I was so terrified something would happen. I couldn't bear the thought of losing you too. I let it affect my behavior toward you, and that was wrong."

"It's okay."

"I promise to be there for you from now, *really* be there. I know that's what Gareth would want, and that's what I want too," Serena said, pulling me in for a hug.

I wrapped my arms around her shoulders, squeezing tightly. There was the slightest scent of sage clinging to her shirt. It made me smile.

When she pulled back, lines of worry creased her forehead. "Are you ready?" She was referring to the Summit, of course.

No. "I think so. I have no choice but to be ready."

"You're going to do fine, Lainey. I know it."

"Serena, have you . . . I mean, could you See—"

"No," she answered with a sad shake of her head. "I'm afraid with everyone's future so uncertain, it's difficult to See much of anything right now. But don't worry, I don't have to See your future to know the outcome. I know you can do it." She smiled. "We should head down. They've probably arrived by now."

I swallowed. "Do you really think I can do this?"

"Of course, but it's not a matter of what I believe." She paused, looking at me. "What do you believe?"

"I believe in Maggie."

She wrapped a reassuring arm around my shoulder. "Then go save her."

Overhead, the sky was dark with ominous black clouds. Low peals of thunder rumbled, and lightning flashed every few seconds. The storm would be upon us soon. I eyed the skyline. "I hope that's not some kind of sign from the universe that this is going to go badly."

Serena's eyes flicked nervously to the clouds.

Zia and some of the others had cleared out one of the

outdoor spaces used for horse training to conduct the meeting. There was a semicircle of chairs in the middle of the large dirt arena, all occupied by people I'd never seen before.

"That's Ajay," Serena whispered in my ear, indicating a tall, broad-shouldered man with dark hair and eyes, and warm reddish-brown skin. "He's the leader of the Shifter faction. Next to him is Lyra, Fae faction, and Brandon, head of the Lycans." The woman next to Ajay was tall and slender, with delicate features, pale skin, and rich chocolate-brown hair. The brawny man next to her wore a red-and-black flannel shirt and had dark brown eyes and a matching thick beard.

"On the other side, you've got Tao, who's one of you, representing the witches and warlocks; Mya, leader of the Nymphs; and Adrien of the Vampire clan." I eyed the unsmiling witch with a curtain of long, shiny, straight black hair down her back, warm, light skin, and bright red lips. The leader of the Nymphs had long blond hair that was decorated with tiny rosebuds. Her skin was the lightest shade of lavender. The straight-backed man next to her had slicked-back dark hair and tan skin.

Seeing the faction leaders assembled made my knees wobble. Serena gave my shoulder a squeeze before settling into an empty chair next to Teddy. Zia motioned for me, and I stumbled forward on shaky legs. "This is Lainey DuCarmont," she said. "The witch I was telling you about."

There were murmurs at the sound of my name, and Zia beamed. My family's reputation was already working in our favor. "Lainey, why don't you tell the leaders how you came to be Keeper of the DuCarmont Grimoire, how you came here, and how you plan to defeat the Master."

Zia stepped back, leaving the floor open to me. The faces that stared back weren't unkind, but they were definitely skeptical. Only Mya, who seemed more in her own world than anything else, offered me the tiniest hint of a smile.

"Hi," I said, giving a little wave. My heart pounded in my chest and echoed in my ears; I wondered if anyone else could hear it. "Thank you for coming." I clasped my sweaty hands together and began to tell them my story, from the very beginning when Josephine had appeared outside the comic book shop. It was more than a little weird as I described in detail everything that had happened to me in the last few weeks. Their faces didn't change much until I got to the part about the Gathering—that's when their expressions hardened.

"And that is when you slaughtered my people!" Brandon exclaimed, leaping to his feet. His size and stature were even more intimidating up close, and I jumped back, my heart in my throat. "My own brother is dead because of you!"

His words had the same effect as a physical punch to the gut, and all the air in my lungs evaporated.

"My partner too." Adrien sniffed, rising to his feet in a single fluid motion. "And my best friend."

Ajay stood up. "We lost countless in our ranks as well."

"We've all suffered losses," Zia said, coming to stand at my side. "But what we need to focus on here is the chance to move forward."

"As long as she's part of the plan, the Lycans will never

ally themselves with the Hetaeria," Brandon spat, his face a grid of angry lines.

"Now look," Zia began, but I held up a hand.

I took a deep, shaky breath and moved back to the center. "I won't deny it. I won't stand here and try to lie to you or make excuses for my actions. People died that night because of me." The words were ash on my tongue. I kept going. "All I can really say is that I'm so sorry. I never meant to hurt anyone."

"Apologies don't bring back the dead," Brandon snarled.

"No"—Tao stood up, dusting her hands on her pencil skirt—"but they are a start." She faced the other faction leaders. "We are not here to put this girl on trial. We've come to hear talk of a weapon, of a plan that will rid us of the Master for good. Perhaps if we put aside our emotions for the time being, we can get back to the task at hand."

She gave Brandon a pointed look before turning to me. "So tell us, Lainey DuCarmont. How are you going to stop the Master?"

I didn't waste any time. Despite my emotions wreaking havoc on my insides, I stood up straight and told them of the spell and my plan. "Because of the dark magic, the Master can only sustain his level of power for so long before he's weakened. Once that happens, I use the spell on him, siphoning away whatever magic is left. Then we end him."

The faces of the faction leaders were incredibly hard to read. I held my breath and waited.

"How do we know if it will work?" Tao asked, tapping a manicured red nail against her chair.

Ajay turned to Zia. "You're asking us to put an awful lot of faith into a girl whose magic can't be trusted."

"She's been training," Teddy said, standing up. "With me." The look on her face was the same one I'd seen when she'd stopped the windstorm: forbidding. The faction leaders fell silent, no one daring to challenge her. It seemed I wasn't the only one with a reputation.

"And," Zia added, after a few seconds, "we're not going to just ask you to blindly trust us, Ajay. Per your request, we're going to show you exactly how the spell will work."

She motioned toward the door. Julian walked over to us, carrying Maggie in his arms. She was unconscious, and she looked so much worse than she had even a few hours ago. It was a reminder that more was at stake here than just the factions' allegiance.

I turned to Teddy, who had stepped up to my side. My hands were shaking. "I'm not sure I can do this."

"You can," she said simply. "You must."

We moved closer to the table where Julian had gently placed Maggie's supine body.

"For your protection," Teddy addressed the faction leaders, "we'll be using a muric barrier. You will be able to see through it, but you won't be able to hear or touch what's happening on the other side." The faction leaders murmured their approval while I let out a breath of relief. The barrier had been my idea. The Master was desperate for the spell I was about to use—we couldn't risk him getting his hands on it if one of the faction leaders was compromised.

Teddy raised her arms, palms outward, murmuring under her breath. What looked like a thin layer of shimmery gauze fell between us and the faction leaders.

"Doesn't look like much," I said, eyeing the barrier.

"Strength cannot be determined by appearance alone," Teddy replied. "It will hold. They won't be able to hear a thing."

I nodded, trying my best to ignore the eyes boring into me. I placed two shaky hands over Maggie's body and then looked at Teddy.

"This will be just like before," she said. "Close your eyes and take some deep breaths."

This was the easy part. I followed her instructions, closing my eyes and waiting until everything around me had faded away. In the quiet of my mind, the power of the Grimoire and my own magic vibrated, humming with warm, familiar energy.

"When you're ready, access the Grimoire and find the siphoning spell."

I took another deep breath and delved in the magic, ignoring the prickling of my spine, the twisting of my gut, the voice inside me pleading, *Don't do this. Don't do this. Don't do this.* It wasn't too late to tell Teddy and Zia about the dark magic, and I stilled for the briefest of moments.

They were all waiting for me. Even with my eyes closed, I felt them watching.

"Lainey?" Teddy whispered. "Is everything okay?"

I started to answer, to spill my secret, but underneath my hands, Maggie sucked in a labored breath. The sound rattling in her lungs was enough to quell my indecision.

I kept my lips clamped together. Maggie's life depended on this. "I'm fine."

I found the spell more quickly than I had the first time. That same voice, cold and nefarious, began to whisper. I still couldn't understand the words, but as they swirled within me, my entire body recoiled.

I whispered the incantation anyway. "*Et Caperia Fineum.*"

As soon as the words were out of my mouth, the icy sensation was back. It shot through my entire body and wrapped every inch of me in its chilling tentacles.

I gasped, my eyes shooting open. The tiny mouse and the magic within it had been so inconsequential, so small, that the effects of the spell had been awful but bearable. I knew it would be more difficult with Maggie, but this, *this* was agony.

The pull of the dark magic was so strong it squeezed the air from my lungs. The energy from my own magic was always warm, filling me with vitality. This energy was dark, yanking and spiraling inside me, sapping the heat from my body.

I bucked against the unnatural current shooting through me, the slice of a thousand ice crystals against my skin. I studied Maggie's face. *I don't want to lose my best friend. I don't want to lose my best friend. I don't want to lose my best friend.*

A tiny wisp of vapor, tinted silver, rose from Maggie's arm. The current pulled it upward and into my outstretched palms. I shrieked when it dissolved in my skin, sending more icy shards up my arms.

Maggie remained unconscious on the table.

"*Et Caperia Fineum!*" I tried again, louder, with more focus. The words elicited a greater column of vapor, but Maggie's back arched off the table, and a sickening gurgle erupted from her throat.

"Maggie!" I screeched, trying to hold my hands steady as the magic drew the vapor toward me. When it hit my skin, I saw stars, gasping and whimpering.

Teddy gripped my shoulder. "Lainey! You need to stop!"

But I could see the wound on Maggie's arm was beginning to heal. The jagged bite marks were disappearing, the dark lines on her skin receding. It was working.

Holding my hands steady, I shook Teddy off of me. "*Et Caperia Fineum!*" I bellowed, clenching my jaw as another burst of electric energy exploded underneath my skin, the ice giving way to flames, burning hot and fast. Engulfed in flames, every inch of me burning, I channeled everything I had into the spell. My heart hammered in my chest, and my strength dwindled with each erratic beat.

Keep going. Just a little more. The wound on Maggie's

arm was nearly completely closed now, the redness and the swelling fading.

Keep going. Don't stop.

Maggie's eyes fluttered and then opened. She blinked rapidly, her forehead scrunching as she tried to make sense of what she was seeing. Teddy bent over, murmuring to her. She nodded, locking eyes with me.

I let out a wild cry as the maelstrom raging inside me burned brighter. My entire body trembled, and my heart no longer pounded in distinct beats, but rather a constant hum. My vision blurred, and all sound became distorted.

"*Et Caperia Fineum,*" I muttered under my breath, one last time as the inferno blazed. The magic itself was in control now. I was no longer driving the energy; it drove me. I was simply a vessel for the flames to incinerate.

Droplets of sweat dripped off Maggie's forehead, and a strange look crossed her face right before she opened her mouth and screamed.

Stop! Stop! Stop! But I couldn't move or speak. I was trapped in the vortex of energy, sucking the life out of both Maggie and me. Teddy screeched at me as she yanked on my arm.

Behind the barrier, the faction leaders had risen to their feet, their mouths forming shouts I couldn't hear.

Zia rushed forward, but she was trapped behind the muric with the others.

"The counterspell!" Teddy screamed at her, though she still held on to me. "Pull it down!"

Zia shot forward, understanding her mother's plea. She placed her hands against the invisible barrier that separated us, her mouth moving soundlessly.

Teddy gripped both my wrists, trying to pull me away, but she couldn't shake me. Maggie seized beneath my hands, a frothy foam seeping from the edges of her mouth.

The world spun out of focus, nothing making sense. Then the door to the arena burst open, and Ty sprinted toward me, shoving the faction leaders out of the way.

Lainey!

When the barrier lifted, the connection between us flared to life, and the sound of my name hit me like a wall.

"Lainey, stop!" Ty pushed through Zia and Teddy and grabbed me, his voice the only thing I could hear above the roaring. "You have to stop. You're going to kill yourself!"

Something inside me cracked. It was like my entire body had been submerged underwater for too long. I fought, aching for air, desperate to resurface—but I couldn't move. I was sinking, weighed down by the icy pull of the energy surging within me.

I couldn't move my lips; my entire body was locked in place. I couldn't break the connection with the spell or with Maggie. *We're going to die.* The thought was clear and strong. *Both of us.*

Ty reached out and cupped my face with his hands. "No, you're not. Listen to the sound of my voice. Just let it go, Lainey."

In the depths of my mind, I began to kick and swing my legs as hard as I could, fighting to get to the top.

The magic writhed within me, that sinister energy fighting to maintain control.

I fought back.

Ty's hands never left my face, and a rush of adrenaline rocketed through me as he lent his own strength to my struggle.

At the brink of the end, when my heart felt as though it were about to explode, I broke free. My entire body went limp as the link between me and the magic broke; my head shot from the water and I gasped for air. I would've hit the ground if Ty hadn't caught me, keeping my head from smacking the dirt.

Everything was spinning. I tried to stand, but my legs wouldn't cooperate. "It's okay," Ty said in my ear. "I've got you."

He carefully helped me stand upright, his arm around my waist supporting me. It took several minutes for my eyes to clear, for the dizziness to dissipate. When it did, I wanted to throw up.

All hell had broken loose.

And it was all my fault.

Again.

CHAPTER SIXTEEN

LAINEY

The faction leaders were screaming—their angry voices clashing together like a chorus of snarling dogs. Zia and Serena were attempting to reason with them, but they were outnumbered, their voices lost.

Teddy leaned over Maggie, whispering incantations under her breath. Maggie was still, her eyes closed. My breath hitched as I stumbled over to her, dragging Ty along with me. "Is she . . ." I couldn't get the words out.

"She's alive," Teddy confirmed, not stopping her ministrations to look at me. "But barely."

"What happened?" I whispered. Ty still held me up, and I clung to him, needing to feel connected to something solid—an anchor to hold fast to. His eyes locked on mine, but I broke away, unable—and maybe a little scared—to read what was there. He opened his mouth, but no words came out. Instead, the shouting from the faction leaders reached its peak. It echoed across the space like a roll of thunder rumbling across the sky.

"Count us out!" Brandon shouted. "We'll be better off taking our chances against the Master alone than with her!" He pointed at me, his lips pulled back in a snarl. Growling, he stalked off and didn't look back.

"That goes for us as well," Ajay said, saluting as he trailed behind Brandon.

The other faction leaders were not far behind.

Tao shared a few whispered words with Zia before leaving, and Mya, whose dazed expression seemed out of place, gave me an odd lilting smile before skipping toward the door.

There was no one left, only Serena, Zia, and Julian, staring at the door of the barn that was thrown open to the night.

I sank to my knees, exhausted and confused.

Zia began pacing, her feet kicking up circles of dust as she moved. The muscles in her cheeks twitched as she chewed on words that didn't come out. No one spoke. When she finally whirled to face me, flames of fury danced in her eyes. "What the hell happened?!" she yelled.

"I . . . I . . ." The words refused to come out. I shook my head.

Zia let out a frustrated yell and gripped fistfuls of her own hair in her hands. "Do you know what this means? They've refused us. Every single one."

Julian's usually jovial face was etched with serious lines. "We can still do this."

"Without the numbers?" Zia tipped her head back and let

out a bitter laugh. "At best, we somehow manage to survive for longer than twenty-four hours once the fighting begins. At worst, we're slaughtered before we get within a hundred feet of the Master." She resumed her pacing.

Serena came closer, kneeling beside me. "You have to tell us what happened, Lainey."

"I don't know," I said. "The spell . . ." I broke off, ashamed of the truth. I looked over to Maggie. "I couldn't stop. I saw her screaming, but I wasn't in control anymore."

Serena's forehead scrunched. "How is that possible?"

"It was dark magic." Ty's voice made me jump. "I felt it," he said, squeezing the back of his neck with one hand—a habit I'd seen him do often when he was uncomfortable. "Through the Praetorian bond."

"Dark magic?" Zia's sharp voice called out. She looked at Teddy. "Is that possible?"

Teddy's eyes were wide. "If the spell . . . It's possible, of course, but . . ." She looked over at me. "You knew, didn't you?"

Every eye was on me. "Yes," I whispered, and everyone but Ty flinched at the word. "When I tapped into the Grimoire, I could feel the darkness of the spell. I knew it was dark magic."

"And you used it anyway?" Teddy asked.

"Maggie was going to die if I didn't try."

Zia's face was bright red. "You put everyone at risk today. Not only have you destroyed our chances at an alliance, you nearly killed yourself and your best friend. Well done, little witch. Well done."

"I'm sorry," I said, finding my voice. "I wasn't completely honest, but I had to do this, I had to try." I glanced over at Maggie. "Is she going to be okay?"

"She's weak," Teddy said, "but look."

The skin on Maggie's arm was pristine, unmarred by any wound or scar.

"It worked?"

"We won't know for sure until she wakes up—she got quite the jolt of energy there at the end— but yes, I believe it did."

"Then I did the right thing." I turned to Zia. "I did the right thing," I said again, needing the words to be true.

"You may have saved your friend," Zia said, "but you've cost us all."

"That's enough," Teddy snapped, moving from behind Maggie to face her daughter. "Wars are not won on the shoulders of teenage witches."

"Not now, Mother." Zia waved her hand.

"No," Teddy said, her voice rising. "The many for the few? That philosophy is not yours, Zia. It's your—it's *his*. Do not forget that."

They stared at each other, a silent conversation between the two of them. Finally, Zia threw her hands up. "Fine." Her eyes landed on me. "I'm glad Maggie will be okay, but you still should have told us. We could've figured something else out. If they had just waited to see . . ." She groaned. "I guess there's no point in dwelling. Now we just have to figure out how in the world to defeat the Master when he outnumbers our forces three to one."

The look on her face was a dagger to my heart. I had saved Maggie, but I had failed in every other way. "For what it's worth, I'm sorry," I whispered.

Zia didn't respond. She was too busy mumbling under her breath, the wheels and cogs of her mind spinning rapidly as she tried to come up with a new plan.

Ty hadn't uttered a word, but he reached down a hand and pulled me gently to my feet. I entwined my fingers through his and squeezed. A small pool of warmth glowed in my chest. There were so many things I needed to say. I opened my mouth, but closed it again. *Not now.*

"You, traitor." Zia beckoned to Ty. "Still up for changing sides?"

"I told you: As long as the Master ends up dead, I don't care what side I'm on."

"Good." Zia clapped her hands together. "We're gonna need intel. Without the advantage of numbers, our only option is to be one step ahead of him. We have to know what he's planning. I hope you're ready to pay him a visit, because *you're* going to get us that information."

"Consider it done," Ty said.

"You leave in the morning."

"You're going to send him back to the Master?" Julian asked. "How do we know we can trust him? What if he betrays us?"

"The way I see it, we're damned if we do, damned if we

don't." Zia's eyes narrowed on Ty's hand interlocked with mine. "I think he'll do what we ask. Unless you have a better option?"

Julian shook his head.

"Then he goes. We'll also need to send some people to their home bases. Maybe they can do some damage control, convince the leaders to join us."

"I'll round up some volunteers," Julian said. "But it won't be easy."

"No, but we have to try. And we'll come up with some contingency plans. If war comes to our door without the numbers, then we'll have to get creative."

Julian turned to go.

"When you come back," Zia called after him, "bring me everyone you can think of with any sort of unique talents or magic. We're going to need to get *very* creative."

"Roger that, boss."

"I'll round up the other Seers," Serena said, following after Julian.

"What can I do?" I asked.

Zia face was stone. "I think you've done enough for one day." There wasn't malice in her voice, just cold hard truth—it blistered just the same.

I was surprised to find Maggie sitting up in the bed when I walked into her room a few hours later. "You're awake?"

"I am," she said, smiling. "Thanks to you." She looked exhausted, but her eyes were bright.

"Please don't thank me," I groaned, sinking down on the edge of her bed. "In truth, I . . ." A lump popped up in my throat, making it difficult to speak. "I almost killed you."

Maggie's smile drooped, and she reached for my hand. "Serena stopped by a little while ago. She filled me in . . . Look, Styles, I know you're probably beating yourself up right now, but you shouldn't." She held up her arm. "The bite poisoning is gone. And even though I'm not a Shifter"—her voice cracked on the last word, and she cleared her throat—"I'm alive. I'm alive because of you."

"I wasn't going to let anything happen to you." The floodgates opened for both of us as Maggie held open her arms and we hugged, holding each other tightly.

When we pulled apart, I sucked down a breath. I needed it for what I was about to say. "Mags, there's something I need to tell you, and you're not going to like it."

"Uh oh, that doesn't sound good."

I looked down at the quilt on the bed, focusing on the patchwork squares instead of her face. "I think you need to go home."

Maggie's back straightened. "What?"

"With everything that's happened, I think you'll be safer if you go back home to Georgia."

"You don't want me here?"

"It's not that," I tried to explain. "I just don't think . . . without . . ." I sighed. The words were not coming out right.

"When the war comes, you can't be anywhere near here. I almost killed you today, trying to save you from something that never should have happened in the first place. You're in this mess because of me, and it's only going to get more dangerous."

"We've talked about this, Styles."

"I know, but Maggie—"

"No," Maggie shook her head. "I'm a part of this, and I'm not going anywhere."

"You could get hurt."

"So could you."

"But . . . I'm . . . I can protect myself with magic. You—"

"Are just a human?" Maggie finished for me, her mouth set in a hard line.

"Not *just*, but yes." The words had a visible effect on Maggie. I might as well have sliced her with a knife.

"We're in this together, Styles."

"I know, but . . ." I stood up, unable to be still any longer. "I just can't be worrying about you on top of everything else. I ruined our chances with the faction leaders, and now we have to fight a war that we're not likely to win. I can't deal with the thought that I'm sending you to your death on top of that."

Maggie leaned forward. "I know it's scary, but we just need to—"

"Stop!" I shouted. "Just stop, okay? You need to go home, Maggie."

Maggie's nostrils flared, and the fire in her eyes was easy enough to decipher.

"I'm sorry," I said, lowering my voice. "I didn't mean to yell at you or make you feel bad. I just want to keep you safe."

"You know who you sound like right now?" Her voice was low. She pinned her eyes on me, not waiting for a response. "Gareth."

That single word stole the breath from my lungs.

"He kept secrets from you, about who you are. He loved you, and he wanted to protect you. But those weren't his decisions to make. Just like this isn't your decision to make either. It's mine."

I couldn't speak. My heartbeat thudded in my ears.

She was right. I was doing to her exactly what Gareth had done to me.

"I'm sorry," I choked out, tears burning my eyes, and ran from the room.

Maggie yelled after me, but I didn't turn around.

I shoved open the porch's screen door and stomped down the stairs. Tiny snow flurries were falling from the sky, and I shivered. I hadn't grabbed a coat on the way out.

I made a beeline for the barn, sucking down mouthfuls of the crisp air as I walked. It did nothing for the ache in my chest. It was like I was back underwater, kicking with all my might to get to the surface, but I was stuck—anchored to the bottom.

The barn was warm, and I headed for Birdie's stall. She nickered when she saw me coming.

"Hey, girl," I said, reaching to rub her nose. She nuzzled my shoulder with her head, nostrils snuffling as she sniffed to see if I'd brought any treats with me. "Sorry," I murmured, resting my head against hers. "But I promise I'll bring extra next time."

She let me lean against her, and the feel of her warm, soft coat beneath my fingertips was soothing. With Birdie, there were no questions to answer, no expectations—well, except for treats, of course. Slowly, the ache in my chest loosened a little. "I've made such a mess of things, Birdie," I murmured. "I don't know how to—"

"Lainey?"

I looked over. Ty stood a few feet away, his hands shoved into the pockets of his jeans. In my haste to flee the big house, I'd completely forgotten that he was staying in the barn. He stared at me, his eyes a turbulent sea of emotions. It hurt to look at them for too long. I tore my gaze away, focusing on the straw at my feet. "Sorry, I forgot you were in here."

"Can we talk?"

There was a catch in his voice that made me look up. He took a step forward. "I'm leaving in the morning. At first light. I don't know when I'll be back, but I didn't want to leave without seeing you."

"Why?" I asked darkly. "You're getting everything you want. What's that got to do with me?"

Ty shifted from one foot to the other. "Not everything."

The warmth in his eyes made my heart beat a little faster. I hated myself for it. How was it possible this stupid boy could make me hate him one minute and want to throw myself at him the next? I backed away from Birdie, clenching my fist. "You frustrate me," I said. "So much. Do you know that?"

"I know." He took another step forward. "But what happened back there . . . with the spell and Maggie . . . I couldn't leave without making sure you were okay."

"Maggie's fine," I said, choking on the words. "That's what's important."

"And how are you?"

"I don't know." I swallowed. "If you hadn't come in, if you hadn't gotten through to me . . ." Tears pooled in my eyes, threatening to spill over. "I don't know what would've happened."

Ty closed the distance between us and grabbed both of my hands in his. Part of me wanted to yank them away, but the rest of me ached for his touch.

"You can't beat yourself up about it," he said, looking me deeply in the eye. "You did what you had to do."

"And in return, I gave everyone here a death sentence."

"That's not true. It may have complicated things a bit, but this war is far from over."

"Yeah, well. Time will tell, I guess." I shrugged. I didn't want to talk about it anymore. "So . . . how does it work exactly? The Praetorian bond. How did you know?"

Ty stepped back a little, but he didn't release my hands. "It's not a direct connection, if that's what you're asking. I can't read your mind. It's more an openness between us, an ease of understanding. I can only feel and see what you choose for me to feel and see."

"But back in the Summit meeting, I wasn't trying to communicate or whatever. How did you know what was happening?"

Ty rubbed the back of his neck, looking slightly uncomfortable. "Maybe not consciously, but the feelings were coming down the bond so fast and clear, it was as if you were standing next me, shouting in my ear."

"But I don't understand—"

"Sometimes," Ty continued, his cheeks reddening, "when the connection between a Praetorian and the Calling goes beyond that . . . say, if feelings were involved . . ." He broke off, and swallowed. "Then . . . it's a little easier."

"Oh," I whispered. *Thanks a lot, stupid, traitorous heart.*

We stared at each other for a few awkward seconds.

"I know what happened today and what I said the other night doesn't change anything between us," Ty said, finally breaking the silence. "I know you hate me, but . . ." He ran a hand through his hair. "I need you to know that I meant what I said. I don't know what's going to happen when I go back, and I . . ." He trailed off, his face paling. "I just needed you to know."

The look in his eyes said more than the words. My heart was in my throat, effectively cutting off any reply I might try to give.

Ty stepped back, no longer able to meet my eye. "Well, uh, take care of yourself, Lainey."

He turned, heading for the main doors.

I stood there, unable to move or breathe for several seconds before my brain and my feet finally coordinated. "Wait!"

I ran after him as he pushed open the main doors. A burst of cold air blew through the barn and bit into my skin underneath the thin shirt I was wearing. The dark sky was a swirl of white. In the short time I'd been in the barn, the flurries had morphed into full-blown snowflakes, falling in fluffy sheets and already sticking to the ground.

The first snowfall of the season.

I let out an excited gasp, nearly skidding to a stop, but I caught myself. "Ty!"

He turned around, snowflakes dotting his hair, his eyes a sea of emotions.

"Thank you. I should've said it earlier, but you're the reason Maggie is alive."

"No," he shook his head. "*You're* the reason Maggie is alive."

We fell into another loaded moment of silence, with the snow swirling around us.

"Listen to me," I finally said. "Nothing is going to happen to you. You're going to go there, get the information you need, and then come back."

"It's not that simple. When I'm away from it, it's easier to think clearly, to remind myself of who I really am. But when I'm there, in the thick of it all, I lose myself. It's not always an easy path to find myself again. I'll do what I have to do to get the information the Hetaeria needs, but I'm not sure who I'll be when I come back."

There was a vulnerability in his face that made my breath catch in my throat. The bravado he had shown in front of Zia was gone, and I got a glimpse of a boy who was still very much grieving the loss of his father, a boy whose path was even more uncertain than my own.

Without questioning the consequences of my actions, what it would cost me later, I lifted my hand and placed it gingerly on his shoulder. "You are Ty Marek. You're a Praetorian, and I'm your Calling. As long as I'm around, you'll be able to find your way back to yourself . . . and to me."

Ty's voice was soft. "I thought you hated me."

"I do," I said too quickly. Ty's wince was barely perceptible, but I saw it just the same. I let out a deep sigh. "No, that's not true. I don't hate you, Ty. I hate what you did. I wish you would've just been honest with me. It would've hurt a whole lot less."

In that moment, I felt a flood of emotions wash over me, the exact mirror of my own, but distinctly not mine. Ty leaned forward, touching his forehead to mine. My heart hammered in my throat as I realized what was happening, what he was allowing me to feel.

"For what it's worth, and I know it's not worth much"— his voice was low and deep—"I'm so sorry for what I've done to you. I never wanted to hurt you."

My fingertips gripped his shoulder. "I want to believe that."

With a gentleness that surprised me, Ty pulled back and placed a kiss on my forehead. His lips were warm against my cool skin as he murmured, "Then believe it."

He caressed my cheek with his thumb before stepping away from me. A gust of icy wind wrapped around me, and I shivered.

"I'll see you when I get back?"

I nodded. "I'll be here. Be careful."

"I will. And Lainey? Remember how much of a badass you are. Don't let today rob you of that."

"I'll try," I said, trying to hold back the next words that came pouring out of my mouth. "Just . . . come back, okay?"

Ty gave me another half smile. "Okay." He turned and headed over to the opposite side of the barn, where the tack room was located.

I watched him go until his shadow disappeared in a swirl of snowflakes.

CHAPTER SEVENTEEN

MAGGIE

A thin layer of snow crunched under my shoes as I walked across the frozen grass. My worn Vans were already soaked through, the cold wetness squishing between my toes. I wasn't really worried about it, though. I was human. If the most interesting thing that was likely to happen to me now was a solid case of pneumonia, then so be it.

"It's not like when Thanos got hold of the Infinity Stones and wiped out half the universe," I grumbled under my breath, annoyed at my own snark. "It could've been worse." *I could've died.* The truth wasn't lost on me, and I was grateful that I hadn't ended up a body in a box. But still, I couldn't shake the sour feeling in my stomach. I looked down at my arm. It was strange to see the skin smooth, the scar that I'd celebrated erased, as if it never existed. "Where's an Infinity Stone when you need one?"

Gripping the shoulder straps of my backpack, I walked on, the contents inside gently bouncing around in time to the cadence of my steps. Up ahead, the outer buildings looked vacant. It was strange how the farm had been so full of activity just a few days ago. Now, a hush had fallen, a stillness only made worse by the snowfall.

Oliver's home was the farthest one in the cluster of buildings, and I could see lights on through the windows. Even though it was early, I had expected him to be already up and starting his day. Looks like I was right.

I knocked on the door. As I waited, I swiped at my curls that were flying around in the morning breeze, catching the errant snowflakes still fluttering to the ground.

Oliver opened the door. It was hard to tell if he was surprised to see me. His features didn't change; they were shaped in the same surly lines they always were. I stifled a laugh as "Grumpy Cat" from those internet memes came to mind. "Hey!" I said, cringing slightly at the overly cheerful, almost shrill tone to my voice. "Whatcha doing?"

I pushed past him without waiting for any kind of reply and immediately plopped down on the worn red sofa in the middle of the room.

Oliver gaped at me.

"Got any coffee?" I asked, eyeing the small kitchenette. "I'm generally a morning person, but I could use a good ole cup of joe today. You?" I was talking too much, but I couldn't stop myself.

Shutting the door, Oliver continued to stare—well, it was

really more of a glare—as he crossed the room and opened a cupboard. I was surprised when he tossed a coffee pod at me and motioned at the Keurig sitting in the corner.

"Thanks!" When I returned to my seat on the sofa, steaming mug in hand, Oliver was sitting in a wooden rocker directly across from me, his forehead scrunched.

"What are you doing here?" he asked. There weren't any traces of anger in his voice or even annoyance, but there was something in it that made me pause and take a sip of my coffee before answering.

"Honestly? I need a favor."

"What sort of favor?"

I'd spent the early morning hours going over this speech in my head. "I heard Zia was sending representatives to their home factions. A last-ditch effort to talk some sense into the leaders. I'm guessing you're the one she chose for the Shifters?"

Oliver grunted an affirmative.

I didn't waste any time. "I want you to take me with you."

This time, his lips cracked open in a laugh. "Why would I do that?"

"Because," I said, trying to sound extra confident, "you're gonna need me on that trip."

Rolling his eyes, Oliver leaned forward, resting his elbows on his knees. "Is that so? How do you figure that?"

"Well, I'm totally guessing here, but I'd wager that public speaking isn't exactly your thing. You know, the whole being personable and likable and whatnot. I mean, I'm sure you're not *always* grumpy, but do we really want to risk it at this point?"

Oliver's eyes widened slightly at my words, and I paused, waiting for him to start yelling, but he didn't. Instead, he let out another chuckle. "Do you always say exactly what you think about things?"

I shrugged. "Usually."

"I'm not grumpy."

This time, it was me who chuckled. "You sure? Because you make Squidward Tentacles look snuggly."

"SpongeBob? Really?"

I gulped down another mouthful of coffee and waved my hand. "Everybody loves that cute yellow sponge, and you know it. But seriously," I said. "Take me with you."

"Maggie—" he began.

"Before you say no"—I jumped up from the couch and sloshed coffee on my jeans in the process—"let me tell you what I bring to the table." I cleared my throat. "Not only did I get an A in speech class, but I have moderated over fifteen panels at local cons and was even given a press pass for this year's DragonCon. Obviously, I didn't get a chance to attend, but if I had, I would have rocked it."

"What's your point?" Oliver deadpanned, annoyance starting to creep in.

"My point is, that while you might have the people skills of a cactus, I am absolutely delightful. Don't you think that might come in handy when you're trying to convince a bunch of scared and reluctant Supernaturals to join a rebellion?"

"It's not that simple. I can't just walk into our territory with an outsider."

"I'm not really an outsider. It's not like I don't know what's been going on. I'm not clueless to what the Master's planning."

Oliver rubbed a hand over his mouth. "It's not that."

"Then what is it?"

"You're human."

And there it was. My unfortunate reality like a slap to the face. The words sucked the wind right out of my sails, and I sank back down onto the sofa. "Yeah, I am," I whispered. "But don't you see? That's exactly why I have to go with you."

I held out my arm, the pristine skin offending more than the old scar ever had. "When I had that scar on my arm, I was one of you. Without it, I go back to just being human? To being on the outskirts?" I shook my head. "No, I'm a part of this, and scar or no, Shifter or not, I'm going to do my part in the fight against the Master."

"It's not your fight."

"It *is* my fight," I said, my voice trembling, not with tears or nerves, but with the fire coiling in my gut. "Who are you to tell me it's not?"

There was so much more I wanted to say. To everyone else, my Shifter bite was something unfortunate that had happened. But to me, it was a golden ticket. A letter to Hogwarts. A key to the Tardis. I'd spent my life between the pages of comic books, going on adventures with characters on screen or in books. That bite meant that I didn't have to wistfully follow along on someone else's adventure—I could go on my own. I had a shot at being the hero in my own story, the possibility of saving the day and doing something that really mattered. And now it was all gone. Just like my scar.

I wanted to tell him everything and make him understand, but I kept my lips pressed together. I didn't want him to see my struggle—only my fire.

Oliver studied my face for a long time.

"You're right," he finally conceded. "It's not my place." He stood up, wiping his hands on his jeans, and walked over to the counter where a pile of supplies were stacked next to an empty backpack. He began loading them inside the bag. "It's not going to be easy. They might very well kill you on sight."

My heart beat wildly in my chest as his words registered. I jumped back up, nearly dumping the remainder of my coffee in my lap. "That's okay. I'm not afraid of a little danger. I'm best friends with Lainey—she's sort of a magnet for danger." The words flew out of my mouth without a thought, an automatic response that made my nose screw up. We hadn't spoken since last night when I'd compared her to Gareth.

"Speaking of your witch friend," Oliver said, turning to face me. "Why not stay here and help her?"

"She wants me to leave. She thinks it will be safer that way, if I go home. But she's wrong. She's my best friend in the world, and she needs my help. So, if she wants me to go, I will."

"I don't think this"—he indicated the two of us—"is what she had in mind."

I shrugged. "Can't have everything."

Oliver finished packing the supplies and shouldered his backpack. "Once we get there, you have to do exactly what I say. Our lives may depend on it. Can you do that?"

"Can the Scarlet Witch manipulate chaos magic?"

"Scarlet Witch?" Oliver's eyebrows scrunched together. "Do we know her?"

It took everything I had not to laugh. "Never mind. It means *yes*."

"I don't really have a whole lot of time to wait for you to pack."

"No worries," I said, pointing to my own backpack. "I came prepared."

Oliver raised an eyebrow. "You knew I'd say yes?"

"I just figured that if I talked long enough and loud enough, that you'd eventually say yes just to get me to shut up."

One side of Oliver's mouth lifted in a grin.

"Is that a smile I see?" I said, my own cheeks lifting. "Further proof that I'm the donkey to your Shrek. Now, let's get going."

I snatched up my backpack from where I'd dropped it near the door and waltzed outside to where Oliver's truck was parked. I shivered in the cold air and pulled the hood of my jacket a little tighter around my neck. Oliver got inside the cab and reached over to unlock the door for me. Inside, the cab smelled like leather and cinnamon.

As we pulled away from the farm, I sent Lainey a quick

text before powering off my phone completely. She'd probably be pissed when she got it, but I was doing the right thing. Maybe by the time we returned, she'd have realized it too.

"So," I said, as the truck began to roll along the main highway. "Where are we going?"

"You'll see," Oliver murmured, not taking his eyes off the road. "We can only take the truck so far. Then we go on foot."

"Oh." *You wanted adventure, remember?* "Alrighty then."

I reached forward to twist one of the dials on the dashboard.

"What are you doing?" Oliver's voice was harsh and loud in the quiet of the cab.

"I'm turning on the radio," I said, rolling my eyes.

"Don't you know you're not supposed to touch someone else's radio? Driver always picks the tunes."

I rolled my eyes again. "Fine. Pick something."

"I prefer no music actually."

"Seriously? You don't like music?"

Oliver arched an eyebrow. "Did I say that?"

"So grumpy," I murmured, relinquishing my control of the radio. "Fine. No music, huh? Guess we'll just have to get to know each other better. So, tell me. Are you a Marvel or a DC fan? Be specific."

"No music means talking?" he asked, gripping the steering wheel a little tighter.

"Yup."

His hand quickly turned the dial, filling the cab with a rich, soulful jazz melody.

I guess I should've been offended, but I wasn't. No matter how cantankerous Oliver might be, this was an opportunity I wasn't going to waste.

Humming along to the song, I focused on the road ahead.

CHAPTER EIGHTEEN

TY

It was nearly midnight, but the city was wide awake. The metro car was full of people, despite it being one of the last trains running into the city. It was practically standing room only. I'd shoved earbuds in my ears, but they didn't help drown out the chatter of the people around me—nor did they drown out my own thoughts, and those were far more distracting.

I closed my eyes and leaned my head against the glass of the window next to me. Everything about this moment felt wrong. Once again, there was a war raging inside of me. My heart was screaming that I was going in the wrong direction, demanding that I return to the girl I'd left in the snow, but there was also the deep, magnetic pull of the darkness that never really went away. Good or bad, right or wrong—I was standing on the edge of a very sharp knife. Like always.

"You are Ty Marek. You're a Praetorian, and I'm your Calling. As long as I'm around, you'll be able to find your way back to yourself . . . and to me." Lainey's words echoed in my ears as I stood up to get off the train, shouldering my bag. "If only it were that simple," I murmured, stepping onto the platform and moving quickly to avoid getting trapped in the swarm of people entering and exiting the train. I'd tried to explain it to her, tried to make her understand, but how could she really?

The sidewalks were packed with people taking advantage of the restaurants and bars within walking distance. Right in the heart of the city, Georgetown was known for its iconic row houses and close proximity to the Potomac River—it was also home to the Master's private headquarters. I'd never been here before, but I knew its location—everyone in the Guard did. The top floor of one of the tallest buildings on this block. Given the Master's taste for the exquisite, I expected nothing less.

Walking up to the glittering housing complex felt very much like walking up the platform to stand in front of a firing squad, and I took a second to make sure my face was casually blank—devoid of any trace of the guilt that chewed at my insides.

I ran through the plan in my head. The last time I'd seen the Master, he'd charged everyone with finding Lainey and the Hetaeria. If Zia wanted information, I couldn't return to him empty-handed. No, I would have to offer the Master something incredibly valuable—something he'd kill for.

I held only a single card to play: the farm.

It was no secret how badly the Master wanted to find and annihilate the Hetaeria. I would be the one to give him the information he needed—my ace in the hole. My single piece of leverage would be enough to get the intel the Hetaeria needed, even if it came at a high cost. I was going to give the Master the exact location of the Hetaerian basecamp.

I hissed through my teeth at the thought. It felt like another betrayal, albeit a necessary one. Finding the Hetaeria an advantage in the war wouldn't be easy. The Master was cunning, and only those who earned his favor were allowed into his circle.

I doubted this is what Zia had in mind when she sent me back, but it was the only way. I could only hope the gamble would be worth it, that I would make it back in time to warn them before the Master used the information against them.

"Name?" the doorman barked at me when I approached. He wasn't human. If you looked hard enough, his scaly green skin shimmered behind the blur of the Glamour he wore. In between blinks, his irises glowed orange.

Taking a sharp glance around to make sure no one was watching, I ignored the question and yanked down the collar of my T-shirt, exposing the mark on my chest.

"Right this way," the doorman barked, opening the door for me and directing me down a private corridor to an elevator.

I murmured my thanks and stepped inside. The panel of controls was different from a typical elevator. There were no buttons with numbers to indicate the floor levels. There was only one unmarked button on the panel. I pressed it, but nothing happened. I pressed it again. Still, the elevator did not move. I bent down to take a closer look. There was no writing on or around the button, but there was a symbol lightly embossed on the surface. Two interlocking triangles that formed an "M." The same mark that was inked across my chest.

I straightened back up, not entirely certain how to proceed. *Wait.* A thought occurred to me.

Reaching into my pocket, I pulled out the small knife I kept there. I sliced the blade across the pad of my thumb, drawing a thin line of red blood, and pressed it back against the button. It immediately glowed red, and the elevator began to move.

"Figures," I mumbled, sucking on my finger to staunch the blood. It made sense, despite my distaste for it. A simple enchantment to ensure those who entered were truly part of the Master's inner circle—not that anyone else would be fool enough to come here.

The elevator moved, slowly and smoothly ascending to the apex of the building. A small chime dinged when the elevator car reached the top floor. The double doors slid open, and I stepped over the threshold, pausing for a second to allow my eyes to adjust to the dim lighting. The space itself was open, a wide room with high ceilings and a shiny marble floor. The walls were draped with heavy onyx tapestries and illuminated by tall candelabras. Small red orbs of light floated through the air, bathing the plush couches and chairs that were arranged throughout the room in crimson spotlights.

The room was full of people, but it was clear after a few steps forward that not everyone in attendance was here of their own will.

A tall Faerie stood in one of the corners, a crowd gathered around her as she conjured objects with magic, illusions that told a story. They listened carefully to her tinkling voice as she told the fascinating tale of a thousand-year battle between a beast and a warrior, but the look in the Faerie's eye was dull and lifeless. Another glance around the room, and I spotted a young girl with a long, flowing dress singing a lullaby about the sea. A thick collar of iron encased her neck. *Siren*, I realized. The collar was a sealant, preventing the full manifestation of her magic and only allowing her to enchant listeners with lovely, but harmless melodies.

There were others in the room too. A Shifter who was Shifting into random animals at the request of an audience circled around him. A Seer doing palm readings and future castings. I didn't want to think about what the Master had done to force them into parading around like circus acts—what he must have threatened. I shook the thought from my head. I had bigger things to focus on.

Various members of the Guard perched on the furniture, watching the performers and mingling. Trays of delicacies and drinks were being carried around the room by a Sprite with a smile as garish as her neon-yellow hair. Low, melodic music played overhead, and the bass pulsated through the room like a heartbeat.

I slipped through the crowd easily, seeking my target. He wasn't hard to find.

The entire back wall of the room was floor-to-ceiling windows—the lights of the city twinkling in the background—and a large leather wing-backed chair was pushed up against them.

Lounging in the chair, with the air of a king, was the Master.

A witch wearing a short black dress was perched on his lap, nuzzling his neck and offering him sips from the glass in her hand. The Master's eyes were half closed, a lazy smile playing on his lips as he allowed the woman to continue her ministrations.

It was strange to see him so at ease, so relaxed—as if war was not imminent, as if he had already secured the victory. He was certainly less formal than I'd last seen him at the Gathering, and though he was clearly focused on pleasure rather than punishment at the moment, I could tell something was off.

His cheeks had lost some of their fullness, making the angles of his face sharp and pointed. He wore his usual crisp black suit, but it seemed to hang on him. Even his hair had a thinness about it. The Alium stood off to the right, blending into the wall with their dark robes, though I noticed they were one less than their usual number of three.

The Master was still allowing the girl to languidly stroke

the skin of his neck with her long fingers. The color of her nails, a bright peachy-orange, clashed against the pallor of his skin. She murmured in his ear, her words lost in the din of the room, and the Master's smile widened at her words.

My lip curled as I watched her drape herself across the Master's lap, desperate for adoration. When she leaned a bit too far forward, arching her back to nip at the exposed skin beneath his chin, the glass in her hand tipped over. The contents spilled onto the Master's lap, soaking the front of his pants.

With a snarl, the Master jumped up, unceremoniously dumping the girl to the floor. She landed in a tangle of limbs, her high-heeled shoes clattering loudly against the marble floor.

The Master stood over her, his eyes darkening. Thick black shadows appeared, rolling around his shoulders, while the woman cowered on the floor. The room grew still.

Growling, the Master examined the stain on his clothing before snapping his fingers. His clothes were instantly dry. The girl on the ground muttered soft apologies for her clumsiness, stumbling over the words as her entire body shook.

The Master sneered, rolling his head back and forth. Then, with a flick of his wrist, the shadows receded, pulling back to hover over his chair like a raincloud. His face relaxed, and he leaned down. All the anger was gone from his face, replaced with a lazy smile. "Come now, love," he purred at the witch. "We must be more careful, mustn't we?" He held out a hand to her.

240

Whimpering, the witch placed her hand in his. Instantly, her face screwed up in a silent howl of pain. Her body jerked violently as if volts of electricity shot through her body. Then she slumped forward and fell hard to the floor. Her eyes were open, but vacant, her mouth twisted permanently in a hideous wail.

With a yawn, the Master snapped again, and the woman disappeared. He rolled his eyes and flicked a piece of lint off his suit while those nearby went back to their casual conversations.

He settled back in his chair without seeming to give a single thought for the witch. A tentacle of shadow drew up behind him and nuzzled him like a cat. He stroked the shadow and grinned a wide, hideous smile.

My blood boiled underneath my skin. So little care, so little regard for the lives he took. For a second, I was transported back to the day my father died—how that same indifference had taken the thing that meant the most to me in this world.

I waited until my breathing was normal again and then pushed through the throng of revelers, not wanting to waste any more time. I stepped forward in front of the Master's chair and bowed deeply. "My lord," I murmured. My voice wasn't loud, but it still carried over the music.

When I didn't hear a response, I looked up.

The Master stared at me curiously. "Marek, is it?"

"Yes, my lord."

"And what brings you to my little soirée?" His voice was flat, bored-sounding.

"I come with information, my lord, about the Hetaeria."

It was as if I flipped a switch. The words sucked the energy from the room, and everyone stilled again, watching me.

"Oh?" the Master ground out the word, a muscle in his jaw twitching.

"I know the location of their basecamp, my lord. I can take you there." I waited, the ace out on the table. It was his move.

"Is that all?" the Master asked, his face jarringly unresponsive to my declaration.

All? I didn't understand. "My lord?"

The Master gripped the arms of his chair. "Tell me something I don't already know, Marek. A report from my Scavengers detailing this information has already come and gone." He leaned back in his chair, smirking. "An incident involving an exceptionally powerful level of magic has been tracked near the eastern shores of Lake Michigan. I think it's pretty clear where my little witch friend and her Hetaerian allies are hiding, don't you?"

"Of course," I said quickly. "My apologies, my lord." My heart pounded in my chest. Without leverage, I had nothing to offer, not a single card to play. I wouldn't even be allowed at the table. I took two small steps backward, inching my feet across the floor.

The Master cocked his head at the movement. "Oh, come now, there's no reason to leave in such a hurry. I'm eager to hear about your travels, your whereabouts, your discoveries." The undercurrent in his words was clear: Provide some other useful, valuable information or be discarded. The shadows around his shoulders were already writhing with anticipation.

I inclined my head, acknowledging his request. My face was casually blank, but inside I was panicking. I had nothing else to give, no other information that he might find useful. Nothing that might spare me from the same punishment as the witch in the black dress. Except . . . *No.*

"Well?" The Master tapped his fingers against the armrest of the chair. "The suspense is killing me."

"As you commanded after the Gathering, my lord, I have spent the last few weeks searching for the DuCarmont girl and the Hetaeria," I answered, trying to stall for time. "I can confirm the location your Scavengers reported."

The Master's eyes narrowed to slits. He was not interested in regurgitated information. He raised his hands, the shadows growing.

"I can tell you everything you want to know about the Hetaeria," I blurted out. "Who's with them, their numbers, and the protection they have on the camp itself." Shame burned my cheeks, but I ignored it, clearing my throat. I had no other choice.

There is always a choice, my own voice echoed back at me.

The room, already hushed, fell deadly silent.

"No one without prior entrance to the camp can cross the boundary line. It's the way the protection wards are designed." The words rolled off my tongue, while my insides twisted. "I know this because I've been there. I've been inside the Hetaerian camp."

The words hung thick in the air. I kept talking, immediately launching into the tale of how I'd lured Lainey to Grand Haven with the Troll, how I'd allowed myself to be injured, and how I had preyed upon her good nature so that she would take me inside the boundaries of the Hetaerian basecamp for healing.

"Their numbers are lower than expected—and even fewer after a meeting with the faction leaders went badly. They are scrambling for allies, my lord, but even with the DuCarmont witch at their side, they are failing to find the numbers. They don't stand a chance against your forces."

"Impressive," the Master said, cocking his head. "If it's true." He rose to his feet, the shadows coiling around him like a cape. "How exactly were you able to lure the witch into your trap?"

My heart stuttered. It was a blunder that would cost Lainey and me both. There was no way around it now. I let out a huff, letting the fiery rage coiling in my gut rise to the surface. "She is my Calling, my lord."

The Master's eyes widened, anger simmering in them like molten lava. "What?!"

A force slammed into me, and the air in my lungs evaporated. I clawed at my throat, at the invisible fingers crushing my windpipe.

"I wasn't aware of it, my lord," I wheezed, fighting against the wooziness from lack of oxygen. "Not until I got close enough. I thought the connection I was feeling was to the other girl, the human."

The Master regarded me for a moment. "Ah yes. I recall your claim on her at the Gathering." The pressure on my throat lifted, and I coughed as the air rushed back into my lungs.

"Right," I said, my voice hoarse. "I've been in your service for many years, my lord. I haven't felt the pull of a Calling before, and I'm afraid I got confused. Had I known, I would've told you immediately. I know how important this could be to our efforts." The explanation was weak, and I waited for the Master to snap my neck with a quick flick of his wrist, but neither the Master nor his shadows moved. "When I realized my mistake, understood that the DuCarmont girl was my true Calling, I plotted a way to get near her."

I hoped the modicum of truth in that statement rang clearer than the lies. I braced myself, but the Master threw back his head, releasing a boom of laughter into the air. "Manipulated the Praetorian bond, did you?" He clapped his hands. "A protector who has gone against the very core of who he is? Oh, you are a wolf among the sheep, Marek. Well done." He let out another peal of gleeful laughter. This time, the entire room followed suit, the levity in the air returning. As the revelers went back to their own amusements, the Master beckoned me forward.

"This news pleases me greatly." He beckoned to a tall, severe-faced man behind me. Crow, the Lycan in charge of training the Master's Guard—who had trained me—stalked forward. The hatred boiling in my gut nearly spilled over.

"I think we need to send a little message," the Master said, addressing Crow. "I want that farm burned to the ground. Take a team and get there as fast as you can. Use Marek's intel and take him with you. He will get you inside the wards. While I gather the remainder of our forces for the final annihilation, you will deliver the message that I. Am. Coming."

Crow's wolfish features were even more pronounced when he grinned. "As you wish, my lord."

I wanted to lunge at him, to wrap my hands around his throat and squeeze until the farm was safe, but my hands stayed loosely at my sides, shame burning me from the inside out.

"And you, Marek"—the Master regarded me—"I have a job for you, a special task that only you can accomplish." He beckoned me closer, as if he were going to whisper a secret. "Your little Calling has something I need. Something of *great* value to me. Bring her to me, and we'll see if my powers of persuasion are as effective on her as they were on her uncle."

My insides ran cold. The single thread of self-control I had left snapped. "I know what you seek. The DuCarmont Grimoire," I said a little too quickly, ignoring the flare of the Master's nostrils at my statement, my knowledge of his secret. "But we don't need the witch. On the farm, I heard talk. The Hetaeria found a way to sever the connection between the book and the girl." It was another lie, of course, but I had to try. "I will bring you that book, my lord, but the girl is of no consequence to you. Not anymore. The book can be opened without the witch."

The Master grinned. "In that case"—he turned to

Crow—"make sure Marek secures the book. Then kill the witch." He let out a laugh. "Consider it her reward for blowing up my house."

The Lycan let out his own chuckle before bowing at the waist and moving back into the shadows.

Kill the witch.

The words rang in my ears, and I had to clamp my jaw to stop the string of curses on the tip of my tongue from flying out. My stupid, foolish attempt at drawing the focus away from Lainey had only drawn a larger target on her back.

Grabbing a glass of wine from the tray of a passing server, the Master faced his guests. "Tonight is a celebration," he crowed. "We will soon have our victory. Let us revel a bit longer, but tomorrow, we prepare for war!" He tossed back the contents of the cup while the crowd grew frenzied, cheering and clapping.

The music volume cranked up at that moment, a wild, lyrical song with an upbeat tempo that enraptured the revelers. The room morphed from a lazy lounge into a pulsing nightclub, bodies swaying and grinding against each other.

No one seemed to notice that the Master's smile had faded, his shoulders shaking with a violent cough. His hand was covering his mouth, but when the fit subsided and he pulled it away, thick onyx blood was smeared across his palm.

Swaying, he gripped the arm of his chair to keep from falling over.

The Alium rushed over and gripped his arms, supporting him. They led him over to an alcove decorated with luxuriant fabrics and tapestries. Strips of gauzy muslin hung from the ceiling and draped together to form a web of color around the tiny space. There were also several layers of curtains suspended from the ceiling—clearly meant to be used for more sensory entertainment, these long drapes served as a privacy barrier between whomever was inside and the rest of the party guests.

The Alium pushed through the drapes, ushering the Master inside.

I slid against the wall, blending into the crowd until I was sure no one was watching me. Then I inched toward the alcove, wrapping myself within the folds of one of the thick drapes for cover. Carefully, I peeked through the labyrinth of fabric.

Just like I'd seen the night of the Gathering, one of the Alium knelt before the Master, a bloody knife in his hand. The other hand dripped blood into a puddle on the floor.

Holding his hand over the blood, the Master spoke a hoarse incantation. As the blood evaporated and the familiar black steam began to rise, I let out a breath.

"What's happening?" the Master asked the Alium who had cut his palm. "Why isn't it lasting as long as last time?"

"My life force is weakening, my lord," the Alium squeaked, his voice softer than I expected and full of apology.

"We'll need to conduct the ritual as soon as possible, then," the Master rasped. He turned to the other Alium. "War is coming, and I won't show weakness."

The other Alium nodded. "Right away, my lord." He handed the Master a glass of water, which he gulped down.

I used the momentary distraction to slip back out into the dancing crowd without notice.

I wasn't sure exactly what I'd seen. The Master was still Blood Reaping, but it wasn't sustaining him like it once had. His appearance tonight was confirmation of that, but what was the ritual he'd spoken of?

A hand fell on my shoulder, a Faerie with long blue hair and cherry-red lips. She was holding a glass of bright-orange liquid. "Dance with me," she purred, batting her eyelashes.

"I'm not much of a dancer," I said, pulling out from under her hand. She pouted, but didn't argue, sauntering away toward a group of Vampires near the opposite wall.

I watched her go, though there was a part of me that wanted to drink whatever was in that glass and dance with that girl until there wasn't a single thought in my head.

It would've been easier than facing what I'd done tonight. I'd panicked, giving away more information than I should have, putting the Hetaeria, *Lainey*, at risk.

"You are a wolf among sheep, Marek," the Master had said, but it wasn't true. I was no wolf.

Tomorrow, the sun would rise, and the Master's men would set out for the farm.

I would be among them.

I would lead them to the boundary line of the farm, and like the worm that I am, I would let them in.

CHAPTER NINETEEN

LAINEY

"Do it again."

Teddy's voice sounded as tired as I felt, but I closed my eyes and reached for the magic within. It was getting easier to access the Grimoire, almost as easy as using my own magic.

"*Incipientius.*" I opened my eyes. The large hemlock tree in front of Teddy's cabin blazed with emerald green flames. The dry, leafless branches crackled in the fire, the vibrant flames a stark contrast to the freshly fallen snow on the ground. The warmth from the blaze kissed my ice-chaffed cheeks.

Teddy stood a few feet away, surveying the tree. When I caught her eye, she nodded, and I closed my eyes once more. "*Extinctius.*" The flames immediately extinguished, snuffing out even the tiniest of sparks and evaporating all traces of ash and smoke. The branches were back to their usual winter wear, not a single scorch mark on them.

"Well done," Teddy said, but her small smile couldn't hide the worry in her eyes. Everyone on the farm had that same look. It'd been a few days since the disaster of the Summit meeting, and we hadn't heard a single word from Ty since he left. Zia said this was to be expected, but it made me nervous. At times, I could feel him through our bond, but the pulses of worry, guilt, and shame that lanced through me did little to settle my nerves.

Representatives had been sent to their home factions, but so far, none of the leaders had agreed to join us.

And Maggie . . . Maggie was gone too. I went to her room the morning after our fight—if you even want to call it that—to apologize, but she wasn't there. There was a text from her on my phone explaining she'd gone with Oliver to the Shifter faction. Zia said it was too late to stop her, and to trust that Oliver would keep her safe, but I knew better. It wasn't Oliver I needed to trust. It was Maggie—and I should've done that the first time around.

I'll make it up to you, Mags. I swear I will.

I took a deep breath, readying myself to practice the spell again.

"Wait," Teddy said, pointing.

Zia was heading in our direction, her face partially covered by the collar of her huge puffy jacket. It would've been comical had I not been distracted by the figure walking next to her—a tiny girl with shiny dark hair and cherub-like features. As they got closer, she smirked at me, and I realized her eyes were a startling shade of purple.

"I've got someone I want you to meet," Zia said. She indicated the child. "This is Cora." I hadn't seen this girl on the farm before. She blinked at me with long dark eyelashes.

"Hi," I said, bending down and extending my hand. "I'm Lainey." I gave her what I hoped was a reassuring smile. I didn't want to frighten her.

The little girl grinned, showing a line of perfectly white teeth, and reached out to shake my hand. But there was something in her smile that threw me off—I only realized it a minute too late. The moment our hands touched, a volt of electricity shot through me, knocking me backward into the snow. The little girl threw back her head and cackled wildly.

"What the—" I mumbled, trying to right myself on the slushy ground. My hand was numb, and my entire arm was tingling.

"Cora," Zia said, struggling to keep the smile from her face, "is a Trickster."

"You don't say." I swiped at the legs of my jeans, now damp from the snow.

"Tricksters are a type of Sage," Teddy explained from beside me. "They are incredibly sneaky and impish, but also fierce. Tricksters specialize in Glamours." There was no smile on Teddy's face at my misfortune, only the same severe lines that had been there for days.

Something niggled at my mind, a recollection of the word. *Trickster*. "Wait . . ."

"Yes," Zia said, reading my expression. "It was Trickster magic your boyfriend used to fool you into thinking he was someone else."

"He's not my boyfriend," I grumbled. *It's complicated.*

"In fact," Zia continued, "it was Cora who was responsible for Ty's disguise during the Troll attack."

Cora grinned again and wiggled her eyebrows as if to say, "Yup! That was me!"—a fact she was clearly proud of.

I resisted the urge to give her a taste of my own magic. "What's she doing here?"

"I have a plan. Something to help ensure your safety during battle, and Cora is going to help with the logistics. You're our greatest weapon, Lainey, and we can't make it easy for the Master to just waltz in and claim you."

"I'm not so sure about that." Ever since the Summit, I doubted whether I was valuable to the Hetaeria at all. I felt more like a liability than an asset.

Zia ignored my comment and kept going. "She needs to detail your face."

"I'm sorry?"

"Bend down, please." This time, it was Cora who spoke, a tinkling, childlike quality in her voice. She grabbed one of my hands—no shock this time—and yanked me closer to the ground.

I tried not to flinch away as she ran her fingers lightly over my face. "And what exactly is the plan here?"

Cora held up a finger to her lips. "You'll see," she singsonged.

When she was apparently satisfied, Cora removed her hands and backed away.

I stood up, shivering a little at the chill from my damp clothing. "How did you know she was the one who helped Ty?"

"Our scouts found her near the scene of the incident. It wasn't difficult to extract information about her involvement."

"We're just going to trust that she's going to help us?" I asked. "How do we know she's not loyal to the Master if she helped Ty?"

"You don't need to worry about that," Cora trilled. "I'm always easily persuaded with the right *incentive*." She tucked her hair behind her ears where an impressively large pair of diamond-stud earrings adorned her petite lobes.

"Incentive?" I rolled my eyes. "You mean bribery."

She winked at me, her grin growing.

"How's the training going?" Zia asked.

"She's doing very well," Teddy answered for me. "She's having no difficulty accessing the Grimoire now."

"Good. And the spell?" Zia's face was as neutral as her words, but I could tell what she was really asking. How likely was I to completely screw up again? Would I be able to actually use the siphoning spell against the Master when the time came?

"We haven't tried it again yet," I said, heat rising in my cheeks. "But we will. I'll be ready, I promise."

Zia gave me a curt nod. "Our lives are counting on it."

Her eyes flicked to her mother for a second before she turned on her heel. Cora waved at me and trailed behind her.

"Right," I grumbled at Zia's back. "Not that you ever let me forget it."

Teddy reached over and squeezed my shoulder. "Don't worry, you will be ready."

"I hope so." I looked down at my jeans, felt for my magic, and then waved my hand. The damp denim dried instantly, as if I had just pulled the jeans out of the dryer. "Much better."

Teddy nodded her approval. "Why don't we take a small break, have some tea?"

I followed her inside and watched as she bustled around the small kitchen, pouring water into a kettle and then setting it on the eye of the stove to boil.

"I'm going to have to try using the spell again . . . sooner rather than later, I guess." The very thought of doing so made me shiver, but Zia's visit was an all too clear reminder that time wasn't on our side. If I was going to use the siphoning spell against the Master, then I needed to figure out how to do it safely.

"I have an idea, something I think we should try." Teddy settled herself on the couch across from me. "We know the spell is imbued with dark magic. What if we countered it with some of our own?"

"How would we do that?"

"I have a theory, but I think you may know someone with a concrete answer: your ancestors. You're able to feel them when you use the Grimoire, correct?"

"Yes, but it's not a conversation or anything. It's more of a feeling."

"Right," Teddy said. "But it *is* possible to communicate beyond this world to the next. There's a place between the two. It's called the Veil."

The Veil. I'd been there before. It was the last place I'd spoken with Josephine.

"The spell has been inside your family's Grimoire for generations. If anyone knows how to safely use it, then it's likely your ancestors. Perhaps we should ask them."

The idea sounded so simple, yet impossible at the same time. "I guess it's worth a shot, but . . . I don't know how to get there, to the Veil."

Teddy smiled. "I do. It's a complicated bit of magic, and it requires that both parties exert and channel tremendous amounts of energy. It's called—"

"A Continuance," I whispered. My heart hammered in my chest as I ran a finger over the place on my arm where Josephine's handprint had been burned into my skin—the very first night we met.

"Yes. How did you—"

"So, how does it work?" I said, eager to keep the conversation going. It was too painful to dwell on Josephine for long.

"I can help you create the link, but it will be up to you and whomever you speak with to sustain it." The tea kettle whistled, and Teddy popped up to move it off the stove. "Either way, you won't have long."

My palms were sweating a little, and I rubbed them against my jeans. "Okay."

Teddy rolled the sleeves of her blouse up to her elbows. "Take a few deep breaths," she directed, walking past me and waving a hand to light the candles that lined the small wooden hearth. "Reach inside, feel for the Grimoire, and focus on the feeling of your family."

I did as she directed, trying to ignore the hammering pulse in my ears.

Teddy walked in a circle around me, her hands floating in front of her as if she were weaving a tapestry. She murmured words underneath her breath. I couldn't make them out, but I felt them settling over me.

Squeezing my eyes shut, I relaxed against the feeling of my magic and the Grimoire's, letting myself get lost in the sensation of love and family. All the sounds from Teddy's living room faded away.

A welcoming, warm darkness wrapped around me.

I took a breath and sank into it.

When I opened my eyes, I was standing in a round clearing at the side of a small, but rushing river. The trees around the clearing were lush and green and giving off a crisp, earthly fragrance. A cool breeze was coming off the water, and I shivered from the magic that teemed with life in this place. Across the river, haze hovered like a large gauzy curtain. Silhouettes glided behind it. *The Veil.*

I smiled. This place was exactly as I remembered it.

"Lainey?"

I gasped at the sound. The voice was as familiar to me as my own.

I turned, my chest heaving, lower lip trembling.

"Gareth," I whispered, choking on the tears that filled my throat.

I'd expected to see Josephine, with her long dark hair and emerald eyes that matched mine, but standing beside a tall tree covered in vibrant green moss was Gareth, the man who had raised me. He wore a dark pair of jeans, a flannel button-up, and the same dopey grin he'd given me every day of my life.

"Hey, Lainey Bug."

With a mix between a laugh and a cry, I crossed the small space between us and threw my arms around his neck. Sobs shook my entire body as Gareth returned the hug, wrapping his arms tightly around me and lifting me off the ground.

"I thought I'd never see you again," I said against his shoulder.

"Me, too, kid." He pulled back, set me on the ground, and smiled. "I'm glad we were both wrong."

"How are you? Are you okay?" I ran my eyes over him, still not quite believing he was standing in front of me.

"I'm good. It's peaceful on the other side."

"I'm so sorry about what happened to you. I should have stopped him, I tried to—"

"Oh no, kid," Gareth said, hugging me again. "There was nothing you could do. It wasn't your fault."

"He tortured you to death then brought you back because of me." The image of Gareth's cold eyes, his unsmiling face still haunted my dreams. "And I—I had to do it!" I sobbed, broken as I remembered the steel in my hand and the way Gareth's warm blood had flowed from the wound I inflicted, how the life had faded from his eyes. "I couldn't leave you like that." The tears flowed freely now, the raw edges of my heart aching.

Gareth held me tighter. "Shhh," he whispered against my hair. "It's alright, Lainey Bug. It's alright."

When my sobs subsided into soft whimpers, he pulled back but kept a tight hold on my shoulders. He bent down until his face was level with mine, his familiar dark-chocolate eyes trained on me. "Listen. What happened to me was not your fault. There was nothing you could have done to save me. Do you hear me? Nothing. The Master is to blame, not you."

"But—"

"No," Gareth interrupted. "I won't let you live another second carrying regret you didn't earn. It breaks my heart to see how much you're hurting because of me." His voice cracked on the last word, and he paused to clear his throat. "You have to let me go."

"I can't," I whimpered, shaking my head. "If I'd done things differently, you might still be alive. Everything I touch,

I ruin. Everyone I love gets hurt . . . or worse. Who else is there to blame but myself?" I let out a shuddering breath, thinking of those my magic destroyed at the Gathering.

"I'm a murderer," I whispered, letting the word hang in the air.

Gareth's eyes filled with tears. "No, sweetheart. You could never be one of those. It wasn't your fault. You have to let it go, you have to forgive yourself."

"I don't know how."

"One breath at a time," Gareth said, squeezing my shoulder. "You're not the monster you think you are."

I snorted.

"Listen to me, kid. I'm not saying this because I think you were in any way to blame for what happened, but because I think you need to hear it." His eyes pierced mine, so full of love and understanding. "I forgive you, Lainey."

Those four little words poured over me, thawing me from the inside out. Tears dripped down my cheeks and Gareth wrapped his arms around me again, holding me tightly.

"I forgive you, Lainey." He was right. I'd needed to hear it. It wasn't an immediate remedy, but those words were the starter stitches for the gaping wound in my chest. I imagined the skin there slowly closing, Gareth's words the silk thread that pulled the edges back together.

"Thank you," I sniffled, wiping my face.

"Promise me you'll forgive yourself."

"I'll try, I promise." And I meant it. "There's so much I

want to tell you, but I don't know how much time I have." I swallowed. "I need your help."

"I know why you're here," Gareth said. "You need a safe way to use the siphoning spell."

I'd forgotten how things worked on the other side. I tried not to grimace, but I was mortified to think Gareth and the rest of my family had witnessed my epic failure. Heat flushed my cheeks. "Yes. Josephine's father was the one who stole the spell," I said, eager to shift our conversation away from me. "So, he must have known how it works, right?"

"Her father knew the spell was powerful," Gareth said, "but not much beyond that, I'm afraid. Spells imbued with dark magic are unpredictable. He didn't know what the Master's plans were for the spell, only that it would be disastrous if he ever got his hands on it."

"So, you don't know a way to use the spell safely then?"

"I didn't say that," Gareth said, his forehead scrunched. "I just wish I had better news."

"That doesn't sound good."

"I'm just going to tell you straight, kid. A spell of this kind, one forged in darkness, was never meant to be used casually. Only someone willing to risk everything would attempt it."

"This is the only way to stop the Master."

"I know, though I wish you didn't have to bear such a burden." Gareth paused, then continued. "There is something you can try, though whether it works or not, I don't know."

"What is it?"

"Your mother doesn't want me to tell you this, but—"

"Mom? How is she?"

"She's good," he said, giving me a soft half smile. "Josephine too. They both miss you terribly, of course, but they're both at peace."

I let out a sigh. "That's good . . . now what doesn't my mom want you to tell me?"

"There might be a way to help counter the negative effects of the spell—but's it very risky. You'll need a conduit."

"A conduit?"

"In its most basic form," Gareth explained, "a conduit is used to channel energy into a source and protect the originator of the energy. Think of it like a surge protector. If you have multiple electronics that need to be plugged into one outlet, you'd need a barrier between the electricity and the electronics to prevent overload. Without it, you could end up frying both the outlet and the electronics."

"So, without a conduit, there's nothing to stop the dark magic from affecting me. Like at the Summit meeting. I almost drained myself and killed Maggie because I couldn't stop, the pull of the dark magic was too strong."

"Yes, exactly. Using a conduit is not a guarantee, but it might be enough."

It was such a simple solution. "That doesn't seem so bad."

"Please understand, I don't know for sure if it will work. It's more than just falling prey to the darkness." Gareth frowned, his face lined with worry. "Using the spell on the Master will require a tremendous amount of energy—you're a

DuCarmont, so you're powerful, but you'd be putting yourself at great risk. What you did with Maggie at the Summit is only a fraction of what would be required to take on the Master. You could burn yourself out completely . . . or worse."

"I could die?" I wasn't surprised to hear it, but the words were still lead on my tongue.

Gareth's face was grave. "Without a conduit, it's an absolute certainty."

The words settled over us for several seconds. Even the sounds in the clearing seemed to quiet under their weight.

"Okay," I said. "So, I need a conduit. Where can I get one?"

"Conduits are common, but in this case, a basic enchanted object won't work. For a spell like this, you'll need something more powerful. You'll need to use a person."

I shook my head. "But wouldn't that put that person at risk?"

"Yes, and in order for the conduit to work, it has to be someone you have a personal connection with, someone you trust completely—a deep, strong bond that cannot be broken."

A pair of crystal blue eyes formed in my mind, but I shoved the thought aside. "Right. Is that it then? The only way?"

"It's all we've got." Gareth reached for my hand. "I wish I could shoulder this for you. I would do anything to keep you safe."

"I just wish you could be there. You and Mom and Josephine."

"We're always with you, Lainey. No matter what you're facing, you never walk alone." He reached out, and I let him pull me close again, inhaling the deep scent of his shirt, memorizing the feel of his reassuring arms around me.

"Could you do me one favor?" His voice was soft.

"Anything."

"Could you tell Serena that I love her very much," Gareth paused, swallowing. His words were thick with emotion. "I want her to be happy, to go on, and to *live*."

I felt his tears on my hair, and I nodded, fighting back my own. "I'll tell her, I promise."

The pressure in the air was dropping, and the magical energy was crackling and popping like bubble wrap—the strain of the Continuance tugged at me. We didn't have long until the connection severed. "Thank you, Uncle Gareth. For everything."

"There's one more thing," Gareth said, pulling back. His eyes fixed on mine, and his expression made the hair on the back of my neck stand up. "Be careful who you trust. Not everyone is what they seem."

"What does that mean?" I thought of Ty and the Troll attack. "Do you mean Ty? He—"

There was a whooshing sound, and all the colors of the clearing twirled into a kaleidoscope of greens and blues and browns. The connection was fading. We were out of time.

Gareth yelled something above the noise, but I couldn't make it out.

He leaned in, trying again. His eyes were wide, frantic. He tried again, but only a few words caught my ear: ". . . in the book."

"What?"

With one final squeeze of my hand, Gareth and the clearing were gone, disappearing in a swirl of color and shadow.

And I found myself back on the floor of Teddy's cabin.

ю•๙

"Well?" Teddy knelt in front of me, her hand on my shoulder. "Did it work?"

"Yeah, I think so." I tried to stand up, but immediately swayed, my head woozy.

"You're drained from maintaining the Continuance." Teddy helped me up and guided me over to the couch. "Rest a few minutes. I'll make you a fresh cup of tea."

"*. . . in the book.*" Gareth's words made no sense. I mulled them over while Teddy busied herself with refilling the tea kettle. *What's in the book? What book? The Grimoire?* I closed my eyes, reaching for the Grimoire's magic, but nothing new came to mind.

"*In the book.*"

"What is, Gareth?" I mumbled under my breath. The queasiness had passed, so I stood up and paced the small expanse of Teddy's living room. When my eyes fell on the leather-bound book sitting on the table, I halted.

Teddy's family Grimoire. Maybe it wasn't *my* Grimoire he'd been referring to.

I picked up the book, flipping through the pages. There was a square of white paper marking the page. I held it out of the way, scanning the pages, but not finding anything helpful or relevant.

Sighing, I shoved the scrap of paper back into the spine of the book. It was then I realized it wasn't a scrap of paper at all. It was a worn photograph with a sentence of scribbled script on the back.

"Emmett's first birthday," the caption read. My blood turned cold. *Emmett?* I only knew one person with that name.

I flipped the photograph over. It was black and white, and featured a much-younger and happier-looking Teddy holding a little boy. She was laughing, her arms wrapped around the child as if she were afraid he was about to jump from her lap. The little boy's face was turned directly to the camera, bearing a wide grin and a handful of teeth.

No. It hit me then what I was looking at. "No," I mumbled, flipping the photo back over. Maybe I'd read it wrong.

But the caption was the same.

It didn't make sense. Teddy had been nothing but kind to me since the day we met. Sure, she'd been reluctant to train me at first, but ever since she'd agreed, she'd been nothing but helpful. *I trust Teddy*, I thought. But then the thoughts crept up in the back of my mind. *Why did she refuse to train you at first? Why isn't she an active member of the Hetaeria? How much do you know about her really?*

"Here you go," Teddy said, two steaming mugs of tea in her hands. When she saw me holding the photograph, the smile vanished from her face.

"Is this . . . is this him?" I asked, hoping that it wasn't, that I'd drawn the wrong conclusion.

But the look of guilt on Teddy's face was far from reassuring. "Where did you find that?"

"Tell me," I said, ignoring the question. "Please, tell me I've got it wrong."

Teddy considered for a moment before placing the mugs on the coffee table and sinking down onto the sofa. "No," she finally said. "No, you're not wrong."

I'd known the truth the minute I found the photograph, but hearing it confirmed out loud still stole the breath from my lungs. "Who are you?" I whispered, trying to understand.

Teddy let out a slow breath. "My name is Theodora Masterson. Emmett Masterson, the Master, is my son."

CHAPTER TWENTY

MAGGIE

There were two cards left in my hand. I stared over the top of them, sizing up my opponent. "You're going down," I said as menacingly as I could.

Oliver rolled his eyes and played a card. A yellow eight.

I almost let out a yell, but managed to keep myself under control. Victory would be so much sweeter if he didn't see it coming. With a coy smile, I placed one of my remaining cards down on the truck's center console, our playing field. A red eight.

"Uno," I said, trying to keep my voice neutral.

Oliver raised an eyebrow, tossing another card down on the pile. A red four. "Uno," he challenged, a smirk playing on his lips.

I moved to draw a card from the stack, sighing deeply to imply that I did not have either a red card or a four in my hand. Then with a wicked laugh, I slammed my remaining card down. A wild draw-four card. "I WIN!" I roared, throwing my hands up in the air and immediately launching into a victory dance.

Oliver leaned back against the window, only slightly bemused. He scooped up the deck of cards, shuffled them, and returned them back to their box while he waited for me to quit flailing. "You done?" he asked when I sank back into my seat, chest heaving.

"Oh, this is just the beginning," I said, grinning. "When we get back to the farm, I'm throwing a parade for myself. I'll be the guest of honor, of course. Maggie Dawson, Uno Player Extraordinaire and Victorious Queen of All Card Games."

"You've lost every single game we've played."

"Until now," I said, holding a finger in the air. "An important distinction."

Oliver rolled his eyes again before checking his watch. "We probably should get back on the road. We still have about sixty miles to go, and I want to get there before it gets too late."

"Roger that, Chief," I said, clicking my seatbelt into the buckle. Oliver pulled out of the parking lot and onto the highway. I gave the Super Walmart, where we'd stopped for snacks—and a quick card game, of course—a big salute.

We'd been on the road for two days, stopping only when necessary. For the first six hours after we left the farm, Oliver had largely ignored me, refusing to answer any of my questions or attempts at small talk and kept turning the radio up louder and louder. It was only after we'd stopped for lunch and I'd found the deck of cards in the glove box that his shell began to crack—even more so once he realized just how much fun it was to beat me at cards.

"I'm not sure what to expect when we get there," Oliver said after we'd been driving for several miles. "But don't forget your promise."

"I know, I know: I have to do exactly what you say. Though I don't recall promising, per se. More like agreed to a suggestion."

Oliver frowned. "This isn't the time for jokes, Maggie. I've known Ajay most of my life. He's fiercely protective of his own, and after the stunt your little witch friend pulled, we'll be lucky if they even let us through the door."

"First of all," I said, pursing my lips, "Lainey saved my life during that little 'stunt,' " I air-quoted. "And second of all, you do realize what you just said was contradictory, right? You're a Shifter. If he's so protective of his own, doesn't that include you? Won't he welcome you with open arms?"

Oliver's forehead wrinkled, his scowl deepening. "We had a bit of a falling out a few years ago."

"Oh." Curiosity was inching down my spine, but the look on Oliver's face kept me from asking any more questions. I knew bad blood when I saw it. "So, what's the plan then?"

"We should arrive in town just before dinnertime. We'll take the gondola up to Mountain Village. Ajay runs a pub there. It's sort of a meeting place."

"Gondola?" All I could picture was one of those skinny boats you always see in pictures of Venice.

"You'll see," Oliver said cryptically, though there was a hint of a smile on his lips.

"And so, what? You're just going to walk into a pub full of Shifters and ask to speak to the manager?"

"Something like that."

It didn't sound like a very good plan to me, but Oliver knew these people far better than I did. While I was hoping there was a little more to that plan, I didn't press.

I pulled my cell phone out of my bag and checked to see if there were any new texts or voicemails. Part of me was grateful that there were none; the other part of me was a little hurt Lainey hadn't tried to reach out. *Well, what do you expect? You asked for space.* Sighing, I shoved the phone back in the front zipper pocket of my bag.

Out the front window, the two-lane highway stretched on, and the beautiful snowcapped San Juan Mountains sat right in front of us, growing bigger every minute.

"They're so pretty," I said, leaning forward to get a better view. I'd lived in Georgia all of my life, and the only mountain I'd ever seen up close was Stone Mountain. The most visually stimulating thing about that hunk of granite was the laser light show performed on its surface every summer. Sweeping views like the one in front of me? I'd only ever seen them on postcards and in movies.

"Just wait till we get into town," Oliver replied. His words were wistful, but there was a steel edge to them that I knew had nothing to do with how much I annoyed him. His hands gripped the steering wheel, and tension rolled off his shoulders with every mile marker we passed. I let the conversation drift back into silence.

The city of Telluride, where the Shifter faction had set up its home base, looked exactly like the set of a movie. Small, charming houses and a rainbow of earth-toned apartment buildings and other dwellings dotted both sides of the road as we entered the city limits, and the voluminous mountains rising high above the town were even more captivating up close. The shops lining Main Street looked to be locally owned and inspired by the town's rich mining history. There wasn't a whole lot of traffic on the roads; nearly everyone was either walking or riding a bike. I wanted so badly to get out and explore, but that wasn't why we'd come.

Oliver pulled the truck over into a parking space and hopped out of the cab. "Come on," he said, heading down the sidewalk. I scrambled to follow him. We didn't go far. He stopped in front of a large brown triangular-shaped building. "Telluride Station" was emblazoned on the front in big white letters. The mountain was directly behind the building, where a system of cables followed the sloping curve of the land. Suspended from the cables were large, enclosed white pods moving up the mountain. It was exactly like a ski lift, only bigger.

"Whoa," I muttered, taking it in.

"That's the gondola," Oliver said, following my gaze. "That's what we're going to take up to Mountain Village."

We followed the crowd inside and stood in line, waiting to board one of the pods. The pulley system was designed to keep moving at all times; it was a little unnerving to hop into a moving cabin, but in no time at all, we were rising up the mountain.

"This is amazing," I said, pressing my face up against the window as we glided high above the tree line until the town of Telluride was nothing but a cluster of blinking lights and color at the bottom of the valley.

"It is," Oliver agreed, though the higher the cabin ascended, the harder his face became.

It only took ten minutes or so to get to the top. Once we exited the station, Oliver turned down a side road and headed toward a little pub nestled at the end of the street.

"It's best that we don't draw any attention to ourselves," Oliver said, standing in front of the entrance. "At least until I speak with Ajay. I haven't been back here in a while, and I'm not sure how we'll be received. Stay close, and don't talk to anyone."

I nodded, and Oliver let out a breath, pushing open the door. He squared his shoulders and walked through the entryway with me trailing behind.

The pub was small and brightly decorated in a rustic style, with wooden tables and stools, a polished concrete floor, and a large stone fireplace. The lights were low, but several neon beer signs dotted the wall behind the bar, casting pools of colored light on the floor. I'd never been in a bar before, but the vibe of the place was warm, friendly, and cool.

I was so busy appreciating the ambience that I didn't notice the tray of stacked steins at the edge of a table until I knocked into it, sending the glasses shattering to the floor. Every head in the room snapped to where we stood, now surrounded by a pile of glass fragments. "Oops," I said. "My bad." *So much for not drawing attention to ourselves.*

Oliver glared at me as a tall guy with broad shoulders and dark hair stepped out from behind the bar. He was older than both Oliver and me, with warm red-brown skin and dark eyes that narrowed on us.

"Well, look what the cat dragged in," he drawled.

Oliver stiffened. "Ajay," he said, his voice carrying across the low music playing in the background. "Can we talk?"

"It depends. What are you doing here?"

"Zia sent me on behalf of the Hetaeria," Oliver said, taking a step closer. "War is coming, and—"

Ajay held up a hand. "You've already wasted your time coming here. Don't waste your breath as well. I'll tell you the same thing I told Zia: The Shifters will not ally with the Hetaeria."

"I know you're just looking out for our people, but—"

"Oh, they're *our* people now?" Ajay challenged. "What about when you up and left? You weren't thinking about *our* people then."

A muscle in Oliver's jaw ticked in his efforts to stay calm. "We're not here to discuss that. We're here because whether you want to admit it or not, war is coming, and it affects all of us."

"I'm not sure how I can be more plain," Ajay said,

chewing on the words. "The Shifters will *not* ally with the Hetaeria."

"Then you doom them to death," Oliver ground out. "How can you stand by and do nothing? Who do you think the Master will come for once his attention is no longer focused on the Hetaeria, when they are no longer a threat? Do you think he will be satisfied? He'll stop at nothing until he rules over us all. You know this."

I stared at Oliver. I usually only managed to pull a few sentences out of him at a time and always with a glare or a scowl. It was strange to see him this way—so impassioned. It was also oddly exciting. Warmth spread up my cheeks.

"I have to do what is right by *my* people," Ajay crossed his arms. "Our best chance is to let this war play out and then appeal to the Master. If we can work with him—"

"You're a fool," Oliver spat. "Do you really think our people are safe up here in the mountains? No matter what deal you make with the Master, he will come for them. They will serve him or die. That's the only option he will give. If you don't join this fight, you condemn them all."

"You do not speak for them," Ajay's voice rose. "Not anymore. You lost that right when you walked away, when you stopped caring for anyone but yourself."

Oliver's nostrils flared, and he shoved Ajay backward. Ajay responded with a shove of his own. Around us, several of the silent patrons had risen from their seats, inching forward. I took it as my cue.

"Okay, so now that we've all established how manly we

are," I said, squeezing between them, "maybe we could step outside, take in the mountain air, have an actual discussion—hold the testosterone, please."

"Maggie," Oliver said. "Get back."

Ajay scoffed. "What's this? You brought a human girl to the heart of the Shifter camp?"

"I didn't give him a choice, really." I held out my hand. "I'm Maggie."

Ajay stared at me, ignoring my hand. "You look familiar."

"People tell me I look like Beyoncé all the time," I said, flipping a curl off my shoulder. "I try not to let it go to my head."

There was a second of silence before Ajay's cheek lifted. A small half smile, but it was enough to ease the tension. "Come out back," he said, waving us on. "We'll have that talk."

Outside, there was a large wooden patio area. A fire blazed in an outdoor fireplace, and dozens of people milled about. Ajay led us to a cluster of unoccupied chairs, grabbing a mug of steaming apple cider off a passing waitress's tray and placing it in my hand. Another server came by and set a tray of appetizers on the table in front of us.

"I know you've already made up your mind," Oliver tried again once we were alone, "but I wouldn't have come if I did not believe in this cause. I believe this is a fight we can win. But the Hetaeria needs the Shifter faction on our side."

"You need our numbers," Ajay countered. "We are nothing more to you than a means to an end."

"That's not true," Oliver snapped.

"Ah, Brother, you forget—I've known you since we were kids." Ajay leaned forward. "You've always been a rotten liar."

I moved before Oliver could react, putting my own hand over his clenched fist. He jumped a little at my touch. "I think it's time to tag me in."

"What?"

I rolled my eyes. "You know, you're down on the mats, things are looking bleak, but your teammate is there, ready to tap in."

Oliver stared blankly. Ajay, who had clearly caught on faster than Oliver, smirked at me over his drink.

"Oh, good gravy," I muttered. Looking behind me, I tossed the contents of my nearly full mug over my shoulder. "Oh, dang, I'm out of cider," I deadpanned, waving my empty mug in Oliver's face. "Want to help a girl out?"

Please, I willed Oliver with my eyes. *Just let me try.*

I'm not sure if he understood the message I was trying to send, but he grabbed my mug with a growl and stalked off into the darkness.

I turned to Ajay, smacking his shoulder with the back of my hand. He raised his eyebrows, though the smirk remained. "What was that for?"

"Oh, don't give me that," I said, shaking my head. "I don't know what happened between you two, but you're intentionally pushing his buttons. Cut it out."

Ajay considered me for a minute, then shrugged. "He's always been easily riled."

"Yeah, well, so is a beehive, but you shouldn't go around poking it with a stick."

Ajay chuckled and leaned forward. "I like you," he said. "Have we met before? I have this feeling that I've seen you somewhere."

"You were at the Summit meeting, right? At the farm?" I pointed to myself. "I was the guinea pig for that demonstration you faction leaders demanded."

"That was you?" Ajay shifted in his chair, the humor gone from his face. "You looked about an inch from death the last time I saw you. You've certainly made a miraculous recovery."

"It wasn't a miracle. It was Lainey. She saved my life."

"That witch was no more in control of her magic than I am of the weather." Ajay tipped his chin down. "You got lucky. That girl could've killed you."

"But she didn't," I said. "Look, I know my best friend. Regardless of what happened at that meeting, I know she can do it. She can beat the Master. She may not have looked like much to you, but the Lainey Styles I know has never let me down, and she's not about to start now. You can trust her."

Ajay considered me carefully. "You're a human. This isn't exactly your fight. What's in it for you?"

"It *is* my fight, same as yours." I plucked a mini corndog off the tray in front of me, not offering any more explanation than that. I bit into it and chewed slowly.

"I see," Ajay said. "And what of Oliver?"

"What about him?"

"Are you and he together?"

"Grumpy Cat Oliver and me? N-no . . . nothing like that," I stammered, though a flush warmed my cheeks. I shoved another corndog bite into my mouth as a distraction.

"Mm-hmm," Ajay purred, a grin lifting his cheeks. "Well, whatever is between you two, it's nice to see him smile again."

"Oliver doesn't smile," I argued. "Except maybe when he beats me at cards, but I don't count that."

"Oh, he smiles all right. Maybe not in the traditional way, no, but I've known him a long time. Trust me, when he looks at you? That's a smile."

The thought warmed me from the inside out, like an entire bag of popcorn kernels popping open all at once. In went another corndog bite; I chewed even slower this time, thinking on Ajay's words.

"Look," I finally said. "Just listen to what he has to say. We came all this way, and the least you can do is stop being a jackhole for five seconds and listen. Think you can handle that?"

Before Ajay could respond, Oliver came stalking back, a fresh mug of cider in his hand.

He sat down next to me, frowning, and handed me the mug.

"Thank you," I said. "Chivalry, as it turns out, isn't dead." I beamed at him.

He huffed before turning his attention back to Ajay. "We don't have a lot of time. I'm not asking you to make your decision tonight, but just hear me out. I think you'll see that joining the Hetaeria is the right call. It's the best chance our people have against the Master." Oliver ran a hand over his face. "Please."

Ajay's face was thoughtful.

Please don't be a jackhole, please don't be a jackhole. I held my breath.

Ajay looked at me and then back at Oliver. "I'm listening."

"Thank you," Oliver said, the tense set of his shoulders easing slightly. "I know the odds seem stacked against us, and in full transparency, they are. Without allies, the Hetaeria is outnumbered. We won't last long on our own."

"Not exactly helping your cause with talk like that," Ajay replied, any trace of the amusement from our earlier conversation gone.

Oliver held up his hands. "You have to trust me on this, which I know is a lot to ask, all things considered, but deep down you know I would never put our people at risk if there wasn't a very good reason."

I stayed quiet, watching Oliver's face. The angry lines that always creased his forehead were gone, and the emotion I saw etched in those grooves instead made it hard to swallow. I cleared my throat quietly, hoping the effect was the same for Ajay.

"Please," Oliver continued. "The Hetaeria needs your help. I wouldn't ask if I didn't believe in this cause, if I didn't believe we could win."

"You make a good argument," Ajay began, and hope welled up in my chest. "But I'm sorry, Brother. This *isn't* a fight you can win," he continued, sucking that hope, like a breath, right back out of me. "If the Master does eventually come for us, we'll be ready, but I won't provoke his wrath unnecessarily."

"But—"

Ajay held up a hand, cutting Oliver off. "I wish we could help you, but the answer is no. You two are welcome to stay as long as you like, but I'm afraid this discussion is over." He stood up. "The Shifters will not ally with the Hetaeria."

CHAPTER TWENTY-ONE

LAINEY

Teddy didn't wait for me to respond, which was probably a good thing. I had zero words. How could she be the Master's mother?

"I know you're probably confused," she said. "Why don't I start at the beginning?" She took a deep breath, settling her hands in her lap. "I met Brigdon Masterson when I was young and foolish, and fell in love with him instantly. He was a powerful and skilled warlock, but he was also incredibly handsome. He had so much charm, and he used it to get exactly what he wanted, including me. My exceptional skills with magic made me desirable, and I was flattered by his attentions. I thought it was love he felt for me, but I was merely a means to an end—a powerful wife to bear him powerful children. Nothing more.

It wasn't long after we were married that I realized how blind I'd been. Behind closed doors, he was violent and cruel.

He desired power above all else and dreamed of ruling over the Supernatural factions as High King. He even had plans for eventually wiping out the human race."

I swallowed. This was all sounding eerily familiar. "It sounds exactly like—"

"Like Emmett?"

I nodded, though hearing the Master called by his real name was jarring.

"Well, of course it does. Where do you think he learned it? Like father, like son." She looked down at her lap, studying her nails before she spoke again. "I used to think it was just fanciful dreams, just talk. I hoped after Brigdon found out I was expecting, he would change, that he would focus on being a father instead of a ruler, but I was wrong. He did dote on Emmett, but as soon as Emmett was old enough to understand, Brigdon began to fill his head, to teach him to hate as he did."

Teddy paused, her face lined with sadness. "I loved Brigdon, but over time, that love turned to resentment and fear," she sniffed. "I was lonely for a very long time. Until . . . I fell in love with another man, a human. His name was Christopher. When I became pregnant with his child, we knew we had to do something. Even if I was able to pass her off as his, Brigdon would eventually figure out she was half-human."

"You mean Zia," I said, as more pieces of the puzzle were snapping into place. "She's the Master's sister." *Whoa.*

"Half-sister, but yes," Teddy confirmed. "Christopher

and I knew Brigdon would kill her if we did nothing, and we convinced ourselves that we were doing it not only for our daughter but also for the greater good."

"You killed him." It wasn't a question. I could see it on her face.

"Yes," Teddy whispered, her voice shaking. "But we made a mistake. Emmett . . . he saw. I tried to explain, but he loved his father very much. He didn't understand." She sucked in a breath and let it out slowly. "He wanted revenge, so he sought out a Sorcerer of dark magic and sold his soul. He has been using dark magic ever since. He murdered Christopher and then came after me."

Unshed tears sparkled in Teddy's eyes. She reached for her mug of tea, taking several small sips while the bleakness of her story settled in. I wanted to say something comforting, but there was nothing I could think of that might make a difference. Like Gareth, some wounds would never fully heal.

"And you fought him?" I asked.

"No," Teddy's voice broke, and she buried her face in her hands. "I ran. I took Zia, and we fled. We've been hiding ever since."

"Just like that? Knowing how he felt about the factions and the human race, you just left? You didn't even try to reason with him? To explain?"

"There was nothing I could say. He had already bought into his father's ideology. His heart was full of hate for those he considered beneath him. He saw what I had done as the worst kind of betrayal . . . I had Zia to think of. I had no choice."

"And now?" I stood up. "He's about to wage a war on everyone."

Teddy winced. "I know. But don't you understand? He's my son. Despite what he is and what's he done, he will always be my child. I could no sooner lift a finger to harm him than I could raise a hand to Zia."

A flush rose in my cheeks. "But he's done terrible things. He's murdered and tortured hundreds."

"I know, and I bear the guilt and shame of those deaths every single day." She pointed to the photograph I still clutched in my hand. "He wasn't always a monster, you know. He was bright and happy. He had a smile that could light up the whole room." A stream of tears spilled down Teddy's cheek. "I failed him in every possible way a mother can fail her child."

My heart ached for Teddy, but my mind was struggling to rationalize it, to understand how she could just stand by and watch as the Master tortured and slaughtered his way to power.

"Zia clearly doesn't feel the same, right?" I asked. "I mean, she's the leader of the Hetaeria."

"No." Teddy wiped her face with her hand. "Zia feels the weight of her brother's actions as strongly as I do, which is why she has taken up the flag as leader of the resistance. She wants to avenge her father's death, unify the factions, and protect the humans. I also think she wants to prove—to herself most of all—that she is nothing like him."

Zia's brusqueness, her desperation, her focus. It was all making sense now. I made a mental note to think less harshly of her.

"This is what you meant the first day I met you, when you told me you weren't really part of the Hetaeria. You said it was complicated."

"It is," Teddy agreed. "Both of my children on warring sides. Where else can I stand but in the middle?"

"But you are helping," I argued. "You're allowing the Hetaeria to house their basecamp here. You're training me to be a weapon against him."

"I am aiding the Hetaeria in whatever way I can, but Lainey, it is all that I can do." She sighed. "I had hoped to explain this in time, and I know I don't have the right to make this request of you, but there's a reason I agreed to train you. It's not simply because he needs to be stopped—I know he does—but from the moment I met you, I saw the kindness in your heart. I agreed to train you because I am hoping that you are strong enough to not only stop him but also spare him."

The words slammed into me. "What? How can you ask that of me?" I whispered, rage boiling in my gut. "After everything he's taken from me?"

"He is my son," Teddy said with a sad smile. "Whatever he has done, he is still one half of my heart."

The taste of rust flooded my mouth, and I realized that

I'd bitten down hard on my tongue. Grimacing, I headed for the door, unable to sit still any longer.

"Lainey, I—"

"No," I said, cutting her off. "I can't listen to this anymore. You're a coward, Teddy." I hated the way those words tasted. I wasn't sure I'd ever be able to look at her—my teacher and mentor—the same way again.

"That may be so," Teddy said softly. "But I had to ask. What mother wouldn't do the same?"

Before I had time to comment, a thunderous boom cracked open the quiet of the night—an alarm so loud, I winced, gripping the sides of my head as it filled the air and pulsated like a heartbeat.

"What is that?" I yelled, turning back to Teddy, whose eyes were wide.

"It's the boundary alarm!" she shouted back. "Someone's broken through the wards."

"What does that mean?"

Teddy's face was grim. "It means we're under attack."

Throwing open the door, I dashed outside. The sky was lit up with an unusual bluish glow. Spheres of azure flames soared through the air with unnatural speed, splitting the darkened sky. Like blazing meteors, they fell upon the farm, igniting everything they touched. Sounds of impact echoed across the valley like the booming of a cannon.

The outer building next to Teddy's cottage burst into flames as one of the spheres hurtled through its roof in an explosion of magic. The shockwave of energy sent Teddy and me sprawling. The impact knocked the breath from my lungs, and I rolled over coughing, covering my head against the sharp fragments of wood and other material raining down on us.

"Teddy!" I choked out. "Teddy, where are you?"

"I'm here!" she called out several feet away.

I crawled over to her, the ground rumbling from the pulses of magic and the explosions that rocked the farm. "Are you okay?"

She nodded, though blood dripped from a cut in her hairline.

Satisfied, I jumped up, surveying the scene. Over half the buildings were blazing with fire, and the tree line was engulfed in a torrent of unnatural blue flames. In the haze of smoke, figures darted in and out of the shadows chaotically, like an anthill that'd been stepped on.

Running in the direction of the big house, I shoved the sleeves of my hoodie up, green lightning already crackling between my fingertips.

Dark shapes moved toward me, a dozen or so, low to the ground and running faster than a human was capable of. *Lycans!* As one neared a burning building, the flames cast just enough light for me to see the shape of its canine body, the long jaw that snapped open and shut, revealing a row of sharp teeth.

Reaching inside, I felt for my magic. It was there, waiting and ready. I flung my arms out toward the pack of Lycans. A streak of green light shot from my palm, expanded, and blasted into the wolves, sending them careening through the air.

I didn't wait to see if they were alive when they landed.

I ran, letting my magic flow through me. I wasn't thinking about it, just feeling. It responded to my every demand, like a physical sword in my hand. My chest heaved, and my muscles ached, but I pushed on, ignoring the obvious strain the magic had on my body.

Around me, members of the Hetaeria were locked in battle with our attackers. Several Hetaerian witches were moving from building to building, conjuring water to extinguish the flames from the spheres.

A Faerie girl with long purple hair darted in front of me, brandishing a broadsword. I'd never met her before but had seen her practicing with the others in the training ring. She was locked in combat with another Faerie, a boy with dark eyes and no shirt—the Master's mark inked across his back. He gripped a cudgel, his teeth bared. The purple-haired Faerie swung her sword with a cry, moving like a wisp of wind. The boy's cudgel met the sword with a clash of steel, and I was temporarily mesmerized as if they were performing an intricate dance, step for step matched perfectly.

One of the buildings behind me exploded, knocking me to the ground. When I staggered back to my feet, the Faeries were gone, lost in the swarm.

The farm was pure chaos, a flurry of surging crowds, hands and bodies working against each other, magic and enchantments flying through the air. I shoved forward, adrenaline pumping through my veins as my magic crackled in my hands.

The mixture of slush, blood, and soot underneath my boots made it difficult to run without slipping. A tall warlock stood near the big house, a ball of blue flames glowing in his hand. "No!" I shouted, watching as he pulled his arm back. Energy shot through my palms, and thick green ropes wrapped around the warlock, squirming like a dozen snakes as they held him. The sphere of flames fell onto the ground. I ran toward the warlock, ripping Gareth's dagger from the sheath I'd strapped on earlier that morning.

Pain exploded in my head as something grabbed me by the ponytail, yanking me backward. I yelped, nearly losing grip of my dagger as a stout Nixie with orange-tinted skin jumped in front of me, teeth bared. The Master's mark on his collarbone stood out, the ink a dark contrast to his skin. I swiped at him with the dagger, but he dodged it with ease, grabbing my arm and twisting it until I saw stars. I cried out as he slammed my arm downward, the force knocking the dagger from my hand.

I kicked my leg out, the heel of my boot connecting with his kneecap. The Nixie swore and loosened his grip. It was enough to twist myself free. My shoulder was throbbing and so was my head. Blood coated my tongue. Keeping my eyes on the Nixie, I spat a mouthful into the snow.

With a yell, the Nixie launched himself at me, and we rolled back and forth until the weight of him nearly crushed my ribcage. I reached for my magic, but he was too fast, slamming a palm over my mouth and nose.

I gasped for air, suffocating under his firm grip. Black spots dotted my vision, and everything inside me screamed for air as my lungs burned and heaved.

The Nixie pushed down harder on my face. With his other hand, he leaned over me and reached for my dagger where it had fallen in the snow.

"Long live the Master," he intoned, angling the dagger at my chest.

I had no air as I reached inside for my magic. Everything was growing dark—even the thread of connection I felt with Ty faded from the lack of oxygen. My magic was a dying ember instead of a roaring flame. Would it be the blade or the lack of breath that killed me first?

I tried to move, but I couldn't feel the rest of my body.

The Nixie smirked and lowered the dagger toward my heart.

CHAPTER TWENTY-TWO

TY

The ground rumbled underneath my feet as I ran, deep vibrations that seemed to unsettle the earth. The darkened sky was tinged with blue, the work of a warlock's deadly flames, and the air crackled with energy. It was enough to make the hair on the back of my arms and neck stand up, though it didn't slow my feet.

The farm was a melee of chaos. The plan—*my* plan—had worked exactly the way it was supposed to. The wards had given us no trouble at all, and I'd led the Master's men right into the heart of the Hetaeria's basecamp.

Dodging my way through the pandemonium, I tried not to allow myself to dwell on the costs of my actions. But it was hard to ignore the stab of guilt every time a body fell to the ground. I imagined my father's face, etched in disappointment. *I'm doing this for you!* I shouted the words in my mind. *"No,"* his voice echoed back, his head shaking sadly. *"You're doing this for you."*

A jolt of shame rocketed through me, and I cried out, wanting to rip the image, the words from my mind. *What do you expect from me? I'm not one of the good guys.* Lainey's face appeared next. *There's always a choice.* They were my own words, whispered back to me.

In front of me, a square-shouldered Shifter, one of the Master's men, prowled toward a young Seer, laughing as he cornered her near the barn. Focusing on my instincts, the years of training, and my father's lessons, I knew what I had to do. I may have unleashed the vipers into the pit, but I didn't have to stand by and watch them strike. *There's always a choice.*

With blood roaring in my ears, I slammed into him from behind. We landed in a tangle of limbs, his teeth snapping and my fists flying. The blade strapped to my back jammed into my spine on impact; I winced but didn't reach for it. I didn't need to. Shifters were strong, and they made for decent fighters, but they were no match for Praetorians, and this one was no match for me.

The Shifter snarled, his features distorting as he began to Shift into a polar bear. Thrusting my arm forward, my elbow connected with his jaw. He howled, and I closed my hands around his throat, cutting off the sound. The Shifter choked and gagged, clawing at my wrists with bear-like claws. Blood dripped down my arm, but I didn't let go.

The Shifter swiped at my face. I hissed as a claw sliced across my forehead, narrowly missing my eye, but causing me to lose my grip. The Shifter knocked me to the side, his jaw snapping. I regained my footing and slammed my fist into the side of his face. With a yelp, he jerked backward. Fire blazed through me, and I pulled back and kicked the Shifter right in his snout. There was a sickening crunch, and his body fell backward, trails of blood dripping from his nostrils. I ripped my sword from its sheath and finished the job.

When I was done, I looked up, and the Seer was already gone. Without a second glance for the Shifter at my feet, I sprang back into the bulk of the fighting. Renewed purpose propelled me forward. I ran, searching. *Lainey.* I needed to find her.

It was difficult to distinguish faces of those swarming around me, so I felt for our connection instead. I let out a breath when a familiar warmth surged through me. She was near, alive. I rushed forward, shoving and swinging at those who got in my way.

I thought I saw a flash of familiar brown hair flying, but then a Faerie girl with a broadsword slid in front of me, blocking my view. The Faerie had purple hair and a fierce expression as she battled one of the Master's Fae, a dark-haired boy with a cudgel. They were equally matched, but a sheen of sweat shone on the girl's forehead.

I swung around and ran up to the dark-haired Faerie, gripping the hilt of my sword. He was so focused on the girl he didn't see me coming. I pulled back my arm, bludgeoning him as hard as I could with the flat of my blade. Bones crunched audibly, the Fae went sprawling backward in the dirt.

The purple-haired Faerie gave me a little wink and raised her broadsword above her head with a wild cry, her wild eyes narrowed on the other Fae.

I didn't stop to watch, though the squelching sound that echoed in my ears was enough for me to know her aim was true.

I pressed on, searching.

Suddenly, something plowed into me, knocking me to the ground. A waterfall of thick, fiery hair fell into my face as Zia crouched over me, her lips pulled back in a snarl. "Traitor!" She spat, "Tell me this wasn't you. Tell me you haven't made a fool of me again." Her eyes were wild, and her face was streaked with blue ash and crimson blood.

Behind her, a Lycan—one of the Master's—crept closer, a wicked grin on his face and a curved blade in his hand.

Ignoring the question, I jerked forward, throwing her off balance, and kicked back up to a standing position. Snatching my sword from where I'd dropped it on the ground, I lunged forward and swung it upward, crashing against the Lycan's own blade. He roared, beads of sweat dotting his forehead, and we grappled steel to steel.

Then Zia was there, blistering energy crackling around her and lifting the ends of her hair. She opened her mouth and cried out. A streak of scarlet light shot from her palm and into the Lycan's chest. He opened his mouth, his lips forming an "O," but no sound came out. He fell backward into the dirt and did not move again.

She whirled to face me. "Tell me, Traitor. Was this your plan all along?"

"This wasn't my doing," I said, panting. "The Master was already planning this attack by the time I arrived. You were right: Lainey's magic was far too powerful for him not to notice, not to track."

Zia's chest heaved, her eyes narrowed on her face. "That may be true, but there's no way they could've gotten through the wards without help." Her lip raised in a feral sneer. "That was all you."

"You're right," I said, sheathing my sword, "but I had no choice. To get the information you needed, I had to offer something else in return. The Master gives nothing for free. You know that."

"You got it then? The intel?"

"I did."

Zia swiped at the blood trickling down her face and sniffed. "The blood of these people"—she gestured to the bodies littering the ground—"that's on your hands."

I swallowed, trying to ignore the way the words gouged at my chest, puncture wounds that throbbed with every beat of my heart.

"Pain is earned, son." My father's voice echoed in my thoughts. *"But you get to choose whether it limits you or reminds you of how hard you've fought. Win or lose, loss or*

gain, how we acknowledge our pain defines us. It is the tether that links us to who we really are, who we are meant to be. Pain is a tether."

"I know." I gave Zia a curt nod.

The bulk of the fighting was beginning to die down.

"They're retreating," Zia mused, watching as a host of figures ran through the shadows, back across the boundary lines.

"The mission wasn't annihilation," I said. "It was to break the Hetaeria's spirit. This is nothing but a precursor of what's coming."

Before I could speak again, explain further, a feeling slammed into me like a physical blow to the chest. Air was forced from my lungs, and I clawed at my throat as both adrenaline and fear shot through me.

Zia gripped my shoulder and said something, but I heard nothing but the pounding of my own heart.

Then the feeling released me. Gasping, I dropped to my knees, clutching at my heaving chest.

"What the hell?" Zia yelled, yanking on my arm.

"It's Lainey," I said, more to myself than to her. The feeling hadn't been my own. It was hers.

The world itself seemed to melt away as I moved. I grabbed my sword and ran, faster than I've ever run before, the connection between us open and flowing.

I'm coming. Over and over, I said the words in my mind,

sending them to her through the bond. *I'm coming. I'm coming. I'm coming.*

Roaring—my own—filled my ears as I shoved through the remaining pockets of fighting, swinging my club and showing no mercy for anyone who stepped in my path. Carnage was everywhere around me, the snow stained red.

"Lainey!" I screamed, but the only faces that stared back at me were strangers.

Then it stopped. The connection between us faded; I could no longer feel it. It was just . . . gone. *No.*

"Lainey!"

I ran harder and faster.

No, no, no.

I found her lying in the snow, curled up on her side.

If I hadn't been looking for her, I'm not sure I would've seen her. But even with her back to me, I knew it was her. Her long brown hair that I so often imagined running a hand through was as recognizable as the curve of her hip, the shape of her ear, visible in the dying glow of blue flames.

Lainey. Her name stuck to my tongue, and I couldn't speak. I dropped to my knees beside her in the snow.

With a gentle hand, I rolled her over onto my lap, pushing the hair off her face. Blood trickled from her mouth, but the rest of her face was unmarred. She looked like she was sleeping.

Instinctively, I reached for her, felt for the bond between

us, but there was nothing. Just a cold silence. An emptiness that could have filled the deepest of chasms.

No. I shook my head. *This isn't happening. Not again.*

"Please," I murmured, running a finger across her smooth cheek. "Please don't do this." Trembling, I leaned forward, touching my forehead to hers. "Stay with me."

Just like I had with my father, my fingers searched for the spot on her neck where her pulse should be. Already, her skin was chilled, her heart no longer pumping life into her veins.

Pain, agonizing and deep, exploded in my chest, and I cried out. It shot through me, puncturing the parts of me that I'd ignored for far too long, ripped open wounds I'd tried to forget.

Every piece of me screamed in torment. My splintered heart shattered, the fragments ripping through me, slicing the soft place where I always kept her into ribbons.

A thousand sharp knives. A thousand gaping wounds.

Broken and raw, I pulled her close, fighting the sob that lodged in my throat.

When my father died, I hadn't shed a single tear.

But now, holding the girl, I—

Tears rolled down my cheeks as I realized the horrible and wonderful truth I'd been denying, ignoring, and lying about for so long.

The remaining threads that were holding me together snapped, and I gave in to the pain, letting it consume me.

"If pain is a tether," I gasped out, choking on tears, "I am unbreakable chain."

Unbreakable.

Broken.

Lainey.

I gathered her in my arms and wept.

CHAPTER
TWENTY-THREE

MAGGIE

I couldn't stand still. Pacing back and forth, my shoes wore a groove into the dirt underneath my feet while the quiet evening air whipped around us.

"Look, Professor X," I said, glaring at Oliver. "I know you and Magneto aren't exactly pals, but I'm going to need you to march back in there and try again."

After Ajay had refused our request to ally with the Hetaeria, Oliver and I retreated to a lookout point across the street from the pub, away from the other Shifters' curious glances. A smattering of shining stars had begun popping up against the blackening sky, but it was difficult to appreciate the beauty while Ajay's refusal hung over us like a cloud.

"He can't just say no like that," I said.

Oliver glared straight ahead, his hands gripping the edge

of the worn wooden bench he sat on. "Oh, he can, and he did," he growled, his face hard. "He won't change his mind."

"We have to keep trying." I flopped down next to Oliver. "There has to be something we can do to convince him."

"If there is such a thing," Oliver said, huffing, "I don't know what it is. I'm a Shifter, not a Seer."

It took every ounce of willpower I had not to smack him. *No shit, Sherlock*, I thought, but out loud, I said, "True, but you know Ajay better than anyone, right? You have history."

Oliver shook his head. "I *used* to know him. Not anymore."

"So, what happened?" It wasn't my business, but I asked anyway, too frustrated to care. "What's the deal with you two?"

Oliver blinked, and for a second I thought he would ignore my question altogether, but then he sighed. "I was supposed to be the next leader of our faction, did you know that? My father was the last leader, and when he passed away, it was my job to step up and fill his shoes. Even though I was young, I was a natural-born leader and well respected among our people . . . or I was before I left."

"Left? What happened?"

"My sister, Sarah, was killed. During one of the Master's raids. We were . . . very close." Oliver frowned, his eyes sad. "I joined the Hetaeria shortly after. That was over two years ago now."

"And that's why Ajay hates you? Because you left?"

"We don't hate each other." Oliver rubbed a hand across

his face. "At least, I don't hate him. It's just . . . complicated. Sarah was Ajay's fiancée. I was out getting supplies, but he was there during the raid. He tried to save her, but it was too late." Oliver paused. "For a long time, I blamed him for her death, for not protecting her. It was easier than blaming myself."

The pain written across Oliver's face pulled at my heart. "I'm sure he did everything he could."

"He did," Oliver agreed. "But by the time I realized that, I had already left, abandoning my people and my responsibility. Ajay became the new leader of the faction, and we've barely spoken since."

"I don't understand. If the Master was responsible for Sarah's death, wouldn't that be motivation enough for Ajay?"

Oliver shrugged. "He's afraid to lose more people. He thinks he's protecting them by keeping them from the fight."

The words settled into a weighty silence. I let out a breath. "Okay, I get it. You were grieving, and he got scared. What about the other Shifters?"

"What about them?"

"You lost your sister," I said. "But they lost *you*, their leader. Don't you think it's time you made that right?"

Oliver stared at me, then shook his head. "They wouldn't want me. Not anymore. Besides, my place is with the Hetaeria." He stood up, rubbing his palms on his jeans. "We're not going to make any ground here. We'll head back to the farm, and—"

"No." I crossed my arms across my chest. "We can't leave yet. You said yourself that the Hetaeria won't last without allies. We have to convince the Shifters to help. *You* have to convince them."

"Why would they listen to me?" Oliver argued. "Ajay already said no."

"Because you're the rightful leader of the faction!" I shouted, the words echoing back at us across the open air.

Oliver shifted from one foot to the other. "That was a long time ago. They won't follow me."

"You won't know unless you ask them." Sinking down on the wooden bench, I turned to him. "I don't know anything about faction politics, but I do know what it's like to wish you could change something that happened to you, to wish it had ended differently." I held up my arm and shoved back the sleeve of my jacket. The sight of that smooth patch of scarless skin still hit me in the gut—the bite that I'd been convinced would change everything now nonexistent. "Not all of us get that chance. Don't waste it."

Oliver studied my face. "What if they don't take me back?" The words were so soft, they nearly got lost in the wind.

I sat up a little straighter, trying not to let the surprise show on my face. "At least you'll know you tried. Isn't that better than wondering?"

Oliver was quiet for a while, before finally nodding. "I should never have left like I did. They deserve better than me."

"You're not giving yourself enough credit," I said. "One mistake doesn't define the rest of your life."

"Yeah . . . maybe." The hard lines of Oliver's face had softened, like he was considering every word.

I leaned over and shoved his shoulder gently with mine. "Oh, come on, Simba, don't you think it's time you go reclaim the Pride Lands?"

He didn't respond right away. But then his cheeks lifted ever so slightly, and I knew my powers of persuasion had won out. "Let's go."

We walked quickly back to the pub. I had to jog to keep up with Oliver's determined gait. Without preamble, he shoved open the door to the pub and marched inside, with me hurrying behind him.

"Ajay!" Oliver shouted, drawing the attention of everyone in the room. "Ajay!"

"I thought I made myself perfectly clear," Ajay said, appearing from behind the bar. "If this is about the Hetaeria—"

"I've come to issue a challenge," Oliver spat. The room immediately broke into dozens of conversations, words of surprise and shock meshing together in a discordant buzz.

Ajay threw the towel in his hand down on the bar and stalked forward. "You show up here after two years and challenge me?"

"I'm only doing what I should have done after Sarah died."

The words had a visible effect on Ajay. He bristled, baring his teeth. "Then come, *Brother*," he sneered. He stormed through the back door, and the Shifters in the pub filed out noisily behind him.

"If things start to go badly," Oliver said, turning to me, "I want you to take my truck and go back to the farm. Tell Zia what happened."

"If things go badly?" I shook my head, not liking the way his eyes were trained on my face. "What does that mean?"

Oliver rolled his eyes. "Scar doesn't exactly hand the Pride Lands over to Simba just because he asks for them, now does he?"

"No, they—" I wasn't entirely sure what it was I'd expected when I'd encouraged Oliver to reclaim his leadership of the faction, but as realization settled over me, all I could manage was a whispered, "Oh."

Oliver smiled a little at that. He pulled the truck keys from his pocket and placed them in my palm, closing his own fingers around mine. "Promise me."

The warmth of his hand enveloping mine surged through me. If he thought I'd actually leave him alone to be . . . Nope, wasn't going to happen. Not that he needed to know that. "Yeah, okay."

His eyes narrowed, as if he were reading my thoughts. "Maggie—"

"It's time," a voice called from the door. A tall Shifter with a grim face beckoned.

Oliver headed toward the door.

"Hey, Oliver!" I called out. There were so many things swirling around in my head, but the words stuck in my throat. "He wins in the end. Simba, I mean." It wasn't exactly what I was going for, but it was close enough.

Oliver nodded, his eyes bright. "I know." Then he turned and strode outside.

I followed him, only a few seconds behind, and found that the back area of the pub had been instantaneously transformed. The couches and lounge chairs had been shoved out of the way. The Shifters from the pub were gathered in a loose semicircle surrounding the open space. Oliver and Ajay stood in the center, facing each other.

I stood at the edge of the circle, fidgeting with my arms—crossed across my chest, down at my sides, I couldn't be still. The air was thick with expectation, and the people around me were murmuring, some with grins and pointed fingers, and others with darting eyes and raised eyebrows.

If some sort of signal was given, I didn't see it. One minute, Oliver and Ajay were chest to chest, glaring at each other, and the next, there was a flurry of color and motion as their solid forms began to distort and change. I'd seen Oliver Shift once before, but it was still jarring to see his limbs elongate, the coarse fur growing on his arms.

A lion with a thick, bushy mane stood where Oliver had been; an enormous brown bear in the place of Ajay. With a roaring bellow, Oliver launched himself at Ajay, his jaws opened wide, sharp teeth gleaming. Ajay responded, swinging his furry arm and knocking Oliver to the ground. Oliver was back on his feet before the gasp had even escaped my lips.

Ajay advanced, roaring. The sound made my eardrums vibrate, and I clapped my hands over my ears. The Shifters around me seemed unfazed, their eyes never straying from the fight.

Oliver and Ajay were wrapped around each other so it was difficult to keep track of whose blood splattered the ground each time canines or claws met skin. They tumbled and rolled, swiping at each other, kicking and biting. I jumped at every snap of jaws, every squelch of teeth against skin, but like the Shifters around me, I couldn't look away.

Ajay and Oliver were evenly matched. A few of the Shifters in the crowd were running a commentary on the fight. I inched closer, trying to catch snippets of their conversation.

"This could take hours," one complained. "They're playing nice."

Nice? With the snarling roars and slashing claws, it seemed to me that they were tearing each other to bits.

I wasn't sure how much time had passed, but as the fight continued, both Ajay and Oliver slowed down, their movements jerky and lacking intensity. When another unspoken signal was given, they broke apart, Shifting back to their human forms.

"Oliver!" I called out, shoving through the crowd. "Are you okay?"

He staggered over to me, his chest heaving. Sweat poured off his body, and when he reached my side, placing a hand on my shoulder to steady himself, his entire shirt was soaked through.

"I'm . . . fine," he wheezed, his voice low enough that only I could hear.

I gripped his arm, helping him stand upright.

With his chest still heaving, he pulled his shirt over his head and wiped his face.

Holy crapkittens . . . I hissed, blowing air through my teeth. He'd been shirtless when I first met him, but up close, with his six-pack abs staring me in the face, it was really hard to breathe.

"S-so . . . u-uh . . ." I stammered. "How are you not bleeding out right now?"

Oliver pointed to three angry red slashes across his chest, the remnants of one of Ajay's well-aimed swipes. "Shifters heal quickly. Hurts like hell but doesn't linger."

"That's . . . convenient," I said, trying not to stare. "What's next?"

"Round two," Oliver said grimly. He winced a little as he rotated his shoulders.

"Well, stop taking it easy on him, will you?"

Oliver looked at me, eyebrows raised, as if I'd caught him in the middle of a lie, then let out a laugh. "Alright, then." He stalked back over to where Ajay was waiting, swinging his arms back and forth.

The prelude lasted only seconds this time. Oliver Shifted into a large gray wolf, while Ajay took shape as a cougar. With a scream that made the hair on my arms rise, Ajay attacked, swiping his massive paw and sharp claws through the air.

Oliver was ready, skirting out of the way and pouncing

atop Ajay's back, sinking his teeth into the skin of the cat's neck. Back and forth they went, but this time, Oliver's skill as a fighter showed. He darted between Ajay's paws, landing blows and bites of his own, all while dancing out of harm's way.

The murmur of the crowd around me grew louder, the energy in the air crackling. With a furious snarl, Oliver flipped Ajay onto his back, his teeth inches from the cat's throat. A single bite was all it would take to end it all.

No one moved.

Oliver, still in wolf form, snarled viciously, then leapt off the supine cat, Shifting as he went. He stood over Ajay in human form, his hard eyes darting over those in the crowd.

Ajay also Shifted back, still lying on the ground. His hair was damp with sweat, and a trickle of blood ran down his chin. "Finish it," he growled. "Do it."

Oliver shook his head.

"It's part of the challenge," Ajay countered, spitting blood into the dirt beside him. "You want to lead this faction, you have to kill me."

I blanched. *Kill?* I hadn't realized that was part of the deal. I glanced around but no one seemed as bothered by the news as I was.

Oliver growled. "And what problem does that solve?" He leaned over, holding a hand out to Ajay. "You are not my enemy."

Ajay stared, but took Oliver's hand, allowing him to pull him to his feet.

"This is not the way," a grizzly looking Shifter said, stepping through the crowd. Heads bobbed in agreement.

"No," Oliver agreed. "But that doesn't mean it's right or that it can't be changed."

The faces in the crowd didn't soften. If anything, Oliver's words incensed them. A few stepped forward.

"I will not kill Ajay," Oliver said, loud enough that his voice projected across the yard. "He is not the enemy. The Master is the enemy, and he's coming for all of us. I know I failed you once before, but I promise you, I will not fail you again. I will not kill this man today, because he is my friend, our brother, and a good man." He reached for Ajay, squeezing his shoulder before turning back to the crowd. "Despite the outcome of this challenge, I offer you the choice. I will respect your decision, but if you'll have me as your leader . . . I'm here to stay this time."

This was it. The moment where Simba reclaimed the Pride Lands or got taken out by Scar and the hyenas. I wasn't sure which way the pendulum would swing—especially given the looks on the faces of the Shifters in the crowd. But then the energy shifted. The expressions of incensed fury gave way to consideration, and a buzz of conversations floated in the air.

Oliver turned to Ajay. "I'm sorry . . . for everything."

Ajay looked taken aback, but then he let out a breath and held out a hand to Oliver.

The two shook, and Ajay addressed the crowd. "Oliver is the rightful faction leader, and he's right. There is a greater enemy we must all face. Together."

The grizzly Shifter stepped closer, holding out his hand to Oliver. "Welcome back, Brother."

Like a spell that had been broken, the remaining tension in the air fizzled into nothingness. The Shifters broke up, several walking over to Oliver to shake his hand and welcome him back.

I let out a deep sigh. "Nice job, Simba. You did it."

A loud bang made me jump as a girl around my age burst through the door and raced across the lawn, heading straight for Ajay and Oliver. When she reached them, she whispered in Ajay's ear, her face grim. The rest of the Shifters quieted.

"Something's happened," Ajay said, clearing his throat. The look on his face sent ice down my back. I stilled immediately, the smile dying on my lips.

Oliver had stiffened, sensing it too. "What is it?"

"We've just received word. There's been an attack on the Hetaerian basecamp."

I gasped, while Oliver swore. "How bad?" he demanded.

"I don't know," Ajay said. "But the attack was just a precursor of what's coming. The Master's forces are already on the move. The war is starting."

"We have to go. We have to get back to the farm." I hurried to Oliver's side. "Right now!" I thought of Lainey and Serena. *Please let them be okay, please let them be okay.*

"Hang on," Oliver said, grabbing me by the arm. "Ajay, based on the intel, what's the likelihood that we'll be able to get back to the farm before the Master strikes again?"

"There's no way to know for sure, but it would be cutting it close."

Oliver turned to me. "Maggie, we can't go back, not just yet."

"What are you talking about?" I demanded, hysteria rising in my throat like bile. "Our friends are in trouble—they need our help."

"I know," he said, holding his hands up. "But the Hetaeria needs allies. If the war is starting, we'll need every bit of help we can get. We have the Shifters on our side, but we need more. We have to try."

"I don't—" I shook my head. "What are you saying?"

Oliver rolled his eyes. "When the Avengers tried to take down Thanos, they didn't do it alone, did they?"

"No, they—" I paused, shock filling my features. *Oliver just made a Marvel reference?* I shoved my wonder aside as understanding settled in. "You mean the other factions? Do you really think we can convince them? Do we have time?"

"If we hurry."

Ajay's eyes flashed. "We can make it work, but we'll need to leave right away."

"Will they listen to us?"

"Just give them the same 'Don't be a jackhole' speech you gave me." Ajay grinned. "Worked for me."

Oliver looked confused, but I just grinned.

"Let's do this," I crowed. "Avengers, assemble!"

Hang in there, Styles. We're on our way.

CHAPTER TWENTY-FOUR

LAINEY

I'm dying.

The thought was clear in my head as the dagger inched its way closer to my heart. The Nixie's gleeful grin grew wider, a layer of fuzzy green moss visible on his teeth.

My body was detached and heavy; the lack of oxygen squeezed my insides. Resignation hung over me, but as the Nixie giggled, ready to claim his kill, a sudden spark ignited, surging through me to replace my scream for air with a battle cry of survival.

I threw my head forward, knocking into the Nixie with as much force as I could muster. The sound of our skulls colliding made a horrible crunching sound, and we both cried out. I was sure I'd broken half my face, but air rushed back into my lungs, and that was all that mattered.

The Nixie was howling, holding his nose. He'd dropped the dagger, and it was laying next to him in the snow. Bucking my hips to displace his balance, I shot upward and grabbed the dagger, swinging it into the Nixie's side. He gasped, the sound sharp and breathy.

I drove the blade in farther. Thick, hot blood gushed from the wound and dripped down my arm. The Nixie slumped against me, his eyes rolling back into his head. Shoving him to the side, I squirmed out from underneath his weight. The blood soaking through my sweatshirt and jeans smelled like river water and dead fish. I plucked the dagger from where it stuck out of the dead Nixie at my feet, trying not to look into his vacant, unseeing eyes. I wiped it clean in the snow and then surveyed the area around me.

Several of the buildings were still on fire from the magical spheres, and people moved among the wreckage, but it appeared the fighting had stopped. Bodies littered the ground, and I tried not to look too closely as I walked through the rubble.

My head was pounding, and the entire right side of my face was starting to swell. Now that the adrenaline was ebbing from my veins, reality was starting to set in. Headbutting a foe always looked so cool in the action movies. In real life, when your life really depends on it? Yeah, not so much.

"Lainey!"

Julian jogged toward me from the direction of the barn. Behind him was . . . *me*.

I gaped at the girl running next to him, a girl whose face

was identical to mine. She wore different clothes, but as she stepped in front of me, it was as if I were staring into a mirror.

I opened my mouth, but not a single word came out. I looked at Julian, my heart hammering in my ears.

"Didn't Zia explain the plan?" he asked, confused by my expression.

I wordlessly shook my head.

The other Lainey began to giggle, a high-pitched, shrill sound that was instantly familiar. Her face began to shimmer and distort, until the features that were so intimately familiar to me melted away to reveal a round, childlike face and a pair of striking amethyst eyes.

"Cora?"

"What happened to your face?" she asked, her lilting voice, like the tinkling of crystals.

"Never mind that, why you are *wearing* my face?"

"Decoys," Julian answered for her. "Zia's idea."

I shook my head and instantly regretted the movement, as it exacerbated the pounding. "Why?" Our encounter from earlier came back to me then, the way Cora's tiny hands had flitted over my face, memorizing every line and detail.

"You're the Hetaeria's most valuable asset," Cora said simply, as if I had asked her about the weather.

Julian confirmed. "Zia wanted a layer of protection in place, just in case the wards ever fell. In case they came looking for you."

Warmth pooled in my chest. I was oddly touched by

this, even though I knew it was more about protecting the "weapon" than it was about protecting me. "Oh, right."

Julian shifted from one foot to the other, his forehead scrunched as if he were chewing on something sour.

"What?" There was something he wasn't telling me.

"Something's happened. Zia sent me to find you." He tilted his head in the direction he'd come from. "You need to come now."

All the fire and warmth that ran through me chilled at the words, and I shivered. "Tell me, Julian. What is it? Is someone—"

I choked on the word, unable to spit it out. Of course there had been casualties. The evidence was literally lying all around us. But who? Serena? I shivered again, the breath hitching in my throat.

"Just . . ." Julian hesitated. "Come see. It's hard to explain."

I followed him through the ruined farm, staring at his back and trying to prepare myself for whatever waited for me. What could possibly be so bad that he couldn't put it into words? Cora trailed behind, humming an eerie little tune under her breath.

Zia stood stiffly against one of the outer buildings. She was covered in grime, with various cuts and shallow injuries, but she was alive. It was a relief to see her standing there, scowling.

"Is it Teddy? Serena?" I asked, my voice low.

"No," Zia shook her head. She opened and closed her mouth several times, as if she were trying to find the right words, but then she sighed. "He won't let anyone come near you."

The words didn't make sense.

But then she shifted to the side, and everything became clear.

Several feet away, Ty knelt in the snow. Cradled in his arms was . . . me.

A decoy version of me, lifeless and still in his arms.

His entire body shook with violent sobs. The sound punched through my chest and reverberated in my ears, a sound of pain so profound I couldn't bear it.

"Oh," I whispered, thick tears blurring my vision.

I felt a tiny hand grip mine. I looked down. Cora was standing next to me. For once, the impish grin was gone from her face. There was only sadness in her large eyes.

"Sometimes we don't realize our own hearts," she whispered, the tinkling of her words like falling tears, "until we lose them."

With tears spilling over, I took a step toward him.

He was holding the decoy delicately in his arms, as if she were made of glass and at any moment she would shatter. His hand stroked her hair, and tears dripped down his chin, as he murmured words too low for me to hear.

Ty, the boy who betrayed me, was broken.

And in that moment, so was I.

My own heart, ragged as it was, cracked open. And there in the center of it was the truth—something I'd known for a while, but wanted to ignore, to forget. Underneath it all, in my most vulnerable and real place, was Ty.

Exactly where he'd always been.

I sucked down a shuddering breath and kept walking. When I got close enough for him to hear the snow crunch under my boots, his back stiffened.

"Go away," he growled over his shoulder. "I said to leave us alone."

The pain in his voice, raw and real, made me ache so deeply, I had to wrap an arm around myself to keep from breaking into pieces.

I took another step.

"I said go away!" he roared, and I winced, more tears slipping down my cheeks.

The air around us was so still the world itself seemed to hold its breath.

"Ty." My voice was barely more than a whisper.

His back straightened, his chest heaving. Then he shook his head, bending back down over the decoy.

"Ty." I said it louder this time, placing my hand gently on his shoulder.

He jerked under my touch, twisting around to face me. His eyes widened as he took me in. His chest began to heave as he looked at me, then down at the decoy, then back at me.

He shook his head. "You're not real."

"I am," I said, my voice shaking. I pointed to the decoy. "That's not me, Ty." I knelt slowly, afraid to move too quickly. "That's not me."

Ty shook his head again, faster this time. "No."

"Ty, it's not me." I reached for him, but he jerked away and leapt to his feet, both hands gripping his hair.

"Why are you doing this?!" he shouted into the air. "Is this what I deserve? My punishment for all I've done?" Fresh tears streaked down his face.

Stepping around the decoy, I moved to stand in front of him. "Listen to me," I said, gripping his arms. "I'm right here, standing in front of you." My lips began to quiver. "I'm *right* here."

Slowly, as to not spook him again, I lifted my hand. "I'm right here, Ty." I tried to reach him through the Praetorian bond, but the connection was weak—my fight with the Nixie had nearly severed it, and I realized I'd somehow blocked it when I used the last bit of strength to fight back. I placed my palm against Ty's cheek, rekindling the link between us. It snapped open under my coaxing, and I shoved everything I was feeling at Ty.

His reaction was immediate. Ty sagged and closed his eyes. When he opened them again, they stared back at me, seeing me—really seeing me—for the first time. "Lainey?"

"I'm right here."

With a sound that broke my heart—a sound of both relief and torment—he reached for me, yanking me close, as his lips crashed down on mine.

He tasted of tears.

I clung to him, returning the kiss with every aching part of me. His entire body was trembling, and I wrapped my arms around him as tightly as I could manage, trying to squeeze the pain out from between us.

Just when I thought my lungs would burst, he pulled away, gasping for breath. He ran his fingers over my cheeks before kissing me again, fast and slow, short and long, as if there were nothing left in the world but him and me.

I felt it then, the same kindling of flame I'd felt on the dance floor at the Gathering. But this time, it wasn't just a spark. It was a blaze of fire—brighter than anything I'd ever felt before.

"I'm sorry," he said, finally pulling away, crushing me to his chest. "I'm so sorry." He murmured the words over and over against my hair, his hand holding my head against his heart. It beat so fast it hummed underneath my ear.

Then he pulled back, searching my face as if to confirm that it was still me he was holding in his arms. "I'm so sorry."

There was so much wrapped up in those words that I didn't have to ask to know that he meant more than just the attack. I reached out, running my thumb across his cheek-bone. His eyes, red-rimmed and shining, stared into mine.

"I forgive you."

He let out a sigh, pressing his forehead against mine. I closed my eyes, letting those words—meant to be a balm for him—ease into the aching parts of me as well. *I forgive you.* The same healing words Gareth had given me passed on to another. I spoke the words in my mind, trying to send every ounce of what I was feeling—warmth, compassion, and the feeling in my heart too complex to name—to Ty through our connection.

And when his lips pressed gently against mine, his fingers grazing the side of my neck, I knew he felt it all.

CHAPTER TWENTY-FIVE

TY

I waited for the breath to return to my lungs, but as I pulled Lainey closer, my chest throbbed. My heart beat erratically, pumping pulses of pain through me—a stabbing, aching pain so torturous I buckled under its weight, its depth.

Fear, cold and slippery, still gripped me. I didn't want to let her go. With her warm body pressed against mine, it was easy to believe she was real, that I hadn't lost her. Without that, when I could no longer wrap my arms around her, how could I be sure that she was really there, alive and breathing? How could I know that the heart beating in my chest wasn't a phantom, the ghost of the girl who had captured it?

Maybe the remnants of pain were meant to be a reminder. The absolute agony I'd felt seeing that girl lying in the snow and thinking it was Lainey still hovered in the air, only a heartbeat away.

I never wanted to feel that way again.

I let out a deep breath, closing my eyes and allowing my senses to overwhelm my mind. The silk of her hair underneath my fingertips. The heat coming off her skin. The feel of her lips moving against mine. The proof of her still-beating heart against my chest.

She pulled back, though not far enough to break the circle of my arms. "Are you okay?" There was a softness in her eyes that made me shiver, a look I thought I'd lost a long time ago.

"You're alive," I replied. "The world could be on fire, and I'd still be okay, knowing that."

She pressed her lips back to mine, and I tasted salt. Both her tears and mine.

This time when we pulled away, my eyes focused on the ugly purpling mass on the side of her face. "You're hurt," I murmured, running my thumb gently over the bruise.

"I'll live," she breathed, leaning into my hand.

The words made the air hitch in my throat, the ache in my chest still throbbing. I looked down at the girl in the snow. The likeness was so uncanny, it turned my stomach, and the bitter taste of acid rose in my throat. "I don't understand though." I indicated the body. "How is it possible that I'm holding you, when the proof that this is all just a dream is lying there, right next to me? I reached for our connection, but I couldn't feel you. I thought—"

Lainey shook her head. "I know what you thought, but I'm right here." She squeezed my arm as a reminder. Then she frowned as she looked down at the girl. "She's a decoy. Someone else from the Hetaeria."

I raised an eyebrow. "I'm not sure I'm following."

"She's been Glamoured with Trickster magic to look like me. It was Zia's plan." Lainey let out a breath, tears welling up in her eyes. "To make sure that in an attack, I would be harder to find. It was supposed to be some kind of protection plan, though clearly it didn't work." She sniffed. "At least not for her. I don't even know who she is, but she gave her life to help keep me safe."

The sadness in her voice made my ears burn, shame creeping up my neck. "It might have been a good plan, if it weren't for me." I swallowed. "I'm the reason that girl is dead."

"What?"

"I lied. I told the Master the connection between you and the Grimoire had been severed, that it was possible to unlock the Grimoire without you. I, too, was trying to protect you. But my plan backfired. Since he thought he didn't need you anymore, he ordered you to be killed on sight. This girl's death is on me."

Lainey stared at me. I tried to pull away, my cheeks flushing, but she held on to me.

"You're not the bad guy here, Ty."

I blinked. If only that were true.

We stared at each other, neither of us saying anything until a purposeful cough sounded behind us.

Zia stood behind us, looking uncomfortable. "We good here?"

Lainey stepped back, nodding. "We're good."

Zia's eyes fell to the girl at our feet. "Someone will be along soon to tend to her." She looked around at the rest of the bodies on the ground. "And the rest of them."

"Who was she?" Lainey asked, her lower lip trembling.

"Someone who believed in this cause. Believed in you," Zia answered. "Come on, there's a lot to do."

Lainey swiped at the tears that were streaking down her cheeks and followed Zia.

"We made the rounds, moved most of the wounded into the big house. I'm calling an emergency council meeting to assess the losses. I need you there," Zia called to Lainey, then she paused, throwing a look my way as well. "You, too, Traitor. It's time to pay the piper."

I fell into step beside Lainey and reached for her hand. Though my eyes could see her living and breathing, I still craved more proof. I needed to touch her, to feel her skin against mine. She didn't object when I entwined my fingers with hers, only squeezed my hand as if she, too, needed reassurance. I wasn't stupid enough to think this changed things between us, that all the old wounds had healed. I still had so much to atone for. But Lainey was alive and next to me. For now, it was enough.

The big house was slightly scorched, and several of the windows had blown out, but for the most part, the house was standing, having sustained far less damage than the outer buildings.

Zia led us inside to the dining room. There was a large

table in the center of the room. Most of the Supernaturals sitting there were unfamiliar to me, but I supposed they were the remaining members of the council. Serena was standing next to the large windows, looking weary and pale but otherwise unharmed. Lainey pulled her hand out of mine and ran over to her, throwing her arms around her.

Without the anchor of her hand, I floated around the room, not sure whether to sit or stand.

The council members murmured to each other, their concerned voices getting louder with each passing minute. Zia stood next to Teddy, whose serious expression matched Zia's as she clapped her hands, drawing everyone's attention.

"Tonight's attack was a clear and orchestrated move by the Master." Zia ground her teeth on the word. "Julian is still checking the inventory, but most of our supplies and weaponry were lost with the outer buildings and storerooms. We expected something like this might be coming, but we were more unprepared than we'd hoped." She looked down at her shoes for a second, drawing in a slow breath. "Many of our people are dead, even more injured."

"I don't understand," a stocky-looking Skipper said, slamming a hand down on the table. "How did they make it inside the wards?"

Everyone began talking at once, echoing the frustration. Zia held up a hand, tying to quell their conversation, but the din grew louder.

I stepped forward. "They made it inside because of me."

"Traitor!" someone shouted.

"Oathbreaker!" another voice chimed in, as nearly every single eye in the room glared at me.

I ignored them, though I couldn't bring myself to meet Lainey's eye as I told them what I'd told Zia, how I had helped the Master's forces get through the wards. "I had no choice. If I didn't give the Master something of value, he would have made me pay for wasting his time."

"So you're not only a traitor, you're a coward!" the Skipper shouted. "You sacrificed us all to save your own skin."

Coward. The word made my blood boil. I was many things, but a coward I was not.

"I did what needed to be done," I growled. "If I were dead, it would be impossible to pass along the information that the Hetaeria needs to win this war."

That got their attention. Everyone at the table quieted, and Zia leaned forward. "So, tell us, then. What information did you willingly sacrifice so many lives for?"

The words were salt in the wound, but I stood stiffly, willing my face into a casual mask of indifference. I would not let them see how the words affected me, what they would cost me later. Sometimes, the greatest wounds are the ones we inflict upon ourselves.

"The Master is gathering his forces," I said, pressing on. "With the men who return from tonight's attack, he'll be able to march his forces right across the boundary lines. He'll be here in three days' time."

Several of the council members gasped, and others leaned back in their chairs, while Zia visibly paled.

"His numbers are large, and his goal is annihilation. There will be no cease-fires, no surrenders, and no mercy." I steadied myself with a breath before continuing. "But the Master is ill. The more dark magic he uses, the greater toll it takes on him. I already told you he's Blood Reaping to counter the effects, but it's not working as well as it once was." I recounted how sickly and wan he'd seemed, how he had coughed up the black phlegm. "He's having to Reap more blood more frequently."

I zeroed in on Zia. "As you already know, Blood Reaping requires a sacrifice from a willing participant. What you don't know is that a willing donor is not where the power of the Reaping lies. There's a ritual that's performed beforehand, a ritual that ties the donor's life force to the blood itself. The donor is not merely giving blood, but years of his or her life."

"That's blasphemy," Serena whispered. "Anyone who used such magic would be cursed."

"The Master clearly doesn't care," I answered. "Once a donor's life force is completely drained, the donor dies. The Master has already drained one of his Alium," I said, recalling how they'd been less in number. "And I heard another Alium say his life force was nearly depleted. The Master is literally sucking the life out of his most devout followers."

The room was still.

"There's more," I continued. "And this is the important part. I overheard the Master telling the Alium that he needs to complete the ritual again before the battle, as not to show weakness, and I figured it out. It means that the Blood

Reaping only works on people he's completed the ritual with. He can't just Reap blood from anyone. If we take out the Alium during the battle, he won't be able to Reap, and—"

"And he won't be able to replenish his strength," Zia said, catching on. "He'll be at his weakest, drained of magic and of physical strength." She turned to Lainey. "That will be the moment to strike. To move in."

The council began to murmur again, the tenor of the air more charged this time.

There was one person who did not seem to be relishing in this news.

Lainey stood. "There's a small problem with that plan," she said, eyeing Teddy, who nodded at her. "I made a discovery of my own today. Before the attack, Teddy and I were working on the siphoning spell, trying to find a way for me to hone it without falling prey to the side effects of the dark magic."

She sighed. "Long story short, I have to use a conduit, something to help me channel the energy."

"A conduit?" one of the council members finally said. "Those are easy enough to find and use."

"No," Lainey said. "For a spell of this magnitude, an ordinary conduit won't work . . . It has to be a person."

"And there's more," Lainey said, catching my eye for the briefest of seconds before looking down at her feet. "It has to be someone I have a strong emotional connection with. Without that, using the spell could drain me of all my power . . . or it could kill me."

The words slammed into my chest as the image of the

dead body lying in the snow flashed in my mind. The ache still resonating in my chest flared up at the sight. I hissed as a new wave of pain seared through me.

Everyone in the room was talking, but I heard little of their conversations as I stepped in front of Lainey. She was the only one in the room. "I'll do it."

"Ty, no—"

"I'll do it."

"You have to understand what you're volunteering for," Lainey said, her brows furrowed. "The spell could kill us both."

"I thought I lost you tonight. I'll do whatever it takes to make sure that doesn't happen, no matter what it does to me."

Lainey's eyes searched mine, so full of questions.

"Ty, I don't know . . . I . . ."

"Please," I reached to brush a finger across her cheek. "I don't know if I can ever make up for everything I've done to you, how I've hurt you . . . but I can do this. Let me do this."

A single tear rolled down her cheek; I wiped it away. *My hands, my blade, my life . . . my heart.* It was all so clear now. I wasn't a good guy, far from it, but I could do this. For her. Whether she succeeded in destroying the Master or not, I wanted to be by her side—even if it meant my own life would be forfeited.

She reached for my hand, interlocking her fingers with mine, and squeezed. "Okay."

"Taking out the Alium is my responsibility," I faced Zia. "It won't make up for the Hetaerian blood on my hands, but I'll spill every drop of theirs to make sure the Master can't Reap."

"Make sure that you do," Zia said, her voice breaking through the stillness of the room. "Now, we just have to figure out the rest of the plans."

"Are we retreating?" the Skipper asked.

"We can't just leave," another argued. "What of the wounded? What of the dead? There are rites to perform."

Teddy's voice was soft. "It doesn't matter where you go. The Master will follow you."

"She's right," Zia said. "At least here, we know the lay of the land. It will be easier to defend ourselves. The Master may know exactly where to find us, but we have the advantage of knowing the area and all its secrets. I vote we stay here."

The rest of the council members voiced their agreement.

"Good," Zia said. "It's settled. Tonight, we rest. Attend to our wounded. Bury our dead. In the morning, we prepare for war."

The room slowly emptied. I hung back awkwardly, unsure of my place as everyone else filed out.

Eventually, only Lainey and I were left in the room.

"Come on," she said, heading for the door. She led me up the stairs and down a hallway, through a door.

I sucked in a breath, realizing we were standing in her room.

"I know you were sleeping in the barn before, but . . ." She trailed off, looking everywhere but at me. "I don't want to be alone tonight," she said, a shyness in her voice.

"What about Maggie?" I asked, realizing I hadn't seen her.

"Maggie's not here right now." Lainey let out a soft sigh. "Will you stay with me?"

"Yeah," I said, my voice hoarse. I cleared it. "Yeah, sure."

She smiled. "Thank you. I'm going to go clean up a bit." She walked to the door of the adjoining bathroom. "There's another bathroom just down the hall if you want to do the same."

In the hall bathroom, I peeled off my grimy clothes. In the heat of the shower, I let my guard down, allowing myself to feel everything I was fighting so hard to keep back. The water washed away all the mire from my skin, and when I felt more in control of myself, I turned the water off and stepped out.

There was a basket of disposable toothbrushes, so I made quick work scrubbing my teeth clean. I wrapped a thick, fluffy towel around my waist; I didn't have a change of clothes, but at least I was clean.

There was a knock on the door. "I thought you might need these," Lainey's voice came through the other side. "Zia keeps extras around the house just in case."

I opened the door. There was a stack of clean clothes in her hands, but it wasn't the clothes that caught my eye. Lainey's cheeks were rosy from the heat of her own shower. Her long hair was wet and curled around her face as droplets of water fell, leaving spots on her off-the-shoulder sweatshirt.

"Thanks," I said, heat coloring my cheeks as I reached for the bundle of clothes.

I threw on the T-shirt and loose pair of sweatpants and walked back toward her room.

Lainey was sitting on her bed, knees pulled up to her chest, waiting for me. "Hey," I said, shoving my hands in my pockets.

She smiled. "Hi."

"How's your face?" I asked, reaching out a finger to tilt her chin up so I could see her injury better. The right side of her face was still swollen and already turning various shades of purple and black.

"It hurts," she said, "but I'll be okay."

"What exactly happened?"

She shrugged. "I head-butted a Nixie."

The words caught me off guard. "What?"

"It always works in the movies," she said, chuckling.

I let out a laugh of my own. "Such a badass."

She grinned. "I know." She ran a finger across the gash above my eyebrow. "What about you?"

"I'm okay. Couple of scratches, a few bumps and bruises, nothing serious."

"Good," Lainey said, yawning. "I'm glad you're okay." She squeezed my hand and fell back on her pillow. Her eyes were already closing.

Reaching for a blanket at the foot of her bed, I unfolded it and draped it across her. Then I slowly lowered myself down beside her, trying not to groan out loud at how soft the mattress felt to my weary and exhausted body. I left several inches between us, not wanting to make her uncomfortable. There was still so much we hadn't said.

After a few seconds, Lainey rolled over and curled up right next to me, her head on my shoulder. There was no hesitation in her face, no worry or expectation. I let out a deep, slow breath.

Taking her cue, I shoved all the anxious thoughts running through my mind away and focused on the singular desire to wrap my arms around the girl I thought I'd lost and hold her through the night.

"Goodnight, Ty," she murmured, snuggling even closer into my side.

I shifted so that her head was pillowed on my chest and wrapped both arms around her. Only then did all the thoughts in my head still.

For the first time in a long while, I felt a whisper of peace.

"Night, Lainey."

I closed my eyes and let the gentle rise and fall of her body against mine lull me to sleep.

CHAPTER TWENTY-SIX

LAINEY

The sun was already streaming through the window, casting its golden fingers on my pillow when I finally decided it was time to get out of bed and face the day. The puffy white clouds and bright, cheerful light were a stark contrast to what I expected to see, as if the universe were mocking us. The farm was about to become a battleground again. Dark skies and thunderclouds seemed much more appropriate.

I rolled over with a groan and pulled the extra pillow closer, burying my face in the soft fabric. A clean, woodsy scent with a hint of spearmint flooded my nostrils; I inhaled deeply. *Ty's scent.* Warmth rose up my neck and flooded my cheeks. We hadn't really talked since the attack, but for the past two nights, I'd fallen asleep with his arms around me. There was so much still hanging over our heads, so many things we needed to talk about, but when we were lying together in the dark with only the soundtrack of our own heartbeats, it was easy to ignore everything else and just listen to the music.

I picked up my phone and pressed Maggie's picture from the list of favorites. *Hi, this is Maggie! I'm not here right now, but if you'll leave me a message, I'll make like Barry Gordon and get back with you in a flash!* I smiled a little at the chipper tone of her voicemail, but there was also a tug in my chest. It was safer for her to be gone—though I could probably argue that a human waltzing into the home base of the Shifter faction was just as dangerous as being here on the farm—but that didn't stop me from wishing she were next to me, throwing out a bunch of comic-book references I didn't understand. I missed her, and today of all days, I needed my best friend.

Sighing, I tossed back the covers and stood up, yelping a little at the stiffness in my neck and shoulders. All the magical drills I'd been practicing with Teddy were taking a toll, those and the farm cleanup. We'd been working nonstop to prepare for what was coming. After throwing on a pair of warm clothes and sturdy boots, and a quick brush of my teeth, I headed downstairs and outside.

The farm looked completely different than it had forty-eight hours ago. The buildings that had been destroyed by the warlock's fire had been demolished. Any lumber that was salvaged had been used to erect large battlement-like structures, strategically placed in a horseshoe pattern surrounding the main house. These towers were designed to mimic real trees, with long, sturdy arms branching from the base. The footholds would give an advantage over those on the ground. Inside, the towers were stocked with medical kits, food, and weaponry. There were even several hidden burrows in case someone needed to hide quickly.

The Sprites and Nymphs had been toiling over the towers, using their elemental magic to ensure the ground underneath was strong, a foundation of stone and hard-packed dirt. They'd also inlaid special saplings in the soil beside the towers, and tall trees had grown overnight, twisting toward and towering over the structures. Their branches were full of enchanted leaves—another odd juxtaposition against the snowy landscape.

The flat expanse of land in front of the structures was rigged with Faerie mines—a messy tactic, but necessary. The pastures behind the house had also been left open with a clear path for the hills if things went badly—a contingency plan we hadn't wanted to make.

The farm no longer looked like a farm at all, but a fortress bordered by a large wooded area. "You're no Helm's Deep," I murmured as I stared at the towers, "but I guess you'll do." I chuckled a little, thinking Maggie would've been proud of my joke. It was better to laugh than to let the fear coiling in my gut capture me in its greedy little fingers, ready to suffocate me.

Zia and Serena stood near the closest tower, surveying our homegrown forest.

"Think it will really work?" I asked, stepping up between them.

"It has to," Zia said. "With our low numbers, we can't hope to beat the Master's forces by strength alone. We simply have to outsmart them. Most in his service are either Supernaturals who have been forced to his side or those whose loyalty has been purchased. Once the war begins and people are dying, that loyalty will be tested."

"By us," I confirmed.

"Exactly. Once we draw them into the trees, we have the advantage. We confuse them. We make it difficult to find us. We make them think our numbers are far larger than they expected. We move from the towers and among the trees like ghosts, while they stumble around blindly."

"And we pick them off one by one," I said. We'd gone over the plan dozens of times before, but I think both Zia and I needed to hear it aloud one more time.

"In theory," Zia said. "But if we have tricks up our sleeves, it would be stupid to think the Master doesn't have some too. That's what worries me the most."

I turned to Serena. She was wringing her hands beside me, but her cheeks had more color than I'd seen in weeks. She'd cried when I'd given her Gareth's message, but she had also smiled—and it was then that I knew she was going to be okay. Her blue lace agate medallion rested at its usual spot against her heart, and the peasant top she wore under her thick wool coat made me smile. We still had healing to do, she and I, but we were mending. Even in the face of war and possible death, it was nice to see.

"Any luck?" I asked her. She, along with the other Seers, had been trying to See the outcome of the battle.

She shook her head. "No, everything is so unclear. With so many possible outcomes, it is difficult to See what is true and what is merely a projection of what could be."

I recalled Gareth telling me how subjective her Sight could be, how a simple action or decision could alter the course of fate.

"It's okay," I said, reaching over to hug her. "We're going to beat him. No matter what the universe says. But, not gonna lie, I wouldn't mind the confirmation that some allies were on their way."

She gave me a grim smile but returned my hug. "That makes two of us."

"Is there anything else that needs to be done?"

Zia was scanning the horizon, meticulously looking over each inch of the farm as though she were checking for a chink in a piece of chainmail. "Now we wait. Julian and the other Skippers are taking the last of the wounded to the designated safe spot. Once they return, we should get ready. I don't think it will be long now. The Master won't wait for the cover of darkness. He's too confident he'll win."

"Okay," I said. "I'm going to head to Teddy's one last time, but I'll spread the word."

Zia pressed her lips together and huffed. "See if you can't reason with her while you're there."

"She's still refusing to fight?"

"She is."

I wasn't surprised, given what Teddy had told me the night of the attack, but I had hoped seeing the destruction of the farm would change her mind.

"My mother will do what she wills." Zia's stony face softened slightly. "She won't listen to me, but maybe you can talk some sense into her."

"I'll try."

I maneuvered through the newly grown trees to where Teddy's cabin stood, now nearly hidden by a thicket of tall, overgrown bushes. The building had sustained minor damage during the attack but had been easily repaired. Teddy stood in her kitchen, preparing vials of various colorful liquids.

"Amplifiers," she explained when she saw me. "They amplify the drinker's power for a few hours. Not a particularly powerful batch, but it's the best I could do in the short amount of time. A good amplifier takes weeks to mature." There was something in her face, a nervous energy.

"I just spoke with Zia."

"And how is my daughter? Ready for battle, I presume?" She busied herself with the vials, not meeting my eye.

"She is. We all are, I guess, whether we want to be or not." I walked closer. "What about you? Will you fight with us?"

"You already know the answer to that."

"Teddy, I know you think there's some goodness left in him or something, but there isn't. We need your help. You're a powerful witch, and there aren't that many of us left. The Hetaeria needs you. Zia needs you . . . *I* need you."

Teddy's face was sad as she reached out to cup my cheek. "You don't need me. We've gone over everything, and we've trained to the best of my ability. You're ready."

"But—"

"I'm sorry," she said, cutting me off. "I won't fight against him. He is my son."

"That may be true," I said, grinding my teeth, "but he's a monster."

"We are all many things," Teddy said, her eyes pleading. "But does that mean that we don't deserve a chance at redemption?"

"He has killed so many. He killed my mom, my uncle. He deserves nothing but a hole in the ground," I said, hot tears welling up in my eyes. "And even that is far better than he deserves."

She didn't argue, only offered me the same sad smile.

Suddenly, it was too warm in the room. Turning on my heel, I stalked back out the way I came. I didn't realize how frustrated I was until hot tears rolled down my cheeks. I headed back toward the main house, blind to everything but my own anger until a hand wrapped around my wrist, yanking me to a stop.

Ty's face was red, and his hair was slick with sweat and curling around his ears. A long broadsword was secured on his back. Several other knives and daggers were strapped to various other places on his body—two at his hips and one just below his right knee. He'd clearly just come from the makeshift smith we'd set up on the far edge of the property. The Fae had been working around the clock to forge as many weapons as possible. "Hey, I was just coming to find you. Are you okay?"

"Yeah," I said, wiping my face. "Just . . ." I trailed off, not wanting to make any excuses. "I'm okay."

Ty nodded, knowing not to press the matter. "I have something for you." He drew a scabbard out from his back pocket. I recognized it immediately. "I hope you don't mind," he said, his cheek lifted in a half smile. "I found it in your room. It was all crusted over with dried Nixie blood. I had one of the Fae clean and sharpen it for you. Figured it might come in handy today."

I pulled the dagger out of its sheath and admired the shine of the bronze blade, running my finger across the careful etching of greenery and daisies. Gareth's handiwork.

"Thank you," I said, strapping the dagger around my waist, grateful to have a piece of Gareth with me.

Ty reached out, lightly running a thumb across my cheek. "I know you can take care of yourself, but I made an oath to you, and I intend to keep it. No matter what happens today, I'll be by your side."

"I know," I said, warmth flooding my cheeks. "Are you afraid to face him?"

"No," Ty shook his head. "I finally know my place in all of this. It's next to you, not him."

I wasn't sure what to say, so instead of speaking, I stepped up on my tiptoes and pressed my mouth against his.

But the moment our lips brushed, a loud alarm began to blare.

"The boundary wards," I said. "He's breeched them. It's happening. *Now.*"

Ty gripped my hand, pulling me through the trees. "We should get into position."

We ran together, up to the big house. People swarmed in all directions—some toward the towers, some to the big house, the barn, and various other positions around the farm—while Zia barked orders from the porch.

"Remember!" she shouted. "Stick to the plan!"

Another thunderous boom echoed across the trees—it was the sound of the wards collapsing.

Ty and I dashed up the tallest westernmost tower, scrambling into position. I stood on the landing at the very top, a place that allowed me to see a panoramic view of the farm. Ty planted himself next to me, his face lined with focus.

I heard the first line advancing before I saw them, a blurred line of black dots heading straight for the island.

As the image cleared, I realized it was not a legion of people that raced toward us—it was animals. The Master's Lycan and Shifter forces bore down on us. The Lycans were, of course, in their wolf forms, but the Shifters were a menagerie of animals that I'd only ever seen in zoos and in movies. Solid black leopards, striped tigers, black and brown bears, mountain lions, and even a rhino raced forward with its horn down.

I was horror-stricken as our own line of Shifters and Lycans made their way out to meet them, also in animal form. There were so few of them compared to the legion of creatures that raced forward. As the two dark lines merged, the sounds of impact were so loud, I winced, covering my ears to the chorus of snarling and howling that filled the air.

It was the signal the rest of the Master's forces were waiting for. They raced over the open land with battle cries on their lips. Witches and warlocks whose magic rippled around them as light and shadow, colorful streaks and balls of energy and fire already slicing through the air. Faeries wielding sharp, curved blades and other weaponry. Skippers Skipping back and forth across the battle lines. Nixies, Sprites, and Nymphs bending the elements to their will.

All coming right for us.

The blood drained from my face.

Just as I felt the fingers of fear wrap around my throat, I saw the Master. He sat atop a skeletal horse the color of night, his shadows swirling around him like a cape. Two figures wearing long robes stood next to him on the ground, their faces expressionless.

"Is that the Alium?" I asked.

"Yes," Ty said, following my gaze. "I take them out, and the Master won't be able to Blood Reap."

"Then that's your target," I responded, never taking my eyes off my own. Inside, my magic—both mine and the

Grimoire's—writhed and squirmed, anxious to be unleashed. I had to be careful not to wear myself out, but I couldn't help but let a sharp streak of electric-green lightning streak across the sky. The resounding crack of thunder made me smile.

I'm coming for you.

Down below, the Shifters and the Lycans battled on. Bodies were dropping to the ground, but I had no way of knowing what side they belonged to.

Two towers over, I caught sight of a flying wisp of Zia's red hair as she popped up from one of the footholds. "Wait for my signal!" she shouted.

The swarm of Supernaturals running toward us was getting closer.

"Now!" Zia yelled, and the earth responded.

The mines buried in the ground exploded; colored flames, debris, and bodies went flying into the air. As planned, the Master's forces had to dodge the explosions, driving them closer to the trees—exactly where we wanted them.

The first few breeched the tree line, and the fighting began almost immediately. I heard a loud voice booming in the darkness— Zia had her hands raised, and the sky began to darken as if night had fallen.

I smirked at the sound of confusion from the enemy force below. They outnumbered us, but we had the element of surprise, and we weren't going to waste it. The rest of the Master's forces poured into the woods, but we were ready and waiting, ghosts in the trees, just as Zia said.

I raised my hands, green lightning at the ready. Beside me, Ty gripped the hilt of his sword, a half smile on his lips.

We fought for hours or maybe a handful of minutes. It was hard to tell. Time was suspended, every second that passed measured in volts of electricity, splatters of blood, and the clash of steel and death.

"*Ventius Ictuum*!" I shouted when a Skipper—one of the Master's—landed on the foothold, swiping at me with a dagger. My gust of wind shot into his chest, knocking him backward onto the ground. Beside me, Ty was squaring off with a green-eyed Faerie with a double-headed axe. The Faerie lunged forward, swinging the axe, but Ty darted out of the way, striking him on the back with his own blade. The momentum sent the Fae flying off the tower with a wail. I stepped backward, nearly tripping over the body of a Nymph with long lavender hair. There was a long knife embedded in her gut, her eyes open but unseeing. I'd never spoken to her, but had seen her around the farm. I didn't even know her name.

Bile rose in my throat, and I coughed, leaning over the landing in case I threw up. But as I looked over the edge, I blanched instead. Those guarding the base of the tower were lying dead on the ground, and over twenty of our enemies were climbing the structure toward us. The Master's forces appeared to have figured out exactly where the ghosts were hiding, and the towers and the trees were thick with hands moving over feet. A quick glance at the other towers showed me they were swarmed as well. In seconds, the towers would be taken. Any advantage they had given us was long gone. We had no choice but to make our stand on the ground.

"Ty!" I shouted, pointing over the side. "We have to go down. There's too many of them."

But before he could respond, the Master's men began to retreat, climbing back down the tower and running through the trees, as if responding to a signal I'd neither seen nor heard.

"What's going on?" I asked, turning to Ty.

"I don't know."

From my position on the landing, I could still see the Master on his horse. He had a hand raised. "He's called them back," I said, zeroing in on the smug expression on his face. "Why would he do that?"

"Whatever the reason, it's not good," Ty grunted, out of breath.

We watched as the Master raised both hands and began speaking. I didn't have to hear the words to know it was an incantation he was chanting.

"He's using magic," Ty said, recognizing it as well.

"Good, that's what we want. The more he uses, the weaker he'll become." The words, intended to sound sure and confident, come out breathy. Ty didn't respond.

The Master's forces had passed through the trees and were stopped on the open land of the island. But for what? What were they waiting for?

Seconds later, our homemade forest rippled with energy, a force so strong it knocked me to my knees. I slammed a palm against my chest to ease the pressure, struggling to breathe under the weight of the magic. Ty was next to me, gasping. Then the pressure lifted. I looked around, but everything looked the same.

Except the body of the dead Faerie.

She was moving.

CHAPTER
TWENTY-SEVEN

LAINEY

I squeaked, the sound a mixture of horror and surprise, as the dead Faerie sat up, the lavender tendrils of her hair whipping around her face. Her eyes were hazy from death, but they focused on me. The knife that had ended her life was still buried to the hilt in her abdomen. She made no move to remove it, but instead flashed a smile at us that made the hair on my neck stand straight up.

Then the smile twisted into a feral snarl, and the girl lunged at me, teeth bared. I was too stunned to move; Ty thrust his sword forward, and the squelching sound it made when it connected with her body was too much. This time, I did vomit over the side of the landing. When I turned back, the Faerie was lying on the ground, her eyes closed this time.

Everything was clear. "He's animating the dead," I choked

out, still tasting acid on my tongue. "Just like he did with Gareth." The realization was worse than any physical blow.

Ty's face was pale. "Why would he do that? He already has us in number."

I remembered the cold, unfeeling glare on Gareth's face. "To break us."

The forest came alive with sound, members of the Hetaeria crying out as their own comrades rose up from where they'd fallen and began to fight their own people with an intensity stronger than the living.

"He's using our own people to wipe us out while he just sits there and enjoys the show." The screams of the Hetaeria grew louder. I shuddered, the tenor of pain in the voices entirely familiar to me. "We have to go now—we have to get to the Master and stop him."

Ty shook his head. "We'll never get there alive. His entire army is just sitting there."

"We have to try." Our carefully thought-out strategy was falling apart. We climbed down from the tower, dodging through the fighting as we raced over to the main house. Birdie and a few of the other horses had been cobbled there, part of the contingency plan. They were skittish and stamping around when we got close. "Hey, girl," I said, reaching for her. Her nostrils were flaring, but she calmed under my touch. "I need you to take me—"

Birdie's ears shot straight up, and she neighed loudly, reacting to something I couldn't see or hear.

But I felt it. The ground was rumbling with vibration.

Something was coming up fast from behind the farm-house. "Oh shit," I said. Was it possible the Master had split his forces, ordered them to attack us from behind?

Beside me, Ty's face was hard, and he gripped the hilt of his sword tighter, as though he had arrived at the same realization.

I heard them seconds before they came racing out from behind the house—hundreds of animals, teeth bared and snarling, all racing for the trees. The horses went wild, rearing up and whinnying. I gripped Birdie's reins, but she ripped them from my hands.

Just when my heart nearly stopped beating in my chest, the most glorious sight I've ever seen came whipping around the other side of the house.

It was Oliver's truck.

The windows were rolled down, and "Carry on My Wayward Son" was blasting through the speakers.

Driving the truck, her curls flying, was Maggie.

"Go, go, go!" she shouted, throwing the truck into park. The back of the truck was filled with people—I recognized Oliver, Ajay, Brandon, and Lyra, the leaders of the factions who had refused to help us. They leapt out of the back, racing into the fight.

"Maggie!" I yelled, but she didn't hear me. When the truck had emptied, she whipped it in reverse, heading back the way she came.

Beside me, Ty was whooping. "Now we've got ourselves a fair fight," he beamed, his eyes sparkling.

I wasn't so convinced.

A wave of fighting Supernaturals poured from the tree line and surged toward us in a clash of steel and magic. I lost sight of Ty in the throng, narrowly avoiding a fireball launched from an enemy Nymph. Grabbing Birdie's reigns again, I threw myself up onto the saddle, guiding her into a gallop. We raced through the trees, dodging the pockets of fighting. I needed a vantage point.

With our allies' help, the Master's dead army was taken care of in minutes. The Master's face was screwed up in a rage. Yelling, he gave the signal, and his army ran back through the trees. The forest and the open battlefield were a chaotic mass of bodies, animals, and magic flying around each other.

There was a booming sound, almost like thunder. The Master had dismounted his horse, and he was gliding toward the fighting, his shadows growing behind him. With a yell, he thrust out his hand. The shadows shot forward into the mass of bodies, a swirl of power that eviscerated anything in its path. Screams filled the air as the Master attacked, dozens of our fighters lost with a single wave of his hand.

"No, no, no!" I didn't even remember what the plan was anymore. Everything had fallen apart. Bodies flew through the air as the Master unleashed his shadows without mercy.

Do something! the voice in my head screamed. Our allies were dying. The Hetaeria was dying. Nothing could stand against the Master and his shadows.

Nothing but me.

I veered right, Birdie's strong legs swiftly moving us

up a small hill, past the bulk of the fighting and closer to the boundary line. I had to draw him away from the farm, away from the people I cared about. It wouldn't matter if the Master got his hands on the siphoning spell if we were all dead. I reached for Ty though our connection, sending him a mental picture of my location. *I need you! We have to end this now!*

Gasping for breath, I felt for my magic. It rushed through me as I held up my hands. Flames, electric green, swirled around Birdie and me until I was a living ball of fire. I raced across the battlefield, my flames acting as both a protectant and a beacon. *Come on, you bastard. Come get me.*

At the top of the hill, I pulled Birdie to a stop, releasing the magic around me. I leapt to the ground and gave Birdie a swift swat on the rump, sending her away from the danger. The fighting still raged, but the shadows had diminished, retreating back behind the Master, who was casually strolling toward me.

He looked older and more frayed than he had the night of the Gathering. His cold gray eyes were trained on my face, malice swirling inside them. Several feet away, two robed figures glided behind him with bowed heads. The Alium.

I stood my ground, the whispers of my ancestors in my ears. They were with me, ready to fight with me.

"Lainey DuCarmont," the Master drawled, stepping in front of me. "We meet again." He swept an arm out, indicating the fighting. "Your darling little alliance has put up quite a fight. I'm impressed, really I am." He leaned in. "But you can't be stupid enough to think you can win. I'm the most powerful warlock there is. Surrender, and I'll spare your life."

"If you're so powerful, why do you need this?" With a quick flick of my wrist, I conjured a worn book. A decoy, of course.

The smirk on the Master's face evaporated. "You will return what is mine, girl."

A laugh bubbled in my throat. "Not gonna happen. You'll never get what you want."

The Master trembled with the effort of keeping his face neutral. He blinked, and one of the shadows lurched forward, snatching the book from my hand.

I yelped, nearly losing my footing, while the Master laughed, curling his fingers around the book. "Stupid little Keeper, I don't need you," he said, cracking open the cover. "I—" He stopped, his eyes frantically scanning the pages.

With a scream of rage, he threw the book down on the ground. The pages, all blank, whipped in the wind.

"What is this?"

"It's a book," I said, mocking him. "Oh, did you think that was actually the Grimoire? And you're calling me stupid?"

The Master glared. "Produce the Grimoire immediately, or I will wipe you and everyone you love from this stinking farm."

"You want the Grimoire? You got it," I said, raising a hand, my magic ready. A jet of green light shot from my palm. The force of it sent him flying backward, and he landed in a heap of limbs and shadow. He was shaking, not from rage or injury—but from laughter. "Oh, you want to play, do you? Fine. But I warn you, girl, I do *not* like playing games."

With a high shriek, the Master lunged at me, his shadows erupting with a blast. They hurtled toward me like cannon fire.

I let out a wild yell as the power of the Grimoire rose up like a rushing wind. Crackling green energy, tangible and rippling like a wave, erupted from within me, swirling around my head and charging the shadows.

I gasped at the pull of magic, the struggle to maintain it.

I could already feel exhaustion rushing over me. I ground my teeth, determined to hold the connection. *If it's this hard for me, then it has to be draining him as well.*

Beads of sweat formed in my hairline and dripped into my eyes.

It was hard to see the Master through the swirling vortex of our power, but his forehead was crunched in concentration.

"Hang in there, kid. We're with you." The sound of Gareth's voice in my ear nearly made me stagger backward. I sucked down a breath as my family's strength blended with mine.

"You've got this," Josephine whispered in my ear. *"Just keep going."*

"Just hold your ground."

I dug my heels into the dirt, the faces of everyone I cared about flashing before my eyes. My arms trembled under the strain, my body's strength dwindling fast. I cried out, but my voice carried only so far before it was lost in the swirl of energy.

The Master's mouth was open in a soundless scream.

Then, with a boom like a cannon, our magic burst apart, both light and shadow flying in all directions.

The wave of energy expanded, knocking into the Master and me.

I was thrown high into the air, my stomach twisting, and then I was free falling.

I didn't even have time to scream as the ground rushed up to meet me.

CHAPTER TWENTY-EIGHT

TY

I'd lost Lainey. I ran through the trees, searching, but the fighting had intensified. Every step I took, I had to fight to take the next. Slashing down with my sword, using my body to push through the swarm, all the while fighting the panic that rose in my throat—the image of Lainey's prostrate body in the snow was all I could see. *She's not dead*, I reasoned with myself. I could feel her through our bond, but that didn't stop the image from consuming my thoughts. I fought harder. Step, slash. Step, swing. Step, punch. *Keep going.*

Pushing through the tree line and out into the open space of the battlefield, I sucked down a mouthful of air. My lungs burned, and my chest heaved from exertion. The faction allies had evened the playing field in terms of numbers, but looking at the fighting, it was difficult to discern who was winning.

Then something tugged at me, a sense of determination so fierce it almost knocked me over. *Lainey.*

"I need you! We have to end this now!" Her voice was loud and clear through our connection.

Shoving my way through the fighting, my sword swinging at anything that got in my way, I searched for her.

She was standing atop a small hill to the east of the fighting. The Master stood facing her, his shadows billowing around him.

I ran toward her, willing my legs to carry me faster.

They were talking to each other, but the conversation looked anything but casual. I could see from the strong set of Lainey's shoulders and the look on the Master's face that she was baiting him. I ran faster.

Then, like lightning, the Master lunged forward, his shadows hurtling toward Lainey. She responded with magic of her own, a bubble of crackling green energy that seemed to explode out of her skin, expanding as it pushed toward the shadows. The two sources of magic collided, swirling around together like a tornado. Lainey, and even the Master, seemed so small in its wake.

Then, like one of the Faerie mines, the vortex of magic exploded. The shockwave of energy slammed into my chest, knocking me, everyone, and everything within a five-mile radius down to the ground. When I got up, Lainey was falling from the sky.

"Lainey!" I screamed, pushing myself as hard as I could.

She hit the ground with a thump and lay unmoving. The Master was also on the ground.

"Lainey?" I touched her shoulder, afraid to do more if she were seriously injured. She groaned, and the sound sent an electric shock right to my heart. She was alive.

"Are you okay?" I asked, bending over her. "Can you move?"

"Ugh," she moaned. "Everything hurts."

Out of the corner of my eyes, I saw the Alium hurrying over to the Master, who was rolling around on the ground in clear discomfort. "Master," one of them said, pulling a curved dagger—the one I had seen them use before—out of his robes. He raised his hand, ready to slice open his palm, but I reacted faster. Pulling my sword from its sheath, I barreled across the small distance between us and stood directly between the Alium and the Master.

"Marek," the Master barked behind me. He'd managed to sit up, but he was pale. Whatever magical tango he'd just performed with Lainey had taken its toll. "Kill the girl!" he ordered. His shadows clung to him, but they were barely wisps of wind, translucent and grainy. He was weak. "Kill her!"

"No," I said, eyeing the Alium and daring them to come forward. The one closest to the Master darted forward in an attempt to reach him. With a roaring deep in my chest, I swung, the power of my sword knocking into him, slicing right through him. He fell to the ground in a heap.

Furious, the Master yelled, "No!" and struggled to his feet, energy crackling around him, regenerating.

The sickly one holding the knife looked at me with the oddest expression on his face. "Please," he mouthed and closed his eyes, not even trying to defend himself against me.

I didn't hesitate. Swinging my blade, I brought it down upon him. I swore I heard a sigh of relief as he fell to the ground. The Master's scream of rage was deafening.

The shadows whirled around me then, no longer translucent. They wrapped around my throat and lifted me off the ground. I kicked my feet, but there wasn't a foothold or leverage. I clawed at my neck, but there was nothing tangible to grab on to. I choked and gagged as my lungs fought for oxygen.

The Master stood now, roaring, as his clawed shadow fingers tightened.

Black spots appeared before my eyes. Just when I was starting to lose consciousness, the shadows released me and fell in a heap on the ground.

The Master was yowling, pulling a dagger from his shoulder. Lainey's dagger.

I turned my head. Lainey was standing behind me, still a little unsteady on her feet, but with a focused, determined look on her face. The arm that she had used to throw the dagger was still outstretched and trembling.

Fire burned in the Master's eyes, and I was already moving, even before the words of retaliation came spewing out of his mouth. With every ounce of strength I could muster, I shoved forward, leaping in front of Lainey and catching the spell directly in the chest.

It ripped through me, a sharpness that sliced down to the bone. I cried out, the razor-sharp pain nearly splitting me in half. When I hit the ground, hot liquid rolled across my skin. *Blood. My blood.* All I could do was close my eyes to the pain.

Lainey screamed my name, and I felt her hands on me, but everything else sounded distorted, seemed so very far away.

"You stay with me, Ty!" Lainey shouted, her lips near my ear. She began to whisper an incantation, her palms held over my body.

A laugh, cold and cruel, mixed with the sound. The Master.

I cried out again when my skin began to stretch, inching together to close the gaps of my wounds. Healing was nearly as painful as the initial injury, and hot tears burned my eyes as I squirmed on the ground.

"It's okay," Lainey said, her own voice thick with worry. "You're going to be okay."

The laughter grew louder, grating against my eardrums.

But then a quiet voice spoke. "That's enough."

I peeled open a heavy eyelid. Everything was fuzzy, but a figure had stepped between the Master and where I lay on the ground with Lainey bending over me.

The Master's laughter died instantly, and there was a comical look of surprise on his face. It was quickly replaced by a twisted smile. He chuckled, clapping his hands together.

"Hello, Mother."

CHAPTER TWENTY-NINE

LAINEY

Teddy looked so calm, while the Master's face was twisted into a sneer, a wild expression in his eyes.

"And to what do I owe this pleasure?" the Master drawled, holding out his hand. "Have you come to join me, Mother? After all these years?"

Teddy frowned, clasping her hands in front of her. "Emmett, I—"

The Master flinched as if she'd struck him. "Do not call me that," he growled.

"It is your name," Teddy replied softly.

"Not anymore."

The Master paced back and forth, while the shadows coiled and wrapped around him like a hundred writhing snakes. Teddy did not seem fazed or frightened. She simply stood with her back straight, a pained expression in her eyes. The conversation between them was wordless, but the more the Master paced, the easier it was to see how his mother's presence affected him.

"If you're not here to join me," he finally said, "then I suppose you're here to stop me."

"No," Teddy shook her head. "I've come only to ask your forgiveness."

A gasp escaped my lips. It was clearly not what the Master had expected, either—his eyes widened at her words.

"You were just a boy when your father . . . when I . . ." She paused, swallowing audibly. "Perhaps if I had been a better mother, if I'd known how to protect you or if I had been honest with you about what kind of man Brigdon was, if I had explained—"

"It would've changed nothing," the Master ground out.

Teddy took a step forward. "I don't believe that. You were once kind . . . happy." She took another step, reaching out her hand. "Please, let me help you. I wasn't there for you, but I'm here now."

The Master's eyes were still wide. He was seething, visibly shaking with rage, but there was a tiny flicker of vulnerability in his eyes. He inched closer, but was immediately blasted backward by a shaft of gleaming scarlet light. His roar of anger echoed across the trees as Zia stepped up next to her mother.

"Brother!" she called out as he got to his feet, nostrils flaring. "Long time no see."

Whatever flash of humanity I'd seen in his eyes was gone; only the flames of hatred were left burning there.

"Don't," Teddy said, holding a restraining hand out to Zia.

"I'm sorry, Mother," Zia said, never taking her eyes off the Master. "But he's not who you think he is. He's not worth your compassion or your love. He's a murderous bastard who deserves nothing but the dirt under our feet."

The Master chuckled and pantomimed raising a glass. "You're too kind, *Sister*." He spat out the word. "Perhaps you're just jealous."

Zia lifted a shoulder. "Yeah, of course. Nothing says 'My life is awesome' quite like being a Blood Reaper. Tell me, are you feeling a little woozy?" Her eyes flicked over to where the Alium lay dead in the grass. "Ah well, bad luck, mate."

The Master snarled, clearly done talking. He raised his arm and snapped his fingers. The shadows behind him responded, manipulating into a long, sharp spear.

"No!" Teddy shouted, shoving Zia out of the way as the shadow spear careened through the air. A cry of pain tore from Teddy's lips as the tip of the spear pierced her skin. The long shaft in her abdomen poured crimson blood.

"Mother!" Zia rushed to Teddy's side, but Teddy held a hand out to hold her back. Groaning, she held a trembling hand over the shadow spear and murmured under her breath until it evaporated in a puff of smoke. She sagged a little as more blood pooled from the wound. Zia ripped a thick strip of cloth from the bottom of her T-shirt and wrapped it quickly around her mother's torso. Teddy turned to the Master, her face pale.

The Master raised his arm again, more shadow spears forming. "Oh, come now, Mother. It's not nice to show favorites."

"Please, Emmett, it's not too late," she pleaded. "Don't do this. We can start over—we can be a family again."

The Master sneered. "I have no family."

The shadow spears shot forward at a deadly speed, and I screamed. "Teddy!"

But Teddy was fast, and despite her injury, she was already murmuring under her breath. Just before they made impact, the shadow spears evaporated into smoke and mist against the shield of Teddy's magic. With a single tear rolling down her cheek, Teddy's eyes narrowed on her son. A stallion of golden fire flared to life in front of her and galloped toward the Master. With a wild cry, he thrust his arms forward, and a swirling lasso of shadow wrapped around the horse's neck.

Zia threw her arms in the air, rushing to stand next to her mother. A powerful wind whirled around them, sucking both shadow and light into a blazing ring of fire. The three of them stood locked in a game of tug-of-war.

I tore my eyes away and glanced down at Ty. He wasn't completely unconscious, but I wasn't sure what he was aware of and what he wasn't. Blood covered my hands, hot and sticky. The Master's spell had left a dozen dangerously deep gashes all over Ty's chest and abdomen. I'd used a basic healing spell to staunch the bleeding, but I wasn't sure how long it would hold. My stomach churned. If Ty wasn't strong enough to be my conduit—. *No*, I chided myself. *He's strong enough.*

He groaned then, and I sighed with relief when I saw that some of the color had returned to his cheeks. "Ty, can you hear me?"

"Lainey? What—"

"We don't have time for questions," I said, helping him up into a sitting position. I pulled him carefully to his feet, wrapping his arm around my shoulder. He staggered a little, but was able to mostly stand on his own, despite the streams of blood that still dripped from his wounds.

"Lainey!" a familiar voice shouted my name. I turned and tears immediately formed at the sight of Maggie running up the hill. Oliver, Ajay, Tao, and the other faction leaders were close behind. The fighting on the battlefield had come to a head, and torrents of people were streaming toward the boundary line, away from the farm.

"They're retreating," I said, turning to Ty. "Just like Zia said they would."

"Loyalty doesn't come from fear," he said, his head rolling slightly. "Loyalty must be earned."

When Maggie was close enough, and I was sure Ty wouldn't fall over, I slipped out from under his arm and ran to meet her, throwing my arms around her. "I'm so glad you're here. I don't know what we would've done if you hadn't shown up."

"Of course I'm here, Styles." She pulled back, grinning at me. "Sam wouldn't let Frodo go to Mt. Doom alone. I wasn't about to let you face the Master without me." Her eyes widened as she took in the maelstrom behind me. "Whoa."

"Yeah," I said, looking over at the faction leaders. "Thank you for coming."

"What do we do now?" Oliver asked, his eyes also on the fight behind me.

"Now, we finish what we started," Ty said, limping over.

Maggie whistled at the sight of him. "Damn, Pretty Face. You look worse than Deadpool with the mask off."

"It's good to see you too, Maggie," Ty said, cracking a half smile, even though the pain was still clear on his face. She winked at him.

"Well, the plan's kind of gone to hell, but I think we can still do this," I said, making eye contact with the faction leaders. "With your help."

Ajay stepped forward. "You have it. What should we do?"

I quickly reiterated the original plan and explained the use of the conduit. "We have to tire him out," I said. "He's most vulnerable when he's drained of power, and"—I looked over my shoulder where the shadows were still swirling—"we're not there yet."

Ajay grinned. "I think we can help with that." He nodded at Oliver. "Let's see what he's got." With a shimmer and a crackle, Oliver and Ajay Shifted into lions and launched into the fray with Teddy and Zia. Tao held up her hands, balls of crimson fire burning there, and then smiled at Mya, who was already calling the wind. Together, they raced forward.

Everything was a swirl of color and sound, light and dark.

My magic pumped through me, itching to be released. I took a step forward, but stopped. I was already pretty drained from my own duel with the Master. I needed to conserve whatever energy I had left for the siphoning spell.

"Don't worry, Styles," Maggie said, reading my mind. "They've got it covered."

"I know."

When the fusion of magic reached its peak, waves of energy pulsed out into the air. The ground rumbled with vibrations, and inside the vortex, the rainbow of light and shadow was growing brighter and brighter, nearly blinding us. Then, as if someone had pressed the button on the detonator of a bomb, it exploded. The pressure in the air bottomed out as a pulse of power shot into the sky—a supernova of color—before the sky blazed black and everything fell silent.

Coughing, I waved my hand in front of my face, trying to clear the hazy fog that clogged the air—the discharge of the pulse.

The Master was lying on the ground, the members of the Hetaeria scattered around him like the numbers on a clock. He was alive, but drained and weak.

Maggie and I ran toward those on the ground.

"Are they hurt?" I called to Maggie as I bent down to check Zia's pulse. It hummed underneath my fingertips.

"I don't think so!" Maggie yelled back from where she was bent over Oliver. "I think they're just stunned or something."

"Zia, can you hear me?" I tapped her cheek lightly.

Her eyes fluttered for a second as her head rolled slowly from side to side. But then she shot upright, chest heaving.

"It's okay," I said, catching her arms. "You're okay."

"Where is he?" she demanded, whipping her head back and forth. I pointed to where the Master was lying, still writhing around, but attempting to pull himself upright.

Teddy stirred from where she was lying a few paces away, though her movements were slow. I let out a breath when I saw Mya's and Tao's movements as well.

Zia looked at me. "Do it now."

A sudden burst of fear clawed at me as I realized the magnitude of the moment.

Murderer. The echo of that word was never far away, but I shook my head to silence the reverberations. *No, I'm not.*

Closing my eyes, I took a deep breath and tried to clear my mind. My magic was waiting, the energy warm and bright. Using it as a guide, I probed at the spot where the siphoning spell was kept, ignoring the dread creeping through me, the icy burn that blazed through me as I spoke the words in my mind. Already, the spell was active, squirming like a worm on a hook.

Gasping, I opened my eyes and sucked down a breath. As Ty limped over to me, his face set with determination, panic bubbled in my throat. *What if I kill him? What if this kills both of us?* His crystal blue eyes stared into mine, and the thought of never seeing them again had me gasping. *Can I really do this?*

"*Yes, you can.*" The reply came through the Praetorian bond. I hadn't even realized I was sending my feelings to him, but when he reached over and linked his hand with mine, I was grateful.

"Whatever happens," he said, out loud this time, "I'm with you."

"I know," I said, squeezing his hand tightly.

With one last breath, I stretched out my arm, holding my free palm toward the Master. "*Et Caperia Fineum.*"

My voice was loud and strong, and the magic reacted immediately. Ice shot through my veins, and I clamped my jaw shut to keep from crying out. Unnatural fingers of darkness crawled over my skin, and even though I expected it, I still gasped at the pull of that sinister energy, strong and unyielding.

The Master, thrown backward by the power of the spell, screamed as thick onyx vapor materialized from his chest— where his heart was housed.

"*Et Caperia Fineum!*" I yelled again, unleashing every ounce of energy and power I had within me. A scream erupted from my lips, and the ice gave way to fire, blazing through me and pulling the vapor—the Master's magic—toward me like a vacuum.

The Master's screams intensified, wails of both rage and pain slicing through the air.

My own voice blended with his as the spell's power rocketed through me, the cold so intense it burned like flames as thousands of ice shards seared through my veins. I was swathed in vapor now, my palm absorbing every molecule and volt of energy.

I wasn't the only one screaming. Next to me, Ty was also bellowing, his hand gripping mine, his face screwed up in agony.

The ice then gave way to a heat that licked through my body, scorching my skin. *Too hot.*

Something was wrong.

The current surging through me was too strong, the heat molten as it incinerated me from the inside out. My eyes were still open, but I saw nothing but red. My entire body convulsed, my heart no longer beating in separate distinct beats, but in one continuous hum that buzzed in my ears. My grasp on the magic was slipping. I was no longer in control.

I felt hands on my shoulders, digging in my shoulders and yanking me back and forth, but I couldn't let the spell go. I was an inferno, burning from the inside out; soon, I would be nothing but chaff for the wind to blow away.

Voices shouted, but I couldn't make out the words. Only the cacophony of screams—mine, Ty's, and the Master's—made sense. I was blind to everything but the blistering white light of power that wrapped around me, charring every inch of me. Tears rolled down my cheeks as I thought of my friends, of my family. *I'm sorry I failed you.*

Ty's hand was suddenly ripped from mine.

No! I fell to my knees, agony slicing through me. I tried to breathe, but my lungs were full of flame. *He's dead!* It was the only thing that made sense.

Until I felt a hand wrap around mine.

Instantly, a blast of cool energy shot through me, cooling and soothing the scorched and aching inches of my skin. I stopped screaming and gasped, air filling my lungs, fresh and full of life. Renewed strength flowed through me, and I opened my eyes, expecting to see Ty.

But it wasn't his hand I was holding.

It was Maggie's.

Her eyes were wide, and her entire body shook from the magic flowing through our linked hands, but she managed a small smile. A sheen of sweat covered her face, and for a second, I started to pull away, but her hand clamped down on mine.

Batman and Robin.

Sam and Frodo.

Lainey and Maggie.

Suddenly, it all made sense. Despite my feelings for Ty, my strongest emotional connection wasn't with him. It was with the person who had always had my back through thick and thin. The person who never let me down and never stopped believing in me, even when I didn't believe in myself.

It was with my best friend, with Maggie.

The power rushing through me now was warm, but not scorching—a bright flame that I could wield. Gripping Maggie's hand, I opened my mouth and shouted, "*Et Caperia Fineum!*"

A burst of energy shot outward, a gust of wind so strong it nearly knocked me over. The onyx vapor poured out of the

Master in a steady stream, rushing toward me. The Master's screams intensified the more I siphoned, morphing into a high-pitched ringing that punched through the air, clawing at my nerves and inching up my spine like sharp claws.

When the last of his magic had been absorbed, it was all over. All of the magic and power volatilized, and I sank to the ground, breathless and woozy.

Maggie knelt next to me, her chest heaving. There was so much I wanted to say, but I couldn't speak, so I squeezed her hand instead. She squeezed mine right back.

It was several minutes before anyone moved. Then, slowly, people began to rise, the air finally clearing.

Ty stood over me, his hand extended. I put my hand in his and let him pull me up. There was a look in his eyes that confused me, but before I could ask about it, there was a cry of shock a few feet away.

Tao was staring wide-eyed at the Master.

The young, powerful warlock who had haunted my nightmares for so long was not the same. A bent and crumpled old man had replaced him, his hair shining silver as he lay curled on his side in the grass.

I'd known that the lifespan of Supernaturals was long and even more so for those who dabbled in dark magic, but without magic of any kind, time had caught up with the Master. There was nothing more than a shriveled-up shell. He was no longer the Master. He was human.

"Magic *always* leaves a mark," I murmured.

The faction leaders cheered and whooped as the sky began

to clear. The sun had returned, and unlike this morning, I was grateful for the feel of its warm rays on my face. Oliver—who had pulled Maggie to her feet and had an arm wrapped protectively around her waist—and Maggie shared a smile, and even Zia looked bemused at our success.

Only two stood frozen, their expressions far from cheerful, the two people with the most to both gain and lose in this final moment.

Ty and Teddy.

Teddy was hunched over, pressing a hand to the wound in her side, tears pouring down her cheeks. Ty stood stiffly, his hands clenched into fists at his sides.

With a broken cry, Teddy collapsed to her knees. Blood poured from her wound, and she swayed back and forth.

"Mother!" Zia caught her before she fell over completely, easing her to the ground.

"Teddy!" I ran over as fast as my weary body would allow. "Is she alright?"

Zia's lower lip trembled as she smoothed the hair from Teddy's face. Tears lined her eyes. "It was dark magic," she said. "I don't think—" She broke off with a sob.

"Someone get a healer!" I shouted over my shoulder.

"It's too late for that, I'm afraid." Teddy's voice was faint. She reached a hand up to cup Zia's cheek. "Shhh, my darling. It's okay."

"It's not," Zia responded brokenly.

"There has to be something we can do." Tears of my own slipped down my cheeks.

Zia swiped at her nose. "She's lost too much blood."

"Lainey," Teddy rasped. "Please," she said, her voice weak.

I knew what she was asking, as unfair as it may be. Her words from earlier came back to me: *We are all many things, but does that mean we don't deserve a chance at redemption?*

I whirled around. Ty stared at the Master, his face an unreadable mask. With a sharp inhale, he limped over to where his sword lay in the grass. Picking it up, he gripped the hilt so tightly his knuckles were white and stalked over to where the feeble old man lay.

I rushed across the grass. "Wait!" I called out.

Ty stilled at my words, but didn't turn.

"You don't have to do this," I said.

"He killed my father." Ty's voice was raw.

"I know." I reached out to touch his arm.

"He deserves to die for what he did, for all he's done. He took everything from me," Ty whispered, his voice breaking on the last word.

"Not everything." I squeezed his hand. "You're still your father's son. You're his legacy."

"Legacy?" He shook his head. "He'd be so ashamed of me, of what I've become."

"I don't think so. He loved you. Remember what you told me that night at the railroad tracks?" I leaned a little closer. "You told me that no one gets to tell me who or what I'm going be. That it's my choice. I know you've been walking the line for a while. Good guy or bad. But this is it, the moment you get to choose."

Ty turned to face me, his eyes swimming with grief and anger. "I've spent years thinking about this moment, imagining what it would be like to finally avenge my father, but no matter what I do"—he shook his head, a single tear dripping down his cheek—"it won't bring him back, will it?"

"No," I whispered, my heart breaking. "It won't." The death of the Master wouldn't bring Gareth back either. Or Josephine. Or my mother. "But there is something you can do: You can forgive yourself."

Forgiveness. So powerful and so restorative. I hadn't realized it until that moment, but the weight I'd been carrying since the Gathering was gone. Gareth had forgiven me, I had forgiven Ty, and along the way, I had forgiven myself too. It was time for Ty to do the same.

His eyes were dark, and the war raging inside him was clear by the agony on his face. I laid my hand against his cheek. "The choice is yours, Ty. Who do you want to be?"

Ty closed his eyes at my touch and let out a deep, shuddering breath. "To live by light and each day's breath. To serve, to give, and others protect," he whispered, his fingers loosening on the sword. "To fight, to love, and do what's right. This spoken seal, my word, my life."

With the final word, he dropped his sword onto the ground. "I choose to be the man my father raised me to be. It may take some time, but I choose to forgive. I have a lot to atone for, but killing him"—he shot a look over his shoulder at the Master—"won't be one of those things."

I smiled at him and wrapped my arm around his waist, pulling him close. "Good."

We hurried over to Teddy. Her eyes were closed, and her skin was ashen. Zia was holding her hand, tears streaking down her cheeks. The other faction leaders stood around her, their faces solemn. She didn't have long.

I knelt down, taking her other hand in mine. Her lungs rattled as she struggled to draw breath, the sound wheezing in her chest. Tears welled up in my eyes.

"You were right, Teddy," I said, leaning down to whisper in her ear. "Everyone deserves a second chance."

They were the words she'd been waiting for.

Her eyes found mine, and with one final squeeze of my hand, her heart stopped beating.

Her face was peaceful.

Zia fell over her mother, her shoulders shaking. I stood up, giving her space. My own tears made it difficult to see, so I wiped my face with the heel of my hand. Smoke billowed over the farm, and as I surveyed the aftermath, the devastation of the war, I knew this wasn't the end. Teddy wouldn't be the only one we lost. The scars of today would last forever.

But there was hope too.

And the chance for a new beginning.

It made the ache in my chest ease ever so slightly.

I walked over to where the Master lay, snoring gently in the grass.

"So what do we do with him now?" Maggie asked, coming to stand beside me.

I let out a breath as a crack of electric green lightning lit up the sky.

"I think I have an idea."

CHAPTER THIRTY

MAGGIE

Two Weeks Later

I stared at the two comic books in front of me, scanning their covers carefully.

"Whatcha doing?" Lainey sat down next to me, two mugs of hot chocolate in her hand. She handed me one with a smile.

"Thanks," I said, accepting the mug. "I'm trying to decide which one of these to give to Oliver."

"Oh," Lainey said, her eyebrows raising. "I didn't realize he was a fan of comic books."

"He's not," I grinned. "But clearly, that's something I have to fix." I held up one of the books. "Which one? Black Panther or Guardians of the Galaxy?"

Lainey scratched her head. "Uh . . . both?"

"I like the way you think, Styles!" I said, slapping the

comics back down. "Now, I just have to get him to actually read them."

"I don't think you'll have much of a problem with that one."

"Because of my dazzling personality and powers of persuasion?" I asked with a grin. "I mean, I'm no Emma Frost, but I can be pretty compelling when I want to."

"Well, that," Lainey said, taking a sip of her hot chocolate, "and I'm pretty sure that he's into you. I think you could tell him to Shift into a giraffe and do a tap dance, and he'd do it."

I shook my head. "Are we talking about the same Oliver? Tall, dark skin, gives Oscar the Grouch a run for his money?"

"That's him," Lainey laughed. "I don't think you realize how he looks at you when you're not paying attention."

"No," I said, though a flush was rising in my cheeks. "He's probably just trying to figure out a way to get me to stop talking."

"Maybe, but did you know he came to see you when you were sick?"

"He did?"

Lainey laughed at the look on my face. "Don't look so surprised, Mags."

"I guess I just didn't think he cared," I replied, flushing again.

"Funny how things turn out, huh?"

I clinked my glass to Lainey's. "I'll drink to that."

The din of voices downstairs floated toward us. "That must be the council," Lainey said. "They're supposed to be meeting to come up with some new laws, make sure that the factions have an equal balance of power, just like the original Hetaeria intended."

"I'm surprised they didn't ask you to sit in on that."

Lainey shook her head. "I'm glad they didn't." She let out a breath. "I'm still taking it one day at a time."

I knew what she meant. We were all still trying to cope with the aftermath of war. In addition to Teddy, the Hetaeria had lost many of their people in the war, as had the factions. There'd been more funerals and ceremonies than I could count. The farm was still in ruins, but come spring, there were plans to rebuild.

I was planning to return home for Christmas in a few weeks, but I'd told Zia not to remove the spell she had placed on my parents. I was still human, and eventually, I was going to have to go back to my old life. But I'd found a second family here, and I wanted to stay for a while and help with the recovery efforts. Besides, even if she didn't say it, I knew Lainey needed me.

I wrapped my arm around her shoulder. "You know I'm here for you, right?"

"I know . . . Maggie, I never apologized for the way I treated you before. I never should have tried to force you to leave."

"You don't have to apologize, Styles. Trying to protect the people you love is a pretty common protagonist behavior." I tapped the cover of the comics. "And I'm pretty much an expert on those."

"Yes, you are," she smiled. "But seriously, you're the reason we're all here. Without you, I never could've done the siphoning spell."

"Ah well," I said, blushing. "What are sidekicks for?"

Lainey shook her head. "No, Mags. You're my best friend, but you've never been just a sidekick. You're the hero of this story. You saved us all."

An unexpected wave of tears welled up in my eyes. All the insecurities I'd felt about not being a Supernatural hadn't diminished entirely. Her words were exactly what I needed to hear. "Thanks, Styles."

"Come on, we better get downstairs. I heard Serena tell Zia that she was making chicken pot pie, and the last time Ajay and Brandon were here, they practically emptied the cupboards. If we want dinner, we better grab it before they get to it."

I laughed. "You go ahead. I'll be right down."

I considered the two comic books for a few more minutes before getting up, deciding that I would, in fact, just give him both. As I passed the hall mirror, I thought about what Lainey had said about Oliver. Then, feeling a little silly, I gave my curls a quick fluff and headed downstairs.

Oliver was standing in the foyer near the front door, holding a manila folder in his hand. "Hey!" I said, bounding down the steps. "I didn't realize you were going to be here."

"Ajay and I have a meeting later with the other faction leaders," Oliver said with a shrug. "We're working on some new trade agreements."

I whistled through my teeth. "Well, look at you, Mr. Leader of the Shifter Faction. Color me impressed." I grinned, then held up the comic books. "I have something for you. I figured it was time we started your education."

"Thanks," Oliver said, taking the comics. "I . . . uh, have something for you too." He glanced over his shoulder at the front door, and I followed him out onto the porch, both curious and a little surprised.

"Here," he said, thrusting the envelope at me, and then looking away, clearly embarrassed.

I opened the folder and gasped.

Inside was a piece of artwork, a colorful drawing of a comic book cover. A vast cityscape of sprawling buildings served as the background, and there in the very center with a swirling purple cape and a power stance that would put Captain America to shame was me, depicted as a fierce and powerful superhero.

I marveled, running my fingers over all the careful little details. The spring of my curls, the twinkle in my eye, the kick-butt sass my comic self was exuding. It left me speechless.

"I like to draw," Oliver mumbled. "No one really knows that about me."

A giggle bubbled in my throat. *Grumpy Oliver, an artist?* "This is amazing," I said, unable to take my eyes off the art.

"It's you," Oliver confirmed. "It's how I see you." The words were soft, and he quickly cleared his throat. "I know comics are kinda your thing. I was thinking maybe we could make one . . . you know, together."

He was looking brutally uncomfortable now, shifting from one foot to the other. It was absolutely adorable. I thought about what Lainey had said and grinned. It really was funny how things turned out.

"That would be amazing," I said with a wide smile. "I always knew I was destined to be in a comic." I leaned up on my toes and surprised us both when I pressed my lips against his.

"Now," I said, when we pulled apart, my heart fluttering wildly. "Why don't we grab some dinner, and then, what do you say we play a little game? I'm pretty sure I saw a deck of Uno cards in the hall drawer."

Oliver beamed at me. "You're on."

CHAPTER THIRTY-ONE

TY

The barn was freezing, but I didn't mind. It was easier to breathe out where the air was crisp, where I could be alone. The farmhouse—the only other main structure still standing—was always so full of people.

Zia had vouched for me with the faction leaders and council and given me a place within the Hetaeria, but distrustful eyes still watched me, and whispers of "traitor" and "Oathbreaker" still lingered behind my back.

I couldn't blame them. After all I'd done, it was only a fraction of what I deserved.

So, I'd kept to myself for the last two weeks, helping where needed, but otherwise keeping my distance. Without that insatiable need for vengeance driving me, I was struggling to figure out where I belonged. I'd chosen to live as the man my father raised me to be, but I hadn't figured out yet what that meant moving forward. I still wasn't one of the good guys, but I wasn't a bad one either. I was just me, just Ty.

I stood near the open double doors, watching tiny snow flurries flutter to the ground, when a figure bundled up in coat and scarf headed in my direction. Lainey.

My heartbeat sped up as I lifted a hand in greeting. I still hadn't gotten over the sight of her cold, dead body in my arms, and every time I touched her, felt her warm skin beneath my fingertips, it was a reminder that I'd been given a second chance, and I wasn't going to waste it.

"Hey," she said, walking inside and shaking the snow out of her hair. "I thought you might be in here."

"Coming to keep me company?" I reached for her, but she twisted away, teasing.

"Actually, I was just coming to visit Birdie." She pulled an apple out of her pocket. "I promised I'd bring her a treat." We walked over to where the friendly brown horse was waiting, nickering happily.

"I've already given her three of those," I chuckled as Birdie gave me an affectionate nudge with her head. "I think she's starting to like me."

"Well, horses are excellent judges of character." Lainey gave me a soft smile, but it didn't reach her eyes. "Teddy told me that."

The look of sadness on her face hit me square in the chest. I grabbed her hand and entwined her fingers with mine, squeezing gently. "How you holding up?"

"I'm just taking it one day at a time, like everyone else," she sighed. "But it's hard. Now that the Master's gone, everything's hitting me. It's like I'm feeling Gareth's death all over again. And now, Teddy's gone too."

"Grief is like that," I said, thinking of my father. "Some days you're fine, and others it hits you like a Mack truck." I gave her hand another squeeze. "It does get a little easier with time."

Her eyes filled with tears. "I know, it's just . . . I don't want to lose anyone else."

"Come here," I said, wrapping my arms around her. "It's all over. You don't have to worry about losing anyone else right now."

"I already have."

The words were so soft, I almost didn't hear them. I pulled back enough to see the tears spill over and roll down her cheeks. "What are you talking about?"

"I have a secret, something I haven't told anyone else yet."

I waited, not wanting to interrupt her.

She sucked in a shuddering breath. "I can't feel the Grimoire anymore." Her voice broke and more tears fell. "I can't feel my family either. I used to hear their voices, but now it's just quiet."

"Are you sure?" I reached up to wipe her tears with my thumb.

"I'm sure." A sob escaped her lips. "They're gone."

"How?"

"I don't know," she said. "But I think it was the siphoning

spell. Teddy said that no one witch was meant to have all that power. Maybe it was the universe's way of putting things back in balance or something. When I used that spell on the Master, I think I siphoned away the Grimoire and my entire family with it. I can't hear their voices anymore, and the magic is just . . . gone."

"How does that work exactly? Does that mean you're not a—"

"No," she said, shaking her head. "I'm still a witch. I'm just an ordinary one now." Her lower lip trembled. "I miss them so much."

With gentle hands, I led her over to a small wooden bench and let her cry on my shoulder. I held her hand until her tears had slowed.

"Can I tell you something? Something my father once told me?"

She nodded.

" 'Pain is a tether,' he used to always say." I smiled a little. "It was a reminder that pain is a part of life, that it can destroy us if we let it, or it can be the link to who we've been, who we are, and who we're going to be."

"Pain is a tether," she echoed.

"I know losing your uncle and losing your family's Grimoire is hard, but you're going to be okay," I said.

"It's just . . . I was Lainey DuCarmont, Keeper of the Grimoire." She drew in another shuddering breath. "If I'm not the Keeper anymore, I'm not sure who I am."

"I know the feeling," I said. "I'm still trying to figure out who I am too. But maybe what we're feeling is just another piece to the puzzle. Maybe it's part of the journey—pain and all. We feel, we seek, and hopefully, we find."

"Seekers," Lainey whispered. "That's what we are now."

"Ty Marek, Praetorian and Seeker." I grinned at her. "I like it."

She straightened, wiping the tears from her face. "Lainey DuCarmont, Ordinary Witch and Seeker." She smiled. "I can get behind that."

"Not ordinary," I disagreed, caressing her cheek with my thumb. "*Extraordinary*."

She gave me a little shove. "Stop, you're just saying that because you lo—" She broke off, flushing bright pink.

Laughter bubbled in my chest as I pulled her face to mine and kissed her.

Feel.

Seek.

Find.

I had a very good feeling we would do just that.

EPILOGUE

Wilhelmina Gunther hummed a happy tune as she wheeled Heritage Creek Retirement Community's newest resident down the hallway. As housing director, it was her job to make sure that each new member of the community was welcomed graciously and warmly.

"We have bingo every Tuesday night, and the local Girl Scout troop comes the second Saturday of every month to do craft time. We also offer karaoke night, bridge club, and baking classes. I think you'll be quite pleased with the programming we offer."

She continued her little ditty as she turned down the corridor that led to the residential housing area. She stopped right outside room twelve, pushing down the brakes of the wheelchair. She gave the door three little knocks and pushed it open with a happy little "Ta-da!"

"Oh!" she said, seeing the occupant sitting by the window.

"Mr. Masterson, come meet your new roommate," she sing-songed, her voice light and airy.

The silver-haired man sitting by the window glared at her.

"Mr. Roberts"—she addressed the new resident in the wheelchair—"I'm happy to report that you lucked out in the roommate department. Mr. Masterson is one of our favorite residents. He tells the most *wonderful* stories."

"They're not stories," Mr. Masterson mumbled. "They're true, you fool!"

"Ah yes, of course, Mr. Masterson," she said. "Warlocks, magic, and shadow monsters, oh my!" She placed a dainty palm against her heart. "How I do love a good fairy tale!"

Mr. Masterson scowled, the effort making him cough uncontrollably. "Oh, you poor dear," Wilhelmina said, pouring him a glass of water from the pitcher on the nightstand. "You just drink this right up, you hear me?"

"Now, I think I'll leave you two to get acquainted. Mr. Roberts, if you need anything at all, please don't hesitate to ask. And, Mr. Masterson, do tell him one of your tales. I particularly love the one about the girl with the green lightning and the magical book. It's absolutely exhilarating!"

She gave both gentlemen a rosy smile and then bustled out into the hallway, shutting the door behind her.

The sound of her cheerful humming echoed down the hall.

ACKNOWLEDGMENTS

It truly takes a village to write a novel, and as I come to the end of this one, I have to stop and thank the amazing people who have stood behind me and supported me along the way.

Most importantly, thank you to my Heavenly Father for grace upon grace. All that I am and all that I have is from you.

To my amazing beta readers: Bethany Atazadeh, Leo P. Carney, Holly Davis, Jessi Elliott, Savannah Goins, Kimberly Goodwin, Mandi Lynn, Emma-Kate McDonald, J. M. Miller, Brent Perrotti, Paige Roberts, Danielle Thaldorf, Kayla Scutti, and Ashley Zarzaur. Thank you for being so excited about this book and for helping me make it the best it can possibly be. Your support means the world to me!

To Geneva Clawson, who critiqued the heck out of this book not once, but twice! Not only did your feedback and incredible line edits help shape this book for the better, but you taught me so much. I never realized how often my characters nodded until you pointed it out! Thank you so much for all your help!

To Karli Cook: Girl, I am SO grateful for you! You came into my life when I needed it the most, and I am so blessed by you and your friendship. Thank you for being amazing and for always being a huge source of support and encouragement for me. When you make it as a big-time author (and you totally will!), I'll be the first in line to buy your book!

To Amy Trueblood: Navigating the publishing world is so much better with a friend! I'm so happy that our paths crossed and I get to experience all of this with you. Thank you for always being so supportive and lending an ear when I needed one. You're one heck of a writer and an even better friend!

Endless gratitude to Megan Naidl and the amazing team at Flux: Thank you so much for all your hard work! Behind every good book are people like you, working tirelessly to make the magic happen. I appreciate all of you so much! And an extra special thank you to the talented Jake Slavik. You brought *Keeper* and *Seeker* to life with your beautiful covers!

I owe a tremendous debt of gratitude to my brilliant editor, Mari Kesselring: Working with you has been an absolute dream! Thank you for being such a champion of this book and for working so hard to make *Seeker* shine! I am a better writer for having worked with you!

To Caitlen Rubino-Bradway, the world's best literary agent: Since day one, you have understood Lainey and me better than anyone else, and neither of us would be here today without you! I am so grateful for all your hard work and support. You really are the best agent in the world, and I'm so glad you're mine! Can't wait to see what the future holds!

To Megan LaCroix: Simply put, your friendship has changed my life. You're not just an incredible critique partner; you're an amazing friend! I know I've said this before, but I'm going to keep on saying it: I couldn't do what I do without you. Thank you for always believing in me! Batman and Robin. Sam and Frodo. Lainey and Maggie. Kim and Megan.

To my mom: I know you're already mentioned in the dedication, but I thought you deserved a shout-out here too. Thanks, Mama. You are the reason this book exists.

To my amazing husband, Jim: You always make me laugh, my love. Thank you for dances in the kitchen, for folding all the laundry I dumped on the bed and promptly forgot about, and for always chasing me around the house with your cold hands. Life with you is a gigantic goat rodeo, and I wouldn't have it any other way! Thank you for never letting me give up on this dream of mine and for being understanding when deadline stress turns me into Cruella De Vil. I love you so much! To my sweet kiddos: Mommy loves you more than anything, including books! Thanks for being the absolute best part of my life!

To my readers: Thank you so much for loving Lainey, Ty, and Maggie as much as I do! You're the bee's knees!

Lastly, and most importantly, thanks to Hershey and Keurig: Were it not for the two family-size bags of Hershey's Kisses and the dozens of coffee pods I went through, I never would have met my deadline. Keep doing what you do. I have a feeling this is only the beginning of a beautiful relationship between us.

ABOUT THE AUTHOR

Kim Chance is an English teacher from Alabama, currently residing in Michigan with her husband and three children. Kim is also a YouTuber who has a passion for helping other writers. She posts weekly writing videos on her channel, www.youtube.com/kimchance1. When not writing, Kim enjoys spending time with her family and two crazy dogs, binge-watching Netflix, fangirling over books, and making death-by-cheese casseroles.